SANDRA BROWN

FRENCH SILK

WARNER BOOKS

A Time Warner Company

WARNER BOOKS EDITION

Cover design and illustration by Andrew Newman

Warner Books, Inc.
1271 Avenue of the Americas
New York, NY 10020

Visit our Web site at
http://pathfinder.com/twep

W A Time Warner Company

Printed in the United States of America

Originally published in hardcover by Warner Books.

First Printed in Paperback: May, 1993
Reissued: July, 1995

15   14

Acknowledgments

During the writing of *French Silk*, I asked the help of several people who gave eagerly and generously of their time, knowledge, and experience. My heartfelt thanks go to Mr. John DeMers of the Fairmont Hotel, New Orleans, and to Mr. Jerry Jensen of the Pontchartrain Hotel, New Orleans. My story would have been impossible to write without the help of the Orleans Parish District Attorney's Office. My thanks to Mr. Harry Connick, Sr., for making his staff available, especially Assistant District Attorney Timothy McElroy, Chief of Screening Division.

A special thanks belongs to Metsy Hingle, who must surely know everybody in the city and who opened doors for me that otherwise would have been closed. Heartiest thanks to Jean Wilson and Jeanne Wilson, the best guides and drivers possible, who got me where I needed to go when I needed to be there and provided me with a wealth of "insider" information. I appreciate Mary Adams for giving me a glimpse into a realm outside my experience.

To my friend and research assistant, Becky Higgins, who tolerated me and learned firsthand what "authoritis" really is, thank you.

And I'm grateful to the beguiling city of New Orleans, that mystical, magical, marvelous place that continues to intrigue and inspire.

SANDRA BROWN

Prologue

❧ ❧

Ablue jay swooped in and perched on the naked
cherub's toe. Too conceited to splash in the fountain with the abandon of the lowly sparrow, the
jay took one sip of water, then jetted from the
courtyard. He seemed disdainful of the serenity enclosed
within the old brick walls which were covered with clinging,
flowering vines. Bumblebees buzzed industriously among the
pastel blossoms. Hanging baskets of ferns still dripped from
a predawn shower. On the waxy leaves of philodendrons and
camellia bushes, drops of rainwater glistened in the bright
sunlight.

"So Rapunzel let down her cascade of lovely, golden hair,
and the prince used the heavy locks to scale the stone wall of
the tower."

Claire Laurent, who'd been listening intently, looked skeptically at her mother. "Wouldn't that hurt, Mama?"

"Not in fairy tales, darling."

"I wish I had long, golden hair." The girl sighed wistfully.

Mary Catherine patted her five-year-old daughter's tumble of russet waves. "Your hair is too lovely for words."

The tranquility of the courtyard was shattered abruptly when Aunt Laurel barged through the screen door. "Mary Catherine, they're here again! And this time they have a paper saying they can take Claire away."

Mary Catherine stared vacantly at her aunt. "Who's here?"

Claire knew. Even if her mother did not, Claire remembered the man in the dark suit who smelled of wintergreen breath mints and oily hair cream. He'd come twice to the house, contaminating Aunt Laurel's parlor with his offensive odors. A woman carrying a large leather satchel always came with him. They talked to Aunt Laurel and Mary Catherine about her as though she were deaf or not there at all.

Claire didn't understand all the words, but she grasped the nature of these conversations. They always left Aunt Laurel distraught, but her mother suffered terribly. After their last visit she had stayed in bed for three days, crying incessantly. It had been one of her worst spells and distressed Aunt Laurel even more.

Claire scuttled behind the wrought-iron chair where her mama was seated, trying to make herself small and invisible. Fear clutched at her throat and made her heart pound in her narrow chest.

"Oh, dear. Oh, dear." Aunt Laurel's chins were wobbling. She twisted the handkerchief clutched in her pudgy hands. "I don't know what to do. Mary Catherine, what can I do? They say they can take her."

The man appeared first. His hawkish eyes darted around the courtyard authoritatively; he was as territorial in bearing as the blue jay had been. Finally his eyes pinpointed the lovely young woman who sat like a living portrait against the picturesque backdrop.

"Good morning, Miss Laurent."

Watching from her hiding place behind her mother, Claire saw him smile. She didn't like his smile. It was as insincere as the garish grin on a Mardi Gras mask. Even outdoors she could smell his sickeningly sweet hair tonic and breath candy.

Aunt Laurel's words had terrified her. Take her where? She couldn't go anywhere without her mama. If they took her away, who would look after Mama? Who would pat her shoulder and sing softly to her when she got sad? Who would go after her when she sneaked out of the house during one of her spells?

"You no longer have a choice regarding your daughter's guardianship," the drab woman in the ugly gray dress told Mary Catherine. She spoke harshly, and the leather satchel weighed down her arm. "This is not a good environment for your child. You want what's best for her, don't you?"

Mary Catherine's finely boned hand fluttered to her chest and fingered the strand of pearls that lay against her lace collar. "I don't understand these things. It's all so . . . confusing."

The man and woman glanced at each other. The man said, "Rest easy, Miss Laurent. Your little girl will be well taken care of." He nodded brusquely at the woman. She stepped around the chair and seized Claire by the arm.

"No!" Claire yanked her arm from the woman's hot, damp grasp and backed away. "I don't want to go with you. I want to stay with my mama."

"Come on now, Claire," the woman cooed through a brittle smile. "We're going to take you to a house where there are lots of other children to play with. You'll like it. I promise."

Claire didn't believe her. She had the pointed nose and furtive eyes of the rats that scurried through the garbage in the alleyways of the Quarter. She wasn't pretty, soft, and good-smelling, and, even though she was attempting to speak kindly, her voice didn't have the melodious rise and fall of Mama's.

"I won't go," Claire declared with the obstinacy of a five-year-old. "I won't go anywhere without my mama."

"I'm afraid you must."

The woman reached for Claire again. This time her grip held, although Claire struggled to free herself. "No! No!" The woman's fingernails dug into her arm, breaking the skin. "Let me go! I'm staying with Mama and Aunt Laurel."

Screaming, she wriggled and kicked and flailed her arms and dug the heels of her black patent maryjanes into the bricks and everything else she could think of to do that might break the woman's hold on her, but it was inexorable.

Aunt Laurel had regained her composure and was berating the man for separating a child from her mother. "Mary Catherine suffers from spells of melancholia, but who doesn't? Hers are just more deeply felt. She's a wonderful mother. Claire adores her. I assure you, she's perfectly harmless."

Heedless of Aunt Laurel's earnest pleas, the woman pulled Claire through the screen door into the kitchen. The child looked back and saw her mother still sitting in her chair, limned in mellow sunlight. "Mama!" she cried out. "Mama, don't let them take me."

"Stop that yelling!" The woman shook Claire so hard that she accidentally bit her tongue and screamed louder, in pain.

Yanked from her stupor by her daughter's wail, Mary Catherine suddenly realized that Claire was in peril. She pushed herself up from the wrought-iron chair with such impetus that it fell over backward and cracked two of the courtyard bricks. She ran for the screen door and had almost reached it when the man clamped his hand on her shoulder.

"There's nothing you can do to stop us this time, Miss Laurent. We have the authority to remove your daughter from these premises."

"I'll kill you first." Mary Catherine grabbed the neck of a vase on the patio table and swung it toward his head.

With a sickening thunk, lead crystal connected with flesh. The blow opened up a three-inch gash on the social worker's temple. When Mary Catherine dropped the vase, it shattered on the bricks. Water drenched the front of the man's dark suit. Roses fell randomly around their feet.

He bellowed in anger and pain. "Perfectly harmless, my ass," he shouted into Aunt Laurel's face. She had rushed forward to restrain Mary Catherine.

While her mouth filled with blood from the cut on her tongue, Claire continued to fight the woman as she dragged her through the house. The man lumbered behind them, stanching the flow of blood from his temple with a handkerchief. He was cursing liberally.

Claire kept her eyes on her mother as long as she could. Mary Catherine's face was distorted by torment as she strained against Aunt Laurel's clutches. Her arms were extended beseechingly toward her daughter.

"Claire. Claire. My baby girl."

"*Mama! Mama! Mama! . . .*"

Claire sat up suddenly in her wide bed. Her chest was heaving and she couldn't catch her breath. Her mouth was arid, her throat raw from having silently screamed in her sleep. Her nightgown was stuck to her damp skin.

She threw off the covers, drew her knees up to her chest, and rested her forehead on them. She didn't raise her head until all vestiges of the nightmare had vanished and the demons of memory had slunk back into their lairs in her subconscious.

She left her bed and walked down the hall to her mother's room. Mary Catherine was sleeping peacefully. Relieved, Claire got a drink of water from the bathroom sink and then returned to her bedroom. She changed into a fresh nightgown and straightened the covers before getting into bed again. It would be a while, she knew, before she went back to sleep.

Recently she'd been plagued by recurring bad dreams that

forced her to relive the worst moments of her troubled childhood. The origin of the dreams was no mystery. She knew their source. It was the same evil presence that was currently endangering the peace and security she had worked so diligently to maintain.

She had thought these past heartaches had been buried so deep that they would never be unearthed. But they were being resurrected by a malevolent intruder. He was a threat to those she loved. He was wreaking havoc on her life.

Unless she took drastic measures to change the course of events, he would ruin the future she had planned.

Chapter One

※* ※*

The Reverend Jackson Wilde had been shot in the head, the heart, and the testicles. Right off Cassidy figured that was a significant clue.

"Hell of a mess."

The medical examiner's remark was an understatement, Cassidy thought. He guessed the murder weapon was a .38 snub-nose revolver, fired at close range. Hollow-tip bullets. The perpetrator had definitely wanted to blow the victim away. Tissue was splattered on the headboard and sheets. The mattress was saturated with blood that pooled beneath the body, which, beyond the devastating damage from the bullets, hadn't been butchered or dismembered. Grisly as it was, Cassidy had seen much worse.

What made this murder scene particularly messy was the identity of the victim. Cassidy had heard the startling news bulletin over his car radio while fighting morning rush-hour traffic. He'd immediately executed an illegal U-turn even though he had no business rushing to the scene without authorization. The policemen who had cordoned off the Fairmont

7

Hotel recognized him and automatically assumed that he was officially representing the Orleans Parish District Attorney's office. None had questioned his appearance in the seventh floor San Louis suite that was crowded with investigators who were likely to destroy evidence in their eagerness to collect it.

Cassidy approached the medical examiner. "What do you think, Elvie?"

Dr. Elvira Dupuis was stout, gray-haired and butchy. Her sex life was constant grist for the gossip mills, but none of the conveyors spoke from firsthand experience. Elvie was liked by few and despised by most. No one, however, disputed her competence.

Cassidy loved having her on the stand *if* she was a witness for the prosecution. He could count on her answers to be forthright and unequivocal. When she took the oath on the Bible, she looked sincere. She always had a profound impact on jurors.

In response to his question, the middle-aged pathologist pushed her eyeglasses more squarely onto her square face. "My initial guess is that the head wound got him. The bullet destroyed most of his gray matter. Chest wound looks a little too far to the right to have burst the heart, although I can't rule it out as the mortal wound until I've cracked his chest. The shot to his balls probably wouldn't have killed him, not instantly anyway." She looked up at the assistant D.A. and grinned mischievously. "But it sure as hell would've thrown a wrench into his love life."

Cassidy winced with empathy. "Wonder which shot was fired first."

"Can't say."

"My guess would be the head."

"Why?"

"The chest wound, if it didn't kill him, would have immobilized him."

"His lungs would have flooded. And?"

"And if somebody had shot me in the crotch, I'd have reflexively tried to protect the area."

"Dying with a death grip around your balls?"

"Something like that."

She shook her head. "Wilde's arms were at his sides. No sign of a struggle or adverse reaction of any kind. I'd guess he felt perfectly at ease with whoever offed him. He might have even been asleep. He didn't see it coming."

"Victims rarely do," Cassidy muttered. "What time would you guess it happened?"

She lifted the corpse's right hand and revolved it around the wrist joint, testing the rigidity. "Midnight. Maybe before." Dropping the hand back onto the sheet, she asked, "Can I have him now?"

Cassidy gave the brutalized body a final once-over. "Be my guest."

"I'll see that you get a copy of the autopsy report as soon as I'm finished. Don't call and start bugging me for it before I'm through or it'll only take longer."

Dr. Dupuis had assumed that he would be prosecuting the case. He didn't qualify his involvement at this point. It was only a matter of time. He would have this case.

Moving aside to give the forensic crew room to maneuver, Cassidy conducted a visual investigation of the hotel bedroom. The articles on the nightstand had already been dusted for prints. A fine, black film clung to everything. Various items were being carefully placed in separate plastic bags and labeled. Robbery could be ruled out as a motive. Among the articles on the nightstand was a Rolex wristwatch.

A police photographer was taking pictures. Another policeman wearing surgical gloves was on his hands and knees, examining the carpet for fibers.

"Has any press been allowed in yet?"

"Nope," the officer on his knees replied.

"Keep them out as long as possible and hold all vital info close to your chest. Our office will prepare a statement later in the day when we know the facts."

The officer acknowledged the instructions with a nod.

Leaving the policemen to do their jobs, Cassidy wandered into the parlor of the suite. Opaque drapes had been drawn across the two walls of windows, making the room appear dim and gloomy in spite of its pastel and white decor. Huddled in the corner of a peach velvet sofa was a young woman, her head bent, her face buried in her hands. She was sobbing uncontrollably. A young man sat beside her. He looked nervous, even frightened, as he tried in vain to console her.

They were being questioned by an NOPD homicide detective. Howard Glenn had been in the department for more than twenty years, although he was a rogue and not particularly liked by his colleagues. His appearance didn't attract companions or solicit friendships. He was dingy and disheveled, he chain-smoked unfiltered Camels, and overall he looked like he belonged in a 1940s film noire. But he was well respected throughout the local law-enforcement community for his dogged method of investigation.

As he approached, Glenn glanced up and said, "Hey, Cassidy. You got here quick. Crowder send you?"

Anthony Crowder was the district attorney of Orleans Parish, Cassidy's boss. He sidestepped the question and nodded down to the couple on the sofa. "Who're they?"

"Don't you watch TV?"

"Not religious programs. Never saw his show."

Glenn turned his head and said out the side of his mouth so that only Cassidy could hear, "Too bad. He's been canceled."

Cassidy glanced over his shoulder into the bedroom where Elvie Dupuis was overseeing the transference of the bagged body from the bed to the gurney. "He damn sure has."

"This is the evangelist's wife, Ariel Wilde," Glenn informed him. "And his son, Joshua."

The young man looked up at Cassidy. Cassidy stuck out his right hand. "Assistant District Attorney Cassidy."

Joshua Wilde shook hands with him. His grip was firm enough, but his hands were soft, smooth, and well tended, not a working man's hands. He had expressive brown eyes and ash-brown hair worn long and wavy on top. He was good-looking, on the verge of pretty. Born a century or two earlier on another continent, he would have frequented fashionable salons and dabbled in writing romantic poetry. Cassidy doubted that he'd ever thrown a baseball, camped out, or played shirts and skins with the guys.

His voice was as southern and cultured as a cask of Jack Daniels. "Find the monster who did this to my father, Mr. Cassidy."

"I intend to."

"And bring him to swift justice."

"*Him?* Are you sure it was a man who killed your father, Mr. Wilde?"

Joshua Wilde was flustered. "Not at all. I only meant . . . I used the masculine pronoun in a generic sense."

"Then it could have been a woman."

Until now, the widow had failed to acknowledge the introduction while weeping into a shredding Kleenex. Suddenly Ariel Wilde tossed her pale, straight hair over her shoulders and fixed Cassidy with a wild, fanatic gaze. Her complexion had no more color than the white plaster lamp on the end table, but she had beautiful blue eyes enhanced by extraordinarily long lashes and the shimmer of fresh tears.

"Is that how you solve murder cases, Mr. . . . what was it again?"

"Cassidy."

"Do you solve crimes by playing word games?"

"Sometimes, yes."

"You're no better than this detective." She sneered contemptuously at Howard Glenn. "Instead of going after the killer, he's been questioning Josh and me."

Cassidy exchanged a telling glance with Glenn. The detective shrugged, tacitly granting Cassidy permission to intervene. "Before we can 'go after the killer,' Mrs. Wilde," he explained, "we have to learn exactly what happened to your husband."

She gestured toward the blood-soaked bed in the next room and shrieked, "Isn't it obvious what happened?"

"Not always."

"Well we don't know what happened," she wailed theatrically before cramming the Kleenex against her colorless lips. "If we'd known he was going to be murdered last night, do you think we would have left Jackson alone in the suite?"

"The two of you left Reverend Wilde alone last night? Where were you?" Cassidy sat down on the edge of the adjacent loveseat. He took a good look at the woman and her stepson. They both looked to be in their late twenties.

"We were in my suite. Rehearsing," Josh replied.

"Rehearsing?"

"Mrs. Wilde sings at all their crusade services and on the television program," Glenn provided. "Mr. Wilde here plays the piano."

Tidy of Jackson Wilde to keep his ministry a family enterprise, Cassidy thought. He already had a jaundiced view of television preachers and had seen nothing so far to dispel the stereotype. He asked, "Where is your suite, Mr. Wilde?"

"Down the hall. Daddy had reserved all the rooms on this floor."

"Why?"

"That's customary. It guarantees our privacy. Daddy's followers often go to any lengths to get near him. He loved people, but he needed rest and privacy between services. He and Ariel stayed in this suite. I took the next largest one so a practice piano could be moved into it."

Cassidy turned to the newly widowed woman. "This suite has two bedrooms. Why weren't you sleeping with your husband?"

Mrs. Wilde responded with a sniff of disdain. "He's already asked me about that," she said, shooting another disparaging glance toward Detective Glenn. "I came in late last night and didn't want to disturb Jackson's rest. He was exhausted, so I slept in the other bedroom."

"What time did you come in?"

"I didn't notice."

Cassidy looked at Josh inquisitively. "Did you notice what time it was when she left your room?"

"I'm afraid not. Late."

"After midnight?"

"Much later."

For the time being, Cassidy let it pass. "Did you speak with your husband when you came in, Mrs. Wilde?"

"No."

"Went in and kissed him good night?"

"No. I used the door opening directly into my bedroom from the hall. I should have checked on him," she said weepily. "But I thought he was sleeping peacefully."

Cassidy glanced up at Glenn and with a stern look warned him not to make the obvious quip. Instead the detective said, "Unfortunately, Mrs. Wilde didn't discover her husband's body until this morning."

"When he didn't respond to his wake-up call," she said, her voice cracking. She used the wadded Kleenex tissue to blot beneath her nose. "To think he was in there . . . dead all that time . . . while I was sleeping in the next room."

Swooning, she collapsed against her stepson. He placed his arm around her shoulders and spoke softly into her hair.

"Guess that's all for now." Cassidy stood.

Glenn followed him to the door. "Smells like yesterday's fish heads, doesn't it?"

"Oh, I don't know," Cassidy said. "It's almost too pat to be a lie."

Glenn made an unappealing snorting sound as he fished for a fresh Camel in the crumpled pack he took from his shirt pocket. "You're shittin' me, right? It's plain to see. They've got the hots for each other and bumped off the preacher to get him out of their way."

"Could be," Cassidy said noncommittally. "Maybe not."

Glenn eyed him shrewdly as he lit his cigarette. "A smart boy like you didn't fall for those pretty blue eyes, did you, Cassidy? And all that crying? Hell, before you got here, they were praying out loud together." He sucked deeply on the Camel. "Surely you don't believe they're telling the truth?"

"Sure I believe them." As Cassidy went through the door, he glanced over his shoulder and added, "About as far as I can piss through a hurricane."

He rode the elevator down alone, and it opened onto pandemonium. The lobby of the Fairmont Hotel was a city block long. Ordinarily, it was a paragon of stately refinement and luxury, with its matte black walls, red velvet furniture, and gold leaf accents—a grand old dame of a hotel. But this morning it was teeming with frustrated, angry people. Police were trying to ignore the aggressive media reporters who were in hot pursuit of the facts surrounding the astonishing murder of Jackson Wilde. Hotel guests who earlier had been rounded up by police and questioned in the ballroom were now being systematically dismissed; they appeared reluctant to leave, however, before venting their outrage. Hotel staff were being questioned while also trying to placate their disgruntled clientele.

Cassidy elbowed his way through the noisy crowd. He overheard one woman with a midwestern twang surmising that a psychopath was loose in the hotel and that they were all doomed to be slaughtered in their beds.

A man was shouting at the top of his voice that "they" were going to hear about this, although it was unclear who "they" were.

Disciples of the Reverend Jackson Wilde, upon hearing of their leader's demise, had contributed to the confusion by congregating in the lobby and making it a temporary shrine.

They were weeping copiously and noisily, holding spontaneous prayer meetings, singing hymns, and invoking the Almighty's wrath on the one who had slain the televangelist.

As he made his way toward the University Street entrance, Cassidy tried to avoid the local media, but to no avail. The reporters surrounded him.

"Mr. Cassidy, did you see—"

"Nothing."

"Mr. Cassidy, was he—"

"No comment."

"Mr. Cassidy—"

"Later."

He maneuvered his way through them, dodging the cameras, deflecting extended microphones, and prudently declining to say anything until District Attorney Crowder placed him in charge of prosecuting Wilde's murder case.

Assuming Crowder would.

No, there could be no assumption to it. He must.

Cassidy wanted this case so badly he could taste it. Moreover, he *needed* it.

Yasmine strutted through the automatic doors at New Orleans International Airport. A redcap, dwarfed by her extraordinary height and dazzled by her legs beneath the short leather miniskirt, trudged behind her carting two suitcases.

At the sound of a car horn, Yasmine spotted Claire's LeBaron parked at the curb as scheduled. Her suitcases were stowed inside the trunk, which Claire unlocked from the dashboard, the redcap was tipped, and Yasmine slid into the passenger seat with a flash of brown thighs and a waft of gardenia perfume.

"Good morning," Claire said. "How was your flight?"

"Can you believe it about Jackson Wilde?"

Claire Laurent glanced over her left shoulder, then daringly pulled into the erratic flow of traffic made hazardous by buses, taxis, and courtesy vans picking up and depositing airline passengers. "What's he done this time?"

"You haven't heard?" Yasmine gasped. "Jesus, Claire, what have you been doing this morning?"

"Going over invoices and . . . Why?"

"You didn't see any TV news? Listen to the radio?" Jasmine noticed that a cassette was playing in the car.

"I've deliberately avoided newscasts all week. I didn't want Mama to catch Jackson Wilde taking potshots at us while he's in town. By the way, we received another invitation to debate him, which I declined."

Yasmine continued to gape at her best friend and business associate. "You really don't know."

"What?" Claire asked with a laugh. "Is French Silk under attack again? What did he say this time, that we're going to burn in eternal hell? That I'd better clean up my act or else? That I'm corrupting the morals of America with my pornographic displays of the human body?"

Yasmine removed the large, dark sunglasses she wore when she didn't want to be recognized and looked at Claire with the tiger eyes that for a decade had graced the covers of countless fashion magazines. "The Reverend Jackson Wilde won't be saying anything about you anymore, Claire. He won't be badmouthing French Silk or our catalog. He won't be doin' nuthin', honey," she said, lapsing into the black lingo of her childhood. "The man has been silenced forever. The man is dead."

"*Dead?*" Claire braked hard, pitching them forward.

"Deader'n a doornail, as my mama used to say."

Claire stared at her, whey-faced and incredulous, and repeated, "Dead?"

"Apparently he preached one sermon too many. He pissed off someone enough to kill him."

Claire nervously wet her lips. "You mean he was murdered?"

A furious driver gave a blast of his horn. Another made an obscene gesture as he steered around them and sped past. Claire forced her foot off the brake pedal and back onto the accelerator. The car lurched.

"What's the matter with you? I thought you'd be applauding. Do you want me to drive?"

"No. No, I'm fine."

"You don't look fine. In fact you look like shit."

"I had a rough night."

"Mary Catherine?"

Claire shook her head. "Some bad dreams that have been keeping me awake."

"Dreams about what?"

"Never mind. Yasmine, you're sure about Jackson Wilde?"

"I heard it in the airport while I was waiting for my luggage. They had a TV on in the Avis booth. People were crowded around it. I asked somebody what was going on, expecting something like the *Challenger* explosion. This man says, 'That television preacher done got hisself shot last night.' And since I have a voodoo doll in the image of one particular television preacher, my interest was naturally piqued. I shoved my way closer to the set and heard the news for myself."

"Was he killed at the Fairmont?"

Yasmine looked at her curiously. "How'd you know that?"

"I heard that's where he was staying. From Andre."

"Andre. I forgot about him. Bet he's having conniptions this morning." Before Yasmine could comment further on their mutual friend, Claire asked another question.

"Who discovered the body?"

"His wife. She found him this morning in his bed with three bullet holes in him."

"My God. What time did she find him?"

"Time? Hell, I don't know. They didn't say. What differ-

ence does it make?'' Yasmine took off her head scarf and
shook loose the long, full Afro for which she was famous.
From her oversized handbag she retrieved several bangles and
slid them over her slender hands. Next, she put on gigantic
disk earrings. With no more than these few cosmetic changes,
the image of the most successful ethnic model since Iman
began to emerge.

''Have they arrested anyone yet?''

''Nope.'' Yasmine applied coral gloss to her lips with a
fine-tipped brush. After dusting her cheeks with blush, she
viewed her exquisite face from all angles in the visor mirror.

Rush hour was over, but as always there was heavy traffic
on the expressway. Claire weaved through it with the ease of
experience and familiarity. She had lived in New Orleans all
her life. Since Yasmine now divided her time between New
Orleans and New York, Claire usually picked her up at the
airport.

''Did the killer leave clues? Did they find the murder
weapon?''

Impatiently Yasmine flipped the visor back into place. ''It
was like a news bulletin, you know? The details were sketchy.
The reporters were after some guy from the D.A.'s office to
make a statement, but he didn't say zip. What's with the
twenty questions?''

''I can't believe he's dead.'' Claire hesitated before saying
the last word, as though she couldn't bring herself to utter it.
''He preached at the Superdome last night.''

''They showed film of that on the news story. There he
was on the TV screen, face red, white hair bristling, screaming about fire and brimstone. He pleaded with every American
to get down on his knees and beg for redemption.'' Yasmine's
sleek brows drew together. ''How could the Lord hear anybody else's prayers with Wilde yelling so loud?'' She
shrugged. ''I'm glad he's finally been shut up. Now he's out
of our hair.''

Claire sharply cut her eyes toward Yasmine. "You shouldn't say that."

"Why not? That's how I feel. I'm sure as hell not going to burst into tears and pretend to mourn his passing." She made a scoffing sound. "They should give the one who plugged him a medal for ridding this country of a pest."

The Reverend Jackson Wilde had used his television program as a forum for his crusade against pornography. He had adopted this issue as his special mission, pledging to eradicate obscenity from America. His fiery sermons had whipped thousands of his followers into a frenzy. Consequently, artists, writers, and others in the creative arts were being virulently and personally attacked, having their work banned and in some instances vandalized.

Many viewed the televangelist's crusade as a threat much more severe than the prohibition of peddling dirty magazines. They considered it an endangerment of rights granted by the First Amendment. The legal definitions as to what was obscene and what wasn't was unclear, and since the U.S. Supreme Court had been unsuccessful in establishing definite guidelines, Wilde's opponents naturally protested using his narrow opinion as the standard by which material was measured.

Warfare had been declared. In cities and towns, battles were being waged in movie theaters, bookstores, libraries, and museums. Those opposing Reverend Wilde found themselves lumped together and labeled "nonbelieving heathens." They were promoted as this era's heretics, witches, and pagans, anathema to every true believer.

Because the catalog for the lingerie line French Silk had fallen under Jackson Wilde's censure, Claire, as its creator, had been thrust into the unwelcome limelight. For months he'd lambasted the catalog, grouping it with hard core pornographic magazines. Yasmine had agreed with Claire's assertion that they should ignore Wilde and his ridiculous accusations rather than try to defend what neither felt needed defending.

But Wilde wasn't easily ignored. When his sermons failed to provoke the response he wanted—a televised debate—he'd used his pulpit to attack Yasmine and Claire personally, citing them as lewd, lascivious, contemporary Jezebels. His sermons against them had heated up even more when, a week earlier, he'd brought his crusade to New Orleans, home of French Silk. Yasmine had been in New York taking care of other business interests, so Claire had had to bear the brunt of Wilde's vicious insults.

That's why Yasmine was baffled by Claire's reaction to the news of his death. French Silk was Claire's brainchild. It had been her conception. Her business acumen, vivid imagination, and instinct for what the women of America wanted had made the mail-order business a stunning success. For Yasmine herself, it had prolonged a waning career. It had been her salvation, although even Claire didn't realize to what extent.

Now the bastard who had threatened to end all that was dead. To her way of thinking, it was cause for celebration.

Claire, however, saw it differently. "Since Wilde had labeled us his enemies, and considering that he was murdered, I don't think we should be heard gloating over his death."

"I've been accused of a lot of things, Claire, but never of being two-faced. I don't mince words. What I feel, I say. You were bred in a hothouse of gentility, while I was scraping and clawing to survive in Harlem. Me, I come on like gangbusters, while you barely flutter the air when you move. I've got a mouth as wide as the Lincoln Tunnel. Your voice would melt butter.

"But there's a limit to even your patience, Claire Louise Laurent. This preacher man was on your ass for almost a year, since the first time he trashed French Silk's catalog from his gilded pulpit. It was like having your baby publicly spanked for being a wicked child.

"You've withstood his narrow-minded censure with a poise and grace that did your southern heritage proud, but truthfully now, deep down, aren't you glad the pious son of a bitch is dead?"

Claire stared vacantly beyond her hood ornament. "Yes," she said quietly, slowly. "Deep down, I'm glad the son of a bitch is dead."

"Hmm. Well, maybe you'd better follow your own advice and think of something else to tell them."

"Them?" Claire snapped out of her trance, and Yasmine directed her attention to the next block. Several TV vans with satellite dishes were parked along Peters Street in front of French Silk. Reporters and video cameramen were milling around them.

"Damn!" Claire muttered. "I don't want to be involved in this."

"Well, brace yourself, baby," Yasmine said. "You were one of Jackson Wilde's favorite targets. Whether you want to be or not, you're involved up to your eyebrows."

Chapter Two

❧ ❧

"**Y**ou've failed to get convictions on your last three cases."

Cassidy had expected that argument. Even so, the criticism stung. Rather than showing his agitation, he assumed a self-confident air. "We knew going in that those three cases were weak, Tony. In each one, all the defense attorneys had to do was say, 'Prove it.' I did the best I could with what little evidence I had, and you damn well know that."

District Attorney Anthony Crowder crossed his stubby, hairy hands over his vest and leaned back in his leather desk chair. "This conversation is premature. The police haven't even made an arrest yet. It might be months before they do."

Cassidy stubbornly shook his head. "I want to work alongside them on the investigation to make certain something vital doesn't slip through the cracks."

"Then I'll have the police commissioner on my back for your butting in on what should be a matter strictly for his department."

"I'm glad you mentioned the P.C. You're buddies. Have a talk with him. See if you can get Howard Glenn on the Wilde case."

"That seedy—"

"He was first on the scene, and he's good. The best."

"Cassidy . . ."

"Don't worry about me overstepping my bounds. I'll exercise all my powers of diplomacy."

"You don't have any powers of diplomacy," the district attorney reminded him. "Since you joined this office five years ago, you've done some good work, but generally speaking you've been a pain in the butt."

Cassidy grinned confidently, unfazed by Tony Crowder's gruff put-down. He knew how the D.A. really felt about him. Unofficially he was Crowder's heir apparent. When his current term was up next year, he planned to retire. It was tacitly understood that Cassidy would get first crack at Crowder's office and his endorsement. He might exasperate the older man, but Crowder recognized in Cassidy the same combination of ambition and grit that had once characterized and driven him.

"I've prosecuted and won more cases for you than any other lawyer in the department," Cassidy said without false modesty.

"I know that," Crowder snapped. "You don't have to remind me. But you've also caused me more trouble."

"You can't accomplish anything if you're scared of making waves."

"In your case *tidal* waves."

Cassidy sat forward and fixed Crowder with a compelling stare. His steady gray eyes had intimidated reluctant witnesses, impressed cynical judges, swayed skeptical jurors, and, in his private life, made sweet talk superfluous. "Give me this case, Tony."

Before Crowder could verbalize his decision, his secretary poked her head around the door. "Ariel Wilde is holding a press conference. It's being broadcast live on all the TV stations. Thought you might be interested.'' She withdrew, closing the door behind her.

Crowder reached for the remote control on his desk and switched on the TV set across the room.

The widow's pretty, pale features appeared on the screen. She looked as frail and defenseless as a refugee angel, but there was steely conviction behind her voice. ''This tragedy will not put an end to my husband's crusade against the Devil's handiwork.'' That won her a chorus of *amens* from the faithful followers who were pressing against the ranks of security people, reporters, and photographers surrounding her.

''Satan knew we were winning this battle. He had to take desperate measures. First he used this corrupt city as a tool against us. City officials refused to provide my husband the 'round-the-clock protection he requested.''

''Oh shit,'' Crowder said, groaning. ''Why'd she have to blame the city? The whole damn world is watching.''

''Nobody knows that better than she does.'' Cassidy left his chair, sliding his hands into his trousers pockets as he moved closer to the television set.

As eloquent tears trickled down her ivory cheeks, the widow continued her speech. ''This beautiful city is rank with sin and corruption. Take a walk down Bourbon Street if you want to see the stranglehold the Devil has on New Orleans. Jackson Wilde was a conscience, whispering into the ear of this city that it had become a moral cesspool, a slimy reservoir for crime and immorality.

''Other than these few here who have come to lend support and mourn his passing, local officials resented Jackson for his divinely inspired honesty.'' The camera panned a somber group that included a judge, a congressman, and several city officials.

Crowder made a rude sound. ''Politicians.''

'Some thought Jackson Wilde and voters made good bed-fellows.''

"I'd rather fuck a goat," Crowder grumbled.

"My husband was treated with an indifference that bordered on hostility," Ariel Wilde cried. "That indifference to his safety cost him his life!"

When the roar of agreement from the crowd subsided, she continued. "Then the Devil used one of his demons to silence his staunchest foe, Reverend Jackson Wilde, with a bullet through his heart. But we won't be silenced!" she shouted, raising her thin arms and shaking her fists. "My beloved Jackson is with the Lord now. He's been granted a well-deserved rest and peace, praise the Lord."

"Praise the Lord!" the flock echoed.

"But my work isn't finished. I'll continue the crusade Jackson began. We'll ultimately win this war against the filth that would foul our hearts and minds! This ministry won't stop until America is swept clean of the offal that fills its theaters and bookracks, until museums supported by your tax dollars are rid of pornography that passes itself off as art. We're going to make this country an ideal for the rest of the world to follow, a country free of smut, a nation whose children are reared in an environment of purity and light.''

A shout of approval went up. Policemen had a difficult time holding back the surging crowd. The camera angle widened to take in the entire chaotic scene. Ariel Wilde, seemingly spent and on the verge of collapse, was led away on the arm of her stepson. Wilde's entourage protectively closed ranks around her.

Random close-ups of the crowd showed faces streaked with tears, streaming eyes pinched shut in soulful anguish, lips moving in silent prayer. The mourning disciples linked arms and began singing in unison Jackson Wilde's theme song, "Onward, Christian Soldiers."

With a precise flick of his wrist, Tony Crowder switched off the set. "Damned hypocrites. If they're so concerned about the welfare of their children, why aren't they home with them teaching them the difference between right and wrong, instead of parading for a dead saint?" He sighed in exasperation and nodded toward the TV. "Are you sure you want to get involved in that mess, Cassidy?"

"Absolutely."

"Off the record, its gonna be a frigging three-ring circus, especially when the police start rounding up suspects."

"Which right now is limited to about six hundred people—everyone in and around the Fairmont Hotel last night."

"I'd whittle it down real quick—to the widow and stepson."

"They're tops on my list, too." Cassidy grinned engagingly. "Does this mean I have the case?"

"For the time being."

"Come on, Tony!"

"For the time being," the older man repeated loudly. "You're putting yourself in a hotspot, and it's bound to get hotter. I hate to think what will happen if you provoke Ariel Wilde. She's as loved and adored as her husband was. You might incite a riot if it ever comes down to arresting her for killing him."

"There'll be skirmishes, sure. I'm prepared." Cassidy returned to his chair and sat down. "I've taken heat before, Tony. It doesn't bother me."

"Doesn't bother you, hell. You thrive on it."

"I like to win." Cassidy locked gazes with his superior. His grin faded until his lips were a thin, firm line. "Which is the real reason I want this case, Tony. I'm not bullshitting you now. I need a win. I need one bad."

Crowder nodded, appreciating his protégé's candor. "There are less volatile cases I could throw your way if a win's all you're looking for."

Cassidy shook his head. "I need a *big* win, and bringing

Jackson Wilde's killer to justice is going to be one of the biggest legal coups of this year, if not the decade.''

"So you're after headlines and coverage on the six o'clock news," Crowder said, regarding him with a frown.

"You know me better than that, so I decline to honor that comment with a rebuttal. Since this morning, I've taken a crash course on Jackson Wilde. I don't like what the preacher was or what he stood for. In fact I disagree with just about everything he advocated. His version of Christianity doesn't jive with the one I was taught in Sunday school.''

"You went to Sunday school?''

Cassidy ignored that barb too and stuck with the point he was trying to make. "Whatever else Wilde was, he was a human being with a right to live to a ripe old age. Somebody denied him that right. Naked and defenseless, he was murdered by someone he trusted.''

"How do you know that?''

"There wasn't a sign of forced entry on any of the doors into the suite. The locks hadn't been jimmied. So either the perp had a key or Jackson let him in. Apparently Jackson was lying in bed, either sleeping or talking to whoever killed him. He was a religious fanatic, possibly the most dangerous one since Rasputin, but he didn't deserve to have someone cold-bloodedly put a bullet through his brain.''

"And heart and balls," Crowder added.

Cassidy's eyes narrowed. "That's quirky, isn't it? The shot to the head and the heart were already overkill. Why the balls, too?''

"The killer was pissed.''

"Good and pissed. It smacks of self-indulgence, doesn't it? Female vengeance, for instance.''

"You think the wife offed him? Like some others of his ilk, you think Wilde had a sweet young thing on the side and Ariel found out?''

"I don't know. I just have a strong hunch the killer was female.''

"Why's that?"

"It only makes sense," Cassidy said. "If you were a woman and wanted revenge on a guy, isn't that where you'd shoot him?"

※

Claire was breathless by the time she reached her living quarters at the French Silk offices. She heard Yasmine and her mother talking together in another room, but she slipped down the hallway unnoticed and went directly to her bedroom, closing the door behind her.

Their arrival at French Silk had created a tumult among the reporters who had the building staked out. They had swarmed Yasmine and her the moment they alighted from the car. Claire was tempted to duck her head and dash inside but knew that avoidance would only prolong the inevitable. The media wouldn't leave until she made a statement. They would continue to be an impediment to her business, an annoyance to her neighbors, and possibly a source of anxiety to her mother.

Never sure of what Yasmine might say, Claire asked her to go inside and see that Mary Catherine was kept unaware of what was happening outside. After mugging for the cameras, Yasmine did as Claire requested.

Dozens of questions were shouted at Claire, but she caught only snatches of one before the next one was hurled at her. It was impossible to answer them all, and she wouldn't have anyway. Finally she held up her hands for silence. Speaking into the microphones directed at her, she said, "Although Reverend Wilde had proclaimed me a sinner and his enemy, I'm terribly sorry about his death. My heart goes out to his family."

She moved toward the entrance to French Silk, but her progress was blocked by the clamoring journalists.

"Ms. Laurent, is it true that despite his repeated invitations, you refused to debate Reverend Wilde?"

"They weren't invitations, they were challenges. I only wanted to be let alone to run my business."

"How do you respond to his allegations of—"

"I have nothing more to say."

"Who murdered him, Ms. Laurent?"

The question stopped Claire in her tracks. She gazed with stupefaction at the balding reporter who had rudely asked the question. Smirking, he met her stare unflinchingly. The others fell silent, expectantly awaiting her answer.

In that startling instant, Claire realized that her conflict with Jackson Wilde wasn't over. He was dead, but she wasn't free of him. Indeed, the worst might be yet to come. Why had the reporter asked her specifically about the murder? Did he have a reliable source in the police department? Had he heard rumors about possible suspects?

Although she kept her features composed, fear, like icy fingertips, tiptoed up her spine. In spite of the sweltering heat and high humidity, she felt chilled to the bone. "Excuse me. That's all I have to say."

She forcibly pushed her way through the reporters and didn't stop until she was safely inside, upstairs in her private quarters. The experience had left her shaky and agitated. Her clothes clung to her damply, and she peeled them off with frantic haste. In the bathroom, she leaned over the sink and bathed her face, throat, chest, and arms with cool water.

Feeling somewhat refreshed, she stepped into a strapless cotton jumpsuit, one of French Silk's most popular items from the summer catalog, and pulled her shoulder-length hair into a ponytail. Emerging from the bathroom, she soberly regarded the massive cherrywood armoire across the room.

Three years earlier, when she had picked out the old warehouse for French Silk's headquarters, she'd converted the top floor into her private apartment. It was only the second address Claire had ever had. Before that she had lived in her great-aunt Laurel's house on Royal Street near Esplanade.

Following Aunt Laurel's death, Claire and Mary Catherine

had moved out of her house, but Claire hadn't yet had the heart to clean it out and sell it. She couldn't bring herself to dispose of Aunt Laurel's things, because the funny lady unkindly referred to as an old maid, had derived such joy from her possessions, probably because they compensated for her lack of a husband and children. The house on Royal Street remained intact.

The cherrywood armoire was the single exception, the only piece Claire had brought with her when she moved. She had always admired it. Its clean lines blended well with the apartment's contemporary design. She had specifically requested that the architect design a wall in her bedroom large enough to accommodate the piece.

Claire crossed to the armoire, pulled open the doors, knelt in front of the bureau drawers, and tugged open the bottom one. It took some effort because it was so heavy, filled to capacity with clippings that had been cut from newspapers and magazines. The dates on them spanned the last several years.

Claire had spent hours poring over the articles, digesting the information they contained and assimilating her reactions to it. She regretted having to destroy them. Collecting them had been like a hobby to her, one she had found habit-forming and fascinating.

But now it would have to be disposed of. Immediately. It would be folly for her to keep printed documentation of every move made by the Reverend Jackson Wilde.

The hotel suite was overrun with people. Some were merely curious hangers-on; others were sincerely trying to help. All seemed confused by the sudden loss of their leader as they wandered aimlessly through the suite, gathering in small groups and then dispersing, shaking their heads and whispering tearfully as though it were a refrain, "I just can't believe it."

After being questioned by Cassidy, Ariel had been moved out of the San Louis suite. Her present accommodations were smaller and less luxurious. Her privacy was limited. The constant ebb and flow of mourners was maddening. She signaled to Josh, who immediately rushed to her side. After a hushed, brief exchange, he raised his voice in order to get everyone's attention.

"Ariel is exhausted. Could we ask you please to clear the suite now and let her get some rest. If either of us needs anything, we'll notify you."

Wilde's entourage filed out, looking forlorn and abandoned. They cast sympathetic glances at the widow, who was curled in a corner of the sofa, her legs tucked beneath her. Her black dress seemed to be slowly consuming her as though she were melting inside it.

As soon as Josh had closed the door behind the last straggler, Ariel sat up and swung her legs off the couch. "Thank God they're gone. And shut that damn thing off. I don't want to look at *her*." She pointed to the TV set. The volume had been muted, but the image of a woman trying to avoid a horde of reporters filled the screen.

"Who's she?" Josh asked.

"That French Silk person. A minute ago they had her name superimposed on the screen."

"So that's Claire Laurent," Josh said, standing back to get a better look. "I wondered what she looked like. She doesn't have horns and a pointed tail as Daddy would have had everyone believe. Nor does she look like a scarlet woman. Quite the contrary, I'd say."

"Who cares what you'd say." Ariel marched to the set and shut it off herself.

"Aren't you curious about what Ms. Laurent has to say?" Josh asked.

"Not in the slightest. She'll get hers, but not today. All in good time. Order me something from room service, will you? I'm starving." She disappeared into the next room.

Joshua Wilde, the twenty-eight-year-old son of Jackson Wilde by his first marriage, called room service and ordered a light lunch for his stepmother. He figured a grieving widow shouldn't have too healthy an appetite. For himself he ordered a muffuletta, a New Orleans specialty sandwich for which he had acquired a taste.

While he waited for their order, he moved to the window and gazed down. People on the street were going about their everyday lives as though nothing extraordinary had happened. Hadn't they heard? *Jackson Wilde was dead.*

Josh hadn't yet assimilated it, although he'd seen the body and the bloodshed. He hadn't really expected the earth to stop turning, but he'd thought something momentous would occur to mark his father's passing. Jackson would never again fill a room with his crackling, parasitical energy, which drained the life force out of everyone else. His voice would never be heard again, whether raised in prayer or laden with malice. Never again would Josh be subjected to one of his father's cold stares, which too frequently conveyed either disappointment or disgust, and always criticism.

Seven years ago, Josh's mother, Martha, had died with as little fanfare as that with which she had lived. Josh received the news that she had died instantly of a stroke while he was in New York, studying music at Juilliard. He never got to say goodbye. Her life had been so inconsequential that her death had barely caused a pause in the well-oiled operation of his father's ministry. When she died, Jackson had been actively expanding his ministry to cable television. He was driven, inexhaustible. Immediately following his wife's funeral, he had returned to his office to get in a few hours' work so that the day wouldn't be entirely wasted.

Josh had never forgiven his father for that particular display of insensitivity. That's why he didn't feel guilty now for the appetite that was making his stomach growl, even though he'd viewed his father's bloody corpse only hours ago.

That's also why he didn't feel guilty about committing adultery with his father's second wife. He reasoned that some sins were justified, although he had no scriptural reference to support that belief.

Ariel was only two years older than Josh, but as she came out of the bedroom dressed in an oversized T-shirt, her long hair held away from her face by barrettes, she looked several years younger than he. Her legs and feet were bare. "Did you order some dessert?"

Jackson always taunted her about her overactive sweet tooth and never let her indulge it without hassling her. "Chocolate layer cake," Josh told her.

"Yummy."

"Ariel?"

"Hmm?"

He waited until she turned to face him. "Only a few hours ago, you discovered your husband's body."

"Are you trying to spoil my appetite?"

"I guess I am. Aren't you the least bit upset?"

Her expression turned sulky and self-defensive. "You know how much I cried earlier."

Josh laughed without humor. "You've been crying on cue ever since that night you came to Daddy with a special prayer request for your little brother after he'd received a life sentence. You wrenched Daddy's heart and sang on his podium at the very next service.

"I've seen you be very effective with your tears. Others might mistake them as genuine, but I know better. You use them when it's convenient or when you want something. Never because you're sad. You're too selfish ever to feel sad. Angry and frustrated and jealous, maybe, but never sad."

Ariel had lost a lot of weight since marrying Josh's father

three years earlier. Then she'd been rather plump. Her breasts
were smaller now, but the areolas were still wide and the
nipples large and protrudent. Josh hated himself for noticing
them beneath her soft cotton T-shirt as she propped her hands
on her hips.

"Jackson Wilde was a mean-spirited, spiteful, self-cen-
tered son of a bitch." Her blue eyes didn't blink once. "His
death isn't going to spoil my appetite because I'm not sorry
he's dead. Except for how it might effect the ministry."

"And you took care of that during the press conference."

"That's right, Josh. I've already laid the groundwork for
continuing the ministry. *Somebody* around here should be
thinking about the future," she added snidely.

As though suffering a splitting headache, Josh pressed the
tips of his long, slender, musician's fingers against his hairline
and squeezed his eyes shut. "Christ, you're cold. Always
scheming. Always planning. Relentless."

"Because I've always had to be. I didn't grow up rich
like you, Josh. You call your grandparents' place outside of
Nashville a farm," She scoffed. "My family had a real farm.
It was dirty and stank of manure. I didn't help groom fancy
horses like you did only when you felt like it. Whether I
wanted to or not, I had to weed the vegetable garden and shell
peas and slop a hog so he'd be fat in November when we
butchered him.

"I only owned one pair of shoes at a time. The girls at
school laughed at me for wearing hand-me-downs. And
from the time I was twelve, I had to ward off the groping
hands of drunken uncles on Saturday nights, then look into
their smug faces from the choir loft on Sunday mornings.
Oh, yes, we always went to church on Sundays and listened
to sermons that glorified poverty. But I never believed a
word of it."

She shook her long, straight, platinum-blond hair. "I've
been poor, Josh. And poor sucks. It makes you mean. It
makes you desperate. You reach a point where you'll do

anything to escape it. That's why my little brother is in prison for the rest of his life. After he got sent up, I knew I had to do something drastic or wind up worse off than he is. So, yes, I cried for your daddy. And if he'd asked me to wipe his butt or give him a blow job on the spot, I would have done that, too.

"I learned from him that money makes all the difference. Being rich and mean is a whole lot better than being poor and mean. When you're poor, you go to jail for your meanness, but if you're rich, you can do what you please and nobody can touch you. I'm a schemer, all right. I will be for the rest of my life because I'm never going to be poor again."

She paused to take a breath. "Don't try to tell me you're sorry he's gone, Josh. You hated him as much as I did, if not more."

He couldn't quite meet her direct gaze. "I guess my feelings could be classified as ambivalent. I don't feel any remorse. But I don't feel relieved, as I imagined I would."

She moved toward him and slid her arms around his neck. "Don't you see, Josh? If we play it smart, this can be a beginning for us. The public loves us. We can go on as before, except that life will be so much better without him harping on us all the time."

"Do you really think our adoring public will accept us as a couple, Ariel?" He smiled wanly over her naïveté. Or was it her rapacity that amused him?

He couldn't hold any of it against her, really. She had not had the advantages he'd grown up with and taken for granted. Even before Jackson Wilde had become a household word, he'd had a faithful and generous following. The offering plates were always full. In addition to Martha's inheritance, it amounted to a sizable income. Josh had never lacked for anything material.

The first time he'd seen Ariel, she was wearing a cheap, loud dress and too much costume jewelry. Her speech and crude accent had been offensive to his ears. Even so, he'd admired the audacity it had taken for her to approach his father and solicit prayers for her convicted brother.

Today she was slim, articulate, and immaculately groomed. But Josh knew that when she looked into the mirror Ariel still saw a plump, disheveled, desperate young woman making a last-ditch effort to alter the course of her life. When she gazed at her manicured hands, she saw garden dirt beneath her fingernails.

"The public will accept our new relationship in time," she was saying, "if we bring the Lord into it often enough. We can say we fought our romantic love for each other because it didn't seem right. But then through prayer and Bible study, God convinced us that it had been His will all along. They'll eat it up. Everybody loves a happy ending." She kissed his lips softly, teasingly, releasing a slender thread of her breath into his mouth. "I need you now, Josh."

He shut his eyes tightly, trying valiantly to ward off the lust that was gathering in his center. "Ariel, we shouldn't be together for a while. They'll think—"

She moved closer, bumping his pelvis with her own. "Who'll think what?"

"The police . . . that Mr. Cassidy from the D.A.'s office. We're bound to be suspects."

"Don't be silly, Josh. We have each other for our alibis, remember?"

Her nonchalance was exasperating, but his attraction to her was based on frustration and forbiddenness. Rather than shaking her, as he felt like doing, he slipped his hands beneath her T-shirt and clasped her around the waist, pulling her roughly against him. His lips ground over hers. He pressed his tongue into her eager, wet mouth while the heels of his hands caressed her pelvic bones.

His sex was swollen and hot. He was impatient with his clothing. But as he went for his zipper there was a knock at the door.

"That'll be our lunch." Ariel sighed. She kissed him one final time, brushed her hand across his distended fly, then drifted out of his arms. "Have the waiter bring the tray into the bedroom. We'll eat first."

❧

"Cassidy?"

"Here." He juggled the telephone receiver while trying to depress the volume button on the remote control and keep from dropping his bologna sandwich and his beer.

"It's Glenn. I've been officially assigned to the Wilde case."

Good, Cassidy thought, *Crowder had come through*. Detective Howard Glenn would be the point person, or the main liaison between him and the police department. Once Glenn selected his platoon of officers to investigate the case, he, Cassidy, would be constantly apprised of developments.

He knew that Glenn was difficult to work with. He was a slob, untidy in every respect—except his detective work. But Cassidy was willing to overlook Glenn's character flaws in exchange for his competence.

"Got anything?" he asked, setting aside the tasteless sandwich.

"The lab report's back. We're going through it now."

"How's it look?"

"No prints other than his, his old lady's, and the housekeeper in charge of the suite. Course, we've got hundreds of partials that belong to the people who stayed in that suite before him."

Although Cassidy had figured as much, it was still dismal news. "Any sign of a weapon?"

"Zilch. Whoever walked into Wilde's suite and offed him walked out with the gun."

The lack of a murder weapon was going to make solving

this case and getting a conviction a real challenge. Luckily Cassidy liked challenges, the harder the better.

"How soon could you get a few phone taps in place?" he asked the detective.

"First thing tomorrow. Who else besides the wife and son?"

"We'll discuss it in the morning. Stay in touch."

He hung up, took another bite of his sandwich, another swig of tepid beer, and returned his attention to the television set. Earlier, he had called the cable station that aired Jackson Wilde's *Prayer and Praise Hour* and asked for copies of all available tapes. The station management had promptly delivered the tapes to his office. He'd then brought them home, where he could watch them without interruption.

The programs were slickly produced. Wilde put on a dazzling show, complete with flying white doves, an orchestra, a five-hundred-voice choir, a gold leaf pulpit, and Joshua's mirrored piano, which resembled the one once owned by the late Liberace.

The format never varied. The program opened with a trumpet blast loud enough to herald the Second Coming. The choir broke into song, the doves were released with a flurry of white wings, and Wilde descended a curved staircase as though he'd just wrapped up a visit with the Almighty, which is exactly what he intimated in his opening remarks.

Ariel, always dressed in pristine white, her only jewelry a simple gold wedding band and a pair of discreet pearl earrings—Wilde stressed that the only treasures they stockpiled were their spiritual rewards—was introduced with the trilling of trumpets in the background. Then the audience got a close-up of Joshua Wilde as he played the introduction to Ariel's first song.

Her singing voice, marginal at best, was greatly enhanced by the orchestra, the choir, and a sound system whose staggering cost would have made a large dent in the national debt.

Ariel threw beatific smiles toward her husband, toward Josh, toward the audience, and toward heaven. Invariably, by the end of the song, at least one eloquent, glistening tear had spilled from her celestial blue eyes.

Cassidy was a skeptic by nature and rarely took anything at face value. Generously allowing for that, he still couldn't understand how anyone of reasonable intelligence could fall for Wilde's glitzy sideshow. His sermons were gross distortions of the gospel. He preached much more vehemently about admonition than grace, more about condemnation than love, more about hellfire than forgiveness. More was said of Satan than of Christ. It was easy to see why he was held in such contempt by clergymen of most organized Christian sects.

It was also plain to Cassidy how Wilde was able to induce such fanaticism in his narrow-minded followers. He told them exactly what they wanted to hear: that they were right and anyone who disagreed with their opinion was wrong. Of course, God was *always* on their side.

After viewing the tapes several times, making notes as he watched, Cassidy switched off the set and headed for his bedroom. An inventory of clean shirts and shorts revealed that he could go another couple of days before a trip to the laundry.

When he was married, Kris had taken care of his wardrobe, just as she had kept the house, done the shopping, and cooked their meals. The divorce hadn't come about because she was negligent. And by most standards, he would have been judged a fairly good husband. He always remembered anniversaries and birthdays. He had a sixth sense that told him when sex was out of the question and on those nights he refrained from asking.

The dissolution of their four-year marriage could be blamed more on apathy than on animosity. It had cracked under external pressure, and their love for one another hadn't been

strong enough to hold things together. Kris hadn't even
wanted to discuss relocating, and, after a pivotal incident that
had unbalanced his perfectly balanced life, he'd been adamant
on relocating.

When word reached him of an opening in the Orleans
Parish, Louisiana, D.A.'s office, he applied for the job and
a divorce on the same day. The last he'd heard of Kris, she
was still living in Louisville, happily remarried and pregnant
with a second child. He wished her every happiness. It certainly wasn't her fault that his work had been more important
to him than she had been and that when his career went awry,
he'd had to reevaluate everything in his life, including their
marriage.

In some respects, he was still shackled to his past mistakes.
He'd been hacking away at those problems for five years and
wasn't yet completely free of them. He might never be. But
his marriage wasn't a link in those chains. It had been a clean,
unemotional break. The only time he thought of his former
wife was when he needed sex very badly and no one was
available or when he was out of clean shirts. That wasn't fair
to Kris. She deserved better than that. But that's the way it
was.

He stripped and got into bed, but his mind was too preoccu-
pied to settle into sleep. He realized, to his surprise, that he
was also semierect. Lust for a woman hadn't caused it. It was
residual excitement looking for an outlet. He was super-
charged, mentally and physically.

As he lay there, sleepless, he reviewed the facts of the
Wilde case, acknowledging that there were damned few of
them. All he knew for certain was that it was going to be a
difficult, jealous bitch of a case that would consume his life
for months, if not years.

Undaunted by the prospect of that, he was itching to get
started. He'd overseen the writing and issuance of the press
release that gave an account of the murder. It was now a
matter of record that he would be heading the investigation

and prosecuting the case when it came to trial. He'd asked for the opportunity and it had been granted. He couldn't blow it. He had to prove to Crowder that his trust wasn't misplaced.

Cassidy also had to prove it to himself.

Chapter Three

The building was located on North Peters Street, one block from where it merged with Decatur. It was last in a row of scarred brick warehouses that had thus far withstood the path of progress in this old industrial district of the French Quarter. Most of the buildings, including the nearby Jax Brewery, had been gutted and redeveloped into fashionable eateries and shopping malls.

The renovation had resulted in a discordant blending of authentic New Orleans with crass commercialism. The old-timers, who wished to preserve the mystic atmosphere of the Vieux Carré considered such commercialization an abomination, a desecration of the district's uniqueness. Those who clung to it did so with tenacity and defiance, as the facade of French Silk evinced.

The ancient bricks had been painted white, although the side of the building that was exposed to the intersecting street bore the cruel marks of age. In keeping with Creole architecture, there were glossy black shutters on all the windows. Black grillwork simulating balconies had been added to the second and third floors. Above the entrance, suspended from twin black chains, was a discreet sign bearing the name of the business written in cursive.

Cassidy soon discovered, however, that the front door was also a facade and that the real entrance to the warehouse was a heavy metal door on the Conti Street side of the building. He depressed the button and heard a loud school bell ringing inside. A few seconds later the door was opened.

"What do you want?" The woman who confronted him was built like a stevedore. RALPH, spelled out in blue letters and centered in a red heart, had been tattooed on her forearm. Her upper lip was beaded with perspiration that clung to the hairs of a faint mustache. She looked no more like she belonged in a lingerie factory than a linebacker did at a debutante ball. Cassidy's heart went out to Ralph.

"My name is Cassidy. Are you Claire Laurent?"

She uttered a sound like a foghorn. "Is that supposed to be a joke?"

"No. I'm looking for Claire Laurent. Is she here?"

She gave him a suspicious once-over. "Just a minute." Propping the door open with her foot, she picked up a wall-mounted telephone and pressed two digits on the panel. "There's a guy here to see Ms. Laurent. Kennedy somebody."

"Cassidy," he corrected with a polite smile. He was no Schwarzenegger, but he could hold his own in an ordinary brawl. Still, he'd hate to tangle with this Tugboat Annie.

She glared at Cassidy while waiting for further instructions. Cupping the mouthpiece of the telephone, she spat past his shoulder. Finally she listened, then said to him, "Ms. Laurent wants to know what about."

"I'm from the district attorney's office." He removed the leather folder from his breast pocket and flipped it open to show her his ID.

That won him another glare and a slow, distrustful once-over. "He's from the district attorney's office." After a moment she hung up the telephone. "This way." She didn't looked pleased about her boss's decision to see him. Her rubber soles struck the concrete floor like each footfall might have a cockroach beneath it. She led him past row upon row of boxed goods that were being labeled and loaded for shipping.

Large fans mounted in the walls at ceiling level were blowing hard and noisily. But they succeeded only in circulating warm, humid air. Their blades interrupted the sunlight streaming in, creating an effect like a strobe and lending a surreal atmosphere to the warehouse.

Cassidy felt a trickle of sweat running down his side and forgave the woman her sweating upper lip. He shrugged off his suit jacket and held it over his shoulder. Then he loosened the knot of his necktie. As he moved across the warehouse, he noticed that it was spotlessly clean and highly organized. The busy workers, seemingly unaffected by the heat, chatted happily among themselves. A few glanced curiously at him, but none had glared at him like Tugboat. He supposed that suspicion was the nature of her job, which was obviously to keep out the scumbags and undesirables like himself.

When they reached the freight elevator she slid open the heavy double doors. "Second floor."

"Thank you."

The doors clanged shut, sealing him in an elevator larger than his apartment's bathroom. On his way up, he rolled his shirtsleeves up to his elbows.

He stepped into a corridor that ran the width of the building. Branching off it were other hallways and offices, from which he could hear sounds of clerical activity. Directly in front of him was a set of wide double doors. Instinctively he knew that he would find Ms. Laurent behind them.

Indeed, the doors opened onto a carpeted, air-conditioned office that was exquisitely furnished, complete with a smiling receptionist behind a desk made of glass and black lacquer. "Mr. Cassidy?" she asked pleasantly.

"That's right." He hadn't expected so plush an office above an ordinary warehouse. He shouldn't have removed his jacket and loosened his tie. However, he didn't have time to correct that before the receptionist escorted him to another set of double doors.

"Ms. Laurent is expecting you. Go right in."

She opened the door for him and stepped aside. He went in and received the next in a series of surprises. He had anticipated a glamorous office that lived up to the lavish reception area. Instead, this was a work space—*space* being the operative word. There seemed to be acres of it. The room was as wide as the building and half as deep. A wall of windows offered a panoramic view of the Mississippi River. There were several drawing tables, each outfitted with a vast assortment of implements, and three headless dress forms, and easels, and a sewing machine, and swatches of fabric . . . and a woman.

She was seated on a high stool, bending over one of the drawing tables, pencil in hand. As the door closed behind Cassidy, she raised her head and looked at him through a pair of square tortoiseshell eyeglasses. "Mr. Cassidy?"

"Ms. Laurent?"

After removing her glasses and leaving them and the pencil on the table, she came toward him with her right hand extended. "Yes, I'm Claire Laurent."

Her face, figure, and form weren't at all what he had expected. For a moment, while he clasped her hand courteously, his head went a little muzzy. What had he expected Claire Laurent to look like? Another Tugboat Annie? Another petite doll like the receptionist? She was neither. It hardly seemed that she and the doorkeeper belonged to the same species, much less the same sex. For while Claire Laurent was wearing wide-legged trousers the color of ripe tobacco and a loose, tailored silk shirt, there was certainly nothing masculine about her. Nor was she pert and cute like the secretary.

She was tall. Slender. She had fashionably wide shoulders. Her breasts were compact but definitely discernible. Supported by lace, he guessed, because he caught glimpses of it between the soft lapels of the ivory shirt. Her eyes were the color of expensive whiskey, and if whiskey had a voice, it would sound like hers, like a blend of satin and woodsmoke.

"You wanted to see me?"

He released her hand. "Yes."

"Can I offer you something to drink?"

She indicated a sitting area comprised of a divan with deep cushions and a low table between two upholstered chairs. In one of the chairs was a basket overflowing with what appeared to be crochet or knitting. On the table were several crystal decanters reflecting the late afternoon sunlight and casting rainbows on the white plaster walls and hardwood floor.

"No, thanks. Nothing."

"May I hang up your jacket?" She reached for it.

He almost passed it to her before thinking better of it. "No, thanks. I'm fine. Sorry to be so casual, but downstairs is a sweatbox."

Because she wasn't what he'd expected, it had cost him a few seconds of control. Cassidy liked always to be in control, and somehow he wanted to pay her back for stealing that from him. Feeling ornery, he had spoken the statement innocently, but he'd intended it as a dig, which she'd have to be a real airhead to miss. She wasn't. Not by a long shot.

Her eyes flickered defensively, but she obviously decided to let it pass. "Yes, it can sometimes get uncomfortably warm. Please, sit down."

"Thanks."

He moved to one of the chairs and sat down, draping his jacket over his knee. She sat on the divan, facing him. He noticed that her lipstick was wearing off, as though she'd been pulling that full lower lip between her teeth while deep in concentration. Her hair was a light shade of auburn that shimmered like fire in the sunlight. She must have been raking her hands or her pencil through it because the curls and waves were tousled.

Immediately, he knew several things about her. First, Claire Laurent was a working woman. She wasn't hung up on feminine affectations and vanity. She was also a woman trying to hide her nervousness behind hospitality. Only the pulse beating at the base of her elegantly smooth throat gave her away.

From her throat, his eyes moved to the trinket hanging from a black silk cord around her neck. She followed his gaze down and said, "It was a gift from my friend Yasmine."

"What's in it?" The small vial lying against her chest contained a clear liquid. "A love potion?"

His gray eyes connected with hers with an almost audible click. Suddenly Cassidy wished that he hadn't gone to bed last night with a semi-hard-on. He also wished that his errand here today weren't an official one.

She removed the stopper from the vial. At the end of the short wand was a minuscule spool. She raised it to her lips and blew through it. Dozens of tiny, iridescent bubbles burst from it and drifted up and around her face.

He laughed, partly because the bubbles surprised him and partly to release some of the energy building inside him.

"A whimsical distraction for when work gets me down," she said. "Yasmine frequently gives me gadgets like this because she says I take myself too seriously." Smiling, she recapped the vial.

"Do you?"

She met his direct gaze. "Do I what?"

"Take yourself too seriously."

He knew from her reaction that he'd overstepped his

bounds. Her smile congealed. Still cordial, but with a hint of impatience, she asked, "Why did you come to see me, Mr. Cassidy? Is it regarding that hot check I reported to the D.A.'s office?"

"Hot check? No, I'm afraid not."

"Then I'm at a loss."

"Reverend Jackson Wilde." He tossed out the name without preamble. It lay like a gauntlet between them. She didn't pick it up but merely continued to gaze at him inquisitively. He was forced to elaborate. "I assume you've heard about his murder."

"Certainly. Didn't you see me on TV?"

That took him aback. "No. When was that?"

"The day Reverend Wilde's body was found. The day before yesterday, wasn't it? Reporters came here to get my statement. It must not have been as dramatic as they wanted, because I didn't make the evening news."

"Were you relieved or disappointed that you were cut?"

"What do you think?" Her smile had disappeared.

Cassidy took another tack. "What do you know about the murder?"

"Know?" she repeated with a shrug. "Only what I read in the newspapers and see on television. Why?"

"Were you acquainted with Reverend Wilde?"

"Do you mean had I ever met him? No."

"Never?"

"No."

"But he knew you." She remained silent, although she didn't look quite as calm, cool, and collected as she had a few moments ago. "Didn't he, Ms. Laurent? Well enough that your opinion was sought by the media when he was found dead."

She wet her lips with a dainty, pink tongue that momentarily distracted him. "Reverend Wilde knew me by name, as the owner of French Silk. He condemned me from his pulpit as a pornographer. 'Smut-peddler' is how he referred to me.''

"How did you feel about that?"

"How do you think I felt?" Suddenly giving vent to the agitation he'd sensed behind her calm facade, she stood up and rounded the divan, so that it was between them.

"I'll bet you didn't like it one damn bit."

"You're absolutely right, Mr. Cassidy. I didn't. The term *smut* doesn't apply either to my business or to my catalog."

"Did you know you were on Wilde's hit list?"

"What are you talking about?"

Cassidy removed a sheet of paper from the pocket of his jacket, which still lay across his knees. He shook out the folds and handed it to her, yet she made no move to take it from him.

"Among Wilde's personal effects," he said, "we found this handwritten list of publications. *Playboy, Hustler*, all the girly mags you'd expect. Along with the French Silk catalog."

That morning when he and Howard Glenn had discussed the few facts they had on the case, Glenn had expressed little interest in this list. The veteran detective was focusing his investigation on Ariel and Joshua Wilde. To his way of thinking, they were the most likely suspects.

He was probably right, but Cassidy hadn't wanted to leave a single clue dangling. His offer to check out French Silk had earned him an indifferent shrug from Glenn, who obviously felt that he was wasting his time.

Having met Claire Laurent, Cassidy didn't think so. She hardly fit a criminal psychological profile, but she was sure as hell intriguing and she had had a real ax to grind with the late preacher.

She stared at the sheet of paper for a moment, then gestured at it angrily. "I don't know anything about this list. My catalog has nothing in common with those magazines."

"Apparently Wilde thought it did."

"He was wrong."

"Ms. Laurent, your company was targeted for defamation and harassment until you were forced out of business. According to the date on this, Wilde made a holy vow a few weeks before his death and signed his name to it in his own blood."

"Obviously he was insane."

"He had thousands of devoted followers."

"So did Adolph Hitler. Some people are sheep who have to be told what to believe because they can't think for themselves. If they're told what they want to hear often enough, they'll follow anyone and adhere to any misinformation they're fed. They're brainwashed. I pity them, but they're free to make their own choices. I only want to be let alone to make mine. That's the only quarrel I had with Jackson Wilde. He presumed to impose his beliefs on everyone. If he didn't approve of my catalog, fine. But who gave him the right to condemn it?"

"He would say God had."

"But we only have Wilde's word on that, don't we?"

She was drawn up tighter than a guitar string threatening to snap. Her breasts rose and fell, disturbing the liquid in the small bottle hanging from her neck. Cassidy learned something else about Claire Laurent in that heated moment. Beneath her cool reserve beat a passionate heart.

He suddenly realized that he was standing, although he didn't remember rising to his feet. "You had a real problem with the televangelist and what he might do to your business, didn't you, Ms. Laurent?"

"He was the one with the problem, not I."

"He had pronounced you his enemy and pledged not to let up on you until he won."

"Then it was his own crusade. I wasn't a participant."

"Are you sure?"

"What do you mean?"

"Hadn't open warfare been declared between the two of you?"

"No. I ignored him."

"Where were you the night of September eighth?"

Her head snapped back. "Pardon me?"

"I believe you heard me."

"September eighth was the night Wilde was murdered. Am I to understand that you're implicating me?"

"That's the general idea."

"You can go straight to hell."

With her succinct words still electrifying the space between them, the double doors opened behind Cassidy. He whipped his head around, almost expecting Tugboat Annie to come barging in with a bent to forcibly evict him from the premises.

The woman who came in looked too delicate to bend the wings of a butterfly. "Oh, my goodness!" she exclaimed when she saw Cassidy. Flattening her hand against her chest, she said, "I didn't know we had a caller. Claire dear, you should have told me I'd be receiving this afternoon. I would have changed into something more appropriate."

Composing herself, Claire moved to the other woman and took her arm. "You look as lovely as always, Mama. Come meet our guest."

As he watched them approach, Cassidy wished to hell he had control of this situation. He'd lost it when the amazon downstairs had let him in, and he'd never fully regained it. The tenuous hold he'd been grappling for had slipped away with the appearance of the woman at Claire's side.

"Mama, this is Mr. Cassidy. He's . . . he's here on a business matter. Mr. Cassidy, this is my mother, Mary Catherine Laurent."

"Mrs. Laurent," he said. Demurely she extended her hand. He had an insane impulse to bend at the waist and kiss it, for that seemed to be what she expected. Instead he gave her fingers a light squeeze and released them.

Soft brown hair waved away from her smooth, youthful

face. As she looked up at him, she tilted her head to one side. "You're the spit and image of your daddy, Mr. Cassidy. I remember when he attended the cotillions in his dress uniform. My goodness, we girls swooned over him."

She laid her fingers against her cheek as though trying to stave off a blush. "He knew he was good-looking and shamelessly broke all our hearts. He was quite a rascal until he met your mama that summer she came visiting from Biloxi. The first time he saw her she was wearing an apricot organza dress and had a white camellia pinned in her hair. He was instantly smitten. They made such a lovely couple. When they danced together, they seemed to scatter fairy dust."

Baffled, Cassidy looked to Claire for help. She was smiling as though what her mother had said made perfect sense. "Sit down, Mama. Would you like some sherry?"

Cassidy caught a whiff of Mary Catherine Laurent's rose perfume as she sat on the chair next to his and decorously pulled her skirt over her knees.

"Since it's coming up on five o'clock, I suppose I could indulge in a sherry. Mr. Cassidy, you'll join me, won't you? It's quite improper for a lady to drink alone."

Sherry? He'd never tasted the stuff and didn't care if he ever did. What he could use right now was a solid belt or two of straight Chivas. But Mary Catherine's inquiring smile was too much for even a jaded prosecutor like him to resist. God forbid that he'd ever have to put her on the witness stand. One smile from her and a jury would be convinced that the moon was made of Philadelphia cream cheese if she said it was.

"I'd love some," he heard himself say. He cast a smile toward Claire; she didn't return it. Her expression was a frosty contrast to her warm coloring, made even rosier by the hues cast by the late-afternoon sun.

"Tell me all about the naval academy, Mr. Cassidy,"

Mary Catherine said. "I was so proud for your parents when you received the appointment."

With the help of a basketball scholarship, Cassidy had attended junior college in his small hometown in Kentucky before laying out a year to work and raise enough money to attend a university. He sure as hell had never been a candidate for a military academy. A voluntary stint in the post—Vietnam army had helped him finance law school after his discharge.

"It was everything I'd hoped it would be," he told Mary Catherine as he accepted the glass of sherry she had poured for him from one of the glittering crystal decanters.

"Claire, would you care for some?" Mary Catherine lifted a glass toward her daughter.

"No, thank you, Mama. I've still got work to do."

Mary Catherine shook her head sorrowfully and said to Cassidy, "She works all the time. Way too much for a young lady, if you ask me. But she's very talented."

"So I see." He had already noted the framed designs hanging on the walls.

"I tried to teach her knitting and crochet," the older woman said, pointing to the basket now at her feet, "but Claire Louise's only interest was in making clothes. She started out with paper dolls. When the wardrobes in the books ran out, she would draw, color, and cut her own."

The woman smiled fondly at her daughter. "The fashions she designed were much prettier than the ones in the books. She went from paper dolls to sewing. What year did you ask for a sewing machine for Christmas?"

"I was twelve, I believe," she replied tightly. Cassidy could tell she didn't like being discussed in front of him.

"Twelve!" Mary Catherine exclaimed. "And from the day she got it, she spent all her spare time sewing, making garments from patterns she bought or those she designed herself. She's always been so clever with cloth and thread."

Her cheeks blushed and she ducked her head coyly. "Of course, I don't approve of some of the things Claire makes now. There's so little to them. But I suppose I'm old-fashioned. Young women are no longer taught to be modest, as my generation was." She took a sip of sherry, then gazed at him with interest. "Tell me, Mr. Cassidy, did your uncle Clive ever strike oil in Alaska? Such an unpleasant and risky business, petroleum."

Before he could answer the question about his nonexistent uncle Clive, the door behind them opened again. This time it was accompanied by a rush of air, as though it had been thrust open from the other side. He was so startled by the appearance of the woman who entered that he shot to his feet, almost spilling his sherry.

"Thank God!" she exclaimed when she spotted Mary Catherine. "I was afraid she'd sneaked out again."

The new arrival was at least six feet tall, with limbs as long and graceful as a gazelle. Her spectacular body was wrapped in a short, white terrycloth kimono that skimmed the middle of her thighs. Another towel had been wrapped like a turban around her head. Even without makeup her face was captivating—widely spaced agate eyes; a small, straight nose; full lips; a square jaw and a well-defined chin; high, prominent cheekbones. The haughty carriage of African royalty was in her walk as she came farther into the room.

"Sorry, Claire. I let Harry go early and decided to take a quick shower. When I came out, Mary Catherine had vanished. Everyone else has gone home for the day. Christ, I thought I'd really goofed this time."

"Everything's fine, Yasmine."

"Who's he?" She turned to Cassidy with frank curiosity.

Claire made rudimentary introductions. He shook a hand as long as his, but much more slender. Even up close, her skin was flawless, seemingly poreless, the color of heavily creamed coffee. It was dappled with beads of water, indicating that she hadn't even taken the time to dry off. The robe was undoubtedly all she had on, but she exhibited no modesty at all as she broke a dazzlingly white smile for him.

"Pleased to meet you, Mr. Cassidy."

"The same. I've admired your work."

"Thanks." She looked to Claire for clarification, then back at Cassidy. "Am I supposed to know who you are and why you're here?"

"No."

A short, awkward silence ensued. Finally Claire ended it. "Yasmine, would you please take Mama back upstairs? She can take her sherry with her. I'll be up for dinner as soon as I conclude my business with Mr. Cassidy."

Yasmine looked at her friend quizzically, but Claire's expression remained impassive. "Come on, Mary Catherine," she said. "Claire has business to attend to."

Mary Catherine didn't argue with the plan. She rose and extended Cassidy her hand again. This time he figured what the hell, and raised the back of it to his lips. She simpered and smiled and asked him please to extend her regards to his family. Then, trailing the mingled scents of roses and sherry, she drifted out of the room on the arm of the stupefying Yasmine.

As soon as the door closed behind them, he turned to Claire. "I'm sorry. That can be tough. My father was afflicted with Alzheimer's for several years before he died."

"My mother doesn't have Alzheimer's, Mr. Cassidy. It's just that she often confuses the present with the past. Sometimes she believes people to be someone else, someone she knew before."

"Before what?"

"Before she became the way she is," she replied stonily. "She is what some would call off her rocker, daft, batty, one brick shy of a load. I'm sure you've heard all the cruel terms. I know I have. Many times. You see, she's been like this all my life. And, although I appreciate your treating her kindly I don't intend to discuss her mental illness with you. In fact, I don't intend to discuss anything with you.''

She stood, signaling that as far as she was concerned their meeting was concluded. ''I didn't know Jackson Wilde, Mr. Cassidy. If that's what you came here to learn, now you know. I'll show you to the door.''

As she stalked past him, he caught her upper arm and brought her up short. ''You don't get it yet, do you? Or if you do, you're too smart to let it show.''

''Let go of my arm.''

The fabric of her sleeve was so soft and crushable, his fingers seemed to have melted it until he was touching her skin. His knuckles were embedded in the giving fullness of her breast. Slowly, and with a shocking amount of regret, he relaxed his fingers and released her.

''What am I supposed to 'get,' Mr. Cassidy?''

''That I didn't come here for chitchat and sherry.''

''No?''

''No. I came to formally question you in connection with the homicide of Jackson Wilde.''

She drew in a sharp, sudden breath and shivered reflexively. ''That's ridiculous.''

''Not when you consider all that you stood to lose if his plans for your business had been realized.''

''It never would have happened.''

''Maybe you wanted to make damn certain it didn't.''

She ran her hand through her hair and visibly composed herself, unwrinkling the lines of consternation in her forehead. When she again looked up at him, her features were as smooth as a porcelain doll's.

''Mr. Cassidy, as I've already told you, I never met Reverend Wilde. I never corresponded with him directly. Nor did we ever speak by telephone, although I was contacted by personnel within his ministry, challenging me to publicly debate him, which I repeatedly declined to do. I had nothing whatsoever to do with him. I certainly didn't kill him.''

"He placed your business in jeopardy."

"He entertained the delusions of a fanatic," she cried, her composure slipping a notch. "Do you honestly believe that he could have toppled the Playboy empire?"

"But you're much smaller game."

"Granted. So what?"

"So you're also headquartered right here in New Orleans. Maybe when he brought his crusade to town, you seized the opportunity to shut him up forever."

Complacently, she folded her arms across her stomach. "That would have been rather obvious, wouldn't it? You might believe me to be capable of committing murder, Mr. Cassidy, but please, never underestimate my intelligence."

"No," he said softly, as he peered into the depths of her amber eyes. "You can be sure I won't."

His stare lasted a few heartbeats too many, switching from accusatory to something closer to interest. Cassidy became profoundly uncomfortable with it. She, however, was the one to break it. "It's obvious that you don't have any physical evidence linking me to this crime."

"How do you know?"

"Because none exists. I wasn't there." She raised her chin. "You came here because you're grasping at straws, scavenging for a case because neither your office nor the police have arrested a suspect and the murder is now over seventy-two hours old. The widow is accusing the local authorities of laziness, incompetence, and indifference. You're taking a beating from the media, and Wilde's followers are demanding swift and sure justice.

"In short, Mr. Cassidy, you need a scapegoat." She paused to draw a breath. "I'm sympathetic to your problem,

but my sympathies don't extend to having my character insulted and my privacy violated. Please leave.''

Cassidy was impressed by the effectiveness and accuracy
of her speech. It was true that Crowder was getting nervous
over the sticky situation created by the Wilde murder. The
press coverage of the police investigation was becoming more
sly and sarcastic with each report.

Ariel Wilde and the late evangelist's entourage were growing increasingly vocal in their criticism of everyone from
the honorable mayor to the lowliest cop on the beat. The
widow wanted to take Wilde's body to Tennessee for burial,
but the police were reluctant to release it, hoping that, in
spite of Elvie Dupuis's thorough autopsy, they might find
a previously overlooked clue. The whole situation, just as
Crowder had forecast, had grown nasty, a three-ring circus
run amok.

Claire Laurent was correct on all accounts. The sad fact
was that Cassidy didn't have a shred of evidence that could
tie her or anyone else to the murder scene. On the other hand,
since entering this room he'd felt that she was withholding
something. She'd been inordinately polite, but gut instinct
told him she didn't want him here.

When he had been a defense attorney, that same gut instinct
had always told him when his client was guilty despite his
avowals of innocence. It was the sixth sense that let him know
when a witness was lying through his teeth. It was the gut
quiver of either victory or defeat that he felt just before a
verdict was read. That instinct was rarely wrong. He trusted
and relied on it.

He knew there was more to Claire Laurent than what one
saw on the surface. Her eyes might be windows to her soul,
but the shutters were closed. Only occasionally did one catch
a glimpse of the woman living behind them. She was more
than a savvy businesswoman and devoted daughter, more
than a mess of sexy hair, more than a mouth that made him

glad some laws were unenforceable. There were elements to her that she kept carefully concealed. Why?

Cassidy resolved to dig until he knew. "Before I go—"

"Yes, Mr. Cassidy?"

"I want to see a copy of your catalog."

Chapter Four

❦ ❦

Claire was surprised by the request. "Why?"

"I tried buying one at several newsstands and couldn't find it."

"The catalog isn't sold at retail stores. It's mailed to subscribers only."

"What's in it that had Reverend Wilde so hot and bothered?"

"You should have asked him."

"Well, since he's unavailable for comment," he said dryly, "I'd like to see it for myself."

She had thought that once the media stopped hounding her for a statement, her worries regarding the murder would be over. Never had she expected a visit from an assistant D.A., although she congratulated herself on handling the situation well so far. But now she desperately wanted him to leave so that she could collect her thoughts. Conversely, she didn't want to appear hostile or, more to the point, as though she had something to hide. He had only asked to see the catalog, after all. As long as his questions didn't become too personal, she felt there was no danger in humoring him.

"By all means, Mr. Cassidy. Sit down." She handed him the latest quarterly issue of French Silk's catalog. To avoid looking nervously at him, she gazed through the windows. The sky was streaked with the brilliant colors of sunset. The river had turned the color of molten brass. "It's officially the cocktail hour. Would you care for a drink now?"

"Does it have to be sherry?" he asked.

"Wine or something stronger?"

"Scotch, if you have it."

"Rocks, water, or soda?"

"Rocks."

She prepared his drink and poured herself a glass of blush wine. When she returned to the divan, he was thumbing through the catalog. He let it fall open across his lap, blinked, and yanked his head back as though he'd been clipped on the chin. He released a stunned breath. "Wow!"

Looking at the page upside down, Claire remarked on his assessment. "We try to appeal to feminine fantasies."

With his eyes still fixed on the glossy pages, he smiled with self-derision. "Well, I'm sure as hell not feminine, but I'm close to fantasizing. Forgive me for noticing that this model's practically naked."

"She's clothed."

"In a . . ."

"Teddy."

"That leaves absolutely nothing to the imagination."

"That's our stock and trade, Mr. Cassidy. We sell lingerie and boudoir accessories. And we want our customers to feel pampered, lovely, and desirable when they wear our garments."

"Hey, I'm not Jackson Wilde. You don't have to defend your product or your marketing strategy to me. In fact, how can I subscribe to the catalog?"

When he looked across at her and grinned, an odd sensation flurried in Claire's midsection. She wasn't flirted with often because most of the men she knew were strictly business associates. There were occasional flirtations on airplanes or in elevators, but they rarely went beyond eye contact and a casual greeting. She discouraged anything more. So her reaction to Cassidy's roguish grin was unexpected and startling. She sipped her wine in an attempt to quell it.

"Actually the catalog is Yasmine's bailiwick," she explained. "Not the subscriptions, of course. We use a telemarketing service for that. Yasmine produces it, you could say. She begins with a concept and then designs the layout."

"And models."

He turned the magazine toward Claire. A full-page ad for silk pajamas featured all seventy-two inches of Yasmine reclining on a rumpled bed. The unbuttoned pajama top revealed nothing except the inside curves of her breasts. The bottoms rode about an inch below her navel. Respectable enough. But wet, slightly parted lips and the hungry-tigress look in her eyes made the photograph provocative.

"She sells," Claire said.

He studied the photo for several seconds. "I can see why."

"She's also smart. She began modeling to pay for art school," Claire explained. "Even after her modeling career took off, she continued studying. When we formed our partnership—"

"How and when did that come about?"

"Six years ago. I had a small, local business, making specialty lingerie, mostly for trousseaus. I wanted to expand, so I took my designs to New York in the hope of finding someone to manufacture and market them for me. I wasn't successful," she said ruefully, recalling all the polite but firm no-thank-yous she had received on Seventh Avenue.

"Quite by accident I met Yasmine in one of the showrooms. In friendly conversation she asked what had brought me to New York. Naturally I was star-struck and flattered when she complimented me on my samples. She even ordered some of the items for herself. We hit it off and had several long lunches together. She's gorgeous, no question. But she's also an astute businesswoman who knows that a model's career is short-lived. And she understood what I wanted to do.''

''Which was?''

''Which *is* to design and manufacture a line of unique lingerie and sell it at a price the average woman can afford. Each season we feature new fabrications and designs that we hope will spark the buyer's imagination. We offer goods that are different and exciting but affordable. Women can buy bras, panties, and slips at Penney's. French Silk sells them fantasy garments. We've made sexy lingerie respectable.''

''Jackson Wilde didn't think it was respectable.''

''I didn't respect him either.''

Cassidy indicated with a slight nod that her point was well taken. ''Back to Yasmine. When did you cut her in?''

''A week following our initial meeting.''

''That soon?''

''I knew it would work. She was looking for a new enterprise where she could utilize her artistic talents. I needed her professional know-how. In exchange for a piece of the business, she introduced me to insiders who could bankroll us. After the first catalog went out, we couldn't fill the orders fast enough. By our third year, we had paid off all our investors. The business continues to flourish.''

''A real success story.''

''Thank you.''

Cassidy turned another page. ''Hmm. You use men, too.''

''That's a recent innovation. Yasmine broached the idea with me; I liked it, and designed some intimate apparel for men.''

''I'll bet Wilde had specific objections to this.'' The ad featured a woman leaning over a handsome young man who was lounging in a wingback leather chair. Her hands, braced on the arms of the chair, were supporting her. Her satin robe was hanging open. ''Is there any doubt at all where the guy's left hand is?''

"Do you think it's erotic, Mr. Cassidy?"

"Hell yes," he said thickly. "Don't you?" He glanced up at her, and Claire felt like she'd been nipped on the belly by sharp but playful teeth.

She lowered her eyes to the ad. "I'm stimulated in a different way. The price of the model's robe is one hundred twenty-five dollars. That's the high-ticket item in that issue. The garments are made in Hong Kong. They cost us a fraction of the sale price. Even figuring in the processing, packaging, shipping, and handling it takes to get the piece to the consumer, our margin of profit is tremendous. I look at that photograph and hope that every woman who sees it is enticed to place an order."

"In the hopes of luring a guy with sapphire eyes and corrugated abs."

Claire laughed. "Why, Mr. Cassidy! You're a disgruntled sexist exercising the double standard."

Her laugh only deepened his frown. "Am I? I don't like to think so."

"But you'd just as soon the young man not be in the picture."

"He's a lot to live up to."

"Now you understand how a woman feels when her lover ogles an airbrushed centerfold. We appeal to our subscriber's fantasy by making her feel that she can be just as lovely as that. The message we convey is that any woman can be beautiful and desirable. 'Wear this and be adored.' Perhaps her only fantasy is to lure a couch potato away from *Monday Night Football*."

After listening carefully to her explanation, he returned his attention to the catalog. Claire lapsed into silence, watching his gray eyes move across the pages. Occasionally he raised his drink to his lips. His mouth was wide, narrow, masculine, softened only by a fuller lower lip and a vertical dimple in his left cheek.

From a purely objective point of view, he was very good-looking. The sprinkling of gray in his sideburns was attractive. His chestnut hair feathered over the tops of his ears in an appealing fashion. Few men were taller than Yasmine, but when Cassidy had shaken hands with her, Claire had noticed that he topped her by two or three inches. He had a trim physique, yet the forearm resting on his knee looked powerful, and there was strength in his heavily veined hand.

After looking at every page, he closed the catalog. "Thanks."

"You're welcome. Do you think Jackson Wilde was justified? Do you think it's smut?"

"Off the record, hell no. It's sensual, erotic, but hardly porno. On the record, I have to be impartial."

It pleased her to know that he wasn't ready to stone her. She placed her glass of wine on the table and stood up. "Take that copy with you. You might decide to order something."

Picking up the catalog, he too came to his feet. "I doubt it. I'm strictly the white cotton Fruit of the Loom briefs type."

"You might enjoy a pair of the silk boxers for lounging."

"I might. Do you own a gun?"

The question stunned her, following so closely behind the disarming statement. "No, I don't, Mr. Cassidy."

"Do you have access to one?"

"No."

"Back to my original question: where were you the night Jackson Wilde was killed?"

She bit back an angry retort and answered calmly, "I don't recall going out. I believe I spent a quiet evening at home."

"Can someone corroborate that?"

"Does it need corroboration? Do you think I'm lying?"

She held his stare even though it stretched out interminably and made her want to squirm.

Finally he said, "Thanks for the drink." He reached for his jacket and slung it over his shoulder, hooking it with his index finger.

"You're welcome."

The wall of windows caught his eye. Twilight had fallen. From this side of her building, one had an unrestricted view of the river. Lights on the levee and the bridge spanning the river sparkled in the glow that ranged from deep purple to shimmering gold. "Great view."

"Thank you."

She'd guaranteed retaining the coveted view by purchasing the property that extended from her corner to the levee and turning it into a parking lot. It was profitable, and it was a safeguard against her view being blocked by a high-rise hotel or shopping center. The land had appreciated a thousand times over since she had bought it, but she wouldn't part with it for any price.

"I'll show you out."

She preceded him out the door, past the glitzy reception desk, and into the elevator. Once they were on their way down, he asked, "What's on the third floor?"

"My apartment."

"Not many people hold to that quaint custom, living above their place of business."

"They do in the Vieux Carré."

"Spoken like someone who knows."

"I was born here and have never lived anywhere else. I even went to college here, commuting every day by trolley to Tulane."

"Happy childhood?"

"Very."

"No major upheavals or crises?"

"None."

"Not even with your mother?"

Claire shrugged. "Because I never knew her to be any other way, I adapted to her illness as any child with a handicapped parent does."

"What about your father?"

"He died when I was a baby. Mama never remarried. We

lived with her aunt Laurel. Shortly after she died, we moved here.''

''Hmm. Your mother still lives with you?''

''That's right.''

''No one else?''

''Yasmine, when she's in town.''

''Who's Harry?''

''Miss Harriett York, our housekeeper and mother's nurse. She doesn't sleep over unless I go out of town.''

''How often is that?''

''Twice a year I travel to Europe and the Orient to buy fabrics. I'm also required to make several trips a year to New York.''

''How often does Yasmine come to New Orleans?''

''That depends.''

''On what?''

''Several things.''

''Like?''

''Like where we are on the next catalog.'' There was no need to inform him that Yasmine's trips to New Orleans had recently become more frequent or why. Volunteering information to him would be foolhardy. As a child Claire had learned not to trust authority figures. They could turn information against you whenever it better served the bureaucracy. For all his manly hands and vertical dimple, Mr. Cassidy was a bureaucrat.

''Is there anything else, Mr. Cassidy?''

''Lots. What's Yasmine doing in New Orleans this time?''

Claire released a sigh of resignation. ''We're consulting on the next catalog. She's developed the concept and has already picked a location for the shoot. Together we're deciding which items to feature and which models to use.''

''What about the rest of the time? When she's not in New Orleans.''

''She lives in New York.''

"Modeling?"

"Until last year, she had an exclusive contract with a cosmetics company. She was bored with it, so now the only modeling she does is for the French Silk catalog. Between her responsibilities here and keeping track of her investments, she stays very busy."

Claire was relieved when they reached the first floor. The ride had never seemed so lengthy, the elevator so small and confining. His penetrating gaze made her want to pull a protective cloak around herself.

He slid open the heavy doors. She muttered a hasty thank-you and stepped into the cavernous warehouse. It was silent, still, and dark now. The fans in the windows stood motionless. The warehouse had acted as a combustion chamber, storing the oppressive heat all afternoon until it now seemed to have texture. It not only settled against the skin but seeped into it and stifled the lungs.

Only strategically placed security lights had been left on. They formed pools of light on the smooth, shiny concrete floor. Claire didn't pause in those circular islands of light. They reminded her of prison movies, of sinister searchlights seeking out doomed escapees.

She unbolted the main door and held it open for her unwelcome visitor. "Goodbye, Mr. Cassidy."

"Are you eager to get rid of me, Ms. Laurent?"

Claire could have kicked herself for being so transparent. She groped for a logical explanation. "Mama's on medication. She has to eat at certain times. I don't want dinner to be delayed on my account."

"Very neat."

"What?"

"That excuse. I'd have to be a real bastard to challenge it, wouldn't I?"

"It's the truth."

His sly grin said he knew she was lying but that he chose to let it drop. "One more question and I'll go. Promise."

"Well?"

"Have you ever been in trouble with the police?"

"No!"

"Ever been arrested?"

"You said one question, Mr. Cassidy. That's two."

"Are you refusing to answer?"

Damn him. She hated giving anyone in authority the upper hand, but refusing to answer would only complicate matters. "I've never been arrested, but I take umbrage at your ask-ing."

"Exception noted," he said unrepentantly. "Good night, Ms. Laurent. We'll be seeing each other again soon."

She was glad she was standing in shadow so he couldn't see her alarmed expression. "I've already told you everything I know."

He subjected her to another deception-flaying stare. "I don't think so." He had rolled the catalog into a tube, which he now used to tip his forehead in a mock salute. "Thanks again for the drink. You stock very good whiskey."

Claire slammed the door in his face, hurriedly clicked the bolts into place, and leaned against the cool metal. She gasped for each breath as though she'd been running for miles. Her heart was beating so wildly that it ached. Her skin was cov-ered with a fine sheen of perspiration, which she attributed to the heat . . . even though she knew better.

Chapter Five

✿ ✿

His tongue flicked over and around her stiff nipples. The caress elicited sounds from her that had pagan origins. "You're killing me, baby," she gasped. "Oh, God, don't stop. Don't stop." She caught his earlobe between her strong, white teeth and bit it hard.

He grunted in pain, but her untamed responsiveness increased his excitement. His fingers made deep impressions in her firm ass as he clamped her to his hips and thrust himself deep inside her. His mouth captured one taut nipple and sucked it hard.

She screamed and clutched handfuls of his hair, bucking against him wildly, lost in the throes of her climax. Seconds later, he came in long, ecstatic bursts, panting and straining and grimacing.

Yasmine's skin was slick with sweat. It gleamed, reflecting the glow of the bedside lamp like polished bronze, except that none had ever been sculpted as exquisitely as she.

She rose above Congressman Alister Petrie's limp, spent body and with adoration gazed down into his flushed face.

"Not bad, sugar," she whispered as she brushed an affectionate kiss across his lips. "You found my G-spot."

Keeping his eyes closed, he chuckled. "Get off me, you insatiable bitch, and pour me a drink."

Yasmine gracefully left the bed and moved to the dresser where earlier she'd arranged a bottle of his favorite brand of scotch, a bucket of ice, and two glasses. Articles of clothing were strewn on furniture and across the carpeting. She was attired only in a pair of large gold earrings that brushed her smooth shoulders whenever she moved her head.

Their love play had begun the moment he'd entered the hotel suite. During a lengthy, tongue-twining kiss, she had guided his hand beneath her skirt, pressing it between her open thighs. "You know what to do, baby. Make me crazy."

"You mean this?" His fingers separated the moist flesh and slipped inside her. "Lucky for you your customers wear your merchandise," he whispered as he stroked her. "What if everybody decided to go without underwear?"

"Everybody would have a lot more fun."

They eagerly shed their clothes without compromising the carnality of the kiss or his manual stimulation. Naked, they fell onto the bed, a tangle of brown and white limbs.

Now, Yasmine mixed his drink while watching him in the mirror. She always loved him best immediately after making love, when his sandy hair was uncharacteristically mussed and his lips were soft and relaxed. They were almost identical in height, but he had more physical stamina than his lean, compact physique indicated. The sheen of perspiration on his smooth chest reminded her of how vigorously he made love, and she felt another tingle of expectation between her thighs.

He stacked the pillows behind his back and sat up against the headboard. Returning to the bed with his drink, she stirred it with her index finger, then ran it across his lips. "How is it?"

He sucked her fingertip. "I taste you," he said huskily. "And me. Delicious. Perfect."

Smiling with pleasure, Yasmine handed him the highball and lay down curled against his side. He kissed her forehead. "You do everything perfect, Yasmine. You are perfect."

"No shit?" Snuggling closer, she applied her mouth to his nipple and damply agitated it with her tongue.

"No shit," he moaned.

"I'd make you a perfect wife."

His reaction was abrupt and negative. He stiffened, and not with heightened desire. "Don't spoil our time together, Yasmine," he urged softly. "These hours are so hard to come by. So precious to me. Don't spoil them by bringing up a topic that makes us both unhappy."

She rolled onto her back and stared at the ceiling. "It doesn't make me unhappy to think about becoming Mrs. Alister Petrie."

"That's not what I meant. You know what I meant."

"I think about it all the time. It's what I want more than anything in the world," she said fiercely.. Tears formed in her eyes and shimmered in the soft light.

"Me too, darling." He set his drink on the nightstand and turned onto his side to face her. "You're so beautiful." His hand glided over her breast. Her nipples were only slightly darker than her skin and very responsive. He bent down and kissed one, raising it with gentle plucking motions of his lips.

"Am I a fool to love you?" she asked.

"I'm the fool."

"Do you ever intend to leave her?"

"Soon, Yasmine, soon. You've got to trust me to choose the right time. This is a difficult situation. It's going to take a lot of finesse to escape it without someone getting hurt, namely you."

They had met a year earlier in Washington, D.C., at a black-tie reception in an African nation's embassy. Yasmine had been invited because she was reputed to have roots in that country. The story had been fabricated by some unknown source, but her agent had liked it and kept it alive for publicity purposes. It certainly had more romance and intrigue than the truth—that her family had lived in Harlem for four generations.

Resplendent in a gold lamé dress, she had been introduced to the handsome young congressman by one of his colleagues. For several minutes Alister had been tongue-tied, but her laughs and gentle teasing soon put him at ease. They ignored everyone else at the reception, eventually left together in a limo provided for her, and concluded the evening in bed in a suburban motel.

It wasn't until the following morning that he confessed to having a wife and children at home in New Orleans. The passion that Yasmine had exhibited in bed hadn't prepared him for the passion of her unleashed fury. She had railed at him, called him scandalously filthy names, and threatened him with voodoo curses that would shrivel his manhood and render it useless.

"You fuck 'em and forget 'em, is that it, Congressman? Well, sugar, you're not dealing with any ordinary dumb chick here. I'm Yasmine. Nobody screws me over and gets away with it."

Once he had calmed her down, he explained the sad state of affairs. "My and my wife's families were friends. Belle and I grew up together."

"Big fuckin' deal."

"Please, Yasmine. Hear me out. You don't understand our society down there."

"I understand enough. I've read the historical novels. I know that the rich white men marry rich white ladies, but take their pleasure in bed with black mistresses."

Groaning her name, he had slumped onto the edge of the bed and plowed all ten fingers through his hair in abject despair. "I swear to you . . . Oh, Jesus, you'll never believe me." He looked up at her imploringly. "I never loved Belle. But once my folks died, hers took me under their wing. I did what was expected of me, what was expedient. I've been a good husband. And I've tried to love her. God knows I've tried.

"You have every right to be angry with me, Yasmine," he'd said. "I should have told you I was married before we left the party together, before things got out of hand. Better still, after meeting you, I should have turned my back and walked away. Because I knew then that, well . . . you dazzled me."

He was a tormented man playing tug-of-war with desire and honor. "But the attraction was just too strong. I was thunderstruck. I simply had to be with you." He bowed his head and stared at the carpet between his shoes. "Now that you know about my family, you've got every right to despise me."

He raised his tortured eyes to hers. "But I'll never forget our one night together. It was the most erotically charged and sexually satisfying experience of my life. Forgive me, but I refuse to apologize for it." He swallowed, visibly emotional. "I'm thirty-four years old. But until last night I didn't know what it felt like to fall in love."

Yasmine's heart had melted. Dropping to her knees, she embraced him. They wept and laughed and then made love again. Since that morning they had met whenever their schedules permitted, stealing a few blissful hours in Washington, New York, or New Orleans. Yasmine didn't feel guilty about her affair with a married man. To her, adultery was just a word. What she shared with Alister was right. It was his marriage that was wrong.

Now, she whispered yearningly, "I get so lonesome for you, baby. I want to be with you all the time. I can't wait for the day when we won't have to sneak around."

"I'm running out of patience too, but I'm making headway."

"How?"

"I've been suggesting to Belle—very subtly, you understand—that perhaps she isn't fulfilled. That perhaps we married before she had a chance to discover herself. That sort of thing.''

"Is it working?''

"I've noticed a coolness.''

Yasmine's heart skipped a beat, and a hopeful smile flickered across her solemn face.

"And we're not . . . you know, sleeping together much anymore. It's been months.'' He drew Yasmine against him and whispered fervently into her hair, "Thank God for that. Every time I had to be with her, all I could think about was you. How you feel and smell and taste. How wanting you drives me insane.''

Their mouths met, melded; desire was rekindled. Yasmine's lips skimmed his chest and belly, then she took his penis into her mouth, using her agile tongue to bring it to steely hardness. Rising, she teasingly drew the glistening tip across her nipples, transfixing him with her shameless sexuality. His face flushed, he clutched at the sheets. When he finally entered her, they were half-crazed with lust. Both climaxed in a feverish rush.

Alister showered while Yasmine languished in the tousled bed. She liked to linger as long as she could amid the linens that bore the musky scents of their sweat and their sex.

Eventually, she forced herself to get up and began dressing. Before he'd arrived, she had discarded her panties and placed them in her large leather shoulder bag. As she reached into the bag for them now, her hand closed around something familiar.

Her revolver.

Alister emerged from the bathroom. "Whoa!'' He dropped the towel he'd been drying himself with and raised both hands in a sign of surrender. "Was my performance unsatisfactory?''

Laughing, Yasmine aimed the gun at the juncture of his thighs. "Bang bang!''

He laughed, too, then gathered his clothing and began dressing. "What the hell are you doing with that?"

"I don't know." He gave her a quizzical glance. "I mean, I thought I'd lost it."

"I wish you had. You shouldn't be toting that thing around."

"Where I grew up, carrying one of these helped ensure survival." She balanced the revolver in her palm. "I thought I'd misplaced it in a piece of luggage on one of my trips between here and New York. I figured it would turn up sooner or later, but I didn't know it was in this bag when I left with it tonight." Shrugging, she tossed the revolver back into her bag. "I'm glad Mr. Cassidy didn't have a search warrant."

"Cassidy? The assistant D.A.?"

Yasmine stepped into her dress. "Oh, I didn't get a chance to tell you earlier. He came to see Claire this afternoon."

"About what?"

"You'll never believe it. Reverend Jackson Wilde."

Alister, straightening his cuffs, checked his reflection in the hotel dresser's mirror. "What about him?"

"He wanted to know what Claire was doing the night Wilde was killed."

Alister turned to face her. "Get real."

Yasmine laughed as she buckled her oversized belt. "That was Claire's reaction, too. That crazy evangelist was a pain in the ass while he was alive, and now he's plaguing us from the grave."

"What's the connection? Other than the obvious."

"Wilde had a 'hit list,' as this Cassidy called it. A list of magazines that he wanted to abolish. French Silk's catalog was one of them. Did you know about that?"

"How would I?"

"Well, you and Wilde were so chummy," she teased.

"I attended a few receptions welcoming him to the city because Belle thought it politically beneficial for me to do so. Personally, I think he was full of shit."

"Amen. I wonder who had the pleasure of shutting him up permanently," she said with a wicked grin. "The police must be scrounging for leads. Anyone on that list would have motivation for killing him, but since French Silk is headquartered here in New Orleans, Cassidy thought that maybe . . . You get the picture.

"Anyway," she continued, sliding on her bangles, "it wouldn't have looked too good for me to be toting around a gun, would it? Especially if the D.A.'s office discovered that I was in New Orleans with you that night and not in New York as everyone believes. If it came down to it, would you vouch for my whereabouts?"

"Don't even joke about it, Yasmine." He took her by the shoulders. "I know Cassidy by reputation: he's ambitious and shrewd and always goes for the jugular. It sounds as though he's grasping at straws to connect French Silk to Wilde's murder, and it might look silly to us, but you can be damn certain that he's serious."

"Well, I'm not worried. He's got nothing on Claire. He can't build a case around her catalog's appearance on a stupid list."

"Of course not."

"Then why the frown?"

"Because I don't want him snooping around you."

"He didn't question me."

"That doesn't mean he won't. If he does, I can't be used as your alibi. Listen, Yasmine," he said urgently, "until I resolve my marriage, in my own time and in my own way, it's imperative that no one find out about us."

"I know that," she said sullenly.

"You can't indicate to anyone—*anyone*—that we're seeing each other."

She was glad he'd brought up the topic because she'd been wanting to address it for a long time. "I want to tell Claire about us, Alister. I hate tricking her and acting out game like having her pick me up at the airport when I've alread;

been in town for twelve hours. Can't I confide in her? She's not going to tell anybody."

He was stubbornly shaking his head before she'd even finished making the request. "No, Yasmine. You can't tell anybody. Promise?"

Angrily she thrust his hands off her shoulders. Her eyes glittered dangerously. "Are you so afraid that word will leak out and reach Belle?"

"Yes, I am. If she ever learned the real reason I want a divorce, she'd try to stop it any way she could. And when she realized that I was determined and that it was inevitable, she'd stall and drag out the proceedings indefinitely."

He sighed and drew Yasmine into his embrace. "Don't you see? Why give Belle ammunition to hurt us even more than we're hurting already? I'm thinking of you. I don't want you dragged into a nasty scandal. No one would understand what it's like between us. The public would think the worst."

She cupped his face between her hands. "I love you, Alis-er. But I'd kill you if I thought you were lying to me."

He turned his face into her palm and kissed it. "I want to be with you more than anything in the world. I want to be married to you, having babies, all of it."

They kissed until tenderness blossomed into passion. "We can't, Yasmine." He moved her questing hand away from his fly. "I'm already late."

"You ain't that late, sugar," she whispered seductively as she opened his zipper.

The time came, however, when he had to leave. It did no good to pout, cry, threaten, or cajole. When he had to go, he had to go. It was as simple as that. She didn't like it, but she had learned to accept it. She made their goodbyes as painless as possible.

"When will I see you?"

"I've got several meetings with the reelection committee this week," he told her as he checked the room for anything he might have left behind. "November will be here before we realize it. Then there's a family reunion in Baton Rouge over the weekend. It'll be hell, but I have to go.''

"Belle and the children will be there?"

"Of course." He tipped up her lowered chin and kissed her again. "How about Sunday night? Here. I'll make up some excuse. They'll be tired after the weekend. I should be able to get away for an hour or so.''

"Sunday night," she agreed, trying to look happy about it. It was five days away.

"If I run into a problem, I'll call you." She had a private telephone line in her bedroom in Claire's apartment; it wasn't answered if she wasn't there.

He was almost through the door when he turned back. "Do you need some money, Yasmine?"

Her wistful smile disintegrated. "For services rendered?" she snapped. "How much do you figure one of my blow-jobs is worth?"

"I merely want to help."

"I should never have told you I was in a cash crunch."

In a weak moment several months earlier she had mentioned to him that her expenditures were running slightly higher than her income. Each month she got a little further behind. Some of her creditors were making threats.

"It's more serious than a cash crunch, Yasmine," Alister said reasonably. "You've been in financial straits for months."

When her contract with the cosmetics line expired, the company had decided against renewing Yasmine in favor of a "new look," a youthful, bouncy blond. Yasmine had pretended to be unfazed by their decision, but it had been a blow to her ego. She'd always known that the life span of a cover girl was short, but when that last major contract had expired, the bitter reality of being a has-been had caused her bouts of depression. At least she hadn't depended exclusively on that contract for her livelihood.

Neither had she taken into account just how lucrative it had been. She hadn't reduced her spending to compensate for the loss. In addition, some of her investments hadn't paid off as well as anticipated. Unreal as it seemed, Yasmine was now broke.

"The situation is temporary, Alister," she said with asperity. "My accountant and I are working out a solution. Things are already beginning to turn around. In any event, I won't take money from you. I'd feel like a whore. Don't offer again."

"What about Claire? She'd be glad to help you."

"It's no more her problem than it is yours. It's mine, and I'll work it out."

She sensed that he wanted to argue further and was glad that he didn't. Instead, he came back and playfully swatted her fanny. "Sassy and sexy. No wonder I love you so much." He whisked a kiss across her mouth. "See you Sunday."

Yasmine and Claire arrived at French Silk at the same time. Yasmine paid her taxi fare, then joined Claire at the door. "What are you doing out at this time of night?"

Claire unlocked the door and turned off the security alarm. "I could ask you the same question, but then I already know the answer, don't I?" After resetting the alarm, they crossed the warehouse toward the elevator.

"Don't be sarcastic," Yasmine said. "Where have you been?"

"Walking. And I wasn't being sarcastic."

"You went out walking alone at this hour? You could have been mugged."

"I know every crumbling brick of the French Quarter. I'm not afraid of it."

"Well, you should be," Yasmine said as they got into the elevator. "When you roam these streets at night alone, you're asking for trouble. The least you could do is carry an insurance policy with you."

"Insurance policy?" Claire looked down to where Yasmine was patting the side of her shoulder bag. "A gun? You bought another one?" They had discussed the revolver when Yasmine reported it missing.

"I didn't have to. The original wasn't lost after all."

"I wish it had been."

They emerged from the elevator on the third floor. Claire quickly checked Mary Catherine's room to make certain she was safely in bed. Claire hadn't been away for more than half an hour, but her mother had been known to disappear in much less time.

"Everything all right?" Yasmine asked when Claire joined her in the kitchen. "I'm surprised you left her alone."

"I had to get some air. I needed to think. I hoped you'd get back, but . . ." She shrugged.

Yasmine flung down the apple she'd taken from the fruit bowl on the counter. "Okay, that's two pricks in a row. Instead of throwing these little poison darts, why don't you come right out and spear me? Say that you disapprove of my affair."

"I disapprove of your affair."

The two women exchanged a hostile stare. Yasmine was the first to break it. She plopped down onto a barstool with a muttered, "Oh, hell," and began picking at the peel of the apple with her sharp fingernails.

Claire went to the refrigerator and poured herself a glass of orange juice that Harry had squeezed fresh that morning. "I'm sorry, Yasmine. I had no right to say that to you. Who am I to approve or disapprove of your private life?"

"You're my best friend, that's who. That entitles you to an opinion."

"Which I should have kept to myself."

"Our friendship's based on candor."

"Oh? I always thought so too, but you haven't been candid. You've never even told me his name."

"If I could tell you about him, I would."

Claire studied her friend's tense facial muscles and red eyes. She'd been crying. Claire sat down on a stool next to Yasmine, removed the apple from her nervous hands, and clasped them between her own.

"I've been rude only because I'm worried. And I'm worried because you're miserable ninety percent of the time. That's why I disapprove of this affair. You're unhappy, Yasmine. Ideally, being in love is supposed to make people happy."

"The circumstances are hardly ideal. In fact it's the worse scenario you can imagine," she said with a bleak smile.

"He's married."

"Bingo."

Claire had been afraid of that, but knowing it for fact didn't make her feel better. "I couldn't see another reason for the secrecy. I'm sorry."

It was evident to Claire that Yasmine's suffering was genuine and deeply felt. This wasn't a capricious romantic adventure like so many of her previous love interests had been. When they had become friends, Yasmine was living a high-spirited social life. Her dates ranged from professional athletes to business tycoons to movie stars to foreign royalty.

About a year ago, Yasmine's whirlwind romances had stopped, and she began going away for unspecified lengths of time to inexact destinations. She was evasive and secretive. She was either ecstatic or abysmal, and her mood swings were swift and drastic. They still were. Besides this secret lover, she saw no one else, as far as Claire knew. Undeniably, her friend was in love, and the love affair was making her dreadfully unhappy.

"Does he meet you here in New Orleans?" she asked gently.

"Actually he lives here," Yasmine replied.

Claire was surprised. "You met him here?"

"No. Actually we met in . . . uh, back east. Last year. It was purely by coincidence that we both have lives in New Orleans, too."

"A convenient coincidence." Claire hated herself for what she was thinking—that the man knew a good thing when he saw it and was taking advantage of Yasmine's ties to his hometown.

"It's not that convenient," Yasmine replied grimly. "He's paranoid about his wife finding out about us before he has a chance to divorce her."

"That's the plan?"

Yasmine whipped her head around. "Yes," she answered testily. "That's the plan. You don't think I'd be having a lengthy affair with a married man unless it was really love, do you? As soon as it's possible, he's divorcing her and marrying me."

"Yasmine—"

"He *is*, Claire. He loves me. I know he does."

"I'm sure he does," Claire murmured, unconvinced. If he loved her so much, why would he cause her this much misery? she wondered. "Does he have children?"

"Two. A boy, ten, and a girl, six. He's nuts about his kids. I've thought of them, Claire. Don't think I haven't. I wonder what a divorce will mean to them. Oh, God."

She propped her elbows on the bar and buried her face in her hands. "When I think of breaking up a family, it makes me sick to my stomach. But he doesn't love his wife. He never has. Sex between them has always been lousy."

Claire's silence must have conveyed her skepticism because Yasmine raised her head and looked at her. "It has," she insisted. "He's told me, but I knew even before that. The first time I went down on him, he was so overwhelmed I thought he was going to cry. And he's told me that his wife would rather die than let him put his mouth 'down there,' even if she could conceive of such a thing. She believes there's no such thing as sex without guilt, so it's straight missionary position all the way.''

Yasmine had never been squeamish when talking about sex. Before this affair, she had frequently regaled Claire with the lurid details of her active love life.

Now, she stabbed the cool marble countertop with her index fingernail. ''I'm the best damn thing that's ever happened to him, Claire. I'd make him a good wife.''

''Then why doesn't he make a clean break? Why torture you both?''

''He can't,'' she said with a melancholy shake of her head. ''The divorce is going to have a profound effect on his career. He's well known. He's in thick with his in-laws and all their friends. Jesus, it'll be a mess. He has to work it out and wait until the time is right. Until then, I have to be patient and look forward to the day we can be together.''

Claire was less optimistic and felt it was her duty as a friend to play devil's advocate. ''Yasmine, affairs like this seldom turn out sunny.''

'' 'Affairs like this'? How the hell would you know what it's like?''

Claire could see Yasmine's temper emerging so she kept her own at bay. ''All I'm saying is that it goes against the law of averages. Men who are well positioned in the community rarely leave their wives and families for their mistresses. Yasmine,'' she asked softly, ''is he white?''

''So what if he is?''

Yasmine's chilly reaction indicated that he was. ''This is the South. New Orleans. Men here have a tradition of—''

''He's not like that,'' Yasmine interrupted vehemently. ''He's the least racially prejudiced person I've ever met.''

Claire forced a smile. ''I'm sure he must be or you couldn't love him.'' She knew when to back down. Yasmine's frame of mind wasn't conducive to an honest discussion. She was wounded, and like any wounded animal she would lash out at anyone who tried to help her. "Forgive me for bringing it up."

"Don't patronize me, Claire."

"I'm not."

"The hell you're not!" Yasmine jumped off her stool. "I doubt if you believe a word I've told you. You probably think he's just screwing me for the hell of it."

Claire pushed back her own stool and stood up. "Good night. I'm going to bed."

"You're running away from an argument."

"Right," she shouted back. "I refuse to argue with you about this because it's a no-win situation. If I say anything negative, you'll leap to his defense. I don't care who or what your lover is. My only concern is your unhappiness. If you want to live like this, that's your business. As long as it doesn't affect your work, it's got nothing to do with me."

"Oh no? What about your jealousy?"

"Jealousy?"

"Don't strike that innocent posture with me, Claire. I can see through it. I'm crazy in love with a guy who's willing to overturn his entire life for me, while your personal life is as sterile as a nun's."

Claire silently counted to ten. When Yasmine was upset with herself, she picked fights in order to redirect her anger. It was a character flaw that Claire, over the course of their friendship, had learned to tolerate. Nevertheless, recognizing it didn't make it any less exasperating. Tomorrow morning Yasmine would be gushing sincere smiles and apologies, calling herself a selfish bitch, and begging Claire's forgiveness, but Claire wasn't up to the exhausting exercise tonight.

"Think what you want to. I'm tired. Good night."

"That Cassidy—does he have a first name?"

"I don't know." Claire switched out the lights on the way

down the hall toward her bedroom. Yasmine didn't take the hint. She was on Claire's heels like a pesky puppy.

"Did you go all cool and haughty on him?"

"I was hospitable."

"Did he realize he was being buffaloed?"

Claire came to a sudden halt and spun around to confront Yasmine. "What are you talking about?"

"You're damned good at equivocating, Claire, but based on my first impressions of Mr. Cassidy, I doubt he takes crap like that from a woman."

"I'm sure he wasn't regarding me as a woman in that sense. He was here in an official capacity."

"He stayed an awfully long time."

"He had a lot of questions to ask."

"Did you have answers?"

Again, Claire gave her friend a hard look. "Only a few. He wanted to connect me to Jackson Wilde's murder, and there is no connection."

"Did you think he was sexy?" Yasmine asked.

"I assume you're referring to the assistant district attorney and not to the evangelist."

"You're equivocating, Claire. Answer the question."

"I didn't give Mr. Cassidy's looks much thought."

"Well, I did. He's sexy in a dark, intense way. Don't you think?"

"I don't remember."

"I'll bet he fucks with his eyes open and his teeth clenched. Makes me hot just to think about it."

Yasmine was trying to provoke her. Refusing to be baited, Claire stepped into her bedroom. "I thought you were in love."

"I am. But I'm not blind. And I'm not dead." Through Claire's closed bedroom door, Yasmine added, "And even though you'd like for Mr. Cassidy and every other man to think your drawers could form icicles, neither are you, Claire Laurent."

As she listened to Yasmine's withdrawing footsteps, Claire glimpsed her reflection in the mirrored door of the armoire. Quite unlike herself, she looked agitated, confused, and afraid.

And Mr. Cassidy was the reason.

Chapter Six

A ndre Philippi finished his dinner and neatly placed the silverware on the rim of his plate. He blotted his mouth on the stiff linen napkin, folded it, and laid it aside. He then rang for a room service waiter to retrieve his tray. The roast duck had been a trifle dry and the vinaigrette on the fresh, cold asparagus had had a trace too much tarragon. He would send a memo to the head chef.

As night manager of the Fairmont Hotel, New Orleans, Andre Philippi demanded optimum performance from everyone on staff. Mistakes simply weren't tolerated. Insolence or slip-shod service was grounds for immediate dismissal. Andre believed that hotel patrons should be treated as pampered guests in the finest home.

In the small washroom adjacent to his private office, he washed his hands with French milled soap, gargled with mouthwash to guard against halitosis, and took pains to dry his pencil-thin mustache as well as his lips. He smoothed his hands over his oiled hair, which he wore combed straight back from his receding hairline, chiefly because that was the neatest style he could derive, but also to combat the natural tendency of his black hair to curl. He checked his nails. Tomorrow was his day to have them clipped, filed, and buffed. He had a standing, weekly manicure appointment, which he religiously kept.

Always with an eye on the hotel's operating budget, he conscientiously switched off the light in the washroom and reentered his office. Ordinarily his position wouldn't have warranted a private office, but Andre had more seniority than anyone else, including the upper-echelon executives.

And he knew how to keep a secret.

Over his tenure, he'd been granted many favors because often his discretion had been required by his superiors. He'd kept secrets about their vices ranging from one's predilection for young boys to another's heroin addiction. The private office was just one expression of appreciation that Andre's confidence had earned him.

Other tokens of appreciation from hotel personnel, and from guests who had required his special services, were earning compound interest in several city banks, making Andre a wealthy man. He rarely had occasion to spend money on anything other than keeping his wardrobe up to snuff and buying flowers for his *maman*'s tomb. Elaborate bouquets of flowers as exotic as she were delivered to the cemetery twice weekly. The floral arrangements were more elaborate than the ones his papa had sent her when Andre was still a boy. That was important to him.

He wasn't tall, but his rigid posture gave him presence. Although he wasn't given to vanity, he was meticulous. He checked his appearance in the full-length mirror on the back of his bathroom door. His trousers still had a knife-blade crease. The red carnation in his lapel buttonhole was still fresh. The collar and cuffs of his starched white shirt were so stiff that a tennis ball would have bounced off them. He always dressed in an impeccably tailored dark suit, white

shirt, and conservative necktie. He would have felt comfortable wearing a morning coat and spats, but that might have
attracted his guests' attention to him rather than to the excellent service they were receiving. And that would have been
tantamount to failure. Andre Philippi considered himself a
servant to the guests of the Fairmont Hotel, and he took his
job seriously.

Following a knock on his office door, a young man in a
room service waiter's uniform stepped in. "Are you done
with your tray?"

"I'm *finished*, yes." Critically he assessed the young
waiter's appearance and technique as he replaced the lids on
the serving dishes and loaded them onto the tray.

"Will that be all for you tonight, Mr. Philippi?"

"Yes, thank you."

"You bet."

Andre frowned over the idiomatic parting words, but, generally speaking, the waiter had performed well. No doubt he
would return to the kitchen and joke with his friends among
the hotel's staff until his next assignment. Andre didn't have
many friends.

He'd attended the finest private schools, including Loyola
University. But because he could never claim his father, and
vice versa, he'd always been a social outcast. He didn't mind.
The only world that existed for him was the hotel. What
went on outside its walls was of only negligible interest or
importance to him. He wasn't ambitious. He didn't have his
eye on a corporate position. For him, heaven would be to die
while on duty at the Fairmont. His cramped apartment was
within walking distance of the hotel, but he actually resented
the time he had to spend there. If it were allowed, he would
never leave the Fairmont.

Andre had but one vice. He indulged it now, as a gourmand
might savor an after-dinner liqueur. Opening the lap drawer
of his desk, he gazed down at the framed, autographed picture. Ah, Yasmine. So exquisite. So beautiful. "To a hell of

a guy," she'd written before signing her name with a plethora of curlicues.

He was more than just an ardent fan. For years, he'd had an affection for her that bordered on obsession. It wasn't a sexual attraction. That would have been profane. No, he worshipped her as an art enthusiast might covet an unattainable painting. He admired and adored her and yearned for her happiness, as he had yearned for his beautiful *maman* to be happy.

Eventually he shut the drawer, knowing that there would be other opportunities tonight for him to gaze at the breathtaking face that was never far from his mind. Now, however, it was time for his hourly inspection of the front desk. Things seemed to be running smoothly. He spotted a cigarette butt on the carpet in front of the elevators, but at a snap of his fingers a bellman rushed forward to dispose of it. He pinched a wilting rose off one of the floral arrangements and inquired courteously of returning guests if they were finding everything to their liking. They assured him that, as usual, everything was perfect.

As he traversed the lobby, he shuddered to recall that horrible morning following the Jackson Wilde murder. What an appalling incident to have happened in his hotel!

He didn't regret that the televangelist was dead, particularly. The man had served his own needs before serving others'. His smile had camouflaged a nasty disposition. He had laughed too loudly, spoken too abrasively, shaken hands too heartily. Andre had extended the man and his family every courtesy, but his heart hadn't been in it because he had a distinct personal dislike for Jackson Wilde.

Andre was still holding a grudge. Wilde's murder had cast a pall over the hotel. No hotel could guarantee that such a thing would never occur in one of its rooms, no matter what security precautions were taken. Nevertheless, some local journalists had outrageously suggested that the hotel should share liability.

Well, the lawyers were handling that aspect of it. That was beyond Andre's realm. But it made him queasy to remember the chaotic aftermath—this serene lobby crawling with policemen and reporters and rightfully disgruntled guests who had been interrogated like miscreants. It had been like witnessing a regal dowager being mauled by street thugs.

What should be obvious to the authorities was that someone had walked in off the street, taken an elevator up to the seventh floor, and been welcomed into Wilde's room. After shooting him, and without attracting anyone's attention, the killer had left the same way. Should all the guests in the hotel that night be treated as suspects? Were the police justified to suspect everyone? Andre didn't think so. That's why he had no qualms about protecting those who couldn't possibly have had a quarrel with Jackson Wilde.

As a matter of routine, the policemen had questioned him, too. They seemed not to doubt his statements. Mr. Cassidy, however, was another matter. He had been more thorough and more dogged than that disheveled detective with two first names. Cassidy hadn't outright accused Andre of lying, but the prosecutor seemed to know that he was concealing information.

"Look, Mr. Philippi," he had said, scooting closer to Andre in a gesture designed to inspire confidence, "I don't care what drug deals might have gone down in the rooms upstairs that night. Nobody's going to get hauled in by vice if they were with a prostitute who handcuffed them to the furniture and took dirty pictures. I don't care who was banging whose wife. What I *do* need to know is the identity of every person who came through the doors that night. I know you keep a tough vigil on the lobby area. You see a lot of people. Someone you consider insignificant might not be. Any scrap of information could be vital."

"I understand, Mr. Cassidy," Andre had replied, his face impassive. "But I've already listed everyone I saw that night.

I've instructed the staff to give you their full cooperation. You have access to our computer."

"Which you and I both know saves only what it's told to save. Data can be deleted more easily than it's entered." Cassidy had raised his voice, demonstrating his impatience. When he realized this, he took another tack, assuming the tone of a caring parent about to administer punishment. "Why don't you come clean with me, Andre? If you're caught withholding information, you could be implicated. I'd hate for it to come to that, wouldn't you?"

Cassidy could change tactics till his face turned blue and he wouldn't prize anything out of Andre. He was resolved never to reveal information that would compromise individuals he respected. Facts that had absolutely no bearing on the murder of the Reverend Jackson Wilde were none of Mr. Cassidy's business.

Mr. Cassidy wasn't originally from New Orleans. He was under the misconception that the law was absolute, unbendable, and applicable to everyone. No doubt he thought that blanket rules covered everybody. Evidently he hadn't yet learned the code of honor that governed the Crescent City. Outsiders might not understand and adhere to it, but Andre Philippi certainly did.

When Claire entered the kitchen area, her mother was sitting alone at the table in the breakfast nook. She was fully dressed and had applied makeup. Those were encouraging signs. There were days when Mary Catherine couldn't leave her bed, imprisoned there by depression.

"Hmm. Coffee smells good, Mama," Claire said as she clipped on her earrings.

"Good morning, dear. Sleep well?"

"Yes," Claire lied. As she stirred cream into her coffee,

she looked over her shoulder and smiled at her mother. Her smile congealed when she saw the familiar face that filled the screen of the portable TV in the étagère. It was tuned to a morning news program.

"She really shouldn't shout like that," Mary Catherine remarked. "It's so unflattering. A lady should cultivate a soothing speaking voice."

Ariel Wilde was ringed by reporters, all eager to broadcast her latest and most vicious criticisms of the city, parish, and state authorities that had thus far declined to release her husband's body for transport to Nashville.

Claire gingerly sat down across from her mother. She watched Mary Catherine rather than the TV.

"Mrs. Wilde should be allowed to bury her husband as soon as possible," Mary Catherine said, "but it's hard to work up sympathy for people who are so unpleasant."

"Why do you say they're unpleasant, Mama?"

Mary Catherine looked at her with bald surprise. "Why, Claire, have you forgotten all the trouble this preacher caused you, all the horrible things he said? He was a detestable human being, and apparently so is his wife."

This is one of her lucid days, Claire thought. They occurred rarely, but on such days Mary Catherine made perfect sense and was fully aware of what was taking place around her. When her eyes were clear and her voice was resonant with conviction, one could easily doubt that she was ever any other way. Claire, looking at her now, wondered what triggered these bouts of sanity and the all-too-frequent lapses. For decades doctors had tried and failed to diagnose and cure the problems.

"The things that man said about you were so hateful," she was saying. "Why couldn't he have minded his own business and left you alone?"

Claire was stunned by her mother's vehemence. "I don't have to worry about him anymore, Mama."

Mary Catherine's lips turned up into a beatific smile. "Oh

yes, I know. He died of three gunshot wounds." Abruptly changing the subject, she pushed a plate of croissants toward Claire. "Have one, dear. They're wonderful."

"Just coffee for now," Claire said distractedly. "Mama, I've been wanting to talk to you about something very important."

"I love this weatherman, don't you? He has such a nice, conversational manner."

"Mama?" Claire waited until Mary Catherine's attention was again focused on her. "Do you remember meeting Mr. Cassidy the other day?"

"Of course. Only a few minutes ago, they showed his picture and quoted him in a news story. I didn't know when I met him that he's so important. He'll be prosecuting the Jackson Wilde case for the district attorney's office."

"That's right. And because Reverend Wilde had been so hostile toward me, Mr. Cassidy wanted to meet me. He might be coming back."

"Oh, how lovely. He was very nice."

"Well, he . . . he's not always nice. In his work, he often must ask people a lot of questions. Personal questions about their lives, their backgrounds. He must delve into their pasts and try to uncover things that they'd rather remain private." She paused to let that sink in. Mary Catherine gazed back at her inquisitively. "If Mr. Cassidy should come back and start asking you about the years we lived with Aunt Laurel, what would you tell him?"

Mary Catherine was nonplussed. "I suppose I'd tell him how lovely it was."

Claire, sighing with relief, took her mother's hand and clasped it warmly. "It was, wasn't it? We had some wonderful times in Aunt Laurel's house."

"I still miss her, you know. This Sunday after mass, let's take some flowers to her tomb." Mary Catherine stood up and moved toward the built-in desk. "Now, Claire, you'll have to excuse me. I've got to make a shopping list before

Harry gets here. She's so forgetful, if I don't write down everything we need at the market, she doesn't remember a thing.''

Mary Catherine began adding items to her shopping list while Claire watched her, a disturbed frown on her face. It was inevitable that Cassidy would come back. She only hoped it wouldn't be today. She was glad that Mary Catherine was enjoying a good day, but she'd just as soon Cassidy talk to her mother when she couldn't converse so lucidly about Jackson Wilde and his murder.

✦

The cold-water tap was on full blast, and it was still only lukewarm. Cassidy supposed he should be grateful that at least it was a powerful spray. As the water struck the back of his neck, it worked out some of the tension. But not all of it.

Eventually he soaped, shampooed, rinsed, and stepped out of the shower. By that time, his coffee had brewed. He followed the rich smell of New Orleans coffee and chicory into his postage-stamp-sized kitchen and poured a cup. Scalding and bitter, it gave him twin jolts of caffeine and optimism. Maybe today would produce something.

He padded to the front door of his Metairie condo and opened it to get his morning paper. The woman who lived across the narrow stone walkway was putting letters into her mailbox.

She looked him over and grinned with amusement. ''Good morning, Cassidy.''

He gripped the knot of the towel wrapped around his waist ''Good morning.''

''I haven't seen so much of you lately.''

Ignoring the double entendre, he said, ''I've been busy.''

''So I've been reading.'' She nodded toward the newspaper he'd tucked under his bare arm. From there her eyes ventured to the water-beaded hair on his lower belly. "Have you had a chance to use that sample soap I gave you last week?"

She worked at Maison-Blanche, representing an international cosmetics line. She was constantly leaving samples from their men's collection on his doorstep. Thanks to her, he had more cosmetics than the female impersonators who pranced in the clubs on Bourbon Street. He stuck to Dial and a splash of shaving lotion, but he hated to hurt her feelings. Feeling a tingle from every hair follicle that she was studying, he said, "Yeah, it was great."

"Smell good?"

"Hmm."

She looked into his face and her eyes lingered. They'd run out of things to say. He recognized her soft expression for what it was. He toyed with the idea of inviting himself into her condo for croissants and coziness, but dismissed the thought before it was fully formed. "Well, I'm running late. 'Bye."

He closed the door seconds before the knotted towel slipped over his buns, then fell to the floor. His neighbor, Penny or Patty or Peggy or something like that, was pretty and available, as far as he knew. She'd made overtures before, which he'd ignored for one reason or another, chiefly due to lack of time and interest.

Maybe this morning he should accept her subtle invitation. Maybe getting laid was just what he needed to improve his outlook. "Hell, I doubt it," he muttered. If it were that easy, he could have climbed out of this slump days ago. Women weren't that hard to come by.

He kicked the wet towel out of his path and stalked naked into the kitchen. He sipped his coffee while waiting for his toaster to spring two slices of wheat bread. Opening his *Times Picayune*, he noted that the Wilde murder story had been demoted to page 4. But there in black and white was an article suggesting that the authorities were baffled. Incompetence was strongly suggested. For those who didn't already know—

and since the media had been saturated with reports, it seemed impossible that the facts weren't known to everyone—the crime scene was restaged according to the press release Cassidy had helped compose.

The reporter quoted him as saying that the combined forces of the police department and the district attorney's office were following several good leads, which was true, and that an arrest was imminent, which was a lie. They weren't even close to arresting anybody. They didn't have shit.

His toast popped up. He buttered both slices, sprinkled them with sugar and cinnamon, and bit off a piece. Claire Laurent sprang to mind. Her mouth would taste like warm butter and cinnamon-sugar.

"Dammit." He braced his hands on the countertop and leaned forward, his chin lowered to his chest. Even though his shower wasn't five minutes old, he began to perspire; the tiny droplets trickled down his sides, chest, back, and belly. Arousal curled around his sex like tendrils of mist off a bayou, taunting and teasing and, to his greater frustration, causing quite a reaction.

Ever since his visit to French Silk, he'd been suffering night sweats. Like malaria, the debilitating symptoms recurred night after night. They made him weak, made him crazy, made him horny. He wanted to blame his adolescent malady on the product French Silk manufactured. If a normal guy looked at enough models wearing skimpy underwear, he would get turned on. It was a rule of nature. Every garment featured in the French Silk catalog was sexy. Either sexy/sweet, sexy/cool, or sexy/hot. But always sexy.

Those glossy pages were a definite turn-on, but he'd studied centerfolds since about age twelve and had never been plagued with a fever like this. The difference was the woman who inspired the catalog. Claire Laurent was as provocative as the merchandise she peddled. He couldn't get her out of his mind, and not necessarily within the context of his investigation. He had wondered more than once if those damn bubbles she'd blown weren't in fact a voodoo love potion.

"How'd it go at that underwear place yesterday afternoon?" Crowder had asked him at their routine morning meeting.

"You mean French Silk?"

"Is there another one involved in this case?"

"It's quite an operation. I had no idea the business was that expansive."

"I don't care about the business. Did you talk to the Laurent woman?"

"Yes. At length."

"Anything?"

"She says she never met Wilde."

"And?"

"That's essentially it."

"Did you believe her?"

For reasons he didn't fully understand, Cassidy had answered evasively. "She didn't give me a reason not to." Because Crowder expected elaboration, he provided it, telling him about Mary Catherine Laurent and the model, Yasmine.

"I know who she is," Crowder said. "Saw her on Johnny Carson once. A real heart stopper."

"Yes, she is. Ms. Laurent, that is the mother, is mentally incapacitated."

"You don't say. In what way?"

Crowder had asked for specifics. Cassidy didn't have any. He doubted that Crowder wanted to hear that his cock got hard every time he thought about Claire Laurent. Not an auspicious sign for an assistant D.A. trying to build a murder case, especially one on which his career was balanced. This was the kind of juicy, well-publicized case that ambitious young prosecutors had wet dreams about. And it belonged to him.

He'd been granted a golden opportunity to prove to

Crowder that he was capable of taking over the reins when the older man retired. He needed to convince the voting public that he was the right man for the tough job. And he needed to prove to himself, as he had strived to do for five years, that he was one of the good guys and didn't belong behind bars himself.

All that was going to be doubly difficult to achieve if one of his suspects made him sweaty and horny.

Claire Laurent *couldn't* have committed cold-blooded murder. *Look at the way she treats her mother*, he argued with himself.

That logic wasn't worth spit and Cassidy knew it. He'd known serial killers who could weep on command, especially around their mothers.

So forget sentiment. Look at it from a practical viewpoint. It wouldn't have made sense for her to kill Wilde. She would risk more by killing him and getting caught than she would if his plans to ruin her business had panned out. Right? Right. She wouldn't have done it.

Even so, something about that situation at French Silk was askew. What was odd about it? He mentally recalled everyone he had encountered: Tugboat Annie, the receptionist, Claire, Mary Catherine, Yasmine. Suddenly it occurred to him. "No men."

No men. All the warehouse workers were women. Harry, the housekeeper, was a nickname for Harriett. Was that exclusivity significant? Was French Silk a prime example of reverse sex discrimination? Was there more to the relationship between Claire and Yasmine than friendship and business?

The thought left a bitter taste in his mouth, stronger than the coffee and chicory. He pitched the dregs into his kitchen sink.

No, that couldn't be. He would have sensed it. They'd silently communicated on the level of confidantes, but not lovers. In any event, Claire Laurent was no killer.

On the other hand, she struck him as a woman who, if she

had already killed a man, wouldn't have any compunction about blowing his balls to smithereens just for the hell of it.

His telephone rang. "It's Glenn."

"Good morning."

The detective grunted as though he disagreed. "I got a call from the P.C. He says the Wilde woman—and that pun is to be taken literally—is demanding that we release the body. We've got to let it go, Cassidy."

He plowed his fingers through his damp hair. "Shit. I guess we don't have a choice. But give me one more crack at her and the stepson."

"We've taken their statements. I've questioned them a dozen times myself. It's going to start looking like harassment."

"I know, but I want to try one more time. I'll be there in half an hour."

The interview with Ariel and Joshua Wilde got off to a bad start. They were already seated in Cassidy's office when he arrived. The widow was dressed in black silk, making her look frail, wan, and unarguably innocent. "Mr. Cassidy, we're leaving for Nashville in a little over an hour. We don't want to miss our flight."

"I apologize," he said, rounding his desk and sitting down. "I ran into some traffic. I'll see that you get to the airport in plenty of time, if it means a police escort."

That seemed to appeal to her. She settled back in her chair. "Thank you."

"I was informed on my way in that the casket with Reverend Wilde's body will also be aboard that flight."

She dabbed at her eyes with an embroidered handkerchief. "Jackson was murdered more than a week ago. Not only have you failed to arrest his assassin, but you've prevented me from burying him."

Cassidy mentally applauded her. She was damned good. Her knees were chastely covered by her skirt; her pale, straight hair was held back by a black velvet headband. She had made no attempt to be alluring, and yet she exuded an inexplicable charisma.

Her stepson laid a comforting hand on her shoulder. "This has been a grueling ordeal for us, Mr. Cassidy. Especially for Ariel."

"I'm certain it has "

"We want to take Daddy's body home, bury him, and then rest. However, we plan to return to New Orleans as soon as the culprit is apprehended. I want to ask him personally why he did it."

"I'd like to ask that myself." Cassidy opened the file that one of the legal clerks had handed him before he came in. "For clarity, I'd like to recheck some times with you." He shuffled paper to make the question look legitimate. "You—the three of you, along with a few of the entourage—arrived at the hotel . . . when?"

"Ten-o-five," Ariel replied impatiently. "Mr. Cassidy, we've been over this a thousand times."

"I know it seems repetitive, but sometimes in the retelling of events, a witness remembers something he's previously forgotten. Please indulge me."

She exhaled a longsuffering sigh. "We arrived at ten-o-five. We were all hungry. We ate in the Sazerac, on the lobby level. I'm sure the staff can verify that."

"They have. Did anyone leave the table at any time?"

"I don't think so. Josh, do you remember anyone leaving the table during the meal?"

"No. Why is that important, Mr. Cassidy?"

How the perp got into the Wildes' suite was still unclear. Cassidy thought someone from the inner circle could have had access to a key and been waiting for Wilde when he returned from dinner. "Just thought I'd check."

"I don't remember anyone leaving until we'd finished," Ariel told him. "We all rode in the elevator together, getting off on our designated floors."

"Was it a convivial group?"

"Everyone was still full of the Spirit."

"The Spirit?"

"The Holy Spirit. That night's service had been particularly blessed."

"I see." Cassidy rifled through more papers. "So, Mrs. Wilde, you, your husband, and Josh got off the elevator together on the seventh floor?"

"That's correct. Jackson always reserved a floor exclusively for us, so the family would have absolute privacy."

"Hmm."

"I kissed Jackson good-night at the elevator, then went to Josh's suite to practice our songs for the next evening's service."

"Do you always sing on a full stomach, Mrs. Wilde?"

"Pardon?"

Cassidy leaned back in his chair and threaded a pencil through his fingers as he closely regarded the two. "I've known a few singers. I've never known one who liked to sing right after eating. A full stomach crowds the diaphragm, doesn't it?"

"What does that have to do with anything?"

"You said you went to Josh's suite to practice."

"I can explain that," Josh said hastily. "When Ariel and I are rehearsing outside the auditorium, we're only working on timing, rhythm, that kind of thing. She doesn't sing full voice until we're in the auditorium, where the sound technicians can set mike levels."

"Oh," Cassidy said. "That must be why nobody heard you singing that night."

"No one else was on the seventh floor, remember?" Ariel sweetly reminded him.

"That's true. But the rooms above and below Josh's suite were occupied, yet the occupants never heard any singing or piano playing."

"What are you implying, Mr. Cassidy?"

"That maybe you went to Josh's suite to make music of a different sort."

The widow shot to her feet and glared down at him. "How dare you!"

"Nobody can corroborate your story, Mrs. Wilde."

"No one can dispute it either."

"And I think you planned it that way."

"Think what you want."

"I think that in order to continue your affair, one or both of you slipped back down the hall that night and shot your husband while he was asleep. You left him there all night, then the following morning staged this dog-and-pony show for the press and the public."

Her blue eyes narrowed menacingly. "The Devil is using you."

"Very possibly," Cassidy replied blandly. "He's always found me willing."

"Are you prepared to arrest us on the basis of this hunch of yours?" Ariel asked loftily.

"Without any evidence? You know as well as I do, Mrs. Wilde, that I couldn't make any charges stick."

"Precisely." She turned and sailed through the door.

Josh remained, but he shared her agitation. "That accusation was uncalled for, Mr. Cassidy. Rather than upsetting my stepmother with nasty allegations, why aren't you out beating the bushes for the real killer?"

"Come off it, Josh." Cassidy deliberately lapsed into the familiar form of address. If he was going to wear either of them down, it would be Josh. "I know you're boinking her. I wouldn't give a damn . . . unless you iced your old man so you could keep on boinking her."

"Stop saying that!"

"Then talk to me, dammit." He slapped the surface of his desk with his palms.

After a moment of tense silence, Josh asked sullenly, "What do you want to know?"

Cassidy curbed his temper, knowing intuitively that Josh would retreat if he wasn't handled with finesse. "Look at it from my perspective, Josh, and see what conclusions you draw. Ariel's young, pretty, talented, and in love with her young, handsome, talented stepson, who returns her love. Only there's a hitch. She's married. The unwanted husband gives her a motive I can't discount. And she was the only person other than your father who had a key to that suite."

"What about the maids? The hotel staff? Professional burglars don't need keys. They break into locked hotel suites all the time."

"Jackson was killed by someone familiar, someone he didn't mind seeing him naked and sprawled on the bed."

"It wasn't Ariel."

"Was it you?"

The younger man blanched. "My father and I had our differences, but I didn't kill him."

"Did he know about your affair with his wife?"

"I don't know what you're talking about."

Cassidy's reclining chair sprang erect, practically catapulting him across the desk. "Don't bullshit me, Josh. Did he?"

The younger man squirmed beneath Cassidy's hard gray stare. Eventually his shoulders slumped slightly and he looked away. "No. I don't think so."

Ah-ha. He now had a confession that they were involved in an illicit relationship. He screened his happy reaction. "You think you were clever enough to conceal it from your father, when I guessed thirty seconds after meeting you?"

"It isn't that we were so clever," Josh said with a mirthless laugh. "It's that he was so egomaniacal. He would never suspect Ariel of choosing me over him."

Cassidy looked him in the eye and believed him. "He was a real son of a bitch, wasn't he?"

"Yes, he was."

"Did you hate him?"

"Sometimes."

"Enough to kill him?"

"Sometimes. But I didn't. I couldn't. I wouldn't have the nerve."

Cassidy believed that, too. Joshua Wilde was named after the Hebrew warrior of the Old Testament, but it was a misnomer. Undoubtedly Jackson Wilde, with his thunderous voice and avenging-angel temperament, had been sorely disappointed in his mild-mannered, soft-spoken son. A kid could stockpile a lot of resentment against an overbearing, supercritical parent. Better parents than Jackson Wilde had been blown away by their stressed-out children. But Cassidy didn't think Josh had it in him to put a bullet through a man's head.

"What about her?" Cassidy asked, pointing his chin toward the door through which Ariel had made her huffy exit. "Think before you answer, Josh. We might turn up incriminating evidence at any moment, something we missed before. If you protect Ariel, you're an accessory, and the punishment's the same. Did she kill him?"

"No."

"Could she have done it without your knowledge? Did you make love with her that night, Josh?"

He cast his eyes down but answered without hesitation. "Yes."

"Did she leave your suite at any time?"

"No. Not until she left for good, sometime in the wee hours."

Too late for the murder, which Elvie Dupuis had placed between 12:00 and 1:00 A.M. "You're sure?"

"Positive."

"Do you *suspect* her of killing him?"

"No." He shook his head so adamantly that several locks of hair fell over his brow.

"How can you be so sure?"

He raised his head and met Cassidy's stare head-on. "My father was Ariel's ticket to greatness. Without him, she's zero."

It was a dead-end street. They were guilty as hell. The rub was that Cassidy didn't know if they were guilty only of adultery or of a sin more grievous. But even if they had offed Wilde, he had no evidence to hold them. "Have a nice trip," he said in a clipped voice.

Joshua Wilde was taken aback. "You mean I can go?"

"Unless you want to sign a confession."

"I've got nothing to confess and neither does Ariel. I swear it, Mr. Cassidy."

"You may have to yet—in a court of law. For the time being, goodbye."

Cassidy watched him go, wondering if he was releasing a murderer onto an unsuspecting public. Although, he reasoned, the only danger Ariel and Josh posed to the general public was fleecing them of hard-earned cash in the name of the Lord.

Querulous and feeling at odds with the world, he snatched up his phone after its first shrill ring. "Cassidy." It was Crowder, who wasn't too pleased to hear the results of the interrogation. "The bottom line is they walked," Cassidy summarized.

Crowder had several choice comments about the widow and the ruckus she had left in her wake. "She's flying off to Nashville smelling like a rose, looking like a goddamn martyr, and leaving us with a stinking pile of shit to shovel. Cassidy, you there?"

"What? Oh, yeah, sorry. Shit. Right."

"What's the matter with you?"

Cassidy was gaping at the stuffed folder that Howard Glenn

had just carried into his office and dropped onto his desk with a triumphant flourish.

"I'll call you back." Cassidy hung up, leaving Crowder in midsentence. He looked up at Glenn, who was standing at the edge of his desk, a smug grin on his unshaved face.

"Hey, Cassidy. This might be the break we've been looking for. Let's go."

Chapter Seven

❧ ❧

"**I**t's yours, isn't it, Miz Laurent?"

"Where did you get it?" Claire asked the unpleasant man who confronted her with the stance and glower of a gladiator.

"One of my men found it in the garbage dumpster a few blocks from here. Didn't you figure on us checking the contents of the garbage bins located near anyone involved in the Wilde case?"

"I'm not involved," Claire said evenly.

"This indicates otherwise." He brandished the incriminating folder an inch from her nose. She batted it aside.

"Glenn, back off," Cassidy said abruptly. The odious man frowned at him, but took a couple of steps backward. Cassidy turned to Claire. "Frankly, I thought you were smarter than this. Why didn't you just throw the folder in the river along with the murder weapon?"

She had thought that the rooms in her apartment, which had been designed for maximum light and spaciousness, would make her feel less claustrophobic. But the moment she'd admitted Cassidy, the walls had seemed to start closing in, especially since he was accompanied by the detective, whom she regarded with unconcealed distaste. He was repugnant to her, not so much because of his unkempt appearance but for his mean, suspicious smirk.

When she spotted what they'd brought with them, her heart had lurched and her palms had grown damp. She felt trapped, afraid, but she was determined not to show it.

"Come clean, Miz Laurent. What about this?" Detective Glenn dropped the folder onto the bar in her kitchen. Dozens of clippings spilled out and scattered across the glossy surface.

Claire hated being backed into a corner by someone in authority. Her instinct was to fight back, as she had done as a five-year-old. But she was no longer a child. She couldn't kick and claw and bow her back. It would be futile to lie. They had her. They knew it. She knew it, too. The best she could do was brazen it out.

"It was mine," she admitted. "Considering that Reverend Wilde was murdered, I thought it would be imprudent for me to keep the file."

" 'Imprudent'?" Glenn snorted. "Is that a fifty-cent word for fuckin' crazy?"

Claire's eyes snapped furiously. Her back went rigid.

Cassidy stepped between her and the detective. "Excuse us." He pushed the detective toward the door. After a whispered but heated discussion, Glenn shot her a dirty look before going out, soundly pulling the door closed behind him.

"Thank you," she said to Cassidy as he came back around. "I don't believe I could have stood him for another second. He was thoroughly obnoxious."

"I didn't do it for you. I did it for me. I've got a lot of questions to ask. It was obvious that Glenn was going to get nowhere with you, so I asked him to give me a shot."

"What questions?"

"What questions! We've got incriminating evidence on you, Ms. Laurent."

"A collection of clippings?" she asked scoffingly. "Hardly, Mr. Cassidy. I was about to make myself a sandwich for lunch. Would you like one?"

Never taking his eyes off her, Cassidy flipped back his suit jacket and propped his hands on his hips. He gazed at her as though trying to figure her out. "You're a cool customer, aren't you," he said tightly. "As well as a liar."

"You never asked me if I kept a file on Jackson Wilde."

"I'm surprised you didn't deny ever having seen these." He gestured at the pile of clippings on the bar.

Claire rounded the bar and moved toward the refrigerator. "Denying it would have really made me look guilty, wouldn't it? Is shrimp salad all right?"

"Fine."

"Wheat bread or white?"

"Christ," he muttered, raking his fingers through his hair. "Don't you ever stop with the southern hospitality?"

"Why should I?"

"Because Glenn is downstairs waiting to arrest you, and you're talking wheat or white."

"I won't be arrested, Mr. Cassidy, and we both know that." Having taken all the ingredients from the refrigerator, she kept her back to him while she made the sandwiches. She hoped he wouldn't notice that her hands were trembling.

In hindsight, disposing of the file seemed like a desperate measure taken by someone with bloodstained hands. She'd been foolish to toss it into the dumpster. Nothing should have been left to chance. Why hadn't she done as he quipped and thrown it in the river? Of course, on the day following the murder, things had happened so quickly that she hadn't been thinking clearly. She'd made an error in judgment, and it was proving to be a costly one.

She'd also underestimated Cassidy and the seriousness of

his initial interrogation. His questions had made her uneasy and cautious, but they hadn't been cause to panic. Finding the folder had changed everything. Now he was more than mildly curious about her feelings toward Wilde. He actually suspected her of killing him. He would be watching her, looking for the slightest scrap of evidence. But Claire had had plenty of practice at thwarting authority figures. The first lesson she had learned was never to be intimidated.

She turned to face him. "You haven't got enough evidence to make an arrest stick, Mr. Cassidy. I had collected a few articles relating to Jackson Wilde. That's hardly a smoking gun."

"The gun's in the Gulf by now," he said as he picked an olive off the plate she handed him. "Carried away by the river's current."

"More than likely." Since the bar was covered with the clippings, she nodded him toward the glass-topped table in the dining room. "Tea or a soft drink?"

"Tea."

"Sugar?"

"Nothing."

After returning with two glasses of mint-sprigged iced tea, she sat across from him. He picked up half of his sandwich and took off a corner in a strong bite. "Some of those clippings are years old."

"My interest dates back several years."

"You have that much interest in religion?"

"No, Mr. Cassidy," she said with a retiring smile. "I'm Catholic by birth, but have never embraced any organized church. I certainly wasn't enamored of charismatic televangelists. Wilde attracted my attention because I believed him to be one of the most dangerous men in America."

"So you considered it your civic duty to ice him?"

"Do you want to hear my explanation or not?" she snapped.

He gestured for her to go ahead.

"You're very rude, Mr. Cassidy."

"Yes, I know."

Their stares locked and held for several seconds. Claire wasn't about to back down, so she began speaking. "Unlike some of the other TV preachers, Wilde threatened to rob people, not of their money but of something much more valuable—their rights guaranteed by the First Amendment. About the time French Silk's first catalog went out, he began his crusade against everything he considered pornographic. From the beginning, his message bothered me tremendously."

"Because his influence could hamper your business?"

"No, because I never wanted to be placed in a position of having to defend my work. I saw that as a very real possibility, and as it turned out, my prediction was right. French Silk's catalog has nothing in common with child pornography and bondage magazines, but it was being lumped in with them and lambasted in the same breath. Reverend Wilde was waging war against freedom of the press."

"You can't have carte blanche freedom, Ms. Laurent. Hand in hand with freedom goes responsibility."

"I agree." She laid down her sandwich and leaned slightly forward. "The thought of men, women, and children being exploited for profit makes me sick to my stomach, but that crime won't be solved by banning quality erotica from museums and bookshelves.

"Censorship belongs in one's mind and heart and conscience. If you don't approve of R-rated movies, spend your seven dollars on something else. If you oppose a television show's scripts, switch channels and don't buy the products that sponsor it. But give those who don't share your views the opportunity to watch whatever they like.

"It's not the privilege of the government, or an appointed committee of so-called experts, or one preacher to dictate what people—*adults*—should or should not be permitted to see. When Hitler came to power, one of the first things he did was burn the books that he deemed unsuitable.''

"So everybody who has a hang-up over *The Catcher in the Rye* is a neo-Nazi?"

"Please, Mr. Cassidy. Don't be insulting. I only meant that it's fascist for those who don't approve of something to forcibly impose their opinion on everybody else.'' Claire felt a heated flush rising in her cheeks. She was so close to this issue that sometimes she sounded as dictatorial and uncompromising as Wilde.

"I didn't enter this war willingly, Mr. Cassidy. Given the choice, I would never have been a part of it. I was drafted into it when Wilde began name-calling from his pulpit. I chose to ignore it as much as possible and declined his repeated invitations for a public debate, but one probably would have been inevitable."

"You were arming yourself by keeping those clippings."

"Exactly. The only thing that file proves is that I had thoroughly researched my opponent so I'd know what I was going up against if and when the time came."

"Why didn't you show me your collection of clippings and explain this the other night?"

"I had already thrown it away."

"You could have mentioned it."

"I could have, yes. But you're under pressure from city hall to bring in a viable suspect. Wilde's followers are demanding a culprit to bring to trial. I didn't want to be your scapegoat, even temporarily. If all you'd done was taken me downtown for formal questioning, it could have adversely affected my business and family."

"I still might do that."

"You'd be wasting your time. I've told you everything I know."

He regarded her closely. "So that red ink mark underlining

the date that Wilde would appear in New Orleans was merely coincidence.''

Color and heat rushed to her face again. "I remember underlining that, yes. I can't explain why I did. I was holding a red pen while I was reading the article," she said with a shrug. "It was reflexive.''

He'd eaten quickly and cleaned his plate. He wiped his mouth with his napkin and laid it next to his plate. "On the surface, that all sounds so damn reasonable. It's almost too reasonable an explanation, Ms. Laurent. It's as though you rehearsed what to say just in case that folder turned up to haunt you.''

"Would you care to have some coffee with your delusions?''

His lips tilted into a half-smile. "No, thanks.'' She carried their plates from the table into the kitchen. "I thought Harry would do that for you," he said conversationally, following her as far as the bar that divided the two rooms.

"Ordinarily she would. She took Mama out this afternoon.''

"How convenient.''

"What do you mean? What do my mother's outings have to do with you?''

"I needed her corroboration on where you were the night Jackson Wilde was killed.''

Claire drew a quick breath. "I won't have my mother interrogated, Mr. Cassidy. Understand that and spare yourself the time and effort. Mama wouldn't remember the events of this morning, much less what happened a few weeks ago. If pinned down, she couldn't possibly give you a credible answer, and any attempts to force one out of her would only cause her distress, which I won't allow.''

"You can't expect Glenn and me to take your flimsy answer to that all-important question as a concrete alibi.''

"You've got no choice," she replied, shuddering at the

mention of the detective's name. "You'll have to take my word for it. I was at home that night."

"You didn't go out at all?"

The hard glint in his eyes caused her to hedge. Nervously, she pushed back her bangs. "Perhaps I did. It would have been a brief errand, because I can't leave Mama alone for extended periods of time, especially at night. Frankly, Mr. Cassidy, I don't remember. The date held no significance for me."

He gave her an extended stare, then asked, "Where's Yasmine?"

"She went back to New York yesterday."

As she had known would happen, the morning following their spat, Yasmine had been contrite and apologetic. They'd hugged, made up, and worked hard to finalize the layout for the next catalog. Yasmine had dashed to her bedroom to answer her telephone several times. Twice before returning to New York she had spent the night out, returning the following morning looking depressed and dispirited. But Yasmine's affair with her married lover was her business. She would have to deal with it.

Claire had enough problems of her own, all of them sparked by the man who kept staring at her in the same penetrating way as the Human Resources personnel once had, as though she were a case study and they were looking for irregularities in personality or behavior.

"What's this?" He gestured toward a framed item on the kitchen wall.

"That's Aunt Laurel's recipe for French Silk." Cassidy angled his head quizzically. "I'd had trouble coming up with a name for the lingerie," she explained, smiling at the memory. "Yasmine and I had deliberated over it for months and couldn't agree on anything. One cold afternoon, I got in the mood for chocolate pie and began thumbing through Aunt Laurel's recipe box. 'French Silk,' " she said, pointing out the name written in a spidery cursive. "That was it. I knew ıt the minute I saw it. Aunt Laurel was so pleased when I told her I was naming my company after her recipe. It made her feel a part, as if she'd contributed to it.'' Her expression turned wistful. ''She died only a few weeks after that.''

Leaning nearer the frame, Cassidy read the ruled card. ''·'Gradually cream sugar into the mixture of butter and melted chocolate, add vanilla, beating constantly on low.' Sounds delicious.''

''It is. It's rich and sensual and feels on your tongue the way I want my lingerie to feel against bare skin. The very name implies self-indulgence.''

When she stopped talking, Claire realized how still they had become, how close, how soundless. He was looking at her mouth, then into her eyes, and if his hearing was as keen as his eyesight, he could hear her heartbeat.

He cleared his throat and put space between them, as though he too had found the long silence uncomfortable. ''That's all interesting, but back to the reason I'm here. Your only beef with Jackson Wilde was this First Amendment issue, right?''

''That's right.''

''Nothing else?''

''What are you driving at, Mr. Cassidy? Is your method of investigation to shoot in the dark until you hit something? That's not a very economical way to spend the taxpayers' money. Your time would be much better spent hunting down the actual murderer. And my time would be—''

''Are you and Yasmine lovers?''

The question was as unexpected as a falling star and rushed at her with about as much impetus. She stared at him, aghast, her lips parted, her eyes wide. ''Whatever gave you that idea?''

''Well, are you?'' When she began to laugh, his expression grew darker. ''Wilde also stirred up a lot of homophobia in this country. The gay activist groups were on his ass about several issues.''

"I see. You figured that he was my enemy on two accounts?" she asked with amusement. "Honestly, I'm not laughing at you, Mr. Cassidy. I'm only imagining how Yasmine would react to your question. Don't you read the tabloids? She's had scores of lovers over the years, all men, and has diligently cultivated a reputation as a femme fatale."

"That could be a pose."

"She'd be crushed to hear you say that. Even if you believed I'm inclined toward lesbianism, how could you possibly think that Yasmine is anything but heterosexual?"

"Because this setup is a little out of kilter, that's why."

"Setup?"

"Your business here."

"How so?" Claire asked, genuinely curious.

"I've been here twice and have yet to see a man. I know cutthroats on death row who would run from that amazon you've got guarding the door downstairs. Every employee I've seen is female, from those folding tissue paper into boxes, to those driving the forklifts. What have you got against men?"

"Nothing."

"Are you married?"

"No."

"Ever been?"

"No."

"Engaged?"

She hesitated. "No."

He raised his index finger as though to snag the lie on the tip of it. "Try again."

Claire felt her temper ignite like kindling. "Have you been prying, Mr. Cassidy?"

"I've been doing my job. Tell me about your relationship with David Allen."

"Damn you! Did you bother him?"

"I didn't have to, but I will if you don't start talking."

Claire was seething, but he'd won the contest of wills. "It

was a long time ago," she said curtly. "Before French Silk. He wanted to marry me."

"What happened?"

She started to tell him that it was none of his damn business, then thought better of it. Any hostility on her part would only make matters worse. Yasmine, who had more experience handling men, had doubted that Cassidy would take any crap from a woman. Claire thought she was probably right. Besides, this wasn't really dangerous territory. They could traverse it without mishap.

"David expected me to commit Mama to an institution," she said softly, lowering her eyes. "I wouldn't hear of it. He issued an ultimatum, so I returned his engagement ring."

"You didn't love him as much as you love your mother?"

"Obviously not."

"No serious affairs since then?"

"Don't you know?"

"Not yet. I can keep digging, or you can spare me the manpower and yourself the embarrassment and just tell me."

"Is my personal life pertinent to your investigation?"

"Maybe. Let's go with it and see where it leads." He sat on a barstool and folded his arms.

Demonstrating her dislike for the topic, she finally said, "I've had a couple of emotional entanglements, but nothing really serious since my breakup with David. Does that satisfy you?"

"For the time being." He turned away and for several moments dallied with the clippings scattered across the bar. "Where's your father, Ms. Laurent?"

Claire shifted her weight. "I told you before. He died shortly after I was born."

"You don't remember him?"

"No. I was too young."

"What'd he die of?"

"Heart attack, I believe."

Watching her, he eased off the barstool and advanced on

her slowly, until he was standing inches from her and she had to tilt her head back in order to look into his incisive eyes.

"You're lying to me again. On your birth certificate there's a big fat question mark in the space for the father's name."

"You son of a bitch." She drew her hand back to slap him, but he caught her wrist, stopping her hand inches from his cheek. Tears of rage and frustration formed in her eyes. "You have no excuse for delving into my private life."

"A corpse with three bullet wounds gives me a damn good excuse."

Claire wrenched her wrist from his grip, then drew her crossed arms close to her body and hugged her elbows. "Well, since you're so smart, Mr. Cassidy, what else did you learn on your nasty little fact-finding mission?"

"The Laurents, your grandparents, were the crème de la crème of New Orleans society, an old family with lots of old money. The apple of their eye was their only child, Mary Catherine. She attended the finest parochial schools and was being groomed to assume her place in society.

"But following one of those cotillions she mentioned to me the other day, she was seduced by one of the rich young gentlemen in attendance. She became pregnant. When she acknowledged her condition and told her parents, she refused to name her partner. Unfortunately, he never came forward to claim responsibility for the child she was carrying. Her parents did what they believed was justified—they disowned and disinherited her. Only her aunt Laurel, her father's maiden sister, took her in.

"The scandal knocked society on its proper ass and took its toll on the family. Within two years Mary Catherine's parents were dead, shamed to death some said. Before he died, her father altered his will and left his considerable estate to the Church."

"Which also treated my mother like an outcast even while espousing mercy, grace, and forgiveness," Claire added.

"But they obviously allowed her illegitimate daughter to attend catechism school."

"No, Mr. Cassidy. I learned Christianity from Aunt Laurel. She was a dotty old maid. Most people considered her life pointless. But she loved my mother and me unconditionally. During Mama's spells, it was Aunt Laurel who reassured me during thunderstorms, nursed me when I was sick, and helped me through the trials and tribulations of childhood. She was the only person I ever knew who actually lived Christianity the way Jesus intended it to be. She didn't preach. She exemplified."

"But my account of your mother's history is accurate?"

"Very. Her cousin Charles was thorough to the nth degree."

"How do you know my information came from him?"

"Because he's the only one left from that branch of the Laurents."

"Do you have contact with him?"

She laughed bitterly. "No, Thank God. Never. He's as stiff-necked and pompous as the rest of them. From what Aunt Laurel told me about them, I'm not surprised that they banished my mother when she needed them most."

"She was just a kid."

"Seventeen." She cocked her head to one side. "You're slipping, Mr. Cassidy. You sound almost sympathetic."

"It was the early sixties, for Christ's sake."

"Actually the late fifties. Eisenhower was still president. America hadn't lost its innocence. Proper young ladies didn't have erogenous zones."

Cassidy shook his head with misapprehension. "But even then, families didn't disown their daughters for getting pregnant."

"The Laurents did. My grandparents never spoke to my mother again. As far as they were concerned, she ceased to exist and so did I."

"She never disclosed who your father was?"

"No."

"And he never acknowledged you, even secretly?"

"No. I'm sure he was afraid of the consequences. He was a member of the same social circle and apparently enjoyed the benefits. He saw what happened to my mother and didn't want the same to happen to him. I don't blame him really."

"Bullshit."

"Excuse me?"

"You wouldn't be human if you didn't hold him accountable."

Claire, feeling like an insect pinned to a corkboard, took a cautious step backward. "Are you trying to make a point, Mr. Cassidy?"

"Whoever killed Wilde had a grudge against men."

"You've deduced that? How clever."

"Not so clever. It was an obvious case of overkill. He was shot one extra time."

"You're referring to the shot to his groin."

"How'd you know?"

"It was in all the newspapers that Wilde had been shot in the testicles." She shook back her hair and faced him defiantly. "So, because I was born on the wrong side of the blanket and have numerous women on my payroll, you've leaped to the brilliant conclusion that I'm the one who pulled the trigger on Jackson Wilde."

"Don't be cute."

"Then don't be ridiculous," she said, raising her voice. "I've freely admitted that I abhorred everything that man stood for. I disagreed with virtually everything he said. So what? Many did."

"True. But only the livelihoods of a few were being threatened, so that places your name high on the list of suspects."

"You're wasting your time investigating me."

"I don't think so. I've caught you in too many lies."

"I explained about the clippings."

"I'm not talking about that."

"I lied to you about my father only to protect my mother. Surely you'll concede that she's suffered enough humiliation without my sharing her past with you."

"I'm not talking about that lie, either," he said.

"Then what? The suspense is killing me."

He turned his back on her and stalked to the door. He wore his dark suit well. The tailored vest snugly fitted his trim torso, and there was no wasted fabric in his trousers. It would have been a luxury if she could have concentrated on his considerable attractiveness as most women would.

But Claire saw him through the eyes of a frightened child. She couldn't separate the man from the bureaucracy he represented. She'd learned at an early age to fear, loathe, and strike out against it. She projected her antipathy for it onto him.

How dare he dig into her mother's sorrowful past? It had caused Mary Catherine so much grief that, in order to survive, she had barricaded herself inside a dream world. Her delusions were rose-colored but as protective as iron gates. They had guarded her against heartache and scorn for three decades. It was unfair that her misfortunes should be exposed for strangers to scrutinize again.

He had reached the door. His right hand was on the knob. Claire knew she was about to test the limits of his patience, but she couldn't help herself. She charged him, taunting, "You're bluffing."

He came around quickly. "You told me that you'd never met Jackson Wilde." He raised his free hand and crushed a handful of her hair in his fist, tugging her head back. Lowering his face close to hers, he spoke rapidly and softly, with emphasis and urgency.

"You didn't spend a 'quiet evening at home' the night he was killed. I got several videotapes from the local cable company, which had been hired to document Wilde's New Orleans crusade. One of the tapes was a recording of the last service he conducted. It was recorded in its entirety.

"When Wilde extended an invitation at the conclusion of the service, hundreds of people flocked to the podium from every tier of the Superdome. Among the first to reach him was a young woman who clasped his hand and spoke to him face to face."

He stared at her hard, as if to imprint the image of her face on his brain. Then he released her hair and opened the door, adding as he went out, "It was you, Claire."

When his telephone rang, Andre Philippi jumped guiltily and slammed shut his desk drawer. The bell was like a conscience, reminding him that he was gazing at his beloved's photograph on company time.

He answered the telephone and, with crisp and businesslike enunciation, identified himself. "How may I help you?"

"*Bonsoir*, Andre."

"*Bonsoir*," he replied in a warmer tone, instantly recognizing the caller, although the voice was soft and muffled. "How are you?"

"Still shaken by what happened week before last."

Andre's small mouth formed a moue of sympathy. "It was a ghastly night."

"I called to thank you again for your discretion."

"I assure you, no thanks are necessary. I felt no obligation to the police. They herded my guests together like cattle and questioned them like criminals."

"You took care of the details for me?"

"No need for concern. There's no record of your having been here that night."

"Has anyone interrogated you about . . . about it?"

"The police," Andre replied with distaste. "I also spoke with a man named Cassidy."

"Cassidy's questioned you?"

"Twice. But don't worry. I answered only specific questions and didn't elaborate."

"Did my name come up?"

"No! And, *naturellement*, I wouldn't mention it."

"I'm certain you didn't," the caller said. "It's just that . . . well, no one needs to know I was there."

"I understand."

"I rely on your confidentiality. It's enormously valuable to me."

"That's the highest compliment you could pay me. *Merci*."

"I need to ask one more favor, Andre."

"I would consider it an honor."

"If Cassidy, or anybody else, asks about me directly, will you notify me?"

"*Certainement*. Immediately. Although I assure you, your fears are unfounded."

Almost inaudibly, the caller replied, "I hope so."

Chapter Eight

❧ ❧

Ariel Wilde had a captive audience in the board members of Jackson Wilde Ministry. They were bound by deference to her recent widowhood, by reverence for the man who had been interred only yesterday, and by their own fear that a very lucrative enterprise was about to collapse following the demise of its leader.

Ariel was holding court from the head of the long conference table in the boardroom on the top floor of the ministry's office complex in Nashville. Garbed in black, she looked thin and wan, almost incapable of lifting the translucent china cup of virtually colorless herbal tea to her chalky lips. Her weepy eyes, which had contributed largely toward making her the patron saint of the hopeless, seemed to have receded into her skull. They were surrounded by violet shadows of fatigue and despair.

No one except Ariel knew that these evidences of grief washed off with soap and water.

She replaced her cup in its saucer. That tiny clink of china against china was the only sound in the room. The indirect lighting, dark paneling, and plush carpeting encouraged a hushed atmosphere similar to that of the funeral home where Jackson Wilde had, for two days, lain in state inside a sealed casket. Those seated around the conference table waited in breathless anticipation for the widow to speak, sympathizing with her while at the same time trying to conceal their personal anxieties.

"Gentlemen, let me begin by thanking you, individually and collectively, for the support you've given me—and to Josh, during these dark and troublesome days following Jackson's death. You're a living tribute to him. The way you've rallied around me is . . . well . . ." Emotionally overcome, she dabbed at her eyes, letting her tears speak for themselves.

Recovering her composure, she continued, "When Jackson was at the helm, he expected you to give one hundred percent of yourself in dedication to him and to doing the Lord's work. In his absence, you've maintained that tradition. I know I speak for him when I say how proud you've made me."

She gave each of them in turn a gentle smile, then took another sip of tea before cutting to the heart of the matter.

"Unfortunately, none of us expected Jackson's tragic demise. It's caught us unprepared. Who could have predicted that a madman would silence one of God's most effective messengers?"

That earned her a few mumbled amens.

"The Devil expects us to surrender and retreat to lick our wounds. He expects us to buckle beneath the burden of our grief. When he silenced Jackson, he figured he'd silenced us all." As rehearsed, she paused strategically. "But the Devil underestimated us. We're not going to be cowed and silent. The Jackson Wilde Ministry will continue as before."

A dozen dark-vested chests relaxed. The escaping tension was as palpable as steam rising from a simmering kettle. Sweat began to evaporate off furrowed brows. Sighs of relief were sensed if not heard.

Ariel could barely contain her smug smile. She now had them in the palm of her hand. They might consider themselves men of God. No doubt a few of them genuinely believed in their mission. But they were still men, subject to the foibles of every descendant of Adam. They had feared for their futures. Fully expecting her to announce the dissolution of the ministry, they had prayed for a miracle. She'd just handed them one.

Of course, there was always at least one skeptic.

"How, Ariel?" the doubting Thomas asked. "I mean, without Jackson, how can we possibly continue? Who's going to preach?"

"I am."

Everyone gaped at her, flabbergasted. It was obvious that they all doubted her abilities. She gave her head a small shake that sent her platinum hair rippling across her shoulders. It was a gesture of resolution and supreme confidence.

"I—that is, we . . . we thought we'd bring in another evangelist."

"Well, you all thought wrong," she said sweetly. "That's why I called this meeting. So I could explain my plans to everyone at once and save having to repeat myself."

She clasped her hands together on the edge of the table. Her recent frailty had been supplanted by a quivering vitality. The spark of life in her eyes, so faint just minutes ago, had grown into a conflagration.

"Our followers will be curious to know my feelings regarding Jackson's death. He died unexpectedly, violently. That's fodder for at least a dozen sermons. And who better to deliver those sermons than his widow?"

The board members glanced at one another, stupefied and speechless.

"Brother Williams wrote all Jackson's sermons. Now, he'll write mine," she said, nodding to the gentleman sitting to her left about midway down the table.

He coughed uncomfortably but said nothing

"Gradually we'll fade out the emphasis on Jackson's murder and move into other areas. We'll take up where Jackson left off on the pornography issue because it's become so identified with the ministry. I'll continue to sing. Josh will continue to play piano. Occasionally we might bring in a guest preacher, but the reason all those folks tune in week after week is to see Jackson and me, right? He's gone. I'm not. And if you thought he preached hellfire and damnation, wait till you hear me."

They were uncomfortable with her bluntness, but none dared rebuke her. She wanted it understood from this moment forward that she was indisputably the one in charge. As Jackson's word had been law, now hers was.

"Brother Raye?"

He sprang upright. "Yes, ma'am?"

"You canceled the Cincinnati crusade. Why?"

"Well, uh, I . . . I assumed that with the . . . after Jackson . . ."

"Don't ever make a decision like that without consulting me. Reschedule it. We'll conduct the crusade as planned."

"But that's only two weeks away, Ariel. You need time to—"

"Reschedule it," she repeated icily.

Brother Raye furtively glanced around the table in a desperate search for support. None was offered. The others kept their eyes averted. He looked at Josh imploringly, but he was staring down at his hands, turning them this way and that as though they were alien appendages recently sprouted from his arms.

Finally Brother Raye said, "I'll reschedule it immediately, Ariel. If you feel up to it."

"By the time we get there, I will. Right now, however, I'm exhausted." She stood. The others followed suit, slowly coming to their feet with the unsure shuffling motions of boxers who'd gone down for the count and were struggling to regain their wits.

"Josh speaks for me and vice versa," she told them as she moved to the door. "However, I prefer that all questions and problems be channeled directly to me. The sooner I assume Jackson's responsibilities, the better. If any of you have a problem with that . . ."

She opened the door and indicated with her head that they were free to walk if they didn't want to play by her rules. No one moved. They scarcely breathed as she made eye contact with each of them. Finally she took their stunned silence for assent.

Her pale face broke into an angelic smile. "Oh, I'm so glad you've all decided to stay on. That's what Jackson would have wanted and expected from you. And, it goes without saying, that's God's will, too."

She beamed another smile, then extended her hand to Josh. Dutifully, he moved to her side and tucked her hand into the crook of his elbow. Together they left the boardroom.

"That was quite a performance," Josh said as they moved through the building's exit.

"Performance?" Ariel settled against the plush interior of the limousine awaiting them at the curb.

"We're going home," Josh told the driver before closing the partition. He sat back against the deep upholstery and stared through the tinted window, trying to get a grip on his temper before addressing his stepmother.

At last he turned his head toward her. "You could have discussed it with me first."

"You sound mad, Josh. What are you mad about?"

"Don't play your games with me, Ariel. And stop batting your eyelashes like a goddamn coquette at an afternoon soiree. That innocent act doesn't wash with me. Haven't you learned that by now?"

She pursed her lips in pique. "I assume you're upset because I didn't discuss my plans with you before presenting them to the board."

"Have you totally lost your grip on reality, Ariel?" He

was genuinely dumbfounded and it showed. "Do you really think you and I can continue this ministry?"

"I know *I* can."

"Oh, I see. Out of the goodness of your heart, you'll carry me."

"Don't put words in my mouth."

"Why should I?" Josh shot back. "You seem to have all the words you need. But do you know what any of them mean?"

That angered her, because her lack of formal education was a sore point. "You don't think I can hold this organization together?"

"No. Although I believe you've convinced yourself you can." He gave her a long assessing look. "You don't let anything stop you, do you? Not even my father's death."

Seeming unconcerned, she rolled her head around her shoulders, as if to relieve tension in her neck. "Look, Josh, Jackson is dead and there's nothing anybody can do about it. We buried him."

"With more pomp and circumstance than a coronation."

"It got the media's attention, didn't it?"

"Is that why we had to have the choir and orchestra and those fucking, flying doves?"

"The vice president of the United States was there!" she shouted. "Are you too stupid to see what that's worth?"

"To him? About a million votes."

"And to us, a minute and a half on network news. World-wide exposure, Josh." Her anger was full blown now. "Were you, or any of the men on that board of directors, stupid enough to think I'd squander all that free publicity? Did you think I'd be that big a fool? If so, you're the fools. I'm going to milk Jackson's death for all it's worth. It's like a gift. I didn't ask for it."

He turned his head toward the window again, muttering, "Didn't you?"

"What?"

He didn't respond.

"*Josh!*"

He stubbornly kept his head averted. She pinched his arm hard. "Dammit!" he shouted viciously as he turned his head around.

"Tell me what you said."

"I just wondered out loud whether you might have asked for his death."

She leveled a cold blue stare on him. "My, my. You're getting awfully self-righteous lately."

"I figure one of us should have a conscience."

"You're also very full of yourself. You think I'd rid myself of Jackson just so I could have you?" she asked scornfully.

"Not me. But maybe your own TV show." He leaned forward and whispered, "What about that segment of time after you left my suite that night, Ariel?"

A flicker of alarm appeared in her eyes. "We agreed never to mention that."

"No, you insisted that I never mention it."

"Because of what the police might make out of it."

"Exactly," he said softly.

"It wasn't worth mentioning," she said breezily, dusting an imaginary speck off her black dress.

"At first I thought so, too. Now I'm not so sure. Maybe it was worth mentioning. You said you were going to your room to look for some sheet music."

"So?"

"So, despite what we told the police, we weren't rehearsing and didn't need any sheet music."

"I wanted it for later."

"You came back empty-handed."

"I couldn't find it."

"You were gone about fifteen minutes."

"I searched through everything, and I was trying to do it quietly because Jackson was asleep."

'Or dead. You had plenty of time to kill him. I think

Cassidy would be interested to know about that fifteen minutes.''

"You can't tell him without implicating yourself."

Josh, trying to reason it through, continued as though she hadn't interrupted. "You certainly had motivation. Besides Daddy being a tyrant, he was in your way. He got top billing, not you. You were no longer satisfied with taking the backseat; you wanted to be in the driver's chair. You wanted the whole ministry. Beyond your greed, you were tired of his constant browbeating about your mediocre voice, about your weight, about everything. So you killed him and used me as your alibi."

"Listen to me, you shithead," she said, reverting to her pre–Jackson Wilde language. "Sometimes I hated him so much I could have killed him. Easily. But he was also the best thing that ever happened to me. If it weren't for Jackson, I'd still be hustling hash for a living, getting my ass pinched by rednecks, and living off the stingy tips they doled out in exchange for a glimpse of cleavage. I'd only be a lifer's sister instead of one of the most recognized women in America, who gets cards and flowers from the president.

"No, I didn't kill him. But I'll be damned before I'll cry over his death or pass up any opportunities it opens up for me. I'm going to fight like hell to keep what I've got."

The limo turned into the curved driveway leading up to the house. Jackson had been wise enough to know that common folks resented conspicuous wealth, so the house befitted an affluent professional, but it wasn't palatial. Josh despised it. Although large and comfortable, it didn't have the quiet elegance of the home his mother had made for them. This was Jackson's house through and through. His stamp was on every room. Josh had hated every minute he'd spent under its roof.

At the moment, however, he hated nothing as much as he hated himself. For while he was contemptuous of Ariel's cavalier attitude regarding his father's murder, he secretly admired it. He wished he could bounce back as easily and as guiltlessly as she. He resented her resilience and gritty ambition, but he was also jealous of them.

"I know you had your own plans for your life, Josh," she was saying. "They didn't jive with Jackson's. Naturally he got his way, and you're still sulking about it."

"You don't know what the hell you're talking about," he said. "All that happened a long time before you came along."

"But I've heard about it, from you and from Jackson. You had some battles royal over whether you were going to become a concert pianist or join the ministry."

"I don't need you to remind me what the quarrel was over."

"Know what, Josh? Your daddy was right. You and I have cut three gospel albums. All of them have gone gold. The Christmas album we recorded last spring will sell like gang-busters after all this publicity. We won't have to spend one red cent on promotion. It'll walk out of the stores.

"This ministry has made you rich and famous, Josh. It's been a hell of a lot more lucrative than if you'd stuck to playing that classical crap. Think about it." The chauffeur came around and opened the door for her. "I'd like to see you stay on at the Jackson Wilde Ministry for your own sake. But if you decide to split, it makes no difference to me."

With one foot on the pavement, she turned back to add, "Good-looking piano players come a dime a dozen, Josh. And so do lovers."

As he entered the Fairmont Hotel, Cassidy was keyed up, on edge, and wet. He'd had to park a block away and run through a deluge. Making his way toward the lobby bar, he removed his trench coat and shook rain off it, then combed his fingers through his damp hair.

He was sick of rain. For days New Orleans had been

inundated. The weather had been no better in Nashville last week, when he'd attended Jackson Wilde's funeral.

"Just coffee, please," he told the cocktail waitress who came to take his order.

"Regula' o' Nawlins coffee?" she asked in a thick native drawl.

"New Orleans. Black." He'd just as well inject the caffeine intravenously; he wasn't sleeping much these nights anyway, so what the hell. He checked his watch. Still twelve minutes till Andre Philippi reported for work. Cassidy's sources told him you could set your clock by the night manager.

While waiting to see him, he sipped the scalding brew the waitress had brought him. He finally had a lead. He, Glenn, and the police platoon assigned to investigate the case had followed hundreds of tips that had proved worthless. But now he had a bona fide lead.

He hoped to God he did. He needed to produce something. Crowder was growing impatient. He had balked at letting Cassidy go to Nashville. "If you can't find the killer on your own turf, what makes you think you can find him up there? I can't justify the expense. Let NOPD send one of their own."

"By his own admission, Glenn's no good with people. Especially with this group, he'd stick out like a sore thumb. He thinks I should go. Let me go, Tony. Maybe I'll pick up some vibes."

That had won him a withering look. "Vibes my ass. You'd just as well consult a clairvoyant."

"I've considered that, too," Cassidy said wryly.

He had continued to badger Crowder until he wore him down and got his permission to go to Nashville. "I still think it's a wild goose chase."

"Maybe so, but I'm spinning my wheels here."

"Remember you're on a budget," he'd shouted as Cassidy rushed from his office.

Regrettably, Crowder had been right. The trip had been a

total waste of time. Thousands had attended the evangelist's funeral, which had had a carnival atmosphere. The sideshow had attracted curiosity seekers, mourning disciples, and media from around the globe, all jockeying for a glimpse of the coffin, which had been draped in red, white, and blue bunting and smothered with flowers.

Cassidy's credentials had won him a spot near Wilde's inner circle of associates and confidants. If there was a killer among them, he or she masked his treachery well, for each wore the bleak expression of someone cut adrift from the last lifeboat. None had appeared jubilant or even relieved. Besides, if someone within Wilde's organization had offed him, where was the motivation? They would profit only as long as he was preaching on television and conducting his crusades, and raking in love offerings from both. Jackson Wilde was an industry. The lowliest gofer reaped benefits. Glenn's investigation had uncovered that Wilde had rewarded loyalty well.

Like any other business, there was occasional strife within the organization. Personality conflicts. Jealousy. Bickering and rumblings within the ranks. Even so, if one of Wilde's own had pulled the trigger, the person would be cutting off his or her source of income. That didn't make sense.

Perhaps there had been a contributor with a grudge, someone who had gone sour on Wilde. Cassidy had subpoenaed the records; Glenn had a couple of guys plowing through them, but there were tens of thousands of people and organizations who had contributed to the ministry over the years.

The only viable suspects at the funeral had been Ariel and Joshua. Cassidy had scrutinized their every move. Josh had appeared composed to the point of catatonia. Unblinking, he'd stared at the casket. It was impossible to gauge whether he was stunned by, indifferent to, or bored with the whole affair.

The widow had been pious and pathetic in equal proportions. She had asked God's blessings on everyone with whom she spoke. She solicited their prayers. Cassidy pegged her as a butterfly with a steel backbone. Beneath the angelic packaging, the woman was cold and hard and probably capable of murder. The problem was, the only evidence he had on her was circumstantial. He couldn't prove her affair with her stepson, and by all appearances, she had adored and now mourned her husband.

Perhaps the most viable suspect hadn't been at the funeral. Following his last interview with Claire Laurent, he and Detective Glenn had discussed her at length. All they could positively derive was that she was a liar.

Initially she'd lied about the depth of her interest in Jackson Wilde. The discovery of the folder proved that, but only that. She'd tried to keep hidden the unsavory aspects of her past, but that proved nothing except her abiding concern for her mother.

As to the videotape of the crusade service, it proved she'd lied about ever having met Wilde and about being at home the night he was murdered. But it didn't place her in the Fairmont suite with the victim. It didn't connect her to a weapon. Cassidy and Glenn knew that a grand jury wouldn't indict on such circumstantial evidence.

Besides, Glenn was still lukewarm on her. "She's a snotty, condescending bitch, but I doubt she's a killer. I still say it's the wife and son. We know they were there. We don't know that about her."

But the evidence that the detective had turned up that afternoon might be the missing clue that would change his mind about the owner of French Silk. "That little twerp over at the hotel has been lying through his teeth," he' told Cassidy.

"Looks like. Want me to take it?" He was itching to.

"Be my guest. If I get near him, I might throttle the littl shit. Never did trust a guy with a flower on his lapel."

Cassidy hadn't spared a second racing to the Fairmont i time to intercept Andre Philippi.

Cassidy spotted him briskly approaching the registration desk. He tossed a couple of bills on the table to cover his coffee, picked up his trench coat, and crossed the lobby in long, purposeful strides.

Andre wasn't pleased to see him. His face crinkled with distaste. "What is it, Mr. Cassidy? I'm very busy."

"I appreciate that, but so am I."

"Perhaps you could call tomorrow and set up an appointment."

"I'm sorry, but I really need to see you now. I apologize for the inconvenience and promise it won't take but a minute. Do you have an audio cassette player handy?"

"A cassette player?" Andre regarded him suspiciously. "There's one in my office. Why?"

"May I?"

Cassidy didn't wait for compliance. He headed toward Andre's office, trusting the little man to follow, which he did—rapidly. Upon entering the office, Cassidy went straight to the machine, turned it on, and inserted the cassette. "This is highly improper, Mr. Cassidy. If you wanted to see me—"

Andre fell silent when he heard a telephone ring on the tape. He heard his own voice answer, then the start of a conversation that began with, "*Bonsoir*, Andre."

He recognized the voice, all right. Apparently he remembered the conversation, too. As Cassidy watched, he seemed to wilt inside his impeccable black suit. Beads of perspiration popped out on his shiny forehead. His pursed lips went slack. He backed up to his desk, groping for the corner of it before plopping down.

"*Mon Dieu*," he whispered as the tape continued to play. He removed a handkerchief from his hip pocket and blotted his forehead. "Please, please, Mr. Cassidy, turn it off."

He didn't turn if off, but he reduced the volume. He'd expected a reaction, but not one so drastic. Obviously he had more here than he'd originally thought. His impulse was to grab the man by the lapels and shake the information out of him. It took some effort to play it cool.

"Why don't you tell me about this, Andre? I'm giving you the opportunity to explain."

Andre wet his lips and nervously picked at the monogram on his handkerchief. If he'd just been sentenced to death row, he couldn't have looked more distressed. "Does she know that you have this?"

Cassidy's heart was drumming. He was on the brink of learning the identity of the woman on the tape. Philippi assumed he already knew who she was. *Don't blow it!* Cassidy gave a noncommittal shrug. "It's her voice, isn't it?"

"Oh, dear. Oh, my," Andre moaned, crumpling even more. "Poor, poor Claire."

Claire had been talking to Yasmine via long distance for almost an hour. Yasmine was depressed. Claire suspected that she'd had more than a couple of drinks.

"He's always in a rush," she whined.

Selfishly, Claire wished that Yasmine had kept her lover a secret. Since the night she had acknowledged him to Claire, most of their conversations revolved around him and the star-crossed affair.

"He's dividing his time between his family and you, Yasmine. You don't have him all to yourself. That's just one of the consequences of being involved with a married man. You must accept that or end the affair."

"I accept it. It's just that . . . well, in the beginning, our time together seemed more leisurely."

"Now it's slam-bam-thank-you-ma'am."

Claire expected that crack to annoy her volatile friend. Instead, she gave one of her throaty laughs that called to mind jungle felines. "Hardly. This past weekend, he worked me over so good . . ."

"Then I don't understand what you're complaining about."

There was a tearful catch in Yasmine's voice. Claire had never known her to cry over anything, even when the cosmetics line chose another model to replace her. That had been the beginning of Yasmine's financial troubles. Yasmine wasn't aware that Claire knew about her present difficulties. She'd debated broaching the subject with her and offering assistance in the form of a loan. But knowing Yasmine's temper and pride as she did, she'd refrained. She hoped Yasmine would come to her of her own accord before her situation became desperate.

"Sometimes I wonder if that's the only reason he wants me," Yasmine said in a small voice. "You know, what we do in bed."

Claire saw the wisdom of holding her silence.

"I know it's not that way," Yasmine hastened to say. "There's much more to our relationship than the physical part. The shitty circumstances have me upset, that's all."

"What happened?"

"He was in Washington on business this week and told me he could pad the trip to include two days in New York. But his business went longer than expected and he got held up. We were only together for one day.

"When he got ready to leave this afternoon, I thought I was going to die, Claire. I did what I know better than to do. I begged him not to go. He got angry. Now, I can't even call him and apologize. I have to wait for him to call me."

Sitting at her drawing board, Claire rested her forehead in her hand and massaged her temples. She was both concerned and irritated. The only thing to be had from this love affair was a broken heart. Yasmine should be smart enough to see that. She should cut her losses now and stop making a fool of herself. But she wouldn't welcome hearing that or any other unsolicited advice.

"I'm sorry, Yasmine," Claire said, meaning it. "I know

you're hurting, and I hate that. I want to see you happy. I only wish there were something I could do.''

"You're doing it. You're listening." She sniffed. "Listen, enough of that. I got with Leon and finalized the schedule for the shoot next week. Ready to take it all down?''

Claire reached for a pad and pencil. "Ready. Oh, wait," she said impatiently when she heard the call-waiting beep. "There's the other line. Just a sec." She depressed the button and said hello. Seconds later, she clicked back to Yasmine. "I've got to go. It's Mama."

Yasmine knew better than to prolong the conversation. "Tomorrow," she said quickly and hung up.

Claire dashed from her office and chose the stairs in favor of the elevator. She'd been in the apartment less than a minute before running down the two flights to the ground level. As she raced across the darkened warehouse, she pushed her arms through the sleeves of a glossy black vinyl raincoat and pulled the matching hat over her hair.

Since the bolts had already been unlocked and the alarm system disengaged, she flung open the door—and came face to face with Cassidy.

His head was bent against the downpour, which had already plastered his hair to his head. The collar of his trench coat had been flipped up; his shoulders were hunched inside. He was reaching for the bell. When they saw each other, one was as surprised as the other.

"What do you want?" Claire asked.

"I have to see you."

"Not now." She set the alarm, pulled the door closed, and locked it behind her. Sidestepping Cassidy, she dashed through the rain toward the rear of the building. Her upper arm was manacled by his hand, and she was brought up short. "Let me go," she cried, struggling to release her arm. "I've got to go."

"Where?"

"On an errand."

"Now?"

"Now.'

"I'll drive you."

"No!"

"Where are you going?"

"Please, don't bully me now. Just let me go."

"Not a chance. Not without some kind of explanation."

A lightning bolt briefly illuminated his strong features and the resolution carved on them. He wasn't going to take no for an answer, and they were wasting time. "All right, you can drive me."

Still with a firm grip on her arm, he wheeled her around. His sedan was parked in a loading zone at the curb. After depositing her in the passenger seat, he jogged around the hood and got in. Rain dripped from his nose and chin as he started the engine. "Where to?"

"The Ponchartrain Hotel."

Chapter Nine

❧❧ ❧❧

"**I**t's on St. Charles Avenue," she told him.

"I know where it is," he said. "Why the hell are you in such a mad dash to get there?"

"Please, Mr. Cassidy, can we hurry?"

Without further comment, he pulled the car away from the curb and turned onto Conti Street. The French Quarter was quiet tonight. The few pedestrians who were out battled with umbrellas as they moved along the narrow sidewalks. The neon signs advertising exotic drinks and aperitifs, filé gumbo and crawfish étouffée, topless dancers and jazz were blurred at the edges by the rainfall.

When Cassidy stopped at an intersection to wait for crossing traffic, he turned his head and looked hard at Claire. She felt his stare like a stroke of his hand across her cheek and could almost feel again his fist closing around her hair. She hadn't expected him to touch her at all, but particularly not like that.

It had astonished her even more than his calling her by her first name, more than his knowing that she had attended

143

Jackson Wilde's last crusade. Almost a week had passed since then. Wilde had been buried in Tennessee. Claire had had no more contact with either the police or the D.A.'s office and had hoped that Cassidy had redirected his investigation away from her. Evidently that had been too much to hope for.

Now, unable to avoid him, she turned her head and met his penetrating stare. "Thank you for driving me."

"Don't thank me. You'll pay for the ride."

"Ah. Men always exact a fee from women, don't they? There's no such thing as a favor without strings attached."

"Don't flatter yourself, Ms. Laurent."

"I'm not. Isn't it the consensus among men that every woman is beautiful at two A.M.?"

"Sexism in reverse. You have a very low opinion of men."

"You'd decided that before our last meeting. Haven't we exhausted that topic?"

"Look," he said angrily, "I don't want anything from you except answers. Straight, no-bullshit answers."

"That shouldn't be too difficult. What do you want to know?"

"Why you lied to me. No, wait. I'll have to be more specific, won't I? I want to know why you lied to me about meeting Jackson Wilde. You not only met him, you met him eyeball to eyeball. You shook hands with him."

"I suppose I should have told you about that," she admitted contritely. "But it wasn't significant. It wasn't!" she emphasized after he gave her a sharp look. "I wanted to meet my adversary face to face. That's all there was to it."

"I seriously doubt that. If that's all there was to it, you wouldn't have lied about it."

"I didn't tell you because I was embarrassed. It was silly and immature, but I enjoyed having Wilde at a disadvantage. I knew him, but he didn't know me. He thought he'd won my soul. It was a kick to think of how he'd feel if he knew he was welcoming one of his so-called smut peddlers into his flock."

"Okay. I'll buy that."

"Good."

"If only it weren't for the other."

"Other?"

"You also lied about being in the Fairmont that night."

Claire had a dozen denials poised on the tip of her tongue, but one look at his face stopped her from vocalizing any of them. He seemed too confident that he had trapped her. Until she knew what she was up against, it would be safer to say nothing. Otherwise, she might only dig herself into a deeper pit.

As soon as there was an opening in the traffic, he drove through the intersection, turning left toward Canal Street. Steering with his left hand, he used his right to remove something from the breast pocket of his trench coat. He inserted a cassette into the tape player and adjusted the volume.

Claire's heart jumped to her throat when she heard her voice say, "*Bonsoir*, Andre." She stared straight ahead through the rain-splattered windshield. As they drove up Canal, she listened to a recording of a recent telephone conversation she'd had with Andre Philippi.

When it was over, Cassidy ejected the tape and returned it to his pocket. He concentrated on getting around Lee Circle before continuing out St. Charles Avenue. "I didn't know you spoke French."

"Fluently."

"That threw me off. I didn't recognize the voice as yours. Not until your old pal Andre identified you for me."

"Andre would never betray a friend."

"He assumed I already knew it was you."

"In other words, you tricked him." Cassidy shrugged an admission. "Why did you tap his telephone?"

"I knew he was holding something back and needed to know what it was. It's done all the time."

"That doesn't excuse it. It's a gross invasion of privacy. Does Andre know you trapped him?"

"I didn't trap him. He got trapped in his own deception."

Claire sighed, knowing how devastated he must be feeling. "Poor Andre."

"That's exactly what he said about you. Poor Claire. You two certainly have a cozy relationship, always thinking of each other, looking out for each other. How nice it is that you can go to the penitentiary together. Maybe we can arrange neighboring cells."

She gave him a sharp glance, which he responded to with an abrupt bob of his head. "Well, hallelujah. I finally got your attention. Are you getting the picture now? Murder two carries a mandatory life sentence in Louisiana. Now how do you feel about being a prime suspect?"

To Claire Louise Laurent, threats had never been an effective deterrent. They didn't make her quail or concede; they only made her more determined to stand her ground. "Prove that I'm guilty of murder, Mr. Cassidy. Prove it."

He held her stare a dangerously long time. Claire turned her head away as the car approached the hotel. "Just let me out at the curb. I won't be a minute."

"Uh-uh. We're going in together."

"I was only thinking of you. You're already drenched."

"I won't dissolve."

He turned on his emergency blinkers and got out of the car. After helping Claire alight, they ducked for cover beneath the canopy extending over the sidewalk. The doorman tipped his hat to Claire.

"Evenin', Miss Laurent."

"Hello, Gregory."

"It sure is wet out tonight. But don't worry none. She got here before it started coming down too bad."

Claire preceded Cassidy into the landmark hotel where suites were named for the celebrities who had resided in them. The narrow lobby was gracious and very European, furnished with antiques and oriental rugs, redolent of courtly charm and southern hospitality.

Mary Catherine Laurent was seated against the marble wall in a striped chair with gilded swans for arms. Her printed voile dress was dotted with water spots that hadn't quite dried. The brim of her pink straw hat drooped from having absorbed too much moisture. Wearing a pair of snowy white gloves, she sat with her hands clasped in her lap, her legs pressed together from instep to groin, feet flat on the floor. She looked like a young girl on her way to confirmation who'd been caught in an unexpected downpour. A suitcase stood within easy reach near her feet.

The clerk on duty was a woman with a straight bob hairdo and hornrimmed glasses. She rounded the concierge's desk at the rear of the lobby. "I called as soon as she got here, Miss Laurent."

"Thank you very much." Claire removed her rain hat and squatted down in front of her mother. "Hi, Mama. It's me, Claire."

"He'll be here soon." Mary Catherine spoke in a thin, faraway voice. Her eyes were looking into another time and place that no one else could see. "He said to meet him here this afternoon."

Claire took the sad straw hat from her mother's head and smoothed the damp hair away from her cheeks. "Maybe you got the days mixed up, Mama."

"No, I don't believe so. I'm certain I got the day right. He said he was coming for me today. I was supposed to be packed and ready. I was supposed to meet him here." Obviously flustered and disoriented, she raised one of her gloved hands and pressed it against her chest. "I'm not feeling well."

Claire glanced up at Cassidy. "Could you get her a glass of water, please?"

Thoroughly baffled, he was staring down at the two women while his trench coat dripped water onto the floor. At Claire's request, he asked the hovering night clerk for a glass of water.

"Mama." Claire gently placed her hand on Mary Catherine's knee. "I don't think he's coming today. Maybe tomorrow. Why don't you come home with me and wait for him there, hmm? Here. Mr. Cassidy has brought you a glass of cool water.''

She folded Mary Catherine's fingers around the glass. Mary Catherine raised it to her lips and sipped. Then she looked up at Cassidy and smiled. "You've been very kind, Mr. Cassidy. Thank you.''

"You're welcome.''

She noticed his wet coat. "Is it raining out?''

He glanced over his shoulder toward the entrance, where the doorman was exercising admirable sensitivity in trying to appear inconspicuous. It was still raining torrentially. Cassidy replied, "Yes, I believe it is.''

"Can you imagine that? It was so hot when I came in. Maybe I'd best go home now.'' She extended her hand up to him. He took it and helped her from her chair, then helplessly looked to Claire for further instructions.

"If you want to go on,'' she told him, "I can call a cab for Mama and me.''

"I'll drive you.''

She nodded and returned the glass of water to the night clerk. "You have my gratitude. I appreciate your understanding.''

"It's no bother, Ms. Laurent. She never causes any trouble. It's just so sad.''

"Yes, it is.'' Placing an arm around her mother's shoulders, Claire guided her toward the door, which the doorman was holding open for them. "Don't forget her suitcase, Ms. Laurent,'' he reminded her kindly.

"I'll get it,'' Cassidy said.

Mary Catherine was impervious to the peels of thunder and flashes of lightning as they waited beneath the canopy for Cassidy to stow the suitcase in the car trunk. Knowing that her mother was in another realm and virtually helpless, Claire assisted her into the backseat and buckled her in.

During the return trip, only Mary Catherine spoke. She said, "I was sure we were supposed to meet today. The Ponchartrain Hotel."

Claire bowed her head slightly and pinched her eyes shut, keenly aware of Cassidy and his rapacious interest in what was taking place. When they arrived at French Silk, he carried the suitcase while Claire ushered Mary Catherine inside and up to the third floor. In the elevator, Claire accidentally made eye contact with him. She looked away quickly, refusing to acknowledge the unasked questions in his intense, gray eyes.

Once inside the apartment, she steered Mary Catherine toward her bedroom. "I'll be back shortly if you want to wait," she said to him over her shoulder.

"I'll wait."

She helped Mary Catherine undress and carefully replaced the outdated clothes in the closet. After seeing that she took her medication, she tucked her in. "Night-night, Mama. Sleep well."

"I must have the days confused. He'll come for me tomorrow," she whispered. Smiling prettily, peacefully, she closed her eyes.

Claire leaned down and kissed her mother's cool, unlined cheek. "Yes, Mama. Tomorrow." She switched out the lamp and left the room, softly closing the door.

She was exhausted. Her shoulders ached with tension. It seemed a long way from her mother's bedroom door to the large, open living area. Like a firing squad, Cassidy was waiting for her there, armed and ready. She had no choice but to face him. Steeling herself, she moved down the hallway.

She didn't immediately see him when she entered the room. Thinking that perhaps he'd changed his mind and left, she experienced an instant of relief—and several heartbeats of disappointment.

Despite her denials to Yasmine, and to herself, she found Cassidy attractive. Physically, certainly. But there was something else . . . his dedication, tenacity, determination? She was attracted to the same qualities as those which repelled her. She feared him, yet he had demonstrated unusual kindness and sympathy toward her mother. As her eyes sought him through the darkness, all she knew for certain about her feelings for Cassidy was that they were ambiguous.

Through the shadows, she spotted him at the sideboard, in his shirtsleeves. In an oddly intimate way, his trench coat was hanging on the coat tree along with her raincoat and hat. When he turned around, Claire saw that his hair was still wet and that he was holding two snifters of Remy Martin. He joined her in the center of the room and extended one of them to her.

"Thank you, Mr. Cassidy."

"It's your liquor."

"Thank you anyway."

Claire was glad that he hadn't turned on any lights. There was light enough coming through the wall of windows. Occasionally the swollen clouds were illuminated by a flash of lightning that made the entire sky look like the negative of a photograph. But for the most part the storm's temper was spent, leaving in its wake a heavy but nonthreatening rain. Silver streams of it ran down the windows, squiggly rivulets that cast wavering shadows across her as she moved toward the windows. The river was discernible only as a wide dark band lined by lights on both levees. An empty barge was chugging upstream.

The first sip of cognac seared her esophagus. The second spread a soothing warmth through her, starting with a slight sting to her lips and ending with a tingle in her toes. "At times like this, I wish I smoked," she remarked.

"Pardon?"

She listened to his footsteps as he approached her. "I said sometimes I wish I smoked. This is one of those times." Turning, she found him standing closer than she had expected. His eyes were the same color as the rain slashing the windows, and they were focused on her with a breath-stopping intensity.

"Smoking's bad for you."

"Yes, I know. I guess I envy the immediate relaxation it gives the smoker." She ran her fingers up the bowl of the snifter. "Have you ever seen a cigar smoker blow smoke into his brandy snifter before taking a sip?" He shook his head. "It's pretty, the way the smoke swirls around inside the crystal. The smoke is inhaled when the liquor is swallowed. It's provocative, sensual. I think it must make the brandy taste better. Or maybe the cigar. I don't know."

"Who have you seen do that?"

"No one, actually. I saw it in a movie about Sir Richard Burton. Maybe that was a habit unique to him. Maybe it was the vogue in the nineteenth century."

His disturbing gaze remained fixed on her face. "What made you think of that, Claire?"

She shrugged self-consciously. "The rainy night, the cognac."

"Or were you just trying to distract me?"

"Could you be that easily distracted?"

He hesitated a moment too long before giving her a curt no. Then he tossed back the remainder of his drink and returned his empty snifter to the sideboard. When he rejoined her at the windows, he was all business. "What went on tonight?"

"You were there. You saw."

"And I still don't know what happened. She flipped out, right?"

"Yes. She flipped out."

"Look, I didn't mean that to sound—"

"I know you didn't."

"How often does she . . . How often is she like that?"

"It varies. Sometimes there's a buildup. Sometimes it occurs out of the blue. Some days she's perfectly lucid. Others, like the first time you met her, she seems to be confused, senile." Her voice turned gruff. "Sometimes she's as you saw her tonight, completely detached from this world, living in another one."

"What triggers it?"

"I don't know."

"What do the doctors say?"

"That they don't know either. It's happened for as long as I can remember, and her lapses have gotten progressively deeper and more frequent the older she gets. The first I remember them, they were little more than bouts of depression. During her spells, as Aunt Laurel referred to them, Mama would retire to her room and cry for days, refuse to leave her bed, refuse to eat. Aunt Laurel and I catered to her."

"She should have gotten treatment when it started." Claire bristled and turned a glare on him. "That was an observation, not a criticism," he said.

Claire studied him for a moment. When she was convinced that he was sincere, she relaxed her hostile posture. "I know now that she should have been placed under a doctor's care immediately. A depression that deep is abnormal. But I was a child. And for all her good intentions, Aunt Laurel didn't know how to deal with mental illness. She didn't even recognize it as such. Mama was a young woman whose love had forsaken her. Her family had disowned and disinherited her. Aunt Laurel mistook her illness as nothing more than a broken heart."

"A broken heart that wouldn't heal."

Claire nodded. "One day Mama did what she did tonight. She dressed up and sneaked out of the house with a packed suitcase. I was very young, but I remember Aunt Laurel becoming frantic with worry until a policeman brought Mama home. He knew us, you see. He had spotted Mama walking along Canal Street, lugging her suitcase. When he approached her and offered assistance, he could tell she wasn't rational. Thankfully, he brought her home instead of taking her to the police station. She was spared that degradation."

"During these spells, she imagines she's eloping?"

"Yes. My guess is that before my father deserted her, he proposed that they elope. He must have gotten cold feet and left her stranded. Mama imagines that he's coming for her at the designated place. Tonight I'm sure she took a bus as far as the trolley, then rode it the rest of the way out St. Charles to the Ponchartrain."

"That's always been where they were to meet?"

"No. The meeting place changes. She's never quite clear on when or where she's supposed to meet her young man. Rather than facing what's obvious, she always blames herself for not getting the instructions straight."

Claire turned away from the windows and looked at Cassidy. "The night Jackson Wilde was murdered, Mama sneaked out and went to the Fairmont. Andre called and told me that she was in the hotel lobby waiting for her beau, so I went to fetch her. That's why I was there. After I learned what had happened, I asked Andre not to mention my being there. Since my presence there had nothing to do with Wilde, he agreed to safeguard my privacy. I'm sure that you and your colleagues got a thrill out of eavesdropping on our conversation, but you misinterpreted it."

Cupping the bowl of the snifter between her palms, she drained it. Cassidy took it from her and returned it to the sideboard. "Wouldn't it be easier on everyone if you had your mother institutionalized?" he asked.

Claire had anticipated the question. It had been posed to her hundreds of times over the years. Her answer was always the same. "Undoubtedly it would be easier. But would it be best?"

"I can see you've got definite opinions on the subject."

Agitated, she began pacing in front of the windows. "For as long as I can remember there have been people from the medical community, from the social services, and from law-enforcement agencies trying to force me to commit her."

"And before that, they tried taking you away from her."

Claire stopped pacing and whipped around to confront him. "You couldn't leave it alone, could you, Mr. Cassidy?"

"No, I couldn't. That's my job."

"Your job sucks."

"Sometimes," he admitted. "Instead of feeding me that hearts-and-flowers rendition of your childhood, why didn't you level with me and tell me about your run-ins with the authorities?"

"Because they're too painful to recall. I still have nightmares about them. I dream the social workers are dragging me, kicking and screaming, from Aunt Laurel's house. Mama's confused and upset. I don't want to go."

"According to the records, little Claire Louise Laurent gave them hell. I can well believe it."

"Things would be going fine," she said. "Then Mama would have a bad spell and do something to stir them up."

"What about your great-aunt? You described her as a loving, caring parent."

"She was, but the experts," she said, emphasizing the word contemptuously, "didn't think so. She was peculiar and therefore didn't fit their textbook criteria for a perfect parent. They'd come for me. I'd be taken away. On three separate occasions I was placed in foster homes. I ran away time after time, until I exhausted them and they let me return home.

"When I was about twelve, Mama wandered away and was lost for several days. We finally located her in a sleazy hotel, but by then the police were involved. Human Resources got wind of it and came for me. I wasn't being brought up in a healthy environment, they said. I needed direction, stability.

"I swore I would run away from wherever they took me and would continue running away, and that no matter what they did, they couldn't keep me separated from my mother. I guess they finally believed me because they never came back."

All her pent-up resentment was turned full force on Cassidy. "I don't give a damn what the records downtown say about me. I gave them hell, yes. I would still give hell to anybody who tried to separate us. I belong with her. I welcome the privilege of looking after her.

"When she got pregnant, she could have done the easy thing—and at that time the fashionable thing among the wealthy. She could have gone to Europe for a year and put me up for adoption. According to Aunt Laurel, that's what my grandparents urged her to do. Or she could have gone across the river to Algiers and found an abortionist. That would have been even simpler. No one would have known, not even her parents. Instead, she chose to have me and to keep me, even though it meant sacrificing her inheritance, her entire way of life."

"Your sense of responsibility is admirable."

"I don't feel responsible for her. I love her."

"Is that why you don't lock her in where she can't possibly get out?"

"Exactly. She doesn't need locks, she needs love and patience and understanding. Besides, that would be cruel, inhumane. I refuse to treat her like an animal."

"She could get hurt out wandering the streets alone, Claire."

She slumped down onto the padded arm of the white-upholstered sofa. "Don't you think I know that? Short of locking her in, I take every precaution to guard against her wanderings. Yasmine does, too. So does Harry. But she has the cunning of a young girl about to elope. Sometimes, in spite of our diligence, she gets past us, like tonight when I thought she was safely asleep."

For a long moment, conversation died. Distant thunder broke the silence, but it wasn't intrusive. Claire folded her arms across her middle and looked up to find Cassidy regarding her with that damned absorption of his. His stare made her uncomfortable for a variety of reasons, and she wondered if he was as aware of the quiet darkness as she.

"Why do I always feel like you're looking at me through a magnifying glass?" she asked resentfully.

"You invite close inspection."

"I'm not that much of an oddity, am I?"

"You're an enigma."

"My life's an open book."

"Hardly, Claire. I've had to pry every scrap of information out of you. You've lied to me every step of the way."

"I went to the Fairmont that night to get my mother," she said wearily. "There was no reason to tell you that."

"You lied about your childhood, which you would have had me believe was bloody terrific."

"Is anyone completely honest about his childhood?"

"And you lied when you told me you'd never been arrested."

She dropped her head forward and exhaled around a bitter laugh. "You have been thorough, haven't you?"

"The day we met, you told me not to underestimate you. Don't ever underestimate me, either." Placing his finger beneath her chin, he tilted her face up. "Tell me about it, Claire."

"Why? I'm sure you already know. I assaulted a policeman."

"The charge was dropped."

"I was only fourteen."

"What happened?"

"Wasn't it in the records?"

"I'd like to hear your side."

She pulled in a deep breath. "A friend of mine from school was staying with me."

"You were hiding her. She was a runaway."

"Yes," she said sharply. "I was hiding her. When the policemen came to take her home, she became hysterical. One tried to handcuff her. I tried my damnedest to stop him."

"Why were you hiding her? Even when they threatened

you with jail, you never told the police why your friend was hiding in your house."

"I gave her my word that I wouldn't. But that was years ago and she . . ." She made a gesture with her hands that said it didn't matter anymore. "Her stepfather was sexually molesting her. She was being raped, sometimes sodomized, every night while her mother looked the other way and pretended it wasn't happening."

Muttering swear words, Cassidy dragged his hand down his face.

"It got to a point where she couldn't take it anymore. There was no one for her to turn to. She was afraid that if she told the nuns, or a priest, they wouldn't believe her. She was also afraid of reprisal at home. When she told me, I offered to hide her for as long as she wanted to remain hidden."

Claire stared into space for a moment, recalling how furious she'd been over the futility of her own actions. "Two weeks after they returned her home, she ran away again. She must have left the city. No one ever heard from her again."

"You could have spared yourself a police record and told them what was happening."

"What good would it have done?" she asked scornfully. "Her stepfather was a millionaire. They lived in a gorgeous house in the Garden District. Even if someone had believed her, it would have been swept under the rug and she'd have been sent back. Besides, I had promised her I wouldn't tell." She shook her head. "The consequences I suffered could hardly compare to what she went through, Mr. Cassidy."

"Tell me about Andre Philippi."

She gazed at him belligerently. "What do you want to know?"

"You both attended Sacred Heart Academy."

"Grades seven through twelve," Claire said. "Sister Anne Elizabeth is Mother Superior. Or she was when Andre and I were students there." She tilted her head; her hair brushed her shoulder. "Is it incriminating that we were classmates?"

"Tell me about him," he said, ignoring the dig. "He's a funny little man."

Instantly her aspect changed. She dropped all vestiges of fun and flirtation. Even her voice assumed a hard edge. "I suppose that athletic, macho types like you might think Andre is 'funny.' "

"I didn't mean anything derogatory."

"The hell you didn't."

"Is he gay?"

"Is that important?"

"I don't know yet. Is he?"

"No. In fact, he's got a schoolboy's crush on Yasmine."

"But he's not intimately involved with anyone, male or female?"

"Not to my knowledge. He lives alone."

"I know."

"Of course you would."

"I have a file on him," he said. "I have a file on all the employees of the Fairmont Hotel, even those who weren't on duty that night."

"Do you have a file on me?"

"A fat one."

"I'm flattered."

Cassidy was frowning. "What about Andre's parents? What's his heritage? I couldn't tell."

"Is that question racially motivated?"

"Shit," Cassidy said. "No, it's not. And would you stop being so goddamn defensive?"

Claire weighed her options and saw the advantage in telling Cassidy about Andre. If she didn't, he'd go prying on his own, and it seemed that the more he pried, the more precarious her situation became.

"Andre's mother was a quadroon. Are you familiar with the term?" He nodded. "She was an exceptionally beautiful woman, somewhat like Yasmine. Although she was intelligent, she never graduated from high school. Instead, she trained herself in the skills necessary to her profession.''

''Which was?''

''To be a companion to men. She learned the techniques from her mother. She began taking clients when she was fifteen.''

''She was a prostitute?''

The word offended Claire and she let him know it. ''A prostitute hangs out on street corners and hustles passersby. There's a distinction here. Andre's mother cultivated multidimensional relationships with gentlemen that often lasted for years. In return they compensated her well.''

''Were these 'gentlemen' white?''

''For the most part.''

''And one of them was Andre's father.''

''That's right. He was a prominent businessman who couldn't claim the child but accepted responsibility for him.''

''Do you know who he was?''

''Andre does, but he's never disclosed his identity to me.''

''And even if you knew, you wouldn't tell me.''

''No. I wouldn't.''

Cassidy ruminated on that for a moment. ''Because his father was well-to-do, Andre could attend the finest schools.''

''Yes, but he was an outcast. The other children said unkind things about his *maman* and taunted him with ugly names. I was considered somewhat of an oddball too, because I didn't have a normal family life. It was natural that Andre and I develop a friendship.

''His mother was devoted to him and vice versa. Just as her mother had done for her, she coached Andre on food and wine, etiquette, how to dress, how to differentiate between quality and junk whether it be jewelry, linen, or antique furniture.

''Before Andre's father set her up in a house, she took Andre with her when she met her gentlemen. He waited for her in the lobbies of luxury hotels where people of color weren't even allowed until the early sixties.

"Perhaps because he was granted that privilege, he fell in love with the hotels. To him they were finer and more sacred than cathedrals, because not everybody could enjoy them. He had a place in them that was prohibited to other children. He dreamed of managing one." In a faraway voice, she added, "I'm glad his dreams came true."

"What about his mother?" Cassidy asked. "Does she still have a clientele?"

"No, Mr. Cassidy. She took her own life by slashing her wrists with a straight razor. Andre found her in the bathtub one afternoon when he came home from school."

"Jesus."

"If you aren't prepared for the stink, you shouldn't exhume the past."

He pulled an angry frown. "Do you think I'm enjoying this?"

"If you don't, then why do you persist in dredging up the ugliness in everyone's life?"

"It's one of the least pleasant aspects of my work, Claire. But it's still my work."

"Answer a question for me," she said suddenly.

"What?"

"Should you be calling me Claire?"

They stared at each other for a long moment, the tension thick. At last he turned away from her. "No, I shouldn't.'

"Then why are you?"

He turned back around slowly. His eyes seemed to acquire tactile qualities; they touched her everywhere at once. "You may be a liar, Claire, but you're not stupid," he said huskily. "You know why."

She held his stare until the pressure in her chest became unbearable. The only thing worse would have been to stop looking at him, and she couldn't bring herself to do that. She felt drawn to him, linked by invisible tethers.

They had remained so still that when he finally moved, she jumped reflexively. But he only raised his hand to rub the back of his neck as though the muscles ached.

"Back to Andre. He called you that night and told you your mother was at the Fairmont."

She nodded. It was difficult to speak. Her heart was still racing.

"You went to pick her up?"

"Yes."

"Alone?"

"Yes. In my car."

"What time was that?"

"I'm not sure."

"Claire."

"I don't know," she cried, shaking her head impatiently. "It was after the crusade, because, as you know, I attended that earlier."

He held his temper in check, but she could see it wasn't easy. "Give me an approximate time."

"Midnight, maybe. No later."

"How did Mary Catherine get out of here without your knowing?"

"I told you she can be very resourceful. She went downstairs, undid the locks, and disengaged the alarm before opening the door."

"Even during one of her 'spells,' she can be that lucid? That functional?"

Claire avoided looking at him. "Sometimes."

"Okay, so you drove to the Fairmont."

"I illegally parked across the street. I knew I wouldn't be but a minute, and I wasn't. I rushed to Andre's office, he handed Mother over to me, and we left. I probably wasn't there more than two minutes."

"Did anyone else see you? Other hotel personnel?"

"I don't know. I suppose you could ask."

"Count on it." He shoved his hands into his pockets and

stared out the rain-streaked windows. In spite of the grilling he was subjecting her to, Claire noticed that he had a very masculine profile, a manly stance, from his damp hair to the toes of his shoes. "You saw Wilde that night at the Superdome. Then later you were in the hotel where he was found murdered. And you took pains to keep it a secret."

"How many times do I have to explain? I wanted to protect my mother from gossip and speculation. Is that so difficult for you to understand?"

"You stayed in the lobby area of the hotel?"

"Yes."

"You didn't go to any other floor, no other area of the hotel?"

"No."

"Did you use the elevator?"

"No."

He turned and braced his hands on the padded arm of the sofa, bracketing her hips. Leaning into her, he asked, "Then why in hell didn't you tell me this sooner? If it was so damned innocent, why did you lie to me?"

"Because you were trying to implicate me. My name was on Wilde's hit list, and you seemed to think that was important. You had that folder of clippings that I had stupidly tried to destroy. That was two strikes against me already. I was afraid that if you knew I was anywhere near the Fairmont that night, you'd do just as you've done and jump to the wrong conclusion."

"*Is* it wrong, Claire? The only reason you went to the Fairmont that night was to pick up your mother?"

"Just like tonight."

"While you were there, you didn't have your old pal Andre Philippi sneak you into Wilde's suite?"

"Would Wilde have lain there nude and calmly talked to me, a total stranger?"

"How did you know he was lying down nude?"

"Because it's been in the newspaper every day for a month

that he was found nude in bed. Besides, even if I had been determined to kill Jackson Wilde, do you think I would have involved someone else?''

''Dammit, I don't know!'' he shouted.

His agitation plain, he hung his head between his shoulders. He was so close that she could smell the rain in his hair and on his skin. Even in the darkness she could see the growth pattern of the hair on the crown of his head. If she had turned her head the slightest degree, her lips would have brushed the temple where a vein ticked with frustration.

Eventually he raised his head and looked searchingly into her eyes. ''It's so damned neat. You had motivation. You had opportunity. You even had an insider who could help you carry it off. Claire, you've got to admit that from where I stand you look guilty as hell.''

''Then why the long face? Isn't this what you wanted? I thought you'd be pleased to finally nail a suspect. What's wrong?''

With slow, deliberate movements, he placed his hands on her shoulders and pulled her up to stand dangerously close to him. ''What's wrong? I think I've found the killer.'' He slid his fingers up through her hair and encircled her head. ''But I didn't want it to be you.''

Then suddenly his lips were pressed firmly against hers. Before Claire could recover from her initial shock, he tilted his head and deepened the kiss. An involuntary sound escaped her when his tongue separated her lips. It brought with it the taste and texture of a man, a delicious blend of cognac and brawn. Angry and aroused, he kissed her masterfully, brooking no resistance, although at first she was too dumbfounded to stop him and within seconds was too caught up in the kiss to try.

He raised his head only long enough to switch angles and slide his hands from her head to her waist, pulling her against him. He was hard. Desire, like the petals of a spring blossom, opened in her midsection. She moved against him.

"Oh, Christ," he muttered and buried his face in her neck. Deftly he undid the buttons of her blouse. He unfastened the clasp of her bra and slid his hands into the loose cups. His palms skimmed over her first, then his hands caressed her.

His kiss turned wilder, hungrier. Claire clutched handfuls of his shirt, because to let go would mean to topple backward, not only because he was bending her back at such a dramatic angle but because her equilibrium was suffering the effects of his kiss, his touch.

His lips tugged at hers while his tongue plumbed her mouth again and again as though searching for the answers he craved. Their bodies were combustible, each as hot as the other. Within his stroking hands her breasts were full and flushed, their centers raised and responsive.

The intensity of the embrace was frightening. Claire's fiery response scared her. She imagined her control disintegrating, like dry kindling being rapidly consumed by a greedy flame. Soon she would have no control left, and that was the most terrifying prospect of all. All her life people in authority had been trying to tell her what was best for her. She was conditioned to resist.

"Stop!" She averted her head and pushed his hands away. "It was a good try, but you won't get a confession out of me this way."

He released her immediately and stepped back. He clenched his fists at his sides. His breathing was labored, his voice raspy and uneven. "You know damn well that's not why I kissed you."

"Isn't it?" she shot back defiantly.

He turned and stomped away, snatched his trench coat off the coat tree, and yanked open the door. Light from the corridor spilled in, silhouetting him in a bright wedge of it.

For several moments they stared at each other across the gloom, then he stepped through the door and slammed it behind him.

Claire collapsed onto the sofa arm. Covering her face with

her hands, she moaned with a repentant attitude that would have made Sister Anne Elizabeth proud. "Oh, God, no. No."

Willingly, ecstatically, she had kissed the man who could, and probably would, condemn her to prison for the rest of her life.

She answered the door wearing a roomy T-shirt over patterned leggings. "Cassidy," she said with no little surprise. "Did you lock yourself out?" She glanced across the walkway that separated their condos, looking for a clue as to why he'd shown up on her doorstep at that hour of the night.

"No. I saw your lights were still on," he remarked, as though that explained everything.

"Come in." Patty-Penny-Peggy moved aside, and he stepped into a living area much like his own, except much better decorated and far neater. "Rough night weather-wise," she said, indicating his trench coat.

"The worst of it is over, I think."

"Sit down. Would you like a drink?"

"No, thanks."

"Oh." She flashed a quick, puzzled smile. "I'd offer you some grass, but I guess that wouldn't be too cool, huh?"

"No."

"Are you hungry? Have you had dinner?"

"I don't remember," he said honestly. "I don't think so, but I'm not hungry."

"Well, sit down. I'll turn on some music. What kind do you like?"

"I'm not particular." He took off his coat and tossed it over the arm of a chair, but he didn't sit down.

She switched on a CD player and a Randy Travis song began to play. "Do you like country?"

"It's okay."

She studied him for a moment, then propped her hands on

her hips. "Look, Cassidy, I'm glad you dropped by, but I'm at a loss here. What's going on?"

"I came to fuck."

She blinked twice, obviously taken aback. Then her lips spread into a wide grin. "Why didn't you just say so?" She pivoted on her bare heels and headed for the bedroom.

Cassidy followed.

Chapter Ten

❧ ❧

Ariel unwrapped a bite-size Snickers and popped it into her mouth. Her teeth split the chocolate covering, crunched through the peanuts, and sank into the caramel and nougat. She savored the luscious combination of flavors as the candy melted and oozed on her tongue. After maximizing the greatest caloric pleasure from it, she sucked the sticky caramel off her teeth.

Candy wrappers littered the coffee table in front of the divan. As a kid, treats had been prohibited on her family's budget, and Ariel had been lucky if she got a piece of stick candy every few weeks. For the past several years she'd been making up for the deprivation; she couldn't get enough.

She stretched for the sheer pleasure of seeing, hearing, and feeling her silk lounging pajamas slide against her legs. The mirror across the room reflected a woman of leisure, surrounded by nice things all belonging to her. Ariel liked that. Indeed, she wanted to crow about it.

The house she'd grown up in had had indoor plumbing, and that was about the only amenity it could boast. It had been distinctly ugly, the large rooms spartanly and cheaply furnished. She shuddered with revulsion at the memory of it. She had never invited friends over because she was ashamed of her family's old, creaky, ugly farm house. She was also ashamed of the people who lived there. Her brother had been meaner than sin and had terrorized everybody. Her parents had always seemed old, although now she realized that weariness had aged them beyond their years. Nevertheless, that didn't make her feel any more kindly toward them. She was glad they were long dead and buried.

She wished she could bury her memories of poverty as easily and as permanently. But whenever she started feeling complacent about her present life, those recollections would emerge from their dormancy to taunt her. They reminded her of who she'd been before she threw herself on the mercy of the Reverend Jackson Wilde.

Those impoverished days are over forever, she vowed as she gazed around her living room. Objets d'art filled every nook and cranny. Most of the pieces were gifts from Jackson's followers. He had frequently suggested that they give some of the things away, but Ariel had refused to part with a single item, no matter how cluttered the house became. If she had to install extra shelving, or store things in the attic and under the beds, she would keep everything that came her way. For Ariel, possessions were tantamount to security. She would never be without them again. As she reaffirmed that pledge, she unwrapped another Snickers and devoured it with hedonistic relish.

When Josh came in carrying a cup of coffee and the morning newspaper, he noticed the candy wrappers immediately. "Is that your breakfast?"

"What of it?"

"Not exactly oat bran, is it?" He sank into an easy chair, placed his cup at his elbow, and unfolded the paper. "It's a miracle. We're not front-page news anymore."

Watching him almost soured the candy in her stomach.

Lately, Josh was about as much fun as a forty-year plague. They still made love every night. He was skilled and ardent and had an artist's sensuality. His fingertips played her body as they did the piano keys, with strength and sensitivity.

But half the excitement of sleeping with him had been the thrill of cuckolding Jackson. Since secrecy and guilt were no longer adding spice to the affair, the lovemaking had grown bland. Even after an orgasm, she hungered for something more.

Yet, she couldn't account for her restlessness and dissatisfaction. The Cincinnati crusade had gone exceptionally well. Two TV shows had been taped and were ready for broadcast. During the tapings, the auditorium had been packed to capacity.

Ariel had sung. Josh had played. Several disciples had tearfully testified to what Jackson Wilde and his ministry had meant to their lives. Then Ariel had taken the podium and begun her heartrending sermon. It had taken days to memorize. Each crack in her voice, each gesture, had been carefully choreographed and rehearsed in front of her mirror. The time and effort had been well spent. Before she was finished there wasn't a dry eye in the place, and the offering plates were overflowing with greenbacks.

Those who, weeks before, had been skeptical of her ability to continue the ministry without Jackson's stern leadership had been effusively complimentary. She'd proved them wrong. She was just as charismatic and persuasive as her late husband had been. People had flocked by the hundreds to see her, considering every word she spoke a precious gem. The world was in her pocket.

So why was she feeling vaguely discontent?

It just still wasn't enough. She had hundreds of thousands of followers, but why not millions? Suddenly she sat up. "I don't think so."

Josh lowered one corner of his paper. "Pardon?"

"I don't think it's so bloody wonderful that we're no longer front-page news." She swung her legs off the divan and began to roam around the room. She fidgeted, straightening tasseled cushions, rearranging crystal vases, and repositioning porcelain shepherdesses.

"Well, if it makes you feel any better, here's our ad on page fifteen of section two."

He turned the paper toward her so that she could see the ad. Across the top, printed in the ministry's trademark typeface, was the title of their television show. Beneath that was a full-face drawing of her, holding a microphone in front of her mouth, tears rolling down her cheeks. The date and time of broadcast were printed beneath.

Ariel critically studied the ad. " '*The Jackson Wilde Prayer and Praise Hour*,' " she read. "Jackson Wilde is dead. Why haven't we changed the name of the program?"

"To what?"

"Why not *The* Ariel *Wilde Prayer and Praise Hour*?"

"Why not *The Prayer and Praise Hour*?"

"Because that's too plain. Besides, people need an individual to identify with."

"You, I suppose."

"Well, why not? I'm the one doing most of the talking now."

Josh watched her over the rim of his coffee cup as he took a sip. "Call the damn show anything you please, Ariel. I really couldn't care less."

"That's readily apparent."

He tossed the newspaper aside and angrily surged to his feet. "What the hell is that supposed to mean?"

"It means that if it weren't for me, this whole outfit would have collapsed after Jackson died. You don't have the balls to hold together a scout troop, much less a ministry like ours. It's a good thing you've got me. Otherwise, you'd be out hustling gigs with tent revivals."

"I'd be a lot happier doing that. At least I wouldn't feel like a carrion bird picking at a dead man's corpse."

One carefully penciled eyebrow arched. "If you're so unhappy, you know where the door is."

Josh glared at her, but, as she had known he would, he backed down. He went to the piano and after running through several chords he began playing a classical piece with all the verve and courage he lacked in dealing with sticky situations.

When finally he had calmed down, he looked up at her, but continued to play. "You know what's really pathetic? You don't realize what a joke you are."

"Joke?" she repeated, affronted. "To who?"

"To everyone within the organization. You're blinded by your inflated self-importance. People are laughing behind your back. Why do you think two of the board members have already resigned?"

"Because they didn't like having a woman calling the shots. I threatened their masculinity. Who gives a damn? We didn't need them."

"This ministry, which you brag about holding together, is crumbling, Ariel. Only you're too pumped up with ego to see it." He ran his hands over the keys, completing the piece, then began another. "Daddy's probably sitting up there somewhere in heaven, having a good laugh on us."

"You've gone soft in the head."

He grinned at her knowingly. "You're still scared of him, aren't you, Ariel?"

"You're the one who's scared."

"I admit it," he said. "You don't."

"I'm not scared of anything or anybody."

"He's still got you under his thumb."

"Like hell."

"Why do you eat like a lumberjack and then go throw it up?" He finished the piece on a fortissimo that punctuated his question.

Ariel's cocky defensiveness wavered. "I don't know what you're talking about."

"Oh yes you do. You've been doing it for months. As

soon as you've eaten, you go into the bathroom. You binge on things like candy bars, then force yourself to throw up. That's a sickness. Bulimia.''

She rolled her eyes. "Who are you, the surgeon general? So I watch my weight. TV cameras add at least fifteen pounds. I don't want to look like a white whale when I descend that freaking staircase.''

He reached up and encircled her narrow wrist, turning it up so that she could see how much his long fingers overlapped. "You don't simply count calories, Ariel. You stuff yourself, then you make yourself vomit.''

She yanked her hand away. "Well, what if I do? Jackson was always on my case about my weight. I had to do something to keep it off.''

"Didn't you ever figure him out?" Josh asked with a rueful smile. "He was a master at preying on a person's weakness. That's how he exercised mind control. He constantly hinted that my mother was stupid, until she began to believe it. For the last few years of her life, she was afraid to offer an opinion on anything at the risk of being ridiculed.

"You know his bit with me. He let me know at every turn that I lacked the musical talent I craved. Every chance he got, he reminded me that I was only good enough to pound out gospel music and was mediocre at that.

"With you, it was your weight. He knew you were self-conscious about it, so he used that to keep you humble. He was as sly as Satan, Ariel. He was so subtle, you didn't even know you'd been gigged until you realized that your self-esteem was lower than shit.

"You should have ignored him when he teased you about your 'baby fat' and your overactive sweet tooth. You were always slender enough. Now you're on the verge of emaciation. Besides, as you noted only moments ago, he's dead. He can't harp on you anymore.''

"No, he's got you to do it for him.''

Josh shook his head in resignation. "You're missing the

point, Ariel. I'm not being critical. I'm worried about your health. I—''

"Wait, Josh, I've got an idea." She reached down and mashed her hands over his, causing the keys to crash discordantly.

He pulled his hands from beneath hers. "You bitch! "If you ever—''

"Oh, stop. I didn't hurt your precious hands. Listen, what you said earlier, about us not making news any longer? Well, you're right. We've got to do something to correct that.''

He was experimentally flexing his fingers. "What do you have in mind?" he grumbled.

"Since we got back from Cincinnati we've been holed up here in Nashville, out of sight and out of mind. It's time we shook things up, generated some headlines. It should be made plain to the cops in New Orleans that the grieving widow and son haven't forgotten that Jackson Wilde was murdered in cold blood.''

"Are you so sure that reminding them of that is a smart idea?"

She shot him a icy look. "Jackson had legions of enemies." Making a steeple of her index fingers, she tapped them against her lips. "One in particular in New Orleans."

"Tell me what it means."

Cassidy was in a bad mood. Dealing with Detective Howard Glenn wasn't improving his state of mind. The day after he had accompanied Claire to the Ponchartrain to pick up Mary Catherine, Cassidy had recounted to Glenn all that had transpired. All except the kiss.

"So she didn't deny that it was her voice on the tape?" Glenn had asked.

"No, because she had a good reason for being at the Fairmont that night."

"To plug the preacher."

"Or to pick up her mother, as she claims." Glenn had regarded him skeptically. "Look, Glenn, they couldn't have staged that business last night. Mary Catherine Laurent's mental instability is genuine and Cl . . . Ms. Laurent protects her like a mama bear."

He had filled him in on Claire's relationship with Andre Philippi. "It dates back to childhood. So it's reasonable that he lied to protect her privacy and that's the extent of it."

Glenn had searched for a place to extinguish his cigarette butt. Cassidy offered him an empty Styrofoam cup. "Jesus," Glenn had said as he ground out the butt, "the deeper we dig the more interesting it gets."

"But we've got to dig with finesse."

"Meaning?"

"I want to get to the bottom of this, too. Maybe there's something there, maybe not. But you can't approach a woman like Claire Laurent reeking of Camels and tossing out obscenities. I still think it's best if you leave her to me."

"Oh?"

"She finds you personally distasteful."

Glenn settled his rump more comfortably in his chair and rested one ankle on the other. "How does she find you, Cassidy?"

"What are you implying?" he had snapped, tossing down his writing pen.

Glenn had raised his hands in surrender. "Nothing, nothing. It's just that I couldn't help but notice that she's a good-looking broad. And you're not exactly a troll. All things considered—"

"All things considered," Cassidy had interrupted tightly, "I'm going to prosecute Jackson Wilde's killer no matter who it is."

"Then you've got no reason to be so touchy, do you?"

From then on, their conversations had been strictly business. Cassidy had chided himself for swallowing Glenn's bait. He wouldn't have if his conscience hadn't been so sorely pricked by Glenn's implications, and he reckoned that the detective knew that. He hadn't brought up the possibility of a conflict of interests since, but Cassidy was certain he hadn't forgotten the exchange.

This morning, Glenn was into guessing games. He'd ambled in and scattered several computer printouts across Cassidy's desk. Thousands of names were listed on the sheets, a few of which had been circled with red crayon. Cassidy randomly picked one. "Who's this Darby Moss?"

"Not a name you forget, is it?" Glenn asked rhetorically. "Years ago when I was still on a beat, I busted him for assault. He worked a hooker over pretty good. Put her in the hospital. Moss flies in this slick little hustler of a lawyer from Dallas, his hometown. Got the charges dropped. Pissed me off good. So when his name showed up on this list of contributors to Wilde's ministry, it set off bells. I went to Dallas over the weekend and found ol' Darby alive and kicking. He owns three adult-book stores."

Cassidy's brows drew together. "You don't say."

"Yeah. Regular jerk-off joints. You name a perversion, he stocks a magazine that caters to it, along with dildos, inflatable pussies, all kinds of shit. Curious, huh? When I got back, I started running matches through the computer and all these other names sent up red flags. In one way or another, they're all dealing in the very stuff Wilde preached against."

"What does that tell us? That when they chipped in, he turned off the heat?"

"Looks like. And that's not all." He scanned the sheet until his finger landed on another name circled in red. "Here."

"Gloria Jean Reynolds?"

Glenn smugly slipped a piece of notepaper from the breast pocket of his dingy white shirt and handed it to Cassidy.

Cassidy silently read the name, then raised inquiring eyes to Glenn, who shrugged eloquently.

The phone on his desk rang. Cassidy picked it up on the second ring. "Cassidy."

"Mr. Cassidy, it's Claire Laurent."

His gut clenched reflexively. Her soft, smoky voice was the last one he had expected to hear. She was never off his mind, but the fantasies he entertained weren't always of convicting her of murder.

The romp with his neighbor had provided only short-term relief. When he left her condo, he still wasn't sure what her name was, and that made him feel he was on the level of a maggot. He had used her in the worst way a man could use a woman. His only absolution was that she had also gotten from him what she had wanted—and had asked for on numerous occasions.

"Hello," he said to Claire with feigned casualness.

"How soon can you get here?"

The question took him aback. Was she about to confess? "To French Silk? What's up?"

"That will be obvious when you arrive. Please hurry."

She hung up before saying anything more. He held the receiver away from his ear and regarded it curiously.

"Who was that?" Glenn asked as he lit a cigarette.

"Claire Laurent."

Glenn's eyes narrowed as he looked at Cassidy through a cloud of smoke. "No shit?"

"No shit. I'll catch you later."

Leaving the detective, Cassidy pulled on his suit coat, hurried from his office, and ran to catch the elevator before the doors closed. He upbraided himself for his haste, but justified it by recalling her tone of voice. Although it had been as low and hushed as always, he had sensed another quality in it. Irritation? Fear? Urgency?

Within seconds he was on his way, driving skillfully fast

toward the French Quarter and cursing the traffic along the way.

Just as Claire had said, he saw the reason for her call before he even reached French Silk. A throng of people, at least two hundred of them, were picketing in front of her building. He had to read only a few signs to know who had organized the protest march.

"Dammit." He parked illegally and shoved his way through the curious onlookers until he reached a policeman. "Cassidy, D.A.'s office," he said, flashing his ID. "Why aren't you breaking this up?"

"They've got a permit."

"What idiot issued that?"

'Judge Harris."

Inwardly Cassidy groaned. Harris was ultraconservative and had been a real fan of Jackson Wilde. At least he had appeared to be to garner votes.

The cop pointed out a picket that a grandmotherly type was holding aloft. "Is that catalog really that hot? Maybe I ought to get one for my old lady. We could use something to jazz up our sex life, ya know?"

Cassidy wasn't interested. "How long have they been at this?"

"An hour maybe. Long as it stays peaceful, we gotta let 'em picket. I just wish to hell they'd sing another song."

The marchers had sung the chorus of "Onward, Christian Soldiers" three times since Cassidy had arrived. They were taking full advantage of the media coverage, which was extensive. All the local television stations were represented by minicams and scrambling reporters. One news photographer with a 35mm camera had climbed the lamppost across the street to get a better angle.

Cassidy irritably pushed his way through the parading ranks of Wilde's disciples toward the side door of French Silk. He depressed the bell.

''I warned you not to come near that goddamn door again!''

''It's Cassidy from the D.A.'s office. Ms. Laurent called me.''

The same woman he'd met before pulled open the door, confronting him like a side of beef that was quivering with indignation. Her eyes were mere slits of hostility in her broad, ruddy face. ''It's all right,'' he heard Claire say from behind the tattooed amazon.

She stepped aside. ''Thanks,'' he said tersely as he came in. She grunted and closed the door behind him.

Claire looked beautiful, although not in her customary, composed fashion. Her cool reserve was gone. Her whiskey-colored eyes were sparkling with vexation. There was color in her cheeks. She was obviously upset, but her disheveled hair and clothing made her sexier, more exciting, more appealing than ever.

''Do something, Mr. Cassidy,'' she demanded. ''Anything. Just make them go away.''

''I'm afraid there's nothing I can do. They've got a permit. You'll just have to tough it out.''

She flung her arm toward the door. ''While they're exercising their rights, they're violating my right to privacy.''

''Calm down. One demonstration isn't going to significantly hurt your business.''

''I'm not concerned about my business,'' she said angrily. ''Didn't you see the TV cameras? We're getting a free commercial out of this. But they're wreaking havoc on the Bienville House,'' she said, referring to the pink-walled hotel across the street. ''Delivery trucks can't get through. Their chef is having apoplexy. The guests are complaining. And the manager, whom I've been friends with for years, has called twice, rightfully demanding that I put a stop to this madness.

''Not only that, I'm afraid for my employees. When the first shift tried to leave a while ago, they were booed and hissed at like they were scum. That's when I called you. I don't want my employees affected by any of this.''

"I'm sorry, Claire. You've got Ariel Wilde to thank."

"Ariel Wilde and *you*."

"Me?" he repeated, flabbergasted. "How the hell can you blame this on me?"

"I was never picketed before, Mr. Cassidy."

"Look, I don't like this any better than you do," he said, bending down and bringing his face closer to hers. "Ariel wants to make the NOPD and my office look like a bunch of buffoons. This is her way of reminding the public that we haven't solved her husband's murder case yet. She needed another dose of free publicity and chose this way to get it."

"Let her have all the publicity she wants. I don't care. Just leave me out of it. I don't want to be involved."

"Well that's tough, because you're already involved."

"Because you've been lurking around here so much!" Claire shouted.

"No, because you've lied to me from the beginning."

"Only to protect myself, my friends, and my family from your snooping."

"I'm only doing my job."

"Are you?"

That left him with nothing to say because his job description didn't include kissing the suspects he was questioning, which is what he'd been doing the last time he'd been with her. She suddenly seemed to remember that, too. She took a hasty step backward. There was a catch in her throat. "Just leave me in peace, Mr. Cassidy, and take all of them with you."

She gestured toward the door, but before her sentence was completely formed, a brick came crashing through the window directly above them. It shattered. Cassidy looked up, saw what had happened, and threw his arms around Claire. He dived for cover behind a tower of packing crates, pressing her against his chest and bending his head over hers, pro-

tecting her as best he could from the falling shards of glass.
The workers scrambled in every direction, trying to escape
injury as glass rained down, splintering into tiny pieces as it
struck the concrete floor.

When it finally stopped, Cassidy relaxed his tight embrace.
"Are you all right?" He swept her hair off her face. examining the delicate skin for nicks and cuts.

"Yes."

"Sure?"

"Yes, I'm fine. Is anyone hurt?" Her employees were
slowly emerging from cover.

"We're all right, Miss Laurent."

When Claire turned back to Cassidy, she uttered a small
gasp. "You've been cut." She reached up and touched his
cheek. Her fingers came away smeared with blood.

He took a handkerchief from his hip pocket and used it to
wipe her fingers clean before blotting his cheek. Surrounding
them were bits of glass as fine as dust and as shimmering as
diamonds. Bending down, he picked up the brick that was
responsible for the damage. Using Magic Marker, someone
had printed on it FILTHY DAUGHTER OF SATAN.

"All right," Claire said softly as she read the poorly printed
words. "That's enough." She strode to the door, her feet
crunching on the broken glass.

"Claire, no!"

Unmindful of his shout, she pulled open the door, stepped
onto the sidewalk, and marched up to one of the policemen.
She tugged at his shirtsleeve to get his attention.

"I thought you were supposed to be keeping this demonstration peaceful."

"That brick came out of nowhere. I'm sorry, ma'am."

"You're sorry, but my employees could have been seriously hurt."

"Their permit to picket doesn't extend to throwing
bricks," Cassidy said.

The policeman recognized him. "Hey, you're Cassidy, aren't you?"

"That's right. And I'm here representing District Attorney Crowder. As of now, their permit has expired. Disperse this crowd. Call in reinforcements if necessary, but clear this area immediately."

"I don't know," the cop said dubiously. The protesters were now clasping hands and praying. Cassidy was glad. As long as their heads were bowed and their eyes were closed, they wouldn't notice Claire. "Judge Harris—"

"Screw Judge Harris and his permit," Cassidy said in a low, rough voice. "If he doesn't like it, he can take it up with the D.A. later. For now, get these people away from here before more damage is done."

"If somebody gets injured," Claire said, "there's going to be hell to pay from Mrs. Wilde and from me."

Finally reaching a decision, the cop went quickly to the man who was leading a loud, long prayer. "Excuse me, sir. Y'all violated the conditions of your permit. You're gonna have to disperse." The leader, who obviously liked the sound of his own voice, didn't want to be silenced. In Jesus' blessed name, he began strenuously to protest. A shoving match ensued.

Cassidy swore. "I was afraid of this. Get inside, Claire."

"This is my fight. I'll handle it."

"Handle it? Are you nuts?"

"They've been misled about me. If I explain to them—"

"A mob can't be reasoned with." He had to raise his voice to be heard above the rising shouts. Soon he'd have a riot on his hands.

"There she is!" someone in the crowd shouted.

"It's her!"

"Smut peddler! Pornographer!"

"Ladies and gentlemen, please." Claire held up her hands for silence, but the insults only grew nastier. Photographers nearly trampled one another trying to capture her image and voice on their videotapes.

"Get inside!" Cassidy tried to take her arm, but she resisted.

"Claire Laurent is a whore!"

"French Silk is filth!"

"Down with porn!"

Cassidy had to lean down in order to hear what Claire was saying to him. "All I want from them is an opportunity to be heard."

"Dammit, now's not the time for a speech."

The crowd was pressing against the human barricade of policemen who had rushed into action. Voices were raised in anger and hatred. Faces were contorted with malice. Pickets were being brandished like weapons. One spark was all that was needed to make the whole ugly scene explode.

It was instantly and effectively defused by the unexpected appearance of Mary Catherine Laurent.

Beautifully dressed and coiffed, looking as though she were about to enter a courtyard for a garden party, she stepped through the door of French Silk pushing a tea cart. On it were rows of Dixie cups filled with what appeared to be red Kool-Aid. A tall, spare woman wearing a white uniform followed her, carrying a tray of cookies.

Claire followed Cassidy's startled gape. "Oh, Mama, *no!*" Claire tried to waylay her, but she determinedly wheeled the dainty tea cart toward the surging, hostile crowd.

"I'm sorry, Claire," Harriett York said as she passed with the tray of cookies. "She insisted on doing this and got so upset when I tried to change her mind, I thought—"

"I understand," Claire interrupted quickly. She moved to Mary Catherine's side and placed her hand beneath her elbow. "Mama, you'd better go back inside now. This isn't a party."

Mary Catherine looked at her daughter with incredulity. 'Well, of course it's not, Claire Louise. Don't talk foolish.

These people are here on behalf of Reverend Jackson Wilde, aren't they?''

"Yes, Mama. They are.''

"I listened to enough of his sermons to know that he'd be ashamed of his followers for conducting themselves this way. I think they need to be reminded of that. Reverend Wilde said many ugly things about you from his pulpit, but he also advocated loving one's enemies. He would never have condoned violence.''

She went straight to the leader of the group. Those around him fell silent, and the silence rippled outward until all the name-calling ceased. Mary Catherine gave the man a smile that would have disarmed a Nazi officer. "I've never known anyone who could be cruel and unkind over cookies and punch. Sir?''

She took a Dixie cup from the cart and extended it to him. To refuse the gesture from a woman so utterly guileless would have been bad P.R. for the Wilde ministry and apparently the man realized that. He was fully aware of the mini-cams recording the bizarre occurrence. Disgruntled, he took the cup of punch from Mary Catherine.

"Thanks.''

"You're quite welcome. Harry, pass the cookies around, please. Who else would care for punch?''

Cassidy watched, shaking his head in disbelief. One by one the pickets were lowered and the crowd began to disperse. "They could use her at the U.N.''

Claire stepped around him and approached her mother. "Thank you, Mama. That was a lovely gesture. But you'd better let Harry take you upstairs now.''

"I'm glad I could help. They were creating such a ruckus.''

Claire kissed her mother's cheek, then signaled Harry to take her back inside. An employee retrieved the tea cart. Claire asked others to collect the empty Dixie cups and napkins and to sweep up the broken window glass that had fallen onto the sidewalk.

"When you're finished out here, return to work," Claire told them. "Let's try to make up for lost time. Mr. Cassidy, you're still bleeding. Perhaps you'd better come upstairs and let me tend to that cut on your cheek."

As they rode the elevator up, she asked, "Does it hurt?"

"No."

"Would you admit it if it did?"

"What, and ruin my—what was it?—'athletic, macho-type' image?"

She smiled with chagrin. He smiled back. They continued looking at each other until the elevator came to a jarring halt on the third floor. Mary Catherine was playing gin with Harry when they entered the apartment.

She looked up from her hand of cards. "Have they gone?"

"Yes, Mama."

"Everything's back to normal," Cassidy said. "Thank you for what you did. But I wish you hadn't placed yourself in danger like that. The police had it under control."

"Sometimes it's more expedient for one to take matters into one's own hands."

"Come on, Mr. Cassidy," Claire said, steering him toward the bedroom. "Blood's dripping on your shirt."

"Gin," he heard Mary Catherine say as he followed Claire into a spacious bedroom. It was decorated monochromatically, in shades of white and ivory. The furnishings were contemporary except for a massive armoire against one wall. Louvered shutters were drawn against the afternoon sun, which cast striped shadows across the king-size bed. He couldn't help but wonder how many men had slept there with her. She had confessed to having only a few meaningful relationships following her broken engagement, but that could be another in her series of lies.

"In here," she said over her shoulder, indicating that ne should follow her into the adjoining bathroom. It looked like a 1930s' movie set. The walls were mirrored. The tub, set into the floor, was three feet deep and twice as long.

As gorgeous as it was, it was a room inhabited and used by a real person—a real *woman*. A peach-colored slip hung from a porcelain hook mounted on the back of the door. On the white marble vanity was a wide array of perfume bottles. A fluffy white lambswool puff hadn't been replaced in the glass container of body powder, and its silver lid was askew. A strand of pearls spilled out of a satin jewelry box. Two cosmetic brushes, a tube of lipstick, and a pair of gold earrings hadn't been put away. And the bubble-blowing necklace was also there.

Everything personified Claire Laurent. Beautiful. Classy. Elegant. Sensual. Cassidy was enchanted by the saturation of femininity. Like a kid in a toy store, he wanted to touch and examine everything.

"I think I've got some peroxide in here." A spring-loaded latch came open when she depressed a seam in the mirrored wall. A section swung out, revealing a medicine cabinet. "Sit down."

His choices were a vanity stool with a white velvet cushion, the commode, or the bidet. The vanity stool didn't look solid enough to support him. The bidet was out of the question. He sat down on the commode lid.

Claire approached him with a snowy washcloth, which she had moistened beneath the gold faucet. "You'll ruin that," he said, yanking back his head. "The bloodstain might never wash out."

She gave him a strange look. "Things are dispensable, Mr. Cassidy. People aren't."

The cut was on the ridge of his cheekbone. He winced when she applied the cold, wet cloth to it. "Why don't you drop the 'mister'? Call me Cassidy."

"What's your first name?"

"Robert."

"That's a respectable name." She dabbed the cut with the cloth, then tossed it into the basin and took a cotton ball from a crystal canister and soaked it with peroxide. "This might sting."

He gritted his teeth as she swabbed the cut, but it was only mildly uncomfortable. "Too Celtic."

"And 'Cassidy' isn't?"

"I didn't want to be Bob or Bobby. Since high school, it's been Cassidy."

She removed the cotton ball and took a Band-Aid from a metal box in the medicine cabinet. He watched her hands as she peeled open the sterile wrapper and protective tapes, but he looked directly at her as she pressed the bandage over the wound.

Her breath was on his face. He caught a whiff of her perfume, which emanated from the cleft between her breasts—breasts that he had touched. Her blouse gaped open slightly as she leaned forward, and it took tremendous self-discipline not to peek.

"There. That should do." She touched his cheek; her fingertips were cool. She turned away to replace the items she'd taken from the medicine cabinet.

This was crazy. This was nuts. He would fuck up big time if he let this get out of hand, but, Jesus . . .

He reached out and bracketed her waist with his hands, turning her around to face him again. "Claire?"

She drew her hands back as though to keep from laying them on his shoulders. "You'd better soak that shirt in cold water or the bloodstain will set."

"Claire?"

Involuntarily it seemed, her eyes moved up from the bloodstain on his shirt to connect with his. "I don't want to talk about it," she said in that husky whisper that echoed in his dreams every night.

"Don't misunderstand, Claire. It's not my standard operating procedure when questioning a female suspect to kiss her."

"No?"

"No. I think you know that."

His gaze moved over her, taking in her lovely face, her smooth throat, the breasts that enticed him, the narrow waist and gentle flare of her hips. Acting instinctively, his hand moved from her waist to splay open over her abdomen. It wasn't an intimate caress. Not really. There were probably three layers of clothing between her skin and the palm of his hand. But it felt intimate in the utter quiet of this most private room of hers.

He felt overwhelmed by the wrongness of it.

She was his prime suspect. It was his job to pursue criminals and bring them to justice. His career hinged on this case. It would either make him a shoo-in candidate for the district attorney's job or forever keep him rooted in the ranks of assistants. He would either earn position and power or remain just another prosecutor trying to trip up drug dealers on tax evasions. He would either be able to redeem himself or forever be condemned for that one major mistake that marred his soul like a dark blot.

Now, here he was, on the verge of committing another grievous blunder. He couldn't let it happen. He wouldn't be derelict in his duty again.

He lowered his hands. Claire backed up as far as the dressing table. "I don't think you should touch me like that anymore. It could cost you your case. Because if I was ever indicted, Cassidy, I'd make sure everybody knew about your conflict of interests."

"And I'd deny it," he stated without hesitation. "It would be your word against mine, Claire. No witnesses."

"Sort of like the Wilde murder. I can't prove that you kissed me. And you can't prove that I killed Jackson Wilde. So why don't we call it even and drop the whole thing before my life is disrupted even more?"

She turned and left the room. He followed her into the bedroom, where she had almost reached the door when he posed a question: "Why did you contribute to Jackson Wilde's ministry?"

She stopped dead in her tracks. Turning to face him, she suddenly grew pale and nervously wet her lips. "How did you know about that?"

While Cassidy stared at her, his optimism took a brutal beating. "I didn't," he said quietly. "Lucky guess."

Claire sank down onto the end of an upholstered chaise. After a moment she glared up at him. "Very clever."

"Don't bother lying. I've got the records. Your name would have popped up sooner or later and all the data will be there. So tell me the truth, okay? How much did you give him and for God's sake why?"

"About six months ago, I sent in a contribution check for fifty dollars."

"Why?"

"I had watched his program. Anyone sending in a minimum offering of fifty dollars was entitled to receive three books of prayers, devotionals, inspirational anecdotes, that sort of thing. They were represented as hardbound volumes, with gilt lettering and such. If the books arrived and weren't all they were cracked up to be, I was hoping to accuse him of mail fraud or whatever the appropriate charge would be."

"How were the books?"

"Exactly as advertised." She left the chaise and moved to the built-in shelves, returning with the three volumes, which she handed to Cassidy for inspection. "He was too smart not to deliver what he had promised. At least something tangible like books." She spread her arms wide. "That's all there was to it. I swear. It was a test, and he passed. I'd forgotten about it."

Cassidy didn't detect a sign of deceit either in her expression or her straightforward gaze. He wanted badly to believe her. But there was that other matter she still had to clarify. He said, "Gloria Jean Reynolds."

Claire's reaction was visible and quick, a blend of puzzlement and astonishment. "What about her?"

"She made a contribution, too. Considerably more than yours. A thousand dollars."

"What?" The question escaped her on a gust of breath. "Yasmine contributed a thousand dollars to Jackson Wilde's ministry? Why?"

"That's what I intend to find out."

Chapter Eleven

❧❧

When a knock sounded on Congressman Alister Petrie's office door, he tossed down his pen and frowned. He had specifically asked not to be disturbed.

"I'm sorry, Congressman," his secretary said hurriedly when she poked her head through the door. "There's someone here to see you. I know you requested that no calls be put through, but I thought you'd want me to make an exception."

She was usually so mousy and reserved that her excitement got his attention immediately. Her lined face was flushed and there was an unusual twinkle in her colorless eyes. Whoever was paying him this unexpected Tuesday-afternoon visit must be damned important.

He stood and adjusted his necktie. "I trust your discretion, Ms. Baines. If it's someone I should see, then by all means show him in."

She ducked out of sight. Alister almost peed in his pants when Yasmine appeared in the open doorway. Like an idiot, he cut a guilty glance toward the sterling silver frame holding the photograph of Belle and the children in the place of honor on his desk.

Thankfully, Ms. Baines, who stumbled in behind Yasmine, was too star-struck to notice his guilty reaction. She was yammering about how surprised she'd been when the famous fashion model—her personal favorite for years—had strolled into the office and asked for an audience with Congressman Petrie.

Alister, partially recovered from his initial shock, plastered on the smile that had helped him win his first congressional seat. "This is indeed an honor, Miss . . ."

"Just Yasmine, Congressman Petrie. It's a rare privilege to see you, too."

It sounded like a cordial greeting, but it blared its double meaning to Alister, especially with the emphasis she placed on the words *rare* and *see*. There was a sly glint in her spectacular eyes as he rounded his desk and approached her. If his gait appeared rubbery to Ms. Baines, he hoped she attributed it to his meeting a star and not to his confronting a mistress obviously up to mischief.

Yasmine was wearing a white dress made of some soft, clinging fabric that hugged her body. The vee where it overlapped across her chest was filled with gold chains of varied designs. Her trademark bangles encircled both wrists. Gold spheres the size of golf balls dangled from her ears. A leopard-print scarf as large as a tablecloth draped one shoulder and extended to the hem of her dress in both front and back.

She looked fabulous and she knew it. As cool and haughty as a temple priestess, she stood her ground and let him come to her, which he did, hand extended like a penitent. The bitch.

He clasped her hand. In high heels she was a couple of inches taller than he. He resented having to look up, even slightly, to meet her eye to eye.

"I'd love to flatter myself and think this is a social call."

She laughed, tossing her ebony mane. "I heard one of your campaign speeches last week. I liked what you had to say and decided to contribute to your campaign. We need more men like you in Congress.''

''Thank you. I'm . . . speechless,'' he stammered, grinning disarmingly for the sake of his still-gaping secretary.

''May I?'' Without waiting for permission, Yasmine moved to a maroon leather seating ensemble that Belle had given him for his last birthday.

''Of course, Yasmine, sit down. Ms. Baines, you'll excuse us please?''

''Certainly. Would you like something to drink? Coffee? Tea?''

''No, thank you,'' Yasmine replied, flashing her brilliant smile. ''But you might ask my escorts if they would like something.'' She slid the slender strap of her lizard handbag off her shoulder and laid it in her lap.

''Escorts?'' Alister asked thinly. Jesus, this must be a nightmare. How many people knew she was here? Had she led a frigging parade down Pennsylvania Avenue?

''Bodyguards, from the looks of them,'' Ms. Baines whispered. ''I'm sure that because of who she is, she has to take them with her everywhere she goes.''

Yasmine merely smiled placidly, letting the woman draw her own dramatic conclusions. The secretary, grinning giddily, backed out and pulled the door closed behind her.

Alister's hands were clenched into fists at his sides. As he approached Yasmine, he wished he could hit her very hard across her flawless face. ''What the fuck do you think you're doing?'' He kept his volume low, but his fierce expression conveyed the full measure of his rage.

He had never used gutter language in front of her except playfully in bed. But in the neighborhood where she'd grown up, that was the vernacular and she wasn't intimidated by it. She came out of the chair like a shot, dumping her handbag onto the floor. The scarf slipped from her shoulder and also fell to the floor.

"What's the matter, sugar?" she sneered. "Aren't you glad to see me?"

"I want to know if you've lost your frigging mind. Are you trying to ruin me? Who saw you come strutting in here? Jesus, did the press get wind of this?" He dragged his hand down his face as one horrendous possibility after another flashed through his mind like a hellish slide show. "What are you doing here?"

"Making my campaign contribution." She unbuttoned the cuffs of her sleeves and, before he realized what she was about to do, peeled the bodice of her dress off her shoulders. It dropped to her waist, caught there by her wide belt. She smiled as she slowly withdrew her arms from the sleeves.

His anger metamorphosed into lust. His eyes moved down to her thrusting, conical breasts. The nipples were dark and pointed, arrogantly offered to him.

"I've been missing you so bad, sugar," she crooned as she slowly inched the skirt of her dress up her thighs.

Heart pounding, lungs laboring, palms sweating, blood rushing to concentrate in his loins, Alister tracked the slow ascent of her hemline with his eyes. Her hosiery came to midthigh, where it was clipped to the suspenders of a garter belt. He groaned involuntarily when she revealed the small triangle of lace that insufficiently covered her mound and its dense thatch of curls.

"Christ," he muttered. Sweat was oozing from his forehead and trickling down his face. "If someone walks in—"

"No one will. Even the president couldn't get past Hans and Franz out there. I told them nobody, but nofuckingbody, was to come through that door."

While he stood transfixed, she hooked her thumbs beneath the elastic band of her panties and pulled them down her legs. After stepping out of them she twirled them around her index finger. "You'd better sit down, sugar. You're looking a little pale."

She gave his chest a light push and he toppled over backward, landing on the leather love seat—the gift from his wife. He didn't think about that. He didn't think about anything except the thundering desire in his cock. He reached for her.

"Not so fast." She stood in front of him, fists propped on her hips, legs slightly spread. "Why haven't you been to see me, you lousy bastard?"

"Yasmine, be reasonable," he panted. "Can you imagine what my schedule has been like? I'm campaigning, for Christ's sake."

"With your smiling wife at your side?"

"What am I supposed to do, leave her at home?"

"Yes!" she hissed angrily.

"Wouldn't that make everyone, especially her, a little suspicious? Think about it." He reached for her again, and this time she allowed his hands to fold around her derriere. "Do you think this separation has been easy for me? Christ, you're insane to come here, but you can't imagine how glad I am to see you."

"You didn't seem so glad at first," she reminded him. "I thought you were about to have a stroke."

"I was shocked, stunned. This is dangerous as hell, but . . . Ah, God, I can smell you." He leaned forward and burrowed his face in the cleft of her thighs, nuzzling, gnawing, kissing her madly through the giving fabric of her dress. "Too bad you can't bottle this."

Yasmine clasped his head between her long, slender hands. "Sugar, I've been miserable. Couldn't eat. Couldn't sleep. I lived for a phone call."

"I couldn't risk it." He raised his head to her breasts and took one of her nipples into his mouth.

"Yes," she moaned. "Hard, baby, suck hard."

He took a breast in each hand and squeezed hard while he suckled until his jaws ached. She straddled his lap and grappled with his clothes until his throbbing penis was sandwiched between her stroking hands.

He shoved his hands beneath her skirt, grabbed her hips, and brought them down hard as he thrust into her. She tore at the buttons of his monogrammed shirt, then sank her long nails into his chest. He grunted with a mix of pleasure and pain, and roughly scraped his chin against her raised nipples, burning them with his whisker stubble.

She rode him frantically, squeezing and pulling like a tight, wet fist, like a mouth. Through the fog of passion, he dimly heard the telephone in the anteroom ring and his secretary's muffled answer: "Congressman Petrie's office. I'm sorry but the congressman is presently engaged."

Alister almost laughed as Yasmine rolled her hips forward, then backward, as she crammed her breast into his mouth. *I'm "presently engaged" fucking my brains out with my mistress*, he thought. Wouldn't that rock the foundations of the Capitol? Wouldn't his constituents be astonished? Wouldn't his foes have a field day?

She came before he did. Closing her arms tightly around his head, she whispered an erotic chant in his ear, "Ohsugarohbabyohgodohyesohfuck," while one spasm after another gripped him deeper and tighter inside her.

His climax wasn't as vocal but was just as tempestuous. For a full sixty seconds afterward she clung to him, her head resting on his shoulder.

When she sat up, her torso was gleaming with perspiration, the sheen enhanced by the gold chains suspended from her neck. Her tiger eyes still smoldered. She was so damned gorgeous she took his breath . . . what was left of it.

"I love you, you son of a bitch."

He chuckled, wincing slightly as he slipped out of her and realized they'd made quite a mess. "I love you, too." Ever aware that there was nothing between him and ruination except a door, he wondered worriedly how long they'd been in there. Nevertheless, he couldn't hustle her out without dispensing some reassurances.

"When I don't call, I'm only protecting you. You've got to

believe that, Yasmine. I'm constantly surrounded by people. I can barely take a leak without somebody following me into the john. I'm working day and night when I'm here. And it's even tougher to see you in New Orleans.''

She cupped his face and brought his mouth up to hers for a slow, wet kiss. "I understand. Truly I do. It's just that I've been so lonesome for you. Can we spend the night together tonight?''

He was torn by indecision. It might be wise to indulge her. On the other hand, the risks of getting caught in Washington were tremendous. "I really can't. I'm scheduled on a five o'clock plane this afternoon. There's a fund-raising function tonight in New Orleans that I can't miss.''

"What flight are you taking? I'll go, too. We can meet tonight after your function.''

Damn! The situation was getting treacherous. "I can't, Yasmine. It takes days to set up our meetings. You know that.'' She looked angry and crestfallen and suspicious. Quickly he drew her against him and kissed her again. "Jesus, I wish we could. Later in the week, I'll come to New York. Give me a few days to make the arrangements.''

"Promise?''

"Promise.''

She pulled her dress back into place and replaced the scarf on her shoulder. Alister's shirt was hopelessly wrinkled; he hoped it wouldn't be noticeable beneath his suit jacket. His lap was uncomfortably sticky, too, but there was no help for that.

Yasmine withdrew a check from her handbag and placed it on his desk. "I hope this contribution doesn't get me into trouble.''

"Trouble?'' He was readjusting his necktie.

"Hmm. One's come back to haunt me. Remember my telling you that I sent an offering to Jackson Wilde under my real name?''

"Yeah? So? You said you thought it might be worth a try to bribe him."

"Well, it wasn't. I lost a thousand dollars I couldn't afford to lose. My follow-up letter was returned with a handwritten message: 'Nice try.' I never knew if Wilde himself or one of his flunkies wrote it, but apparently he wasn't into taking bribes."

"Either that, or you didn't offer enough."

"Right. Anyway, Assistant D.A. Cassidy found out about it. He called me in New York. I admitted that I had half-heartedly tried to bribe Wilde so he'd leave Claire and me alone. He asked to see the letter, which I'd thrown away the minute I read it.

"That's only half of it. Unknown to me, Claire had also sent Wilde money. She chewed my ass for not telling her about my offering. I turned it around and reminded her that she hadn't told me about hers, either. We had a quite a row over it."

"What's the big deal?"

"The big deal is that Cassidy isn't buying our explanations and is reading more into it."

"According to the newspapers, he's trying to scrape up a case out of nothing. Don't worry about it."

"I'm not. It'll blow over." She gave him a sidelong look and winked. "Besides, I had a damn good alibi the night the preacher was killed, remember?"

"Right. You were in New York."

"No, I was sixty-nining with you." Laughing, she opened his lap drawer and dropped her panties inside. "A little something to remember me by, Congressman."

"I don't need anything to remember you by." He wasn't a politician for nothing. He knew when to stoke and just how much. Feigning urgency, he pulled her against him. They embraced and kissed once more. He tried to hide the impatience behind his kiss and ignore the desperation behind hers.

At last she was prepared to go. Then, with her hand on the doorknob, she turned back. "Alister, if I ever found out you were lying to me, I'd be pissed."

"Lying?" He took her hand and rubbed it against his fly. In a low voice he said, "There are some things a man can't lie about."

For once she didn't welcome the chance to fondle him. When he let go of her hand, she let it fall listlessly to her side. "I just thought you ought to be forewarned, sugar," she said. "I don't get mad. I get even."

Her throaty contralto had an undertone that bothered him. Before opening the door, he assumed another hearty smile for the sake of his secretary. He and Yasmine shook hands. He thanked her profusely for her financial support, even though she didn't even reside in his state. She left, flanked by two bulging body builders stuffed like sausages into cheap black suits.

"Well, I'm flabbergasted," Ms. Baines gushed, laying a hand against her bony chest. "Can you believe that?"

"No, I can't."

"And she's so nice. You'd expect somebody famous like her to be conceited, but she's like normal folks."

"Hmm. Well, back to work, Ms. Baines. Please hold all calls unless you hear from Mrs. Petrie."

"Oh, she called while you were with Yasmine."

Panic and nausea seized him. "I'll call her back right now."

"That won't be necessary. She only called to confirm the time of your flight. She said she'd be at the airport to pick you up."

"Oh, fine." He turned toward his private office, but came back around as though it were an afterthought. "Did you mention that Yasmine had come to see me?"

"No, I didn't."

"I'll tell her tonight. I've heard Belle talk about this model. She's always saying she wishes she were that thin." Chuckling, he tugged on his earlobe in a way he knew looked boyish and endearing. "Women always want to be as skinny as models. Can't for the life of me understand why. It's so unattractive. Oh, by the way, she left a check for five hundred dollars. Every penny counts, of course, but it's hardly worth making a big deal over. Probably just a publicity stunt."

He went in and closed his door, hoping that he'd left Ms. Baines with the proper impression—that he'd dismissed Yasmine's visit and campaign contribution as nothing but an isolated gesture from a quirky celebrity.

Behind his desk once again, he opened his lap drawer and took out the panties, crushing the lace in his fist. This thing had gone too far. At some point, it had gotten way out of hand. He didn't need this shit on top of all his other pressures. It was a problem that had to be dealt with soon. But how?

Yasmine had already caused him more trouble than all his other mistresses put together. Until now, this extramarital affair had been worth the additional trouble. Although her veiled threats didn't really frighten him, who could predict what a volatile woman like her might do? He had to take her warnings with some degree of seriousness.

If she wanted to, she could make his life hell. She had the media contacts and the high public profile to wreak havoc on his chances for reelection. She could destroy his family. Dammit, he liked things the way they were and he wanted them to stay that way.

"Hell," he muttered, plowing his fingers through his hair. This time, he didn't see a way out.

The only solution was to call quits to the affair. He'd be sacrificing some quality pussy, but the flip side to that coin was that he'd be sacrificing his lifestyle and career if he was caught. As he stashed Yasmine's underwear in his suit coat pocket for later disposal, he resolved that at his earliest opportunity he'd tell her their affair was over.

"I'll tell her tonight. I've heard Belle talk about the model. She's always saying she wishes she were her size."

Chapter Twelve

❧ ❧

Claire was fitting a pattern on one of the dress forms in her studio when the telephone rang.

"Claire, turn on CNN. Quick." It was Yasmine. They hadn't spoken for several days, since their quarrel when Claire had confronted her about making a generous contribution to Jackson Wilde's ministry.

"What's going on?"

"You'll find out soon enough, and you're going to shit a brick. Hurry or you'll miss it." She hung up.

Intrigued, Claire switched on the portable TV that kept her company when she worked into the wee hours. Because Yasmine had prepared her, she wasn't surprised to see Ariel Wilde on the screen. The interviewer was asking her about the recent demonstration outside French Silk, which she freely admitted having instigated.

"Our adversaries would like to believe that since Jackson's death we've retreated from the fight against pornography. Let me assure them that we haven't. This ministry, under my leadership, intends to double its efforts to stamp out all forms of obscene material.''

The reporter asked, "Why did you pick up the cause with the French Silk catalog? There are other publications much more graphic.''

Ariel smiled sweetly. "The publishers of the more graphic magazines make no bones about being prurient. They don't try to disguise what they are. While I abhor their products, I admire their honesty. At least they aren't hypocritical, like Ms. Laurent, who doesn't even have the courage to debate me.''

"Her catalog is tastefully done, Mrs. Wilde. It's sensual, but I'd hardly call it prurient.''

"It pictures men and women on the verge of coitus. How lewd can you get?''

Evidently embarrassed, the reporter cleared his throat. "The photos merely suggest—''

"Then you agree that the pictures are suggestive?''

"I didn't say that.'' He hastily referred to his notes, but before he could pose another question, Ariel said, "I think it's significant that Ms. Laurent's business is headquartered in New Orleans.''

The interviewer pounced on the bait. "Significant in what way?''

Ariel pretended to reconsider. "I'd better not say anything further. My attorney has advised me to avoid this subject. However, I feel compelled to point out that one of my husband's most publicized targets is located in the very city in which he was murdered.''

Claire saw red. Her gasp filled the silence in the cavernous room. She found herself walking toward the TV set, although she didn't remember leaving her seat.

"Are you implying that Ms. Laurent had something to do with your husband's murder?'' the reporter asked.

"She's being investigated by the D.A.'s office,'' Ariel replied evasively.

"Based on what evidence?"

"None that I know of. I'm certain they're questioning her because of her background."

The reporter looked at her with puzzlement.

"Claire Laurent," she said, "is the illegitimate daughter of a mentally unbalanced woman." She lowered her eyes and assumed a sorrowful expression. "With no more guidance than she had as a child, is it any wonder that her life, even her professional life, is ruled by her passions? Think about it. She obviously possesses talent. Why would she squander her creativity by making sleazy lingerie and advertising it in such a vulgar manner? And why else would she choose for her business partner a woman who, for years, has flaunted her immoral lifestyle?"

"You're referring to the model, Yasmine?"

"Yes. These three women—Ms. Laurent, her mother, and Yasmine—are of such low moral character, I'm sure the same question has occurred to the D.A.'s office as occurred to me: Is publishing a filthy magazine their only crime?"

Claire switched off the set. If she listened to another word she was going to implode. Rage had sent blood rushing to her head. Her earlobes throbbed with it; it clouded her vision.

Ariel Wilde had unmitigated gall. How dare she say those things on a national broadcast? Heretofore, Claire had ignored her snide criticism of the French Silk catalog, but now the invectives had become personal. Ariel had slandered Mary Catherine and Yasmine and all but accused her of murder. How much longer could she stand back and do nothing? Passive resistance didn't work on the Jackson and Ariel Wildes of the world. It was time to act.

She paced while weighing her options. As much as she loathed the thought of it, there seemed no way around making a public statement. When she had cooled down enough to speak, she made a telephone call.

"Newsroom."

"This is Claire Laurent."

She had begun by calling a local network affiliate. Her name had been in the news often enough that it was instantly recognized. "Yes, ma'am. What can I do for you?"

"How would I go about calling CNN?"

"We string for them sometimes. I can get their ear."

"If they're interested in my rebuttal to what Ariel Wilde is saying about me, have a reporter contact me."

"Yes, ma'am. I'm sure someone will call right away."

"I'll be standing by."

Claire hung up, hating what she had just done. She considered privacy a precious commodity. She guarded hers ferociously, mainly for Mary Catherine's sake, but also because Claire intuitively felt that notoriety was tarnishing. In her estimation, to be on public display lessened a person's worth. Publicity seekers were beyond her comprehension. Unlike Yasmine, who thrived on being in the limelight, Claire was content to remain anonymous in the background. For that reason, Yasmine was the one whom people associated with French Silk.

Claire resented being forced to go public. She was also afraid. Between now and her interview, she had to think of words that would negate Ariel Wilde's statements, while keeping her secrets intact.

The following night she was lying in bed watching a replay of her interview with the CNN reporter when her bedside telephone rang. At first she considered letting it ring. Then, obstinately, she lifted the receiver, but said nothing.

"Claire, are you there?"

"Cassidy?"

"Why didn't you say something?"

"Because every time I've answered the telephone tonight it's been someone telling me to go to hell."

"Wilde's people?"

"Undoubtedly. Most shout an insult and then hang up."

"I guess Ariel's pissed. First that picket line of hers back-fired. She got the TV coverage she wanted, but Mary Catherine made her people look like thugs. Then you really put her in her place today. I caught your act earlier."

"It wasn't an act."

"Figure of speech," he said. "You articulated well."

"I meant every word. If Ariel Wilde, or anyone in her organization, maligns my mother or Yasmine again, I'll file a suit for damages that will pitch that ministry into financial chaos."

"You were very convincing."

"Thank you."

"But you didn't deny her veiled allegations that you were somehow involved in her husband's murder." He paused for a response, but Claire remained stubbornly silent. Eventually he said, "If you want, I can pull strings and get your telephone number changed immediately."

"No, thanks. The calls are a nuisance, but the novelty will wear off soon and they'll stop."

"Why don't you turn on your answering machine?"

"Principle. If I'm here, I answer my telephone. I refuse to let them rearrange my life."

He said nothing for a moment, then asked, "Have you had any more protesters outside your door?"

"No," she said, smiling for the first time in twenty-four hours. "I think Mama cured them of that."

"Speaking of your mother, is Harry there to watch her?"

"She's spending the night. Why?"

"I'll tell you when I get there. Meet me downstairs."

"Cassidy, I'm already in bed. I'm tired."

But she was talking to a dead line. She slammed down the phone. If he wanted to see her, he could have made an appointment for the next day. She should let him stand down-stairs ringing the bell to no avail.

But, she swung her legs over the side of her bed and went

into the bathroom. It looked the same as before, yet she knew she'd never enter it again without thinking of him, disheveled and dripping blood on his shirt. He'd looked roguish and rowdy, and her feminine instincts had responded then as they did now with the memory of his strong hands resting on her waist.

She had threatened him with exposure, citing how a romantic dalliance with her might hurt his cause. She had failed to tell him how damaging such a dalliance could also be to her.

She dressed in a pair of jeans and a white cotton pullover, not wanting him to think she had primped in anticipation of seeing him. She took the elevator down to the first floor. He was ringing the buzzer by the time she reached the door.

"You're right on time," she said when she opened it.

"One of my virtues."

He hadn't dressed up either. She'd never seen him in anything except a suit. Tonight he wore jeans, a casual shirt, an ancient Levi's jacket, and jogging shoes. "Why did you want to see me?"

"Come out here."

"Why?"

"I can think more clearly out here." She looked at him quizzically. "There's too much damn ambience in there," he added brusquely.

The commercial district several blocks away was in full swing, but within two blocks on either side of French Silk the street was dark and still. When she turned after securing the door, Cassidy was at the curb, pacing the pavement where the protesters had marched.

"You look upset," she remarked.

"You could say that." He stopped and faced her. "This offering business—"

"I explained that."

"Yeah. So did Yasmine. But it doesn't seem plausible."

"That's your problem."

"Temporarily," he said shortly. "What time did you

me you went to the Fairmont that night to pick up your mother?''

Claire hadn't expected the sudden shift in topic. The question made her throat constrict. ''I . . . I told you I wasn't sure, but I guessed around midnight.''

''What took you so long?''

''Pardon?''

''Andre Philippi says he called you at eleven. At that time of night, it takes about five minutes to drive from here to the Fairmont. I know because I drove it tonight. Your trip took an hour longer than it should have. What delayed you?''

''Cassidy, I said I got there *around* midnight. It might have been eleven or eleven-thirty. I told you I wasn't sure.''

''You're lying!'' He slammed his fist into his opposite palm. Claire fell back a step. ''You didn't leave for the Fairmont Hotel to collect Mary Catherine until almost midnight because you didn't speak directly to Andre until then. When he called at eleven, he spoke to your answering machine, didn't he? You had to call him back.''

He came toe to toe with her. ''You weren't here when he called at eleven. You said tonight that you answer your phone if you're here, right? Andre left a message on your machine, so you'd know where Mary Catherine was when you came in and discovered her gone.''

Claire's heart was hammering. ''I can explain that.''

''Save it. I'm sick of your lies. I'm right, aren't I?'' He grabbed her arm and hauled her close to him. ''Aren't I?''

Coming into contact with the solid strength of his body startled her, but she resented his high-handedness and wriggled free of his grasp.

''Yes, you're right,'' she flung up at him. ''I have a habit of checking Mama's room when I come in. That night, her bed was empty and her suitcase was gone, so I knew what had happened. I was about to go out and look for her when I noticed the message light. I called Andre back immediately.

He told me he had spotted Mama in the lobby of the Fairmont, taken her to his office, and given her some sherry. She was groggy and disoriented when I got there, as she often is after the worst of her spells. I drove her home and put her to bed. That's the truth.''

"Oh, I believe you, Claire," he said. "I just want to know where the hell you were between the conclusion of the crusade and midnight. Did you make two trips to the Fairmont? One to murder Wilde and another to pick up your mother?''

She said nothing.

"You could drive a barge through the space of time you've got to account for," he said, raising his voice.

"I went for a walk."

Obviously he'd been expecting a more elaborate lie. The simplicity of her explanation caught him off guard. "*A walk?*"

"That's right. A long walk. Alone. Through the Quarter."

"At that time of night?" he asked skeptically.

"I often do. Ask Yasmine. She chides me about it all the time."

"Yasmine would cover any lie you chose to tell."

"It's not a lie. It's the truth."

"Why'd you pick that particular night to take a walk?"

"I was upset."

"Murder is upsetting."

Pivoting on her heel, she stalked toward the door of French Silk. "I don't have to take that from you."

"The hell you don't." His arm shot out and caught her sleeve, bringing her back around. "I'm royally pissed off at you, Ms. Laurent. I should have you downtown right now being fingerprinted and fitted for jail issue. You won't look so hot in puke-green broadcloth, Claire. And the undies don't come from the French Silk catalog either.''

A tremor of fear rippled through her. Her greatest fear was of being incarcerated. It wasn't claustrophobia that panicked her, but the loss of freedom. She wouldn't be able to tolerate the constant supervision, the inability to make choices, and the deprivation of privacy and independence.

Cassidy's face was taut with anger. One lock of dark hair had fallen over his brow. His eyes shone with a demanding and piercing glint. For the first time, Claire was actually afraid of him. He might lose patience with her and make good his threat. She needed to talk, and talk fast, because she couldn't spend one night, one minute, in jail.

"I came home from the crusade and—"

"What time?"

Nervously she ran her fingers through her hair. "I swear to you, I don't know the exact time. Shortly after ten, I think."

"I can live with that. The service concluded at nine-twenty. By the time you fought Superdome traffic, that would put you here around ten."

"Harry had stayed with Mama. When I got in, I dismissed her, although later I wished I hadn't. I was restless, couldn't sleep. I tried to work, but all I could think about was Jackson Wilde."

"Why?"

"I'd seen him on TV, but that was nothing compared to seeing him in person. He was a dynamic speaker. He exuded such power, exercised such control over the minds of his audience. Even though I disagreed with everything he preached, I was impressed by the charisma with which he preached it. The people sitting around me were enthralled. Until that night I hadn't fully grasped the strength of his influence. I became afraid that he might actually be able to destroy French Silk. When I went down to the podium and looked him in the eyes, I felt like David looking into the face of Goliath."

She looked up at Cassidy with appeal. "You'd have to understand what this business means to me to know how I felt that night. I can only describe it as panic. Everything I'd worked so hard for was being threatened by an overwhelming force. I had visions of all that I'd struggled to build being knocked down.''

Cassidy said softly, ''I can understand that, Claire, better than you know.'' Then once again his eyes focused sharply on her. ''Did you feel so threatened that you sneaked into his hotel suite and shot him?''

She looked away. ''I told you, I went for a walk.''

''You'll have to do better than that.''

''It's true! I felt like the walls were closing in on me. I felt smothered. Couldn't think. Jackson Wilde's words kept ringing in my ears. I had to get out.'' Suddenly her gaze swung back to him. ''I'll take you.''

''Where?''

''We'll retrace the route I took that night. I'll show you exactly where I went. I'll try to keep the same pace so you'll see how I missed Andre's call.''

Frowning, he pondered it a moment. ''Okay. Where to?''

His hand was riding beneath her elbow as she stepped off the curb and crossed the street. Most of the buildings on that side of Conti Street were vacant and dark. Recessed doorways were deeply shadowed and sinister-looking. Windows and doors were covered with wire mesh.

''Aren't you afraid to walk alone around here at night, Claire?''

''Not at all.'' She looked up at him. ''Are you?''

''Damn right,'' he muttered, casting a quick glance over his shoulder. She laughed and steered him past a dip in the ancient sidewalk. ''I see you know the topography pretty well.''

''Very well. I grew up playing on these sidewalks.'' Pointing out a candy factory with pink awnings, she said, ''They make delicious pralines. Sometimes they'd give us kids the ones that got broken and they couldn't sell. We take a right at the next corner.''

They walked in silence, past the gray stone building

that at one time had been the Louisiana State Supreme Court. They turned right onto Royal Street and she paused outside an antiques shop. "I stopped here that night to browse in this window. There was a marcasite and emerald brooch . . ."

"Marca what?"

"There it is. Third row down, second from the left. See?"

"Hmm. Pretty."

"I thought so. I meant to come back and take a closer look but never got around to it." She lingered for a few moments more, gazing at the array of beaded reticules, oxidized silver services, and estate jewelry, before continuing.

Across the street, two policemen emerged from the Vieux Carré district headquarters of the NOPD. They nodded politely. One spoke to Claire in Cajun-accented French. His partner said, "Evenin', Ms. Laurent." The first did a double take on Cassidy, but if the patrolman recognized him, he didn't call him by name.

They moved past the salmon walls and green shutters of the famous Brennan's restaurant. Claire became aware that Cassidy was watching her closely. She turned the tables and began to study him. "You aren't married, are you, Cassidy?"

"Does it show?"

"No. It's just that most wives wouldn't approve of your working hours." She kept her expression impassive, although she was glad to learn that her sins didn't include kissing a married man.

"I was married," he told her. "I blew it."

"Regrets?"

He shrugged. "Not about her. It worked out best for both of us. I guess you could say I was married to my career. Sort of like you." He paused, giving her an opportunity to comment.

Instead she asked another question. "Any children?"

"No. We never got around to it. Guess that worked out best, too. I wouldn't have wanted to inflict a divorce on my kids." He stopped outside a store front and gazed through the burglary-proof windows. "A gun shop. How convenient."

"Is that the best you can do, Cassidy?"

"Come to think of it, you're too smart to buy a weapon so close to home and in a neighborhood where you're so well known."

She gave him a shrewd look. "You checked, didn't you?"

"Yeah."

From there they moved to a shop whose entire inventory consisted of earrings. "Yasmine is one of their best customers," Claire told him as he stared in awe at the vast variety.

In this elite shopping district, most of the stores were already closed. The silence on the street seemed to envelop them. Bourbon Street was only a block away, but it could have been a hundred miles. Occasionally a few piercingly sweet notes of a jazz trumpet wafted on the sultry air, but they drifted away like lost souls in search of refuge. The wrought-iron grilles that surrounded the overhead balconies added to the aspect of seclusion. Filigree iron gates provided glimpses into inner courtyards where mossy fountains trickled, gas hurricane lamps sputtered, and scarred brick walls guarded secrets.

They came upon a cat scrounging for dinner in a bag of garbage at the curb. Two couples wearing LSU sweatshirts staggered down the street, laughing, talking loudly and profanely, sloshing the Hurricanes they'd taken out in paper cups from Pat O'Brien's. An old man with a mangy beard and wearing an unseasonably heavy overcoat nonchalantly relieved himself against the wall of an alley. An elegant elderly couple, walking arm in arm, passed them, saying, "Good evenin'." A young man wearing tight black jeans, a black turtleneck sweater, and heavy makeup swished past and made a kissing motion toward Cassidy with his glossy scarlet lips.

They turned onto St. Peter Street in front of the Royal Café. Claire pointed out its double balcony to Cassidy. "I think it's the prettiest one in the Quarter."

Jackson Square was closed for the night, but the shops and eateries surrounding it were still open. "I thought about getting a cappuccino here," Claire told Cassidy as she halted in front of a small, intimate bar tucked beneath the historic Pontalba Arms apartments. Two of the outdoor tables were occupied by lovers who were engrossed in each other and impervious to the rest of the world. "But I could smell fresh beignets, so . . ."

She pointed him toward the Café du Monde. They waited for traffic at the curb, where a solo saxophonist was playing for the money passersby tossed into his hat, which lay on the sidewalk. The driver of a horse-drawn carriage and a sidewalk artist who had retired his pallets for the night were having a friendly argument over the football season.

"I agree with the artist," Claire remarked. "The Saints have got to beef up their offensive line if they hope to get in the playoffs this year."

"You could understand those guys?" Cassidy asked.

"Couldn't you?" The sleepy nag harnessed to the carriage was wearing a big floppy hat with bright pink plastic geraniums encircling the crown. Claire stroked her muzzle as she stepped off the curb.

"Not a word. For almost a year after I moved here it was like living in a foreign country. It took a while for my ears to adapt to the accent. I still have trouble sometimes."

"You don't have any trouble understanding me."

"You, Claire, I have the most trouble understanding."

She indicated a table on the open-air terrace of Café du Monde. He held the chrome chair out for her. A waiter in a long white apron approached, his hands outstretched in welcome.

"Ms. Laurent, *bonsoir*. How lovely to see you."

"*Merci*," she said when he bent to kiss her hand.

"And this is?" he inquired, looking at Cassidy.

She introduced Claude, the waiter. "An order of beignets, please, Claude. Two cafés au lait."

"Very good," he said, briskly moving toward the kitchen.

"Obviously you come here often," Cassidy observed.

"It's almost been overrun by tourists, but Mama still enjoys coming here, so I bring her at least once a week."

Claude delivered their order. The yeasty smell of the square, hole-less doughnuts and the aroma of the coffee made Claire's mouth water. She dug in, unabashedly licking the powdered sugar off her fingers. Looking across at Cassidy, she laughed at the powdered sugar ringing his mouth and passed him a paper napkin from the dispenser on the table.

They demolished the beignets, splitting the third one, and sat silently sipping the scalding mixture of coffee and milk. Claire was content to sit and savor the flavor of New Orleans at its best. Too soon, Cassidy got down to business.

"That night," he began, "how long were you here?"

"About thirty minutes, I guess."

He raised an eyebrow. "That long?"

"This is the Vieux Carré, Cassidy. Like the Europeans who originally lived here, we can linger over a meal for hours. The pace is slow. When you cross Canal Street, you should leave behind the American's tendency to bustle, and enjoy life. I resisted eating another order of doughnuts, but I did have two cups of café au lait and spent at least ten minutes with each one."

At her request, Claude replaced their empty cups with full ones. Watching the steam rise from her cup, Claire said, "I had a lot on my mind that night. Jackson Wilde was only one thing that was troubling me."

"What else?"

"Mama. I worry about who would take care of her if something happened to me. For instance if I went to prison." She gave him a puissant look, then lowered her eyes to her coffee, which she swirled in the thick white mug. "And the new catalog was on my mind. I always want the current one to top the last and am afraid the ideas will dry up."

"That fear is common to creative people."

"I suppose. And I was worried about Yasmine."

"Why?"

"It's personal." Her expression dared him to ask her to betray her friend's confidence, but he didn't.

"That was quite a walk." He leaned back in his chair and stretched out his long legs. The old jeans fitted them well, cupping his sex and gloving his thighs. Claire tried to keep her mind on what he was saying. "I suppose if I asked, Claude here would swear on his sainted mother's tombstone that you spent at least half an hour here that night."

"Do you think I'm lying, Cassidy?"

"No," he said. "I think you brought me along tonight so I'd see how well known and respected you are in this community and what I'm up against if I try to convict you. You're even on speaking terms with the neighborhood cops. A good defense attorney would line up all these character witnesses, and even if they couldn't swear that you were walking in the French Quarter that night, they couldn't swear that you weren't."

"If you were my defense attorney, is that what you'd do?"

"Precisely. If the prosecutor didn't have an indisputable piece of physical evidence, I'd make you look like a saint and confuse the jury with facts that weren't pertinent."

"You know all the tricks, I see."

His lips narrowed and his expression turned grim. "*All* the tricks."

There was more to Cassidy than what she knew, Claire decided. The newspapers reported on the A.D.A., not on the inner man. She wanted to pursue that inner man, to discover what made that introspective and regretful expression come across his face occasionally, but she had her own problems.

"You still believe I committed that murder, don't you?"

Sighing, Cassidy looked away and seemed to concentrate on the statue of Andrew Jackson astride his rearing horse, which could be seen through the closed gates of the square across the street. Then he propped his forearms on the small round table and leaned across it. "Here's what I think happened. I think you planned this murder for a long time—from the time you read that Reverend Wilde was bringing his crusade to New Orleans.

"You bought, borrowed, or stole a .38 revolver. You went to the crusade and met face-to-face the man you were planning to kill. By now I know you well enough to know you'd have the integrity to do that. You'd feel like that was the honorable way to kill a man, sort of like your ancestors who met outside the city with pomp and circumstance to duel until one was dead.

"Anyway, you returned home and dismissed Harry. That was a gamble that didn't pay off, but at the time you figured that if she was asked, she could testify that you were home by ten that night. You went to the Fairmont and, using Andre as an accomplice, managed to get into Wilde's hotel suite. You shot him, probably while he was asleep. Then you left and returned home.

"But Fate threw you a curve. Mary Catherine had slipped out. You got home, found her gone, and, ironically, had to make a return trip to the Fairmont to pick her up. I'll bet that wasn't too comfortable for you, returning to the scene of the crime so soon after committing it."

"That's not what happened at all. Do you see how many holes there are in your theory?"

"Hell yes. It's as leaky as a sieve. That's why you're not already in jail."

It took Claire a moment to recover from that remark. She asked, "How did I get into his suite?"

"Simple. Andre gave you a key. While Wilde was having dinner, you let yourself in. Probably hid in a closet to wait. He came in, showered, and got ready for bed. You waited until you were sure he was asleep, then did him."

Claire shook her head. "There's something very basically wrong with that scenario, Cassidy. I would never have involved my friend in a murder plot."

"You might have utilized him without his knowledge."

"By sneaking a key from the front desk?"

"No, by familiarizing yourself with the hotel. There are several odd angles in the hallway on the seventh floor. Maybe you made yourself invisible in one of those bends. When the maid went into the suite to turn down Wilde's bed, you sneaked in behind her while the door was open."

"Very creative."

His eyes scanned her face. "Yes, Claire. Characteristically creative."

She took a sip of cold coffee, willing her hand not to tremble and reveal her nervousness. "How did I know that Wilde would come into the suite alone? Or did I intend to kill Mrs. Wilde, if necessary?"

"That gave me trouble, too. Until Josh and Ariel Wilde told me that they 'rehearsed' every night. Andre could have told you what their routine was. You betted on Jackson going to bed alone."

"Wilde didn't like what I printed in my magazine so he lambasted me from his pulpit. I didn't like what he preached, so I killed him. In effect, what you're saying is that I'm less tolerant and more radical than Jackson Wilde was. You're placing me on the level of the crazies who've been calling and threatening my life."

Cassidy reacted like he'd been goosed. "You've had callers threatening your life? You didn't tell me that."

She hadn't intended to and could have bitten her tongue. "Life threats over the telephone aren't to be taken seriously."

He appeared to disagree. His eyes swept the area as though an assassin might be lurking in the shadows. "We've been here at least half an hour," he said, coming to his feet. "Let's go." He held her chair for her, then struck off down the sidewalk at a fast clip, but stopped when he realized she wasn't beside him. "What?" he called over his shoulder.

"I made one more stop before going home that night. Out there," she said, nodding toward the river.

He returned to her side. "Lead the way." They crossed the military memorial that connected with the paved part of the levee called the Moonwalk. Below them, the river's current gently lapped at the crushed rocks, although at present there wasn't any traffic on the river. The lights from the opposite bank twinkled on the water, which smelled, not unpleasantly, of brine and petroleum and mud. There was a humid breeze, and Claire liked the feel of it in her hair and on her skin. It was soft and gentle, everything that was good about the South.

The Moonwalk was a favorite spot among tourists with cameras, panhandlers, whores, drunks, and lovers. Tonight only a few other pedestrians were taking advantage of the view. When they walked past a couple necking on a park bench, Cassidy's expression turned irascible. "Why don't you give me a break and confess."

"Even if I didn't do it?"

"Please, no. We get plenty of those as it is. Four crazies have already taken credit for offing Wilde."

"Your attitude is certainly cavalier."

"These four guys are chronic confessors," he said dismissively. "We routinely check them out, but none of them was near the Fairmont that night." They reached a tacit agreement to pause and gaze out across the river. After a moment he turned to her. Without prefacing it in any way, he said, "There's a records clerk in the courthouse. Night before last, she invited me over to her house for an evening of spaghetti and sex."

He looked at her pointedly, awaiting a response. At last she said, "She certainly didn't mince words."

"Well, the sex part was implied."

"I see. Did you go?"

"Yes."

"Oh. How was it?"

"Terrific. It was smothered in red clam sauce."

At first taken aback, she then realized that he was attempting a joke. She tried to laugh but discovered she couldn't be blasé about his sleeping with another woman.

"The spaghetti was sensational," he said. "But the sex was only so-so."

"How disappointed you must have been," Claire said tightly.

He shrugged. "And a few nights before that, I slept with my neighbor. It was raunchy, and I'm not even sure what her name is."

Claire's temper snapped. "Are you trying to impress me with your sexual exploits? I'm not a priest. I didn't ask for a confession."

"I just thought you might want to know."

"Well, I don't. Why would I?"

He roughly pulled her against him and held her head between his palms. "Because we're in deep shit here, and you know it as well as I do."

Then he kissed her.

Chapter Thirteen

❧ ❧

Kissing Claire was better than fucking a dozen other women. Her mouth was warm and sweet and snug and he wanted to continue making love to it with his tongue for a thousand years. But he couldn't, so he released her and stepped back.

There was a slight catch in her breath, and her lips were damp and parted, but otherwise her features were composed. She was masterful at concealing her emotions. No doubt she'd developed that trait by having to grow up early. She'd had to deal with adult problems and make adult decisions at an age when most girls were playing with dolls and holding tea parties for teddy bears and imaginary friends.

But, dammit, he'd hoped to provoke more of a response than that unflickering stare. He'd flaunted two lovers, then kissed her intimately. Why didn't she curse him, slap him, go for his eyes with her fingernails?

He'd slept with the clerk for the same reason he'd beaten a path to his neighbor's front door—to seek relief from sexual frustration. Both attempts to get Claire out of his system had

219

failed. While the clerk had been almost pathetically eager to share herself with him, he hadn't found her nakedness as sexy as his fantasies of Claire, unclothed and giving. He'd performed as expected, but only physically. His mind had been elsewhere.

Now, her lack of an overt response angered him. He'd been going through hell these last few days. It was time he spread around some of the misery. "Is this when you got rid of the gun?"

"What?"

Since they hadn't spoken for several moments, the abrupt question took her off guard. "You heard me. Did you come straight here from the Fairmont and throw the gun in the river?"

"I've never owned a gun."

"That doesn't answer my question, Claire," he said, raising his voice. "You've got a legion of friends, any one of whom might have acquired a revolver for you."

"None did. I wouldn't even know how to fire one.'

"Blowing off a man's balls at close range doesn't require sharpshooting skills."

She folded her arms across her middle and hugged her elbows. "It's chilly out here. Can we go now?"

He was supremely exasperated with her and the situation. Nevertheless, he slipped off his jacket and placed it around her shoulders. His hands slid beneath her hair and lifted it from the collar, then lingered. He placed his thumbs beneath her chin and tilted her head up.

"If you came here at all that night, Claire, what did you do?"

"I sat on one of these benches and looked at the river."

"Sat on a bench and looked at the river."

"That's what I said."

Cassidy would have given anything he owned, or ever hoped to own, to know the truth behind her steady amber gaze. But he didn't. And until he did, he was playing with fire every time he came near her. "We'd better go."

They walked in silence back to French Silk. When they reached the door, he drew her around. "Claire, I strongly urge you to retain a criminal defense attorney."

"How close are you to arresting me?"

"Close. Your story is riddled with coincidences. If you're not outright lying, you're concealing the truth. Maybe you're covering for somebody else. I don't know. But you're not being straight with me. I know you're betting against the odds, but there's no statute of limitations on murder. As long as the case remains unsolved, I'll keep digging. Sooner or later I'll turn up the one element that brings everything together." He paused, giving her ample time to refute him. Disappointingly, she didn't. "Hire a lawyer, Claire."

She stared into space for a moment before looking up at him, her expression firmly resolved. "No, I won't do that. I have a business lawyer who handles French Silk's contracts and an accountant who takes care of the taxes. Its growth made them necessary, but I didn't like relinquishing even that much control over something that belongs to me."

She drew a deep breath. "I won't entrust my life to a stranger. I trust my instincts over anyone else's when it comes to what's right or wrong for me. When I was a child, social workers and judges, so-called experts, told me that the best thing for me was being separated from the people I love. Well, they were either dead wrong or unconscionable liars. So I don't trust the system, Cassidy." She shook off his jacket and thrust it at him. "Thank you for the free advice, but I don't want a lawyer."

"Have it your way then," he said impatiently. "But I think you're making a big mistake."

"At least it's *my* mistake."

"And don't leave town."

"The day after tomorrow I'm going to Mississippi."

That struck him like a bolt out of the blue. "What in the hell for?"

"The location shoot for the spring catalog."

"Cancel. Or postpone."

"Out of the question. This has been scheduled for weeks. The crew has been hired. Yasmine can't undo those arrangements. Anyway, we have to shoot before fall sets in and while the foliage is still green. You can't shoot a spring catalog against an autumnal background."

"Interesting, but the judicial system doesn't revolve around photography sessions."

"And I don't coordinate my business with the judicial system's schedule. Your choices are limited, Cassidy. Short of arresting me, you've got to let me go."

His hands were tied. She knew that as well as he did. Without any evidence on which to base a charge, he couldn't detain her any more than he could detain Ariel and Josh Wilde.

Sensing his dilemma, she smiled. "Good night, Cassidy."

"Damn. You're enjoying this, aren't you?" His hand shot out and trapped her jaw, his fingers biting into her cheeks. "Listen," he said, bending close to her face, "up till now, I've gone out of my way to give you the benefit of the doubt. No more, you got that?" He leaned in closer, his voice becoming a growl. "Sure, I want to fuck you, but don't let that go to your head. First and foremost I want to prosecute and convict Jackson Wilde's killer. Don't make the mistake of forgetting that, Claire. This may only be a game to you, but from now on, I play dirty."

She yanked her head free of his grip and shoved him away. "Thank you for the beignets and café au lait, Mr. Cassidy. They should have been my treat."

She slipped inside French Silk and slammed the door in his face. He cursed expansively as he heard the bolts clicking into place.

☙

Ariel impatiently tossed aside her magazine. It was late and she was perturbed. The man in New Orleans had promised to call her tonight no matter how late. It was now well past midnight.

Downstairs, Josh was playing the piano. He'd been at it for hours. That detestable classical music. She couldn't find a tune in any of it. Each song sounded like all the rest. They didn't even have lyrics, so what was the point? She couldn't figure out how anyone could become so absorbed in it. Yet, when Josh played classical piano, he forgot everything else—eating, sleeping, even sex.

Not that she'd missed the sex. She was focused on more important matters now. The picket line had been a fiasco. She had wanted her people to look like crusaders on a divinely inspired mission. Instead, that crazy old broad at French Silk had made them look mean-spirited and stupid. The media coverage had been extensive, but the story had been reported tongue-in-cheek. Ariel Wilde was not going to be a laughing-stock!

To restore her credibility, she had finagled the CNN interview, which, in her critical opinion, had gone exceptionally well. Without being downright libelous, she'd hinted that Claire Laurent was a coward who refused to debate her, that she was a prime suspect in the murder, and that she and everyone else involved with French Silk were immoral scum. Luckily, a devoted follower living in New Orleans had known about Claire Laurent's illegitimacy. Ariel planned to continue hammering home the theme immorality begetting immorality.

But Claire Laurent had appeared on CNN today, looking as regal as Princess Grace in her heyday and talking in that honeyed drawl that seemed to have bewitched the interviewer—and probably a majority of the viewing audience.

She had been articulate and straightforward without seeming abrasive. She'd dismissed Ariel as being delusional but left no doubt that she would take legal action if the persecution continued.

Twice now she'd made the Jackson Wilde Ministry look like a pack of fanatic fools. Ariel simply wouldn't have it. Anyone as cool and controlled as Claire Laurent must have secrets. Why else erect such an impenetrable shield of gentility?

So, Ariel had hired someone to keep an eye on her nemesis and make daily reports. When the telephone on her nightstand rang, she lunged for it. It was the call she'd been waiting for.

"We struck gold on the first try," said the man on the phone, chortling. "For all her denials on TV, she's still a prime suspect. Cassidy went to see her again tonight."

Ariel sat up against the pile of pillows at her back. "Really? How long did he question her?"

"They went for a long walk through the French Quarter."

The more she heard about Claire Laurent's most recent meeting with the handsome, young, sexy prosecutor, the faster the wheels in her brain whirred. She was so busy analyzing the information, she almost missed the most valuable nugget. "Excuse me," she said, interrupting. "What did you say? They what?"

"That's right, Mrs. Wilde. You heard me. They kissed."

Eagerly, Ariel listened to the entire account without another interruption. "Thank you," she said when he'd finished. "Keep me posted on developments. I want to know everything. Remember, you're my eyes and ears." As an afterthought, she added, "God bless, and I'll be praying for you."

Josh strolled in as she was hanging up. "Who's calling at this time of night?" He pulled his T-shirt over his head and began undressing.

"The guy in New Orleans who organized the demonstration at French Silk."

"What a debacle," he muttered as he wobbled first on one foot, then the other, to remove his sneakers.

Ariel wasn't familiar with the word *debacle* but didn't like the sound of it and took his criticism personally. "How could we predict that Claire Laurent's daft old mama wouldn't know any better than to go up against a hostile crowd?"

Josh chuckled as he slid into bed beside her. "You wanted fireworks from them and got Kool-Aid and tea cakes instead."

"It's not funny," she said, slinging off the arm he'd placed across her waist. Throwing back the covers, she left the bed and lit a cigarette, a habit she'd resumed since Jackson was no longer there to forbid it. She ripped open a package of Ding Dongs and stuffed one into her mouth.

"Tomorrow I want to take this show on the road," she told Josh around the mouthful of devil's food cake. "We'll go to several cities and hold only one service in each," Her mind was clicking furiously now. "We'll make them special. We'll call them emergency prayer meetings for the capture and conviction of Jackson's killer."

Groaning, Josh laid his arm across his forehead and closed his eyes. "Ariel, these things take time to plan. You've got to rent a facility—"

"I don't care if we conduct them on football fields," she shouted. "I want a lot of people to attend and a lot of press, and I want you," she said, turning and aiming her finger at him, "to appear shattered by bereavement."

"I'll have to borrow your eyeshadow."

"Go to hell."

She got back into bed, but not until she'd swallowed two laxative tablets to counteract the calories in the Ding Dong. "Not now," she grumbled when Josh rolled toward her and covered her breast with his hand. "I've got too much on my mind."

"It's just as well," he said. "You're so skinny your bones rattle when we make love."

"Fuck you."

"That's what I had in mind, but . . ." Laughing, he burrowed his head in his pillow. Ariel was too wired to sleep. She consumed such vast quantities of caffeine and sugar, it was rare that she slept more than three or four hours a night. Some of the dark shadows under her eyes weren't cosmetically enhanced.

Mentally she reviewed everything she knew about Claire Laurent. Some classy broad, she thought grudgingly. Tall. Naturally sender. Well dressed. Classic features. She was the kind of woman Ariel aspired to be, but she knew in her gut that it wasn't in her genes. She could try from now till doomsday and never achieve that cool elegance. You were either born with it or you weren't.

Claire Laurent was taking long, leisurely walks through the French Quarter with A.D.A. Cassidy, who had never looked at Ariel with anything except suspicion and ill-concealed derision. He seemed to know that no matter how often or how hard she washed, she never felt completely clean. He had kissed Claire Laurent! Shame, shame. The possibilities of how she could use that tidbit made Ariel giddy and almost compensated for her envy.

The snooty bitch had bamboozled him. It was as simple as that. Did he think someone as hoity-toity as Claire Laurent was incapable of murder? *Think again, Mr. Cassidy.*

However you looked at it, he'd been derelict in his duty. Tomorrow morning, even before she called a news conference to announce *Ariel Wilde's Prayer and Praise Hour's* latest undertaking, she had a vitally important telephone call to make.

Cassidy had been forewarned that the chief was on the warpath, so Tony Crowder's imperious summons came as no surprise. "He's waiting for you, Cassidy," the secretary informed him sympathetically. "Go right in."

Cassidy assumed a casual air. "Good morning, Tony. You wanted to see me?" From behind his desk, Crowder glared at him. Cassidy took a seat, crossing his ankle over his opposite knee. "Actually I'm glad you called me in this morning. I've got something to discuss with you."

"I'm taking you off the Jackson Wilde murder case."

"What?" Cassidy's foot hit the floor with such impact that it rattled Crowder's cup of coffee against its saucer.

"You heard me. You're off it. I'm reassigning it to Nance."

"You can't."

"I have. Or at least I will as soon as this meeting's concluded. Which it is."

"Like hell." Cassidy shot up from his chair. "Why're you doing this?"

"I'll tell you why," Crowder thundered. "I'm catching holy hell from everybody about this. The mayor. The P.C. Judges. Especially that tight-assed Harris. Congressmen. Even the freaking governor has put in his two cents' worth. I've got Jackson Wilde coming out my ass, and I'm sick of it. I want an end to it, and so far you've failed to make that happen."

"I'm trying."

"With Claire Laurent?"

Cassidy cautiously assessed the glint in his superior's eyes. Uneasiness crept in behind his anger. "Among others."

"Exactly what are you 'trying' with Claire Laurent?"

"I get the impression that's a loaded question."

Crowder maintained a bead on Cassidy as he reached for his coffee cup and slurped from it. "I got a call this morning from Ariel Wilde."

"Okay, I get the picture," Cassidy said, breathing easier. "She reminded you that we haven't arrested her husband's killer yet, and you felt the need to chew ass. Is that what this is about?"

"That's part of it. Not all."

"Well?"

"Did you take Claire Laurent on a romantic moonlight stroll through the French Quarter last night?"

Although Cassidy's heart had dropped to his knees, he kept his expression impassive. "I went to French Silk and confronted Ms. Laurent with information I'd obtained from other sources." He explained about the telephone calls and the discrepancies in timing. "Ms. Laurent claimed that she had filled that time by taking a walk to cool off after meeting Wilde face to face at the crusade. She suggested that we retrace her steps."

"That included a stop at Café du Monde?"

"Yes."

"And a stroll along the Moonwalk?"

"Yes."

"Which is probably where she disposed of the murder weapon."

"I mentioned that," Cassidy said defensively.

"And what did she say?"

"She maintains that she's never owned a gun of any kind and wouldn't even know how to fire one."

"You don't have to be too good a shot to shoot off a man's balls at point-blank range."

"I mentioned that, too," Cassidy said with a laugh.

"You think this is funny?"

"No. The chuckle was my way of pointing out how alike we are."

"Oh yeah? I've never romanced a suspect."

Cassidy's eyes snapped to Crowder's. "Neither have I," he said, giving Crowder back his hard stare.

"That's not what it looked like to Ariel's spy."

"Spy? What the hell are you talking about?"

"Our dear Mrs. Wilde had one of her flunkies keeping an

eye on Claire Laurent and reporting anything incriminating or suspicious. So far the only suspicious thing she's done is go out on a date—''

"It wasn't a date!"

''—with the man who may very well have to prosecute her in a court of law. Only I'm eliminating that probability by removing you from the case.''

"You can't take me off the case," Cassidy shouted. "I told you how that walk came about."

"Don't play word games with me. Ariel Wilde's man was thorough. He told her every move you made, and she passed the details along to me. You gave Claire Laurent your jacket. You embraced her. You kissed her. Didn't you?''

Cassidy gave a terse nod.

''According to the spy's account, it wasn't a polite little peck, either."

"No," Cassidy said gruffly. "It wasn't."

"Jesus!" Crowder rose to his feet and banged his fist on his desk. "What the hell were you thinking of?"

Cassidy bowed his head. "Shit." After a long, still moment, he raised his head. "I can see how it might have looked to someone who didn't know that circumstances. I *was* questioning her, Tony."

"You were also swapping spit!" he bellowed.

In a much softer, more reasonable tone, Cassidy said, "I was shooting holes in her defense, trying to find the element that's missing from her story."

"So you're sure there's a missing element?"

"Almost positive. I don't know if she's lying to protect herself or someone else, but she's not telling the whole truth. Unfortunately, I can't arrest her on a gut feeling."

'' 'Unfortunately'?'' The D.A. studied him with shrewd eyes that missed nothing. "Are you going to sit there and tell me you don't find this woman attractive?"

"No." Cassidy looked him straight in the eye. "She's extremely attractive to me."

Crowder sank back into his chair and ran a hand over his thinning hair. "I should have become a dentist like my mother wanted me to." Grumbling, he added, "At least you didn't lie to me. And I'd have known if you had. There've been rumors."

"Rumors about what?"

"About your attraction to Ms. Laurent. Glenn complained to the P.C. about it. He came to me with it."

"Christ!" Cassidy exclaimed angrily. "Glenn had no right to—"

"Dammit, he had every right. This is his case, too, remember? He doesn't want it fucked up by a prosecutor with a valentine where his head should be." He shook his head. "I don't want to do this to you, kid. But you leave me no alternative. I've got to take you off the case."

"Don't, Tony." Cassidy left his chair and leaned over Crowder's desk. "I've got to have it. I'll bring the culprit to trial and I'll get a conviction. My career's riding on it. I won't squander this opportunity. Not for anything."

"Not even for a woman you're attracted to?"

"Especially not for that."

Crowder studied him for a moment. "You sound like you mean it."

"I do." Cassidy debated over whether to broach a subject that had always remained closed to discussion. However, last night he had told Claire that from here on, he was playing to win. Crowder needed to be convinced of that, too. "You must have wondered, Tony, why I switched from defense counsel when I came here."

"I thought it was curious that you gave up a lucrative practice in exchange for the salary this parish pays you. But after reviewing your win/loss columns, I considered myself too lucky to have you on my side to start prying. Why bring it up now?"

Cassidy began pacing the length of Crowder's office. "As you said, I had a money-making practice going. I'd racked up an impressive number of wins, some in court, others in plea bargains. Either way, my clients were walking, and I was feeling pretty damn smug about it and very sure of myself.''

"I know the type.''

Cassidy nodded grimly to Crowder's comment. "A particular client retained me to defend him. He was a bad-ass with a list of priors as long as my arm. He'd been sent up for assault but had served only a fraction of his sentence when he was released. A few weeks into his parole, he phoned me. He said I came highly recommended. Said he'd heard I wasn't afraid of anything. Said he was confident I would see to it that he walked.''

He stopped, closed his eyes for a moment, and added, "The hell of it was, Tony, I was confident of it too. I took his case. This time he'd been charged with sexual assault, although the woman had managed to get away before he could rape her.''

He ceased pacing and stared out the window. "The victim was in her early twenties, pretty, good figure," he began softly. "My client had accosted her when she came out of her office building at dusk. I didn't have a prayer. He'd literally been caught with his pants down half a block from the scene. The prosecutor turned down all offers of a plea bargain. He wanted this guy behind bars. The case went to trail. All I could rely on was showmanship, and by then I had it down to a science," he said, making a fist and squeezing hard.

"I pulled out all the stops. By the time I got finished with that girl in cross-examination, the jury was convinced she was a whore who wore miniskirts to work in order to lure her male co-workers. I actually remember thinking how lucky I was that she was chesty because it substantiated my *case*. I made sure the jury's attention was called to her breasts. Christ.''

He rubbed his eyes, attempting to eradicate the disturbing

mental picture of the sobbing young woman he'd stripped and assaulted on the witness stand. "I crucified her, ruined her reputation, painted her up to be a cock-teaser who had teased one cock too many and, as a result, got more than she'd bargained for."

He lowered his hand from his eyes and stared vacantly beyond the window blinds. "It was a brilliantly orchestrated defense. I kept the media apprised of the sordid details, then played their interest for all it was worth. If the jury brought in a guilty verdict, I could always reverse my position and say that my client had been tried in the press.

"But they didn't bring in a guilty verdict." His voice reflected the puzzlement he still felt each time he thought about it. "The jury fell for my theatrics. They acquitted the son of a bitch."

"You were doing what you were paid to do," Tony remarked.

"That doesn't excuse it."

"Half the law community would pat you on the back and envy your success."

"Success? Grossly manipulating the jury and abusing my role as defense attorney?"

"So you went overboard," Tony said. "It's been, what, five years or better? Let it go, Cassidy. Excuse yourself for that one mistake."

"Maybe I could if that were all of it."

"Oh, hell." Crowder leaned back, preparing himself for the worst.

"Two weeks after his acquittal, my client abducted an eleven-year-old fifth-grader off her school playground and drove her to a deserted area of a city park; where he raped her, sodomized her, then strangled her with her training bra. And those were only the crimes that have legal names. The others were—are—unspeakable."

Crowder let several moments of strained silence lapse. "You closed your law office after that."

Cassidy turned away from the window and faced his superior. "Closed the office, shut down my life, relieved my wife of the stigma of being married to me, and left town. That's when I came here."

"Where you've been damned diligent. A real asset to this office."

Cassidy shrugged, wondering if he would ever get over his feelings of inadequacy. Would he ever win a conviction that would atone for that young girl's life? Would he ever be able to face her stricken parents and say, "Finally, I've made amends"? Never. But he would keep trying.

"I won't ever be negligent in my duty again, Tony. I'll never let another psychopath slip through the cracks, never unleash a rapist/murderer onto an unsuspecting public, most of whom have a misplaced trust in us and the legal system."

"Their trust isn't always misplaced. Every now and then we get the bad guy."

Cassidy put all his powers of persuasion into his gaze. "I'm not going to let you down, Tony, because I can't let myself down. I swear I'll deliver Wilde's killer, no matter who it turns out to be."

Tony gnawed the inside of his cheek. "Okay, I'll give you a couple of more weeks," he said impatiently. "But consider your head on the chopping block with the ax hanging over it."

"I understand." Now that the matter was settled, Cassidy saw no need to linger. Both would be uncomfortable if he groveled with gratitude.

He headed for the door, but Crowder halted him. "Cassidy, I have to ask. If you uncover that missing element that indisputably links Claire Laurent to the murder, will it be a problem for you to prosecute when a conviction would mean mandatory life imprisonment for her?"

Cassidy searched his soul, but he already knew the answer. "Absolutely not. I'd do it with no qualms whatsoever."

As he left the office, he pledged to uphold his promise to

Claire, to Tony, and to himself. Under no circumstances would he let his personal interests interfere with his professional duty.

He left the district attorney's building and crossed the street to the police department. Howard Glenn was seated behind a battered, cluttered desk, reclining in a swivel chair, a telephone receiver cradled between his ear and his shoulder. Cassidy came to a halt at the very edge of the desk, his stare boring into Glenn.

"We'll talk later," Glenn said into the receiver, then hung up.

Cassidy said, "The next time you have a complaint about me, don't tattle. Come straight to me with it. Man to man. I'd extend you that courtesy."

"I thought my superintendent—"

"You thought wrong," Cassidy said harshly. "I'm in control of my emotions, of my dick, and of this situation, and it pisses me off that you presumed to have my hands slapped. Don't do it again. If you've got any problems with me, let's hear them now."

Glenn maneuvered his cigarette from one corner of his mouth to the other while carefully gauging the A.D.A. "I've got no problems."

"Fine." Cassidy checked his wristwatch. "It's almost noon. I'll meet you after lunch in my office and we'll discuss our next course of action."

Chapter Fourteen

✣ ✣

The chimes of St. Louis Cathedral rang out as the bride and groom emerged beneath a hail of rice and good wishes from friends and family. Bridesmaids in frothy pink gowns gleefully battled over the tossed bouquet. The bride paused to kiss her weeping mother goodbye, while the grinning groom, impatient with the seemingly endless round of farewells, scooped the bride—lace gown, tulle veil, and all—into his arms and carried her to the long white limousine awaiting them.

From behind the iron picket fence that enclosed Jackson Square, directly in front of the cathedral, Yasmine watched the romantic scene with a volatile mix of yearning and cynicism. That morning, she'd read in the society page that Congressman and Mrs. Alister Petrie would be attending the late afternoon wedding mass. Yasmine, who had arrived in New Orleans the night before, had walked from French Silk to the cathedral and posted herself behind the fence with the hope of catching a glimpse of her errant lover.

Although she'd notified him of her arrival, he hadn't con-

tacted her. She had expected him to arrange an evening of
lovemaking before she had to leave for the location shoot in
Mississippi. She had kept a vigil over her telephone but hadn't
received a call last night or today.

"Guess he was too busy getting ready for the wedding,"
she muttered angrily as she watched the procession of well-
turned-out guests file through the tall, narrow cathedral doors.

But when she spotted him, her anger evaporated and her
heart twisted with love and longing. He epitomized the American dream: a handsome, charming, successful man . . . with
an adoring wife for garnish. Yasmine had seen Belle Petrie
only in photographs. Alister's wife was slight and blond,
pretty in a pale, aristocratic sort of way, and not nearly as
vapid as Yasmine had imagined.

At the sight of Belle and Alister together, all the blood in
Yasmine's body seemed to rush to her head. It pulsated
through her veins with envy. She felt it pounding in her brain,
against her skull, the backs of her eyes, her eardrums.

As Alister moved among the crowd, shaking hands and
smiling, he appeared not to be as miserably unhappy as he
claimed to be. On the contrary, he seemed complacent and
content, a man who had the world wrapped around his little
finger. Nor did Belle appear deprived of anything, especially
marital bliss.

Yasmine could barely contain herself. Her first impulse
was to rush through the gates and brutally attack the man who
had turned her into a woman so desperate and jealous that
she was reduced to spying. Imagine the shock of the formally
attired, bejeweled wedding guests if she were to publicly
expose Alister Petrie, the best among them, as a lying adulterer. Could she ever regale them with lurid accounts of what
he did in bed!

But she couldn't cause a scene without exposing herself as
a jealous fool, and she wasn't prepared to do that. She was
clinging tenaciously to a few shreds of pride, even though it

would have been immensely satisfying to witness Alister's mortification.

She was somewhat mollified when he spotted her. He did a comical double take. His smile collapsed. Appalled disbelief caused his features to go slack. For several moments his jaw hung open, making him look stupid.

As she moved along the fence, Yasmine kept her stare fixed on his fearful eyes. When she passed through the gate, he looked ready to bolt. She took perverse pleasure in moving straight toward him. His tongue darted out to moisten his lips. She got close enough to see sweat popping out on his forehead. At the last possible moment she angled off, walking away from him at no wider a margin than ten degrees.

She took Chartres Street uptown. Although she wanted to gauge Alister's reaction to the close call she'd given him, she didn't glance back once.

Claire and Mary Catherine were eating dinner when she arrived at French Silk. Claire apologized for not waiting for her. "There's so much to do before leaving tomorrow, I wanted to get dinner out of the way early."

"Doesn't matter. I'm not hungry." Yasmine didn't break stride until she reached her bedroom door, which she soundly closed behind her to discourage a visit from Claire.

Having reached the sanctity of her room, the tears that she had stubbornly withheld welled up in her eyes. For the next hour and a half she vacillated between red rage and black despair. One minute she fantasized killing Alister slowly and painfully while his wife watched. The next, she fantasized making love to him until thoughts of all else were obliterated.

Emotionally spent, she lay on her bed, her forearm over her eyes. There was a discreet knock on her door. "I don't want to talk right now, Claire," she called out.

"I wouldn't have bothered you, but something just arrived for you."

"What?" She lowered her arm and sat up. "A delivery?"

"Yes."

Yasmine padded barefoot to the door and opened it a crack. Claire extended her a long, slender, flat box. Ignoring Claire's sympathetic expression, she took the box, thanked her, and closed the door. The box contained a single Sterling rose nestled amid green tissue paper. It was a perfect, flawless bloom of smoky lavender petals. The sweetness of the gesture pierced her soul like a thorn. Mewling with heartache, she cradled the rosebud against her chest and fell back on the pillows, weeping.

Several minutes later the ringing telephone roused her. She rolled toward the nightstand and lifted the receiver. "I just got it," she said, knowing even before he identified himself who the caller was.

"Darling."

The sound of his voice precipitated another bout of tears. "I thought you'd be furious with me for stalking you," she said.

"I was, at first," he admitted.

"You looked like you'd just swallowed a golf ball when you spotted me through the fence."

"If the bride had reached out and grabbed my nuts, I couldn't have been more astonished." They laughed together softly. Then he said, "I can't blame you for spying, Yasmine. I've been a pig. My time and energy have been consumed by my reelection campaign. I'm so damned busy. Everybody pulling on me in a thousand different directions. I've neglected you. Out of necessity, but . . . What I'm saying is, I'm sorry. Be patient with me, darling. When the election is over things will be different. You'll see."

"You and Belle look so happy together, Alister," she remarked as she slowly wound the telephone cord around her finger. His apology had sounded sincere, but she couldn't dismiss the happy picture he and his wife had made as they stood hand in hand in front of the church.

"I suppose she is happy," he said. "She doesn't have the same passions that I do. That *we* do. Since I stopped making love with her, she doesn't even miss it. All she ever wanted was a successful husband and beautiful children. She's got that. She doesn't know what real passion is. God," he moaned. "There's no comparison between you, Yasmine. You've got to know that."

"No, there's no comparison. She's got you and I don't."

"I reside with her," he said evenly. "She doesn't have my heart. It's not her I think about every hour of the day. I want to be with you right now."

"I'll meet you," she offered eagerly.

"I can't. We're involved in this wedding shit for the rest of the evening. Following the reception, there's an after-party and an even more intimate gathering after that. It's essential that I mingle with these people. They're influential. Three-fourths of the money in Louisiana is represented here tonight. I only sneaked away long enough to order the rose for you and to call."

"I'm leaving tomorrow, Alister," she said, trying to keep the whine out of her voice. "I'll be in Mississippi for at least a week."

After a slight pause he said, "Next Thursday night. Can you make a round trip to New Orleans?"

"Yes. Rosesharon is only a two-hour drive from here. It'll be a long night for me, but I've got to see you."

"Thursday then."

After finalizing their plans, Yasmine said breathlessly, "I can't wait."

"Neither can I, but right now I've got to go. Belle will start missing me. This call was supposed to be a quick business call."

"I love you, Alister."

"Oops, there she is. She's signaling for me to rejoin the party. See you next Thursday."

He didn't even say goodbye before hanging up. Dejectedly Yasmine replaced the telephone. For a long while she sat on the edge of her bed, staring vacantly, immobilized by despair. Never in her life had she felt more blue. Even the rose could no longer cheer her. She'd hugged it so tightly, it was already beginning to wilt.

She finally mustered enough energy to move to her dresser, where she gazed at her reflection in the mirror. Even the crying hadn't marred the perfection of her face. She studied her image objectively, then asked, "Why the hell are you putting yourself through this, you dumb bitch?"

It wasn't fair. Alister was at a party, laughing, drinking champagne, dancing, surrounded by people who thought he was bloody marvelous. Here she was: Yasmine, goddess of fashion runways and magazine covers, weeping alone. "What's wrong with this picture?" she asked her reflection.

Men were bastards. All men. From the abusive father who had deserted her mother when Yasmine was still in diapers, to her current lover, they were sorry, low-down, scummy sons of bitches who rarely had to account for their actions. Seldom did one get his just desserts.

Of course there were exceptions. Once in a blue moon one got the punishment he richly deserved. Like Jackson Wilde.

Claire was clearing away the dinner dishes when she heard Mary Catherine cry out. Dropping the sponge into the sink, Claire ran from the kitchen into the living room. Mary Catherine was sitting in an easy chair reading the evening edition of the *Times Picayune*. All the color had drained from her face. Her hands were trembling.

"Mama!" Claire cried in alarm. "What is it?" She rushed to Mary Catherine and caught the newspaper as it slipped from her lifeless fingers. "My God," Claire whispered after reading only a few paragraphs of the front-page story. She lowered herself onto the arm of her mother's chair.

"Does Mr. Cassidy think you killed Reverend Wilde, Claire?"

"He's only doing his job, Mama."

"Did he kiss you?"

"What does it matter?" Claire asked bitterly. "It's been reported that he did."

Mary Catherine covered her face with her hands. "This is all my fault. My sins are reflecting on you. If I hadn't sinned—"

"Mama, stop that!" Claire drew her mother's hands away from her ravaged face. "You were young. You fell in love and gave of yourself. You weren't the sinner. You were sinned against."

"But it says in the newspaper that because of your upbringing you would try seducing the prosecutor to stay out of trouble. Oh, Claire, I'm sorry. I never wanted anyone to judge you by what I did."

"This," Claire said, flicking her hand at the newspaper, "is the handiwork of a wicked, vicious, spiteful woman. Ariel Wilde is trying to make me look guilty in order to turn the attention away from herself. Mrs. Wilde doesn't know you or me. What difference does it make what she thinks of us? Let her believe what she wants to."

"But other people, Mr Cassidy . . ." Her face reflected her torment. In a fast, hushed voice she whispered, "If only he'd come for me as he said he would. I was there, on time, with my things. I'm sure it was today he said we were to meet. But he wasn't there and—"

"Listen, Mama." Claire hastily hunkered down in front of the chair and clasped Mary Catherine's hands. "I just had a wonderful idea. Why don't you come to Mississippi with us tomorrow?"

"Mississippi?"

"Yes. For a vacation. Wouldn't you enjoy a few days away?" Mary Catherine's troubled face began to relax. Claire pressed her point. "Harry can come along to keep you company while I'm working. Please come. I want you there with me."

Mary Catherine coyly laid her hand against her throat, looking as flustered as a wallflower who's just been asked to dance. "Well, Claire Louise, if you really need me there . . ."

"I do, Mama." Claire stood and assisted Mary Catherine to her feet. She whisked the newspaper out of sight. "Start choosing what you want to take with you. I'll call Harry and have her spend the night here. We'll get an early start in the morning. I've rented a van so there'll be plenty of room. We'll stop for breakfast somewhere along the way. Oh, this will be a lovely trip! It's been ages since we went away together."

"Yes, ages," Mary Catherine said as she drifted toward her room. "I'll take that new afternoon dress."

"By all means. You look beautiful in that shade of blue."

As soon as Mary Catherine disappeared into her room, Claire snatched up the evening newspaper and read the infuriating article. It was trash, but it effectively planted in the reader's mind that Claire Laurent, publisher of the scandalous French Silk catalog, was a hussy who had tried seduction as a means of avoiding a murder rap.

Claire tried to locate Cassidy by telephone but was unsuccessful. After cooling down a bit, she reasoned that it was just as well she didn't speak with him. He wouldn't be enjoying the notoriety either. It would be better for them to handle this situation individually rather than as a team, which would only fuel Ariel's hints of an unethical and highly improper affair.

She called Harriet York, informed her of the change in plans, then checked with the proprietors of Rosesharon to make certain they had another bedroom available. As soon as Harry arrived, Claire left her to help Mary Catherine pack while she went downstairs to her workroom to place a long-distance call. She caught her business attorney in New York on his way out to dinner, but he patiently listened while she read him the majority of the newspaper article.

"I warned her not to slander me again," Claire told him when she finished reading. "She's waving a red flag in my face, daring me to sue her."

"That's what worries me," the lawyer said. "She wants to prolong her feud with you and take advantage of the publicity it generates. She's got nothing to lose by pursuing it. You, on the other hand, abhor publicity. Unless you want your private life exposed even more than it already has been—"

"I don't."

"Then I advise you to ignore her."

"Damn!" she muttered. "I know you're right, but I hate to back down. What good are ultimatums if you don't follow through?"

"It's like celebrities who threaten to sue the tabloids for the half-true stories they print. The litigation only creates more adverse publicity. It's a no-win situation. Unless you want all your dirty laundry aired publicly, your hands are tied."

"But how can I allow her to go on saying anything she pleases about me and my family?"

"You can't have it both ways, Claire. If you even hint at whitewashing what can or cannot be said to the media, you've got to be prepared for the backlash. Ariel Wilde could then say you stand for the First Amendment rights of free speech and free press only as long as they benefit you."

Claire sighed. "I never thought of it from that angle."

"I wouldn't be surprised if that's her ultimate goal," the lawyer said. "She'd love to see you eat your words on this censorship issue."

They discussed it for a few minutes more before Claire

said, "I really don't have a better alternative than to continue ignoring her."

"That's my advice. She's a nuisance, but she can't really harm you."

"It's not me I worry about. I couldn't care less what Ariel Wilde or anyone else says about me. It's Mama. When anyone slanders her, I come out slugging. She and Yasmine are the only family I have. We're a tight little group who stands together or not at all."

"I know that. That's why I was so puzzled by that other matter."

"What other matter?"

Then he broke the really bad news.

The two Mrs. Monteiths were almost interchangeable. Grace's hair was a shade darker burgundy than Agnes's, but beyond that there wasn't much difference between the two buxom women. They were sisters-in-law, they explained to Claire as she checked in to the bed-and-breakfast house known as Rosesharon.

"Our husbands were brothers, you see," Agnes told her. "We lost them within months of each other."

"Rather than get into a squabble over who had inherited what in this house, we decided to pool our resources," Grace contributed.

"Each of us loves to cook. It only made sense to capitalize on our hobby."

"The place wasn't fit for guests, though."

"So we sold off part of the acreage and from that revenue hired a fancy decorator to redo the house from top to bottom."

"Well, she certainly did a wonderful job," Claire said, glancing around the wide foyer. The house had been refurbished to antebellum splendor.

"He," Agnes said in a stage whisper, while bobbing her

purplish eyebrows. "Although he was prissier than most females I know."

"Agnes!" Grace admonished with a giggle, which she tried to cover with her veined, age-spotted hand.

As she imprinted Claire's credit card, Agnes said, "Your rooms are ready for you. Juice, cold drinks, and snacks of fruit and cookies can always be found in the kitchen if someone misses the regular meals. Breakfast is served between seven and eight-thirty, but there's always a fresh pot of coffee on the sideboard in the dining room. Lunch is an informal cold buffet. Tea and finger sandwiches are available from three-thirty until five. We open the bar at five, but except for the wine we serve with dinner, there's an extra charge for liquor. One has to mix his own, and we trust our guests to keep their own tabs. Dinner is the only formal meal. It's served at seven-thirty."

Claire liked them and hoped that no one on the crew would take advantage of their hospitality or naïveté. "We'll try to keep to your schedule," she told them. "However, if we get behind, I'll appreciate a little flexibility."

"Of course, dear. You're our first 'working' guests. We've been beside ourselves with excitement. The only thing better would be having a movie filmed here," Agnes gushed.

"And we *love* your catalog," Grace said. "When it arrives in the mail, we fight over who gets to look through it first."

"I'm glad to hear that." Claire was glad that a smile was called for. She couldn't have kept a straight face under punishment of death. "From what I've seen so far, your home will make a beautiful backdrop for our photos."

She'd been impressed since leaving the highway and following the tree-lined, gravel road to Rosesharon. Although the growing season was waning, the lawn and flower gardens surrounding the house were still green and lush. White lawn furniture was grouped in the shade of sprawling trees.

The house itself looked like a wedding cake. The bricks had been painted a pale, creamy pink. The six fluted Corinthian columns and all other trim were white. There was a deep wrap-around veranda shaded by a second-floor balcony. Claire was very pleased with Yasmine's choice.

"We want to make your stay enjoyable," Grace told her. "Remember, this is our home. As our guests, you have the run of the place."

A commotion out on the veranda drew their attention to the front door. A short, wiry young man in a white linen suit and yellow Polo shirt flung open the screen door and made a grand entrance.

"Claire!" he gasped when he saw her. "My God, this is positively fab. Darling!" He kissed her cheeks in turn, then held the light meter, which was suspended from his neck by a black cord, up to her face and checked the reading. "Oh, this is going to be so sweet. I can't wait to begin, *if* I don't expire from the freaking heat first. How do you natives stand it? But the house is fab, really it is. Yasmine said as much, but you know how that bitch is prone to exaggerate."

Leon was one of the most sought-after fashion photographers in New York. His flamboyance was championed only by his talent with lighting and lens. When he wasn't pitching temper tantrums or gossiping bitchily, he could be quite amusing.

Leon hadn't yet stopped talking. "The staircase is to die for. We must have one of the girls languishing on it as though in a swoon." He struck a pose. "Eyes at half-mast, you know. I'll shoot it from above. Perhaps in the late afternoon with sunlight striking just the right spots. Yes, yes," he said clapping his hands. "Someone with lots of hair fanning out behind her head. Moist tendrils clinging to her cheeks. Oh, God, I'm getting chills just thinking about it."

The rest of the entourage trailed in, dropping onto pieces of furniture like wounded soldiers. "Jesus, it's hot," one of the models said as she lifted a mane of streaked blond hair off her neck.

There were four female models and two males. Yasmine

had used them in the catalog before. It was a convivial group, and they were all on a first-name basis—Felicia, Dana, Liz, and Alison. They were young, nubile, and gorgeous. Kurt, the dark, brooding male model, wore his luxuriant black hair shoulder length. He could look either sleek and European or dangerous and untamed. The other man, Paul, was blond and blue-eyed. His "types" were the boy next door and the buttoned-down yuppie.

The stylist, in charge of wardrobe, was known throughout the fashion industry simply as Rue. She was a middle-aged crone who had coarse features and a voice like a cement mixer. She was never without a black, acrid cigarette dangling from her lips.

The makeup artist was a quiet Asian woman with porcelain-like skin and expressive doe eyes. The hair stylist, paradoxically, had virtually no hair. It had been cut very close to her scalp. She compensated by wearing earrings that dangled to her chest.

Leon's assistant, as pudgy and pink as a newborn, was a self-effacing young man who rarely spoke and constantly remained in Leon's shadow.

"Perhaps we should all get settled into our rooms," Claire said. "As soon as you're unpacked, I'd like to have a meeting with Leon and Yasmine to review the shot list."

The Monteiths summoned two valets to help with the luggage. Before everyone scattered, Claire spoke above the noise: "Models, before dinner, I'd like you all to go to the Winnebago for a fitting. Rue has already tagged the garments with your names."

The models divided themselves up two, two, and two. Claire didn't know who was sleeping with whom and made a point not to find out. Too much gossip could jeopardize the camaraderie on a location shoot. If there were any minidramas played out during the course of their stay, she'd rather not know about them.

Mary Catherine was sharing a room with Harry. Leon and

his assistant had a room. Claire and Yasmine were doubling in another. Rue, the hair stylist, and the makeup artist had opted to sleep in the Winnebago. Claire was glad. Otherwise there might not have been a vacancy for her mother and Harry.

Thankfully, she could concentrate on her work, without having to worry about Cassidy questioning her mother. That had been her main reason for hustling Mary Catherine out of New Orleans.

Chapter Fifteen

❧ ❧

Claire was up early and, over coffee, consulted with Leon, Rue, and Yasmine about the shots they had scheduled for that day. "What would you think of using that old-fashioned vanity table in our bedroom for one of the interior shots?" she asked Yasmine.

Yasmine responded enthusiastically. "We could shoot the model from the back, looking into the mirror, and it could reflect one of the guys watching her through the balcony doors. We could close those gauzy curtains so you'd see only the silhouette of a man."

"It'd be a good shot to feature that backless bra you designed, Claire," Rue said around a rattling cough.

"Leon?"

"Sounds fab. But let's wait for a cloudy day to do the interior shots. I want to take advantage of this glorious sunshine while it lasts."

The weather cooperated with Leon's wishes. Conse

quently, the morning sessions went well. By noon they had completed three shots.

"We'll resume after lunch," Claire told everyone as they trooped up the front steps toward the welcome shade of the veranda, where Agnes Monteith was waiting with a cordless phone.

"A call for you, Miss Laurent. A Mr. Cassidy. I told him we were serving lunch, but he was insistent."

"Yes, he would be." Frowning, Claire took the phone but waited until everyone was inside before saying anything. "Hello, Cassidy." Her voice didn't convey any friendliness.

"How's Mississippi?"

"Hot."

"No hotter than it is here."

"Oh?"

"Don't sound so innocent. I'm catching hell from Crowder."

"About that newspaper story?"

"You saw it?"

"Before I left New Orleans. According to Ariel Wilde, I'm quite a tart, aren't I?"

"Much ado about one little kiss."

It hadn't exactly been "one little kiss," but Claire refrained from pointing that out. "You should have thought of the consequences before you kissed me."

"I thought about them. At the time, the consequences didn't seem to matter a whole hell of a lot."

Breathless and feeling overly warm, Claire sank into the nearest wicker chair, wishing she could think of something to say that would fill the awkward silence.

Cassidy said, "Ariel called Crowder even before she went to the press. Apparently she's got somebody tailing you."

The thought of someone, a stranger, covertly watching her made her feel like she needed a bath. "Damn her! Why can't she just leave us alone? Why can't you?"

"Look, the last couple of days haven't exactly be\ picnic for me either."

"I don't suppose Crowder was too happy with you," she remarked.

"He threatened to take me off the case."

"You don't want that, do you?"

"No."

"How is Crowder responding publicly to the newspaper story?"

"He's denying everything."

"How can he?" Claire exclaimed.

"It's their word against ours that I kissed you. Who is Joe Public going to believe, a religious nut or the district attorney?"

"Crowder would lie to protect you?"

"Not me. He'd lie to protect the office. He's a politician first, and supports the establishment as fiercely as you oppose it."

Claire was trying to assimilate it all when a chilling thought occurred to her. "In order to get back in Crowder's good graces, you almost have to indict me. That's the only way you can prove to Joe Public that you're unbiased and that my seductive powers have no influence over you."

"Hell no," he said with asperity. "It's nothing like that.'

"Isn't it?"

"All right, to some extent that's true. But it has nothing to do with politics and Crowder. The only person I have to prove something to is myself. I asked for this case. I *demanded* it. And now that I have it, it's my responsibility to bring Jackson Wilde's killer to justice." In a softer voice, he added, "No matter who it is. That's why . . ."

"That's why what?"

"That's why I obtained a search warrant for French Silk this morning."

His statement produced a severe and gut-wrenching reaction. The thought of her personal things being handled by strangers was untenable. "You can't do that to me, Cassidy!"

"I'm sorry, Claire, but I can. I have. In fact, I'm due there now."

He hung up without saying goodbye.

As she rejoined the group for the cold buffet, she stubbornly maintained her smile and tried to act nonchalant, but apparently she didn't fool anyone.

Mary Catherine pulled her aside. "Is everything all right, dear? You seem upset."

Affectionately she squeezed her mother's hand. "I'm fine, Mama."

"The call was from Mr. Cassidy, wasn't it? Did he ask you about Reverend Wilde again?"

"No. Nothing like that. Are you having a good time? What kept you and Harry occupied this morning?"

Mary Catherine launched into a lengthy description of her activities. Claire found it difficult to concentrate on what her mother was saying. She made appropriate remarks in all the right places, but her mind was on the police search of her private property. God only knew what her employees would think. Later, she would call and assure them that the search was nothing to be alarmed about.

She executed her duties that afternoon, but her mind kept returning to the strangers in uniform who were pawing through her, Yasmine's, and Mary Catherine's bureau drawers, rifling through their official papers, rummaging through their closets, and manhandling their personal things.

She would never forgive Cassidy for this.

"Honey, do you know where my gold cuff links are?"

Alister Petrie emerged from his dressing area with his shirt-tails flapping. He and Belle were due at a campaign fund-raising dinner party in half an hour. They were running late.

He'd arrived home from his afternoon campaign speech with barely enough time to shower and change before charging out again to face another crowd of potential contributors and voters.

"They're here on my dresser."

Belle was seated on the tufted velvet stool in front of her dressing table, pulling a hairbrush through her blond page boy. It was the same page boy she'd worn since high school and was kept silky and sleek by expensive hot-oil treatments and monthly trims.

"Did you have a chance to catch me on the tube?" he asked as he approached her, buttoning his shirt.

"No, darling. I was busy getting ready for tonight. I'm sure you were a smashing success."

He reached around her for the cuff links. "Two TV stations . . ." He yanked his hand back as though it had been bitten by a cobra.

His cuff links were nestled in a tiny heap of lace that he immediately recognized. His stomach quickened. For several unendurable moments he was afraid he was going to be sick all over Belle's jars of beauty creams and bottles of perfume.

His eyes connected with hers in the mirror. Very coolly, she finished clipping on a pair of diamond earrings. "I found those in the pocket of a suit jacket I sent out to be dry cleaned. It's a *wifely* little habit of mine to check your pockets before sending things out. You should have known that and been more careful."

"Belle, I—"

"You what, Alister?" She swiveled around on the stool and gazed up at him with an expression too sweet to be sincere. "You've taken to wearing women's underwear?" She picked up the strands of elasticized lace that supported the small triangle. "What's the term for that predilection? Cross-dressing?"

Now that he had recovered from the initial shock of seeing Yasmine's g-string panties on his wife's dressing table, he started to get angry. Other men had affairs and never had to account for them. Why was he always having to play the penitent?

"Don't talk down to me, Belle."

"Well then," she said, snapping the elastic like a slingshot before letting the garment drop back onto the vanity, "the only other conclusion I can draw is that you're having an extramarital affair."

She stood up and brushed him aside. Of all her affectations, this haughty act grated on his nerves the most. With a few practiced gestures and calculated words, she could make him feel gauche and stupid and small.

He was a United States congressman, by God! No one, not even his wife, was going to humiliate him. He would never confess to having a mistress, much less beg forgiveness.

Belle withdrew a fluid chiffon dress from her closet and stepped into it, working it up and over her willowy hips. "Do me up," she said after pushing her arms through the sequined sleeves.

After he zipped the dress, she turned to face him. "I'm not stupid enough to think you're faithful to me. Of course you've had other women. You have one now and you'll have others. That's not the issue."

"Then why bring it up?" he asked belligerently. She could have discreetly disposed of the panties and avoided this ugly scene. He took heat all day from a dozen different sources. He didn't need to catch shit at home, too.

"I brought it up to point out your appalling stupidity."

Alister saw red. "Now just a goddamn minute. I—"

She held up both hands. "Spare me your righteous indignation, Alister. You can't afford it. Listen to me and heed what I say."

Her eyes narrowed. "If I found out that you're unfaithful to your wedding vows, others will find out. You've been incredibly stupid and alarmingly careless. Sooner or later the odds will catch up with you, just as I did.

"Throughout the campaign you've wooed the public well. You've cultivated a strong, solid constituency." She paused to draw a breath. "How do you think the Bible thumpers, like Jackson Wilde's followers, would regard you if it was revealed that you're an adulterer? Even dead, Wilde is a hot item. We can still use his influence. You've been vocal in your criticism of local law enforcement for failing to find his murderer. But it could all be for nothing if your Christian image was exposed as fraudulent. Are you willing to sacrifice thousands of votes for a few hours of . . ." She flipped her hand out, indicating the panties on the vanity.

"Fucking. It's called fucking, Belle." He took delight in the sudden blanching of her face and the stiffening of her spine. "And if you weren't so prissy in bed, I wouldn't—"

"Don't." She aimed her index finger at the center of his chest. "Don't turn the blame for this on me. This is your mistake, Alister. And I'm informing you now that I won't suffer the consequences of it. I like being Mrs. Alister Petrie, the congressman's wife. That's what I intend to continue being.

"But if you get caught, if you're exposed as a cheating, lying husband, don't expect me to attest to what a wonderful, loving husband and father you are. I won't be made to look a fool.

"Furthermore," she continued, lowering her voice to a more confidential pitch, "you know what it'll mean if I withdraw my financial support from your campaign." Alister felt the blood draining from his face. Belle smiled. "No one knows—yet—that were it not for my legacy, you wouldn't have won your first congressional seat. And without my contributions, you won't win this one. Think about that. The next time you get the urge to fuck—as you so charmingly phrase it—exercise your marital rights."

She tapped the front of his starched shirt with her well-manicured nail. "Making me unhappy would be extremely ill advised, Alister. End the affair. Immediately."

She came up on tiptoe and gave his lips a soft kiss. "You'd better finish dressing or we'll be late. Be sure to allow a few minutes to say good night to the children." At the bedroom door she paused and nodded toward the vanity. "And kindly dispose of those, so I never have to look at them again."

Alister was simmering, and there wasn't a damn thing he could do about it. On the surface they had a perfect marriage. As long as things went Belle's way, life was harmonious. But he suffered no delusions about her. She looked as fragile as a greenhouse orchid. But if crossed, she could be as vicious as a vampire bat.

She was too self-contained to enjoy good, earthy sex. She liked things neat and tidy, organized, well planned, and controlled. It wasn't that he had a lover that had upset her. In truth, she was probably relieved that she didn't have to be inconvenienced so often. What had angered her was the timing of the affair and his failure to conceal it. Belle wasn't running the show. That's what had her pissed.

He approached the dressing table and picked up the lace panties. Too many times his affair with Yasmine had separated him from his better judgment. He shuddered to think of some smart-ass reporter getting wind of his affair with the famous black model. But what was he supposed to do, survive only on the sterile, uninspired sex of his marriage bed? Go completely underground until after the election? It was impossible to keep a low profile during a political campaign. He was like a lightning rod for attracting attention, and he needed that constant public exposure to win voters.

The two interests were incompatible. Something had to give. He couldn't have everything.

As he fingered the lace and thought back to that bizarre afternoon in his Washington office, a smile slowly lifted his lips and he chuckled. "Who says?"

The diner was as gloomy as Cassidy's mood. It was one of those family-owned joints that offered cops a discount in return for meager protection and lousy tips. Detective Glenn had suggested it. It was his kind of place—grimy and depressing. Cassidy wished he were anywhere else, discussing any other topic than the one that had occupied them through uninspired burgers, greasy fries, soggy coconut pie, and countless cups of oily coffee.

"You know, I've been thinking," Glenn said as he lit the next in an endless chain of cigarettes. "Could be one of these gals had a thing going with Wilde. A thing of a romantic nature. Did you ever think of that?"

"No," Cassidy said, offended at hearing Claire referred to as a gal. "Whatever made you think that?"

"That Yasmine's a hot number with a string of boyfriends a mile long. Who's she seeing now? Hasn't been a romance reported in over a year. Strange, huh?"

"You think she was seeing *Wilde?*"

Glenn shrugged. "Maybe those offerings she gave him were payment of a different sort."

"You've had too much nicotine," Cassidy said sourly, fanning the polluted air in front of his face.

"Well, after what we found today, I'd believe just about anything about her." He whistled. "Pretty weird shit."

Cassidy said nothing, but continued to fiddle with the broken napkin dispenser at the end of the booth.

"And the Laurent broad didn't come off smelling like a rose, either, did she?"

"No," Cassidy replied quietly. "She didn't. But what we found still doesn't prove anything."

"No, but it's getting closer." Glenn slurped his coffee. "What'd Crowder think? You told him, didn't you?"

"Yeah, I reported back."

"And?"

"He said for us to take the ball and run with it," Cassidy mumbled reluctantly.

Chapter Sixteen

🌿 🌿

Rain threatened at Rosesharon. The high humidity took its toll on those unaccustomed to it, and tempers were short. During the morning, the clouds became more opaque and the atmosphere grew more sultry. The models who weren't needed retired to their rooms to rest in air-conditioned comfort. Since the weather was too unstable for outdoor shooting, they decided to do some interior shots utilizing the vanity table in Claire and Yasmine's bedroom.

Per Rue's suggestion, Dana was modeling the backless bra. With it she wore ivory satin tap pants, thigh-high hosiery, and ivory satin high heels. Claire had asked the Monteiths where in the nearest town she might locate a wedding gown to borrow.

"Why, we have one!" they exclaimed in unison.

Their niece had used Rosesharon for her wedding several months earlier, and the gown was still stored in their attic. They assured Claire that their niece would be flattered to have it used in the French Silk catalog. It was brought down and removed from its protective hanging bag. Luckily it wasn't stark white, so it matched the color of the sample lingerie. Rue steamed out the wrinkles, muttering all the while. "Just what we needed. More goddamn humidity."

Now the bridal gown was hanging beside the vanity table, suggesting that Dana was a bride preparing for the ceremony. The vanity had been repositioned so that the three-way mirror reflected the French doors opening onto the balcony. It would be a tricky shot to get without Leon and all his lighting equipment being reflected as well.

"I want Dana holding up her hair," Yasmine said, "so that we get a full view of the bra's construction."

The makeup artist wasn't finished with Dana's body makeup, so Yasmine asked Claire to sit on the stool while they calculated the position of the lighting in conjunction with the mirrors and camera angles.

Claire sat and faced the mirror. "I hardly look like a bride," she said, critically assessing her reflection. Her linen shirt had wilted, and she had sweated off most of her makeup. "Maybe the bride of Frankenstein."

"Lift your hair off your neck," Yasmine told her.

"Gladly." She swept her hair into a double fist, lifting it to the top of her head and keeping her elbows parallel with her shoulders.

Her eyes caught movement at the French doors. Cassidy parted the sheer curtains and stepped into the room. He drew up short. Their eyes met in the mirror.

"Perfect, Claire!" Yasmine cried. "That's perfect. That's exactly the expression I want! Did you see that, Dana? Surprised. Expectant. A little breathless." But when she looked over her shoulder and saw that Cassidy was the cause of Claire's flustered expression, her enthusiasm quickly cooled. "What are you doing here?" she asked, obviously displeased. She turned back to Claire. "Did you invite him?"

"No," she answered, her eyes fixed on the A.D.A.

Leon left the lighting to his assistant and sidled up to Cassidy, laying a hand on his arm. "And who are *you*?"

"He's a cop from New Orleans," Yasmine replied.

Cassidy smiled affably but gently disengaged his arm from Leon's clutches. "I'm not a cop."

Claire stood and motioned the model into place. "We need to get this shot. Everybody ready?"

Dana took her place on the vanity stool. Rue and the other stylists fussed around her. Yasmine went back to consulting with Leon about ways to vary the shot.

Claire, trying to hide her anger, drew Cassidy to a corner of the room. "What are you trying to pull, coming here?"

"I didn't know I was going to be on center stage when I came through the . . . uh . . . the curtains." He was momentarily distracted by Dana, who looked resplendently bridal and mouthwateringly sexy in the golden light Leon was shining on her.

"Our photography sessions are strictly off-limits to visitors," Claire said stiffly, noticing the direction of his gaze. "Parents, boyfriends, even spouses are prohibited. The restriction is enforced to protect the privacy of the models and the creative impulses of everyone else involved."

"Sorry, you'll have to make an exception this time."

"Or what?"

"Or I'll get a court order."

"Another search? Shall I tell my crew to expect a shakedown?"

He frowned and gave her a retiring look.

"How did you know where we were going to be?" she asked crossly.

"I have a whole platoon of investigators at my disposal. Finding you was a snap."

"I'm surprised the Monteiths let you in. I thought the house was closed to all but guests."

"I am a guest."

"What?" she exclaimed. When she realized she'd drawn attention to them, she lowered her voice, but still it conveyed her anger. "We were to be the only ones here. I specified that when I made the reservations."

"The Monteiths had one extra room. My credentials persuaded them into letting me have it."

"I don't want you here, Cassidy."

"No, I'm sure you don't. Especially since I've come with bad news."

She folded her arms across her middle. "That's all you've ever brought me. Well, what is it? Let's get it over with."

He glanced over his shoulder. The others were busy or pretending to be. Like Claire, he must have felt inhibited by them. He drew her out into the hallway for more privacy.

Staring down at the patterned rug, he whispered her name with what sounded like regret, then raised his head and looked at her. "Did you know she practices voodoo?"

"Who, Yasmine?" He nodded, and Claire made a small, assenting motion with her shoulders. "A lot of people in New Orleans have a passing acquaintance with it. After spending so much time there, she developed an interest. She's got some voodoo charms, a few candles that represent—"

"Her room at French Silk was full of all kinds of black-magic crap."

"It doesn't mean anything. Since I've known her, she's dabbled in every religion from Judaism to Buddhism. She sometimes wears a Christian cross and has a bracelet with an Egyptian ankh on it. Those symbols hold no significance for her."

"This goes beyond trinkets and costume jewelry, Claire. They also found a voodoo doll, an effigy of Jackson Wilde."

"It's meaningless!" she cried softly, not wanting to attract the attention of the others. "Is that all they found? You could hardly build a murder case around a silly doll."

"They didn't find anything at French Silk, either in the

offices or the apartment, that could directly link you to Wilde's murder.''

Slowly, so as not to reveal her relief, she exhaled a pent-up breath. "I could have told you they wouldn't, but you wouldn't have believed me.''

"Wait.''

"Ah, there's more,'' she said. "The bad news.''

His eyes seemed to pierce straight through her skull. "The fiber samples from your car's carpet match some that were vacuumed out of Jackson Wilde's hotel room. The tests were conclusive. You've been lying to me, Claire. Damn you, you were *there*!''

Josh tapped on the bathroom door. "Ariel, are you all right?'' The sound of her retching had summoned him from his adjoining hotel room in Tulsa. "Ariel,'' he called, knocking sharply. "Open the door.''

He heard the commode flush. Seconds later Ariel unlocked the door and pulled it open. "God knows I've got precious little privacy, Josh. I would appreciate some while I'm in my own bathroom.''

Even though he'd watched her deteriorate over the last several weeks, he was shocked by her appearance. Her eyes were ringed with dark circles that he was afraid weren't makeup. Her cheeks were sunken, making her face look cadaverous. When she turned her back on him, he noticed her shoulder blades poking out the fabric of her dress.

"You're making yourself sick.'' He followed her to her closet, where she began rifling through the clothes, obviously trying to decide what to wear for the two local television news shows and the newspaper interview that were scheduled for later that day.

"I'm fine except for a headache, which your lecturing is only making worse."

"Eating a well-rounded meal would help your headache."

"I ate like a pig last night."

"And then came in and threw it up."

She shot him an angry glance as she removed a dress from the closet and tossed it onto the bed.

"Ariel, eat something," he pleaded. "You need the nourishment. You've got a hectic day planned."

"Stop nagging me."

"You need to eat."

"I ate!"

She flung her hand toward the room-service tray. He inspected it. The salad lunch was intact except for the coffee. "Coffee isn't a meal."

"I'd like to change now," she said impatiently. "As you said, this afternoon's schedule is hectic."

"Cancel it."

She gaped at him as though he'd sprouted horns. "What?"

"Call off the schedule and spend the remainder of the day in bed."

"Are you crazy? I can't do that."

"You mean you won't."

"All right, I won't. I want that auditorium filled to capacity tonight. I want people outside clamoring to get in so they can pray with us."

Josh swore under his breath. "Ariel, this is insane. We've been on the road for ten days. Interviews during the day, followed by prayer meetings that last for hours. Traveling all night to the next city so it can start again the following day. You're running yourself ragged."

"This trip is getting results."

"It's physically exhausting us."

"If you can't stand the heat—"

"This has nothing to do with that mess in New Orleans, does it? You're not staging these silly prayer meeting to spur the police into action. You're conducting them for your self-image. This isn't a holy mission we're on. This is an ego trip. *Your* ego trip, Ariel.''

"So what if it is?" she shouted. "Aren't you reaping the benefits too? I don't see you complaining whenever the TV cameras focus on you playing the piano. Would your piddling talent get that kind of media exposure if it weren't for me and my ingenuity? Huh? Answer me.''

"I've got more than 'piddling talent.'''

She snorted unflatteringly. "Is that so? That wasn't Jackson's opinion. I felt sorry for you whenever he'd start in on his no-talent son. Now I'm beginning to believe he was right.''

"What do you mean?"

She turned away. "We'll be late.''

"What do you mean?" he shouted.

Her face turned ugly with malice. "Only that your daddy was embarrassed to have you on the stage with us. I couldn't count the times he told me that the only reason he kept you up there was because you're his only son. What else could he do, fire you and hire someone with more flash and charisma like he wanted to do? He always told me that you were virtually worthless to him. You didn't have a head for business, you weren't a riveting speaker, and you had no leadership qualities. He was glad you'd taught yourself how to play a few songs on the piano so you wouldn't have to sack groceries at the Piggly Wiggly for a living.''

Before he realized what he was doing, his hands were closing around her skinny throat. "You lying bitch. You're a goddamn liar.'' He shook her hard while pressing his thumbs against her larynx.

Ariel reached up and clawed at his hands, but his long, strong fingers didn't relax. "Daddy knew I had talent and it scared him. He thought that if I pursued my dreams, I might become greater, more famous, than he was.''

"Let—me—go," she choked.

Suddenly Josh's vision cleared and he saw his stepmother's eyes bulging from their darkly ringed sockets. He released her so abruptly that she reeled against the dresser before catching her balance. Coughing and gasping, she stared at him contemptuously. "You're insane."

Josh's breathing was almost as labored as hers. The latent violence that had unexpectedly erupted frightened him. "He did this to us," he said in a slow, rasping voice. "He's still doing it to us. It's like the bastard isn't even dead."

Again he reached for Ariel and turned her around. With his hand splayed over the back of her head, he pushed her face to within inches of the mirror. "Look! Look at yourself. You look like a ghoul. He's doing this to you, and you're letting him. He's the reason you're starving yourself to death. Now tell me who's crazy."

Disgusted with himself as much as with her, he left her staring at her skeletal image in the mirror.

After lunch, the crew set up on Rosesharon's screened back porch. As a prop, they were using an antique hand-crank ice cream freezer that someone had come across in the Monteiths' detached garage. The blue paint on the wooden tub was chipped and pealing. The rusty metal strips holding the vertical slats together had stained the exposed wood. The freezer was no longer usable, but everyone agreed that it made a terrific prop.

The model, Liz, was seated on a milking stool, wearing a long white batiste nightgown that had a row of tiny buttons extending from the scooped neckline to the deep flounce at midcalf. The first several buttons were undone, and the skirt was bunched in her lap, well above her thighs, which were parted to accommodate the ice cream freezer. The impression Claire wanted to convey was that Liz was laboring over the freezer while Kurt reclined in the white macramé hammock in the background.

"It's sexist," Yasmine said.

"Not if it looks like she's enjoying it," Claire argued.

"It looks like doo-doo," Leon whined petulantly, as he adjusted the focus rings of his camera. "It's not hot enough."

"It's the only damn thing that isn't." Rue coughed and lit a cigarette. "Jesus, how do human beings survive down here? Have they ever even *seen* autumn leaves?"

"Maybe Liz needs some perspiration," the makeup lady ventured shyly.

"And I can spritz her hair with water," the stylist offered. "Make it look sweaty."

"Let's try it."

"For God's sake, hurry. I'm positively melting," Leon said.

"It would help if you took off that godawful shirt," Yasmine told him snidely. He was wearing a long-sleeved flamingo-pink silk shirt.

"But this is one of my best colors."

"The color gives 'putrid' a bad name."

"You bitch. You wouldn't know fashion if it—"

"Please, you two," Claire said wearily. "Let's try to get this shot done."

"I'm going to have these impressions on my buns for life," Kurt complained as he shifted uncomfortably in the hammock.

It had been decided several minutes earlier that he should appear as an indistinct form in the hammock, with only one strong, tanned leg dangling over the side. He was naked, save for his lap, which was covered with a towel that would be removed when they began taking pictures.

"Bear with us, Kurt."

"Did you mean that as a pun?" Rue asked.

Liz's hair had been lightly misted and was now clinging to

her neck and chest in damp, spiraling tendrils. "I like that much better," Claire told the hair stylist. "Thanks."

The makeup artist was misting Liz's face and upper body to simulate a healthy sheen of perspiration. "Hmm," Liz sighed. "That feels good."

"Yes, yes, this is much improved," Leon cried. "This is looking great. Oh, yes. I'm *feeling* it now."

"Give us a glimpse of cleavage, Liz," Yasmine said.

The model leaned forward as though applying herself to the hand crank of the ice cream freezer. "Oooh! Perfect!" Leon squealed.

"Wait," Claire ordered. "We've got nipples." The cool misting of water had caused the model's nipples to peak beneath the fabric of the gown.

"So what?" Theatrically Leon lowered his camera, annoyed by the interruption.

"I don't want them projecting," Claire said. "Give them time to relax."

"You show nipples all the time."

"Under the bras, they're relaxed."

"We've had projecting nipples before," Yasmine said.

"She's right. You have," Leon said. "I should know. I took the goddamn pictures."

"Under opaque fabrics, jutting nipples are fine," Claire explained calmly. "But this looks vulgar. I can detect outline and color, and I don't like it. I don't want it to look like we photographed a wet T-shirt contest."

"You've got a naked man there!" Leon protested in a shrill voice that threatened to shatter the Monteith family crystal.

"But he's only an illusion. He's suggestive without being lewd." Claire kept her voice carefully controlled. "This argument is over."

"Oh, for Christ's sake," Leon muttered. "When did you turn into Miss Goody Two-Shoes?"

"Since Jackson Wilde," Yasmine said drolly.

Claire whipped around, confronting her friend with astonishment and anger. "What a ridiculous thing to say, Yasmine! Wilde was never the barometer by which I gauged what was tasteful and what wasn't. He certainly wasn't my conscience. You know that."

"All I know is, you haven't been the same since he was found dead. Relax. He can't point the finger at you any longer."

Her friend's insensitive remarks infuriated Claire, especially since Cassidy was within hearing. She had broken her strict rule and let him watch from the periphery of the sets, thinking that maybe if she revealed to him this aspect of her life, he would stop probing other areas of it. His presence seemed not to faze anyone except her. He kept her nervous and on edge, although she performed her duties as competently as ever.

She sensed his ears pricking up at Yasmine's remark, but when she glanced at him, his expression remained impassive and didn't hint at what he might be thinking.

Cantankerously she said, "Just take the pictures, Leon, and wrap this one."

They finished within a half-hour and the subdued group began to scatter. Claire said in an undertone to Yasmine, "I'd like to see you in our room as soon as possible."

Five minutes later, Yasmine opened the bedroom door and strode in. "I know you're pissed."

Claire had passed the intervening minutes sitting against the carved rosewood headboard of one of the the twin beds. Behind her back she had stacked pillows stuffed into snowy linen pillowcases that smelled cleanly of Tide and starch. She lowered her clipboard to her lap and removed her eyeglasses.

"Under the circumstances, Yasmine, I thought your remarks about Jackson Wilde's death were uncalled for and in bad taste."

One of Yasmine's perfect eyebrows arched. "Who gives a shit about him or what I said about him?"

"Assistant District Attorney Cassidy gives a shit." Claire

tossed her clipboard aside and swung her legs to the edge of the bed. "I wish you hadn't sounded so flippant about Wilde's murder, or so relieved that he's no longer around to hound us."

"You can't possibly think that a remark, spoken as a joke, could influence Cassidy's opinion on your guilt or innocence?"

Claire declined to answer. Finally she looked up at Yasmine and said gravely, "That's not really why I'm angry with you."

Claire then told her about the conversation she'd had with her business attorney the night before she'd left for Mississippi. The instant his name was mentioned, Yasmine's eyes flashed angrily.

"That weasely bastard. I told him not to tell you."

"Then it's true? You asked him to persuade me to let our stock go public so you could sell your shares?"

"It was worth a shot. I've got to unload my stock. That's the only way I can do it."

"The only way?" Claire cried. "You could have come to me."

"Hat in hand, admitting that I'm broke?"

"Dammit, Yasmine, I've known for months that you're broke."

"Oh, great." The former model dropped to the edge of the other twin bed, looking rebellious and hostile.

Claire softened her tone. "It's nothing to be ashamed of. You're overextended, that's all. It happens to everybody at one time or another. I'll gladly loan you some money until things turn around."

"You're the last person I'd ask for money."

"Why?"

"Because you already carry this business. No, don't start throwing up objections. You do, Claire. You brought it from inception to where it is. You do the lion's share of the work. You're the brains behind it."

"And you're the beauty. My small company would have stayed small if not for your endorsement."

Yasmine shrugged as though her contributions amounted to nothing. "This time a year ago, I was rolling in dough. I guess I thought it would never run out. I mismanaged my money, turned it over to 'financial advisers' who probably screwed me out of half of it."

"You threw it away on lost causes like that thousand-dollar offering to Jackson Wilde."

Yasmine raised her hands in surrender. "Guilty. Anyway, I'm down to double zeros. That's why I hoped I could put my shares of French Silk on the auction block."

Claire shook her head. "I'll never go public. If you insist on selling your shares, I'll buy them."

"And obligate me to you."

"I don't look at it that way. It's self-preservation. You know how possessive I am when it comes to my business."

"I know, I know," Yasmine said irascibly. "Jesus, do you think it was easy for me to approach that fat-mouthed lawyer? I never would have except that I'm in dire need of cash. I've sold my last fur coat and all my good jewelry. Those shares are all I have left to liquidate."

"You could use them as collateral to borrow from me."

"I said no, all right?"

"I don't understand—"

Yasmine vaulted off the bed. "Don't harp on me, Claire. I won't borrow from you, but I'll sell you the bloody stocks. Okay? Can we cap it off now? I'll have some cash, and the company will be saved. Hallelujah and amen! That's the last I want to hear of it because I've got another crisis in my life right now."

"That's no excuse for going behind my back and against my wishes. We've all got problems." She flattened her hand against her chest. "I've been accused of murder."

"By Cassidy?" Yasmine snorted. "He hasn't got anything on you."

"They've matched the carpeting in my car to fibers found in Wilde's hotel room."

Yasmine looked surprised. "Since when?"

"Since they got a warrant to search French Silk."

"*What!*"

"Yes. They found some nasty voodoo stuff in your room, Yasmine, including a doll that looks like Wilde."

"That was a joke!"

"That's what I told Cassidy. He didn't think it was funny."

"Come to think of it, I didn't see him crack a smile all afternoon."

"He believes that I was in Jackson Wilde's hotel suite the night he died. Those carpet fibers place me there."

"How many cars with carpet exactly like yours are in Orleans Parish? Dozens, if not hundreds, right?"

"I'm sure that's the only reason why Cassidy didn't arrest me this afternoon," Claire told her. "He said a good defense attorney would have statistics about all those Chrysler products and how many potential murderers that adds up to." She walked toward the balcony doors. "I'm afraid, Yasmine."

"Balls. You've never been afraid of anything. Not in the time I've known you."

"I am now."

"Of Cassidy?"

"He's part of it. Mostly I'm afraid of not having control over this situation. That's the scariest feeling there is—that you've lost control of your destiny."

"Relax, Claire. Cassidy's not going to put you in jail."

"Oh yes he will," she said with a mirthless laugh. "When he believes he's got enough evidence to get a grand-jury indictment, he'll have me arrested."

"Before or after he fucks you?" Claire looked at Yasmine with stunned surprise. Yasmine shrugged. "The man wants you so bad he's in pain. At any given moment, he looks ready to pounce."

"And read me my rights."

"Uh-uh," Yasmine said, shaking her head. "He wants you on your back, or whatever, moving with him." Before Claire could offer an argument, she continued, "Look, I had my first man when I was thirteen. When you start that early, you develop a sixth sense about these things. I can smell when a man wants it. I know when a woman is ready to give it to him. And you're both ripe to bursting. He walks into a room, and your aura goes neon . . . and vice versa. The sex vibes are so thick, they pollute the air."

"Cassidy bid for the Wilde murder case. He was assigned to it because he's good. A conviction will make him a strong contender for the D.A.'s office. The vibes you sensed coming from him are animosity, not lust," Claire argued. "He's irritated with me for not making his job easier. As soon as he turns up something that places me in that room with Jackson Wilde, he'll do everything within his power to prove me guilty."

"But we know you're not, don't we?"

For several seconds they held each other's stare across the room. Inside Claire's head, her heartbeat was as loud as a pile driver. She felt dizzy.

Finally she said, "I'll draft a check for one-fourth of your shares. That'll give you some ready cash, but you'll still retain a partnership in French Silk. If it becomes feasible, you can buy the stock back for the amount I paid."

"Thanks," Yasmine said, unsmiling.

"Thank me by not going behind my back again."

His fountain pen was missing.

When he put on his jacket for dinner, Cassidy noticed that the gold engraved pen—a gift from his parents upon his graduation from law school—was missing. He kept it in the left breast pocket of his coat and was rarely without it.

He searched the top of the bureau in his bedroom, thinking

he might have overlooked the pen lying among the loose change and other pocket accessories. But it wasn't there. He searched through the pockets of his other jackets, to no avail. He was positive he hadn't left it anywhere. He never loaned it and conscientiously returned it to his pocket after each use.

He mentally retraced every place the jacket had been since he had put it on that morning. Because of the stifling, unseasonable heat, he'd left it hanging on a coat tree in the foyer when he went for a walk around the grounds of Rosesharon shortly after lunch.

Had someone stolen his pen? Why? Among the people at Rosesharon, he couldn't think of one who was likely to rifle through another person's pockets in search of treasure. The staff? He couldn't imagine the Monteiths tolerating thievery among their employees, all of whom seemed dedicated to their guests' comfort and contentment.

The pen was only moderately valuable, but he deeply regretted the loss for sentimental reasons. As he descended the staircase to join Claire's group for dinner, he was as upset as he was befuddled.

Two of the models were loitering at the mini wet bar, a twentieth-century addition to the original house. He squeezed between them to pour himself a Chivas on the rocks. "Don't forget to mark it down," the stunning brunette said.

"No, I won't."

"Are you an honest cop or a dirty cop?" her leggy blond companion asked teasingly.

"I'm not a cop." He smiled engagingly.

"Hmm," she hummed skeptically, while tapping her front tooth with her fingernail. Then she pulled her finger through her glossy, pouty lips. "I'd bet you could get dirty."

He clinked his glass with hers. "And you'd be right."

To their disappointment, he excused himself and worked his way toward Yasmine, who was standing at one of the windows, staring out across the veranda to the lawn, where the shadows were long and deep. "Nice place."

He got the full drop-dead treatment from her tiger eyes. "If you're that trite with a jury, it's a wonder you ever win any cases, Mr. Cassidy."

"I was only trying to make polite conversation."

"Spare me."

He sipped his scotch. "Are those bad vibes I get from you intentional?"

"I don't like cops."

He ground his jaw and succinctly repeated, "I'm not a cop."

"Same as."

She was an incredibly gorgeous woman. Even standing this close, he couldn't find a flaw in either her face or her form, and continuing to look for one would be an endless pleasure. But he didn't like her. She had an attitude, the kind of arrogance that couldn't be punctured with threats, cajolery, or flattery, the kind he hated to cross-examine on the witness stand. If she chose to lie, dynamite wouldn't shake the truth out of her.

Using the kind of language he knew would draw a response, he asked, "What burr got up your ass?"

"You, for one. Why don't you lay off Claire?"

"Because she may have killed a man."

"Yeah, right. And I'm one of the Seven Dwarfs."

"You don't think she did it?"

Yasmine made a scoffing sound.

"Then that brings me to you. You had just as much motivation as she. Maybe I'm not here to watch Claire at all. Maybe I'm here to keep an eye on you."

Her beautiful lips broke into a wide smile. Propping one hand on her hip, she thrust out her chest and tossed her head like a proud filly. "Well, here I am, sugar. Look your fill."

He chuckled. "You differ from Claire there. She wants me to keep blinders on."

"I don't care if you look till your eyeballs bleed, I just don't want you lurking around bothering Claire. You get on her nerves."

"Did she tell you that?"

"She didn't have to. I know her. Besides her mother, the thing she loves best is French Silk. She's a perfectionist. These shooting sessions are tense and tiresome enough without her getting into a tizzy on account of you."

"Claire doesn't seem to me the kind of woman who gets into tizzies."

"You don't know her the way I do. She never loses her cool. But she simmers, and the coals burn hot until——" She stopped.

He raised a quizzical eyebrow. "Well? Until what?"

"Never mind."

"What was said during your summit conference this afternoon? Did you have words over your remark about Jackson Wilde?"

"Wouldn't you love to know?"

"Yes, I would."

"Go fuck yourself, Cassidy."

He saluted her with his highball glass. "Spoken like you mean it."

"Count on it, sugar. Right now the whole male population is on my shit list."

"Oh? What'd we do?"

"You drew breath." Having said that, she tossed back the remainder of her wine.

"Dinner!" Grace Monteith rang a little bell as she slid open the doors to the dining room.

Cassidy had arranged it so that he was seated across the table from Claire. Although the models were young and lovely and would have made any setting a visual feast, they seemed insubstantial when compared to Claire Laurent—the difference between grape Kool-Aid and the hearty burgundy that Agnes Monteith was pouring into his wineglass.

As he ate his plate of pot roast and vegetables, he assessed his dinner companions, wondering who among them had taken his pen. He was convinced that it had been stolen, probably out of sheer meanness.

Among the three stylists, none looked sneaky enough to pilfer an engraved fountain pen. The models? They'd all been busy that afternoon. It was unlikely that one had had time to rifle through his pockets. And why would one want to?

He had ample opportunity to observe everyone without drawing notice, because Leon dominated the conversation, while his assistant ate neatly and silently at his side.

"I love the old seesaw on the west lawn," Leon said while slathering butter on a yeast roll. "We must do something on the seesaw."

"How about leggings?" Claire suggested.

"Tremendous," Leon gushed. "So good for straddling. The seesaw, that is." He giggled, then sobered while chewing industriously. "Although, I love the idea of contrasting something silk against those rough, rotting boards. Hmm. I'll think about it. While exploring, did anyone else run across that outdoor shower?"

"That was installed for field hands to use after they came in from picking cotton," Grace supplied as she passed around dessert.

"I've got dibs on a shot using that shower," Yasmine announced. "But my idea's a secret."

"I gotta smoke," Rue said, leaving the table to go out onto the veranda. "You girls had better stop stuffing in this rich food or your guts will be poking out tomorrow." No one paid her any attention.

"First thing in the morning," Leon said, "I want the model who's going to wear that long, sheer nightgown—"

"Felicia," Yasmine told him.

"Felicia dear, you get first call tomorrow."

"Shit," Felicia muttered into her caramel custard.

"I want the morning sunlight backlighting her." Leon held his hands in front of his face and formed right angles with his thumbs as though looking through a frame. "We might get lucky and have natural dew. If not, this dear lady has offered to turn on the sprinkler for us." As Agnes poured him a cup of coffee, he caught her hand and kissed the back of it. "Either way, the grass will be wet and sparkly. I see it absolutely glistening. I want the hem of the nightgown to be damp and trailing. Maybe falling off one shoulder. A peek of booby."

"Kurt could be lounging in the background," Yasmine suggested. "Like on the veranda, with his hair down and wearing only a pair of pajama bottoms."

"I love it," Leon squealed. "Don't shave in the morning, Kurt. I just adore those shots that suggest postcoital scenes. Oh, my dear Agnes, your cheeks are positively fiery. Forgive me for being so blunt. Do you think I'm terribly naughty?"

Cassidy, rolling his eyes at the affectation, happened to glance at Claire. She was suppressing her laughter. They exchanged a smile. Even among so many people, it was a private moment.

He immediately squelched the tenderness welling through his midsection. If Claire weren't his prime suspect, he'd be trying his damnedest to get her into his bed. He knew it. So did Crowder. So, probably, did she. Hell, he'd told her as much.

No more private moments, he sternly told himself. *Not even shared looks across the dinner table*.

The Monteiths encouraged them to take their coffee into the double parlors or out onto the veranda, where it was cooler since the sun had set.

Cassidy followed Claire. She paused at the staircase to speak to Mary Catherine and Harry, who were ready to retire to their room. "I'll be up to say good night when you're tucked in," Claire promised.

"Good night, Mr. Cassidy."

"Good night, Miss Laurent, Miss York."

Smiling sweetly, Mary Catherine turned to go upstairs.

Cassidy held the front door open for Claire and they strolled across the deep porch to the railing. Claire sat down on it and sipped the fragrant coffee. "Well, what do you think of us?"

"Interesting," he said.

"How diplomatic."

He wondered if he should alert her that one among her associates was a thief but decided against it. One allegation at a time. He'd already informally accused her of murder.

"You're staring, Cassidy," she said quietly.

"I'm thinking about something Glenn said last night." He noticed Claire's shudder at the mention of the detective's name, but he forged ahead. "It had crossed his mind that maybe Yasmine was Jackson Wilde's lover."

"*What!*" Her cup clattered against the saucer. She set them on the railing. "Your friend is losing touch with reality, Cassidy. If you're thinking along the same lines, so are you."

"It's not so farfetched."

She gazed up at him with incredulity. "Do you ever think before you spout this nonsense? Listen to what you're saying."

Now that he had spoken the theory aloud, it did sound ridiculous, but he pursued it so he could assure Glenn that he'd done so. Besides, you never knew where a blind alley might lead.

"Yasmine has men in general on her shit list. She told me so herself."

"So that makes Jackson Wilde her lover?" she said. "He was Yasmine's enemy as much as he was mine."

"On the surface."

"You think they were carrying on in secret?"

"Possibly."

"Ludicrous. Anyway, she was in New York the night he was killed."

"You're sure?"

"I picked her up the following morning at the airport."

"Could be she was acting out a charade."

"You're grasping at straws, Cassidy."

"Does she have a current lover?"

"I don't see what—"

"Does she?"

"Yes," Claire snapped.

"Who? What's his name?"

"I don't know."

"Bullshit!"

"I swear I don't!"

He looked at her hard and decided that she was telling the truth. "Why the secrecy? Is he married?"

"All I know is that she's devoted to him," she said evasively. "So that shoots your harebrained theory about her and Jackson Wilde all to hell. They never even met."

"You're sure about that, too?"

"Absolutely. She would have told me."

"Right. She doesn't lie and keep secrets, like you." He stepped closer to her. "Maybe you had a thing going with Wilde." The features of her face became taut with anger. She tried to stand, but he placed his hand on her shoulder and pushed her back to the railing. "A well-publicized skirmish would be mutually satisfying for him and you. Maybe you got together and cooked up this little scam."

"Who thought of this, you or Detective Glenn?"

Ignoring her question, he pressed on. "You gave Wilde a cause to crusade against, a cause that created a groundswell across the nation and made him a celebrity preacher."

"In exchange for free advertising for French Silk, I suppose."

"Exactly. You admitted to me that his sermons were actually good for your business, not the other way around."

"Then why would I kill him and put a stop to such a good thing?"

"Maybe you found out you weren't the only one he'd worked a deal with. Maybe he had a whole legion of women—a different broad for every sin."

"You're sick."

"Maybe the love affair went sour. Was your 'offering' to him a blackmail payment? Did you arrange to meet him while he was in New Orleans and work out a payment schedule? Only you decided to end it then and there." She managed to stand and tried to go around him, but he sidestepped and blocked her path. "Where'd you meet Jackson Wilde?"

Flinging back her head, she glared up at him. "I've told you. I met him only once, during the invitation he extended following his sermon in the Superdome."

"And you lied about that. While he was laying hands on you and granting eternal life, did he whisper his hotel-room number in your ear?" He took her arm in a firm grip. "You had a collection of clippings, Claire, documenting his whereabouts for years. He didn't fart without you knowing about it. That's obsessive behavior."

"I explained those clippings."

"It doesn't wash."

"Well I certainly wasn't his lover."

"You're not sleeping with anyone else."

"How do you know?"

Her question hung between them like the reverberation of clashed swords. The air crackled with animosity and suppressed passion.

Finally Claire said, "Excuse me, Mr. Cassidy."

She went around him and slipped through the screen door.

Chapter Seventeen

❧ ❧

Ariel collapsed during the prayer service being held in Kansas City's Kemper Arena.

For half an hour she had held the capacity crowd spellbound. Garbed in white and spotlighted in the otherwise darkened arena so that her hair looked like a shimmering halo, her arms raised beseechingly toward heaven, she had created the illusion of a forsaken angel pleading to be called home.

One moment, her voice had been raised in supplication, her body quivering with fervency; the next, she lay crumpled on the stage. At first Josh thought she had taken her act one step beyond her usual theatrics. Mentally he congratulated her on her thespian instincts and skill. The audience, as one voice, gasped when her small form was swallowed by the voluminous white robe that mushroomed around her like a deflating parachute.

But when several seconds passed and she didn't move, Josh stood, scraping back his piano bench. The closer he got to her, the faster he moved. Either the spotlight was leeching all the color from her face or she was alarmingly anemic. He knelt beside her, anxiously calling her name. When he tried to lift her into a sitting position, she lay as limp as a ragdoll in his arms, her head lolling to one side. This was no act.

"She's unconscious! Somebody call 911! Get an ambulance here at once. Ariel! Ariel!" He slapped her smartly on the cheeks. She didn't respond. He searched for a pulse in her absurdly slender wrist. He felt a heartbeat, but it was feeble. "Move back and give her some air," he ordered those who had clambered forward to offer assistance.

Everyone in the arena was on his feet, creating a din so loud that Josh couldn't hear himself think. Some were praying, some were weeping, some were merely gawking. He told one of the program coordinators to order everybody to leave. "The show's over."

All Josh's efforts to revive Ariel failed. She didn't respond until the paramedics arrived and began their preliminary examination. "What happened?" she mumbled as she began to come around.

"You collapsed," Josh explained. "The ambulance is here to take you to the hospital. You'll be all right."

"Ambulance?" She weakly tried to fight off the paramedics when they strapped her onto the gurney. As they wheeled her to the waiting ambulance, she protested that she was fine and didn't need to go to the hospital.

"You have any idea what caused this?" one of the paramedics asked Josh, who insisted on accompanying them in the ambulance. "Is she diabetic?"

"Not that I know of. I think she's exhausted and depleted. She throws up everything she eats."

The paramedic took her blood pressure and reported his findings to the attending doctor in the emergency room of St. Luke's Hospital. The doctor ordered an IV, but by the time they reached the hospital, Ariel still looked near death. She hadn't regained her color, her lips were chalky, and her eyes were deeply sunken into their sockets. She was immediately wheeled into an examination room from which Josh was barred entrance.

He had plenty of responsibilities to occupy him. Videotape of Ariel's collapse had been broadcast as a news bulletin. Reporters, photographers, and sympathizers converged on the hospital in such numbers that a police barricade had to be erected. Unaccustomed as he was to public speaking, Josh made a moving, impromptu speech to the cameras and microphones.

"Mrs. Wilde has been exhausting herself in her efforts to seek justice for my father's murder. The doctors here have given me every reason to be optimistic. As soon as I know more, I'll share it with you. Please pray for her."

As he sipped vending-machine coffee and waited for information on her condition, Josh tried to assimilate his feelings. Only a few days ago, he'd been angry enough with Ariel to try to kill her. Now, he feared she might not survive. What if she was no longer capable of ramrodding the ministry? What if it dissolved? What would he do with the rest of his life?

He supposed he could get a job with a dance band and be condemned for life to playing at bar mitzvahs and VFW dances. He could go on the lounge circuit and make the rounds of the Holiday Inns. On that dismal thought, he pushed his fingers through his hair and bent his head over his knees in a posture of prayer. "Christ."

He hated the circus the ministry had become, but he sure as hell liked the public exposure it provided him. Ariel was right about that. Even though he despised the hypocrisy of the ministry, it had given him an opportunity to play piano almost nightly. It was steady employment, and to a musician that was a luxury. His audience was loyal and generous. Playing for them, hearing their applause, had given him a self-confidence that he hadn't found anywhere else. He thrived on that approval, even if it was token. Without it, he would die. Or wish to.

What would he do if his showcase collapsed along with Ariel?

"Mr. Wilde?"

"Yes?" The doctor was young and attractive and looked like she should be teaching kindergarten students rather than working the emergency room of a large city hospital. "How is she? Is she going to be all right?"

"Mrs. Wilde was beginning to develop an eating disorder called bulimia, but I think we've caught it in time. She seems to have been in good health before she began the binge/vomit cycle. With counseling and a proper diet, the trend can be reversed. I don't believe it'll permanently damage her health or that of the baby."

Josh went very still and stared at her blankly. "Baby?"

"That's right," the doctor said with a smile. "Your stepmother is pregnant."

Claire Louise Laurent had never experienced jealousy. During her childhood there had never been anything or anyone to make her feel jealous. She'd had no rivals for her mother's love and attention.

She had a healthy self-esteem, which was miraculous considering her unorthodox childhood. She had always been satisfied with her persona and never wished to be someone else. She competed only with herself, always striving for self-improvement without measuring her appearance, possessions, or accomplishments against those of others.

So when this emotion crept up and encompassed her like a fog, she was shocked and shamed by it. Especially since the object of her jealousy was Yasmine.

"This is positively marvelous." Leon breathed the words reverently as though, through his viewfinder, he were witness to a holy miracle. "You're the absolute best, darling. Always were. There'll never be another Yasmine."

"You got it, sugar." She spoke to him over her shoulder while sassily wagging her rear.

The clouds that had threatened rain the day before had disappeared, and, while dark thunderheads were still silhouetted against the horizon, the sun was currently beating down on Rosesharon and the crew collected around the outdoor shower. The temperature was in the high eighties with a humidity to match. Claire blamed her foul mood on the unrelenting, muggy heat, but knew that wasn't the real cause.

Yasmine had kept her brainstorm a secret up to the hour they were ready to shoot. "I want to wear these." She had produced a pair of white, sheer cotton pajamas.

"I wondered what had happened to those," Claire remarked.

"I had them hidden." The two-piece set of white boxers and top didn't look like an item that Yasmine would ordinarily choose. She preferred to model the glamorous garments.

"Aren't they sort of plain for you?"

"Not the way I'm going to use them," Yasmine purred, flashing a wicked grin.

"How's that?"

"Meet me at that old outdoor shower and I'll show you."

Well, her secret is out now, Claire thought sourly as she watched Yasmine strike a series of poses while Leon clicked off picture after picture, keeping his assistant juggling cameras, lenses, and lights.

Yasmine had discarded the pajama top altogether and rolled up the legs of the boxers until they fit tightly around her upper thighs at the crotch. She struck her first pose standing beneath the shower head with her back to the camera. Then she turned on the spout. Water sparkled on her mane of black hair. It glistened on her arms, which she used as gracefully as a ballerina to strike one stunning pose after another. Water trickled down her smooth back in silky rivulets. By now the boxer shorts were soaked and clinging to her taut buttocks. The fabric was plastered to hollows and curves that were sleek, sinuous, and sexy. She was in full command of her body. It was the machine she worked with and was conditioned to perform with optimum precision.

Claire wanted to protest the overt sexiness of the shots, as she had done about the model's prominent nipples the day before. But her motives for wanting to start an argument were different. The fact was, Yasmine looked like a work of art. Such perfection of form could never be labeled obscene. The image she created was erotic, yes, but not pornographic. It was a celebration of human sensuality, not propaganda for moral decay. And since a close-up of the pajamas would be shown in a small box photo beside the large one, Claire couldn't complain that the item would be misrepresented in the catalog.

Not everyone would look as spectacular as Yasmine did in the pajamas, but the fantasy of doing so would sell them by the thousands. Claire would no doubt be applauding Yasmine's inspiration like the rest of the crew were it not for Cassidy, who was gaping at Yasmine like a star-struck, sex-crazed adolescent.

Claire was hot, angry, nervous, distracted, and jealous, and it was all his fault. He was responsible for this unwelcome, juvenile resentment churning inside her.

She should order him to leave the set. But he would demand to know why, and if she said that he was bothering everybody, all the others would deny it, and that would be tantamount to admitting that his presence was aggravating only to her.

Yasmine was undeniably gorgeous, but Claire had never been jealous of her before. Yasmine cultivated her image of savage sexiness, which Claire had always found amusing if she thought of it at all. It certainly had never sparked envy. Yasmine was merely being Yasmine as she stretched and postured for the camera. She was in her element. She wasn't deliberately trying to entice Cassidy.

"You like it, Claire?" Yasmine called over her shoulder.

"Yes," she said dispassionately. "It's very nice."

Yasmine lowered her arms and turned around. She didn't bother to cover her bare breasts. " 'Nice'? It's not supposed to be nice."

"What's it supposed to be?"

"Well for damn sure not *nice*. It's supposed to be attention-getting and arousing. It's supposed to sell these goddamn pajamas, which, frankly, I think are the most lackluster design you've ever come up with. They've got no style, no class, no nothing. I'm trying to put some zing into an item that otherwise would be a major flop."

Yasmine's speech was delivered with such antipathy that it silenced even Leon. A strained hush fell over the set. Even Rue, who collected sarcastic gems to toss out at the most inopportune times, smoked in silence while everyone else found something other than Claire and Yasmine to focus on. They'd heard them clash before, but never to this degree.

Claire's chest felt close to cracking from internal pressure, but she turned to Leon and asked calmly, "Have you got all the shots you need?"

"I think so. Unless you think we need more." He was being uncharacteristically obsequious and soft-spoken, as though afraid he might detonate an explosion.

"I trust your judgment, Leon."

"Then I'm finished."

"Okay. Thanks, everybody. That's it for today. See you at dinner."

Claire turned her back on them and headed for the house. She walked at a fast clip, wanting only to reach the cool, dim privacy of her room, where she could nurse her jealousy in solitude.

She had almost reached the veranda when Cassidy intercepted her. "Why did you do that?" Sweat had made the hair around his face damp. He looked as hot and short-tempered as she.

"I'm in no mood for one of your inquisitions, Cassidy."

"Answer me. Why did you let Yasmine get away with embarrassing you in front of everyone?"

"Yasmine embarrassed only herself. Now, get out of my way." She managed to get around him and made it up several steps before he blocked her path again.

"You didn't approve of erect nipples yesterday, but today Yasmine couldn't have looked more naked if she'd been naked. I don't get it."

"You're not supposed to."

"Why did one set of poses bother you and not the other?"

"Because there's a fine distinction between sensuality and overt titillation. I'm looking for shots that will excite without being offensive."

"You know from experience that it's purely subjective."

"Invariably. But I'm the first judge, and I've got excellent taste," she stated boastfully but confidently. "I trust my judgment on what's quality and what's questionable."

"Did you like Yasmine's poses?"

"I said I did, didn't I?"

"But you didn't sound as though you meant it, and everybody heard that, especially Yasmine."

"My job isn't to stroke Yasmine's ego."

"No, your job is to sell merchandise, and that shot will sell pajamas."

She blew a strand of hair off her forehead. "Is there a point to this, Cassidy?"

"You were suddenly uncomfortable with Yasmine's sensuality. Why?"

"Did you think she was sensual? I don't know why I'm even asking, when it was so apparent that you did. You were riveted." He gave her a strange and quizzical look, which only made her madder. "Well, weren't you?"

"I wasn't particularly mindful of my reaction," he said softly. "But obviously you were."

Claire, realizing that she was dangerously close to revealing too much, averted her head. "Is that all, Cassidy?"

"Not quite. What kind of relationship do you have with Yasmine that allows her to insult you like that? Anyone else would have come back with both barrels loaded."

"Yasmine attacks other people only when she's upset with herself. I understand that."

"She attacked you yesterday with that crack about Wilde. What gives? What reason does she have to be upset with herself?"

"None of your damn business." Executing a hasty sidestep, he parried her attempt to go around him. Seething, Claire glared up at him. "All right, I'll tell you this much. Yasmine is taking the van to New Orleans tonight to see her lover. She plans to return early tomorrow morning."

"Then what's the problem?"

"I think they might have quarreled the last time they were together."

Cassidy gazed at a point beyond her shoulder for a moment. "She's taking the van?"

"Hmm."

"Does she ever drive your car?"

"You're losing your touch, Cassidy." His eyes swung back to hers. "The reasoning behind that question is amateurish and transparent. You want to know if Yasmine was driving my car the night Jackson Wilde was murdered. You fail to recall that she was in New York that night and that *I* was driving my car."

He bore down on her. "I'm relieved that you remember that, Claire. I was beginning to think you'd forgotten that your car connects you to Wilde's murder."

"It appears to."

"Temporarily. Sooner or later a clue is going to mark you as a killer."

She shuddered, spoke low. "Excuse me. I'm going in now." She got through the front door without being apprehended, but he caught up with her in the foyer. He covered her hand where it rested on the balustrade.

"Claire, why do you do that? Why do you just turn your back and walk away when I make those kinds of allegations? Why don't you deny them?"

"Because I don't have to. I'm innocent until proven guilty, remember? I've got nothing to fear from you."

"The hell you don't." He leaned forward, straining the words through his teeth. "You can't continue to simply walk away. I didn't follow you to Mississippi on a whim, you know."

"Then why did you come here? Why impose yourself on me, why interfere with my work? To bully me about nonexistent affairs with Jackson Wilde? To try to place a wedge between Yasmine and me? Divide and conquer? Is that your current strategy?"

"No. I came because I had no choice. The evidence against you is no longer circumstantial. We've got something tangible in those carpet fibers. So far I've kept you from being formally arrested."

"Why?"

"Number one, because I don't want to look like a fool before the grand jury and get you no billed for lack of more solid evidence."

"And number two?"

The pendulum inside the grandfather clock swung back and forth, ponderously ticking off the seconds they spent staring at each other. Finally he replied, "Because I want to give you the benefit of the doubt. But Glenn and everybody else in a position of authority is getting antsy to close this case."

"They're responding to the ranting of a hysterical woman."

"Who happens to be pregnant."

Claire's breath left her body in an audible rush. "Pregnant?"

"Ariel Wilde collapsed last night during a prayer service in Kansas City. If you'd watched the news you would have seen it." There were no TVs in the guest rooms at Rosesharon. During a guest's stay, he was virtually incommunicado with the outside world unless he read the local newspaper, which carried very little national or world news.

Claire's head was spinning. "She's pregnant?"

"That's right," he said tersely. "That practically eliminates her as a suspect."

"Not necessarily."

"Not to you, maybe. Maybe not even to me. But to everybody else's way of thinking, she's off the hook. Which way do you think public sympathy will swing? To the lady epitomizing motherhood and goodness, or to the woman who publishes dirty pictures?"

"It might not be Jackson's child," Claire said, sounding desperate, like someone grasping at a lifeline. "It could be Josh's baby."

"I know that. And you know that. But Joe Average Citizen doesn't. All he sees on his color Panasonic is a saintly, weeping, pregnant widow, who looks like the last thing on her agenda would be adultery with her stepson and the cold-blooded murder of her husband.

"Be prepared, Claire. Ariel will play this for all it's worth. Twice you've experienced the kind of media manipulation she's capable of. The threat of libel suits doesn't faze her. She'll verbally paint the picture of an immoral, opportunistic monster taking her husband's life and imposing tragedy on her and her unborn baby. Because of the groundwork she's already laid, whose face do you think that monster will wear in the minds of most people?" He leaned down closer to her. "Are the grim implications of her pregnancy beginning to sink in?"

They weren't only sinking in—they had found a nesting place in the recesses of her heart where her deepest fears were lodged. It would be folly, however, to let Cassidy see that she was afraid. "What do you want from me?" she asked defiantly.

"A confession."

She made a scornful sound.

"Then, dammit, don't let me accuse you without putting up a fight. Stamp. Scream. Beat on my chest with your fists. Become outraged, incensed. Don't retreat behind that cool facade; it only makes you look guiltier. You can't remain aloof any longer, Claire. Fight back, for God's sake."

"I wouldn't lower my dignity to such a level."

"Dignity!" he bellowed. The features of his face turned stiff with rage. "Jail is undignified, Claire. So is a murder trial. So is life in prison." His breath fell hotly on her face. "Damn you, tell me my suspicions are wrong. Give me something absolute that will shoot down all the facts I have working against you."

"Until I'm indicted, I shouldn't have to worry about defending myself. The judicial procedure—"

"Screw procedure! Talk to me!"

"Mr. Cassidy?" The wavering voice came from Mary Catherine, who was hovering in the dining-room archway. "Why are you shouting at Claire? You're not going to take her away, are you?"

"Of course not, Mama!" Claire exclaimed.

"Because I really can't let you take her."

Claire moved quickly to her mother's side and placed an arm around her shoulders. "Mr. Cassidy and I were just . . . debating something."

"Oh."

Where was Harry? Claire asked herself. Why wasn't she with her mother? "Everything's fine, Mama. I promise. Are you feeling well?"

Mary Catherine formed a tremulous smile. "We're having stuffed pork chops for dinner. Doesn't that sound delicious? I must ask them to trim all the fat off Aunt Laurel's. That's the only way she'll eat pork, you know. Otherwise she get indigestion. Oh, forgive me, Mr. Cassidy, for discussing suc' an indelicate matter in mixed company."

Cassidy cleared his throat. "Quite all right."

"Aunt Laurel wants to get some cuttings from the rose-bushes here to plant in the courtyard. Wouldn't that be lovely, Claire Louise?"

"Yes, Mama. Lovely."

Mary Catherine walked past Claire to the coat tree near the door, where Cassidy's sports coat was hanging. She removed something from the pocket of her skirt and slipped it into the breast pocket of the jacket. Without acknowledging her strange action, she continued the conversation. "Claire dear, your face is flushed."

"It's hot outside."

"Are you perspiring, dear? That's not at all ladylike. Perhaps you should take a bath and change before dinner."

"I plan to, Mama. I was just on my way up."

"You work much too hard. Aunt Laurel and I were talking about it this afternoon over tea. You really should take care." Mary Catherine stroked her cheek lovingly before drifting upstairs and out of sight. The instant they heard her bedroom door close, Cassidy moved to the coat tree and reached into the breast pocket of his coat.

"Well, I'll be damned."

"What is it?" He held up a gold fountain pen.

"Is it yours?"

With a rueful smile he said, "I noticed it missing the afternoon I arrived, after I'd left my jacket hanging here for a while. I figured somebody had stolen it, although I couldn't imagine who would want to. It isn't an expensive pen, but valuable to me because it was a gift from my folks, and both of them are deceased."

Claire pressed her fingertips against her lips and turned her back to him. She leaned against one of the tall, narrow windows that flanked the front door, resting her forehead against the glass, which had retained some coolness during the sweltering afternoon.

Cassidy moved to stand close behind her. "Hey, it's no big deal, Claire."

His voice was soft, gentle, confidence inspiring. When he placed his hands on her shoulders and turned her to face him, she was tempted to rest her head against his chest as she had the window. It would be a tremendous relief to finally unburden herself and tell him everything. "Oh, Cassidy, I wish . . ."

"What?" he probed gently.

She rolled her head across her shoulders. Naturally she couldn't say what she really wanted to, so she said instead, "I wish it weren't so hot. I wish it would rain. I wish we were finished here so I could go home and restore my office and home, which I'm certain the police left in shambles."

She bit her lower lip to stop tears of frustration and fear. "I wish I'd never heard of Jackson Wilde. I wish you'd have told me about your fountain pen. I could have explained days ago."

"I got it back and that's all that matters. Forget it."

But she couldn't forget it and felt compelled to explain her mother's actions. "See, sometimes Mama takes things. She's not stealing because she doesn't realize she's doing anything wrong. She's just 'borrowing.' She never fails to return whatever it is she's taken. It's harmless and innocent, really."

"Hush, Claire." He pushed his fingers up through her hair and whisked a kiss across her lips. "I believe you."

But when he ducked his head for a deeper kiss, she pushed him away and gazed into his eyes. "No, you don't, Cassidy." Suddenly they were no longer talking about her mother or the fountain pen. Claire slowly shook her head. "You don't believe me at all."

Chapter Eighteen

❦ ❦

Yasmine left before dinner. The empty place at the dining table aroused curiosity, which Claire satisfied without going into details. "Yasmine had an appointment in New Orleans tonight, but she's making a quick round trip. She'll be back early tomorrow morning."

Leon was excited about the photographs he'd taken that day. His enthusiasm, heightened by several glasses of excellent dinner wine, prompted him to wax eloquent throughout the meal. He lavished his captive audience with ribald stories about the famous and would-be famous who frequented Manhattan's ever-changing hotspots.

"Of course it's not like in the old days when Studio 54 was in its heyday," he remarked wistfully. "It's a shame that, what with AIDS and drug awareness, no one *really* parties anymore."

Immediately following dinner, Claire excused herself. A Trivial Pursuit tournament was being organized. She knew from past experience that they invariably turned hostile. Pleading exhaustion, she accompanied Mary Catherine and Harry upstairs, where she lingered in their room, chatting with her mother until Mary Catherine's sleeping pill took effect. Mary Catherine didn't mention Cassidy's fountain pen, nor did she give any indication that she remembered taking it.

In her rush to leave for New Orleans, Yasmine had left their bedroom looking like a storm had hit it. Claire spent a half-hour picking up strewn clothing and reorganizing the vanity table. The bathroom was in no better shape. After straightening it, she languished in a tub of cool water, trying to relax and stop thinking about Ariel Wilde's pregnancy and what adverse effects it might have on her.

After her bath, she dusted with talcum, and put on a silk thigh-length chemise that was the color of old, expensive pearls. She twisted her hair into a knot on top of her head and secured it with a clip, then stacked pillows against the headboard of her bed and reclined against them. She intended to switch on the bedside lamp, but the darkness was so soothing. More than she needed to review the schedule for tomorrow, she needed sleep.

But her thoughts weren't restful. Like intractable children, they wouldn't behave and leave her in peace. Her eyes would remain closed for only brief snatches of time before they stubbornly sprang open. The bed, on which she had spent several restful nights, had metamorphosed into a bunk full of lumps and knots. Her pillow became warm too quickly. She flipped it over several times, growing increasingly impatient with her insomnia. Laughter wafted up the staircase from the parlor where the game was still in progress. She wished everybody would shut up and go to bed.

She blamed her discontent on the mattress, the pillow, and the noise, but she knew that the real source of it, like her jealousy that afternoon, was something deep inside herself.

It wasn't in her nature to be out of sorts with her friends and associates, her environment, and herself. She didn't like herself this way.

Yet, she was afraid to look too closely for an explanation. She knew intuitively that whatever had brought about this character change was something she'd rather not acknowledge. Avoidance was preferable to confrontation. She didn't want to deal with whatever was making her crazy. Left alone, maybe it would simply go away.

She heard a noise that sounded like someone moving furniture across the hardwood floors. It was thunder. Vainly willing herself to fall asleep, she listened to the thunderstorm moving progressively closer to Rosesharon. Lightning flashed through the sheer drapes at the French doors. Maybe this time the clouds would deliver a cooling rain. So far all they'd produced was a heightened sense of expectancy to an atmosphere already too thick to breathe.

As the storm came nearer and increased in intensity, so did Claire's restlessness.

Cassidy declined to join the Trivial Pursuit tournament in favor of a stroll around the grounds. However, the stifling humidity and biting mosquitoes quickly drove him back inside.

He didn't stop in the parlor to bid anyone good night but went straight upstairs to his room. He paused to listen at Claire's door, which was next door to his, but could hear nothing. There wasn't any light showing through the crack beneath the door, either, so he reasoned she must have done as she'd said and gone to bed early.

In his room, he stripped to the skin. God, it was muggy even indoors. He considered going downstairs to get a beer from the bar but decided against it. He might bump into Agnes or Grace, who were wont to engage their guests in lengthy conversations. Southern hospitality only went so far before it became cloying. His present frame of mind wasn't conducive to chatter. Tonight he wasn't fit company for anyone except himself, and he was finding himself nearly intolerable.

After taking a quick shower to cool off, he lay down on the bed and lit a cigarette. He'd quit smoking two years earlier, but he was feeling agitated. Besides, he needed something to keep his hands occupied while his mind ran in incessant circles.

Claire had motive. Claire had opportunity. Claire could be directly linked to the crime scene through fibers from her car's carpet. Claire had no ironclad alibi. Claire was his best shot at getting the conviction that he desperately needed for both professional and personal reasons.

But he didn't want Claire to be the culprit.

"Goddammit." The curse seemed to hover in the darkness long after the sound had faded. This was a bitch of a position he had placed himself in. If he followed his conscience and the ethics of professional conduct, he would distance himself from this case. Crowder had already given him a deadline for bringing in a suspect. The number of allotted days was dwindling. If he was summarily replaced, that would be a hell of a thing to live down.

But what if, before the deadline, he asked to be removed? Crowder thought he was too personally involved in the case, so he would probably be relieved by the request. The decision wouldn't damage their relationship. In fact, it would probably win his mentor's favor. Crowder would simply assign the case to someone else.

No, that was no good. That someone else would probably be aggressive and sly and would slap handcuffs on Claire as soon as she returned to New Orleans. She'd be booked for murder two. Fingerprinted. Photographed. Jailed. The thought of it made him sick.

On the other hand, he couldn't live with the thought that

he might let a guilty woman go free because he had the hots for her. Only it wasn't as simple as that. It never had been. Since he had first walked into French Silk and met Claire Laurent, nothing had been easy or routine.

It was as though he'd been bewitched. French Silk had an ambience that mystified and intrigued him. It wasn't the old building itself, or even the French Quarter. He'd been there many times since he'd moved to New Orleans. He'd found it charming, but it had never made him feel as though he had gone through a time warp on the other side of which everything moved in slow motion and nothing was what it seemed.

It wasn't the physical place that had mesmerized him. It was Claire. She exuded a mystique that confounded him. That unnamed quality was dangerously romantic, totally alluring, and potentially disastrous. It had trapped him like an invisible web. The harder he struggled against it, the more ensnared he became. Even now, while he should be plotting a way to catch her, he was devising means to protect her from prosecution.

Crazy, he thought, shaking his head over his own culpability. But he went with it anyway. There was no harm in exploring alternatives, was there? In fact, wasn't that the sensible, responsible, professional thing to do?

Who else was a viable suspect?

Ariel Wilde. She was pregnant now, but she could have offed her husband for a variety of reasons. Nevertheless, it would be tough to prosecute her and emerge a hero. He could always raise doubt as to who had fathered her child. But a good attorney would object to that line of questioning. The judge might rule in defense's favor, and that would be that. Nipped in the bud. The jury would never know about Ariel's affair with her stepson, and Cassidy would be despised for casting aspersions on a saintly expectant mother.

Joshua Wilde. Cassidy's gut instinct told him that the young man wouldn't have the gumption to kill a fly, much less a tyrannical father. On the other hand, he'd had the moxie to boink his old man's wife.

The problem with prosecuting Ariel or Josh was that he didn't have a shred of physical evidence on either of them. It was all circumstantial and conjecture. If the jurors followed the judge's instructions and entertained any reasonable doubt, Ariel and Josh would walk. Assistant District Attorney Cassidy would have lost his credibility and let the real killer, whoever it might be, go free.

That prospect was unthinkable. His main objective was to make sure that didn't happen. Above all else, he was committed to catching the bad guy and convicting him.

Or her.

Thoughts of Claire made him swear liberally as he ground out his first, virtually unsmoked, cigarette and lit another. He envisioned her as she had been that afternoon. Her dishevelment had been fetching, the perspiration having given her skin a healthy glow. The humidity had made the hair around her face curl beguilingly. She had looked hot and bothered. But when he'd confronted her about it, she'd been too damn proud to claim those two human frailties, jealousy and lust.

Feeling restless and mean, Cassidy rolled off the bed and hiked a pair of jeans up over his hips. He didn't bother buttoning them before he yanked open the French doors and stepped onto the balcony. The air was even sultrier than it had been earlier. There wasn't a breath of breeze.

He glanced toward the French doors of Claire's room and saw darkness. She was sleeping. He gazed up at the sky; the low clouds looked swollen and bruised. The smell of rain was pervasive, but he didn't feel a drop. The atmosphere was electrically charged, as though something consequential were about to take place.

No sooner had the thought crossed his mind than a flash of lightning sizzled across the sky just above the motionless treetops.

When the sky was split by a brilliant, jagged fork of lightning, Claire sprang into a sitting position. She held her breath in anticipation of the thunder. It cracked like a whip across the roof of the house, rattling windows and glassware. It was followed by a strong gust of wind. Her French doors burst open, swinging into the room and banging against the interior walls. The sheer draperies billowed like sails suddenly unfurled.

Claire slid from the bed and walked across the room. Rosesharon's trees were swaying in an angry wind that seemed to be blowing in no particular direction. It tore at her hair and molded her chemise to her body. Another bolt of lightning temporarily spotlighted the balcony.

That's when she saw Cassidy. He was standing at the railing, shirtless, smoking, looking straight at her. She started to duck back into her bedroom and seal shut the French doors, but she couldn't move. His riveting gaze had immobilized her. Saying nothing, he pushed himself away from the railing and came toward her with a slow, measured, predatory tread.

Her heart started racing as fast as the frenzied wind. Her mind spun as erratically as anything in the wind's path. She spoke the first inane words that came to her: "I didn't know you smoked."

Cassidy still said nothing but continued moving forward in that same dangerous manner. He didn't stop until he was within arm's reach. Claire felt herself drawn to him by a physical and inexorable tug, as though he had a powerful magnet inside his chest.

Breathlessly she said, "I think a storm is finally about to break."

He flicked his cigarette over the balcony railing, then reached for her, pulling her against him with the force of the next thunderclap. The kiss he ground upon her mouth was as ruthless as the wind. He snapped open her hair barrette and let it drop unheeded to the floor, then moved his fingers through her hair, tilting her head first to one side, then the other, so that her mouth had to obey the rapacious demands of his.

Heat emanated from him, through his skin, through the hair that matted his chest. His unleashed sexual desire seeped into Claire and she responded, suddenly acknowledging it as the source of her recent discontent. It blossomed and spread through her—a sweet, aching need for this . . . for Cassidy.

Her fingers curled into the fleshy part of his shoulders and she arched against him. He made a low, erotic sound. His mouth left hers to seek the hollow of her neck. Claire's head fell back as she welcomed the sucking motions of his lips.

He slid his hand down her back, over her bottom, and tilted her higher and closer to him, pushing his erection against her cleft. He lowered one strap of her chemise and bared her breast. He sought the nipple first, closing his lips around it and madly laving it with his tongue. Soft, glad little cries escaped Claire's parted lips until he took them again in a kiss.

The ferocity of the storm was fully upon them now. The fierce wind howled. Lightning flashed and thunder cracked. Rain fell in torrents. Sheets of it were driven beneath the balcony roof to splash against their bare feet. They were mindless of it all.

Until they heard approaching voices.

In order to enjoy the rain, two of the models had decided to take the balcony route to their rooms instead of the interior hallway. Claire pushed Cassidy away and glanced toward the corner of the house, where at any moment the models would appear.

Taking her hand, he stepped into her room and pulled her in behind him. He latched the French doors just as the models rounded the corner, where they paused to watch the storm.

Cassidy backed Claire against the French doors and they became hopelessly entangled in the sheer drapes. Any objec-

tions she might have uttered were silenced by his kiss. His
tongue entered her mouth and plumbed it seductively. His
hands moved beneath her chemise. They felt warm and strong
against her derriere as he lifted one of her thighs and propped
it on his. His knuckles lightly fanned her pubic hair. Her belly
quickened reflexively and she almost cried out. To trap the
sound, he covered her mouth with his.

Outside, one of the models said, "It's really coming down.
I've never seen lightning like this."

"Shh! You'll wake up Claire."

Claire was fully awake. Every fiber of her body was responding to Cassidy's touch. His fingers separated the lips of
her sex; one slipped inside her. With a subtle flexing motion,
he extended it fully before gradually retracting it again and
again. Claire clutched at him. He ended a torrid kiss and
penetrated her eyes with a hot, hard stare while continuing to
stroke her.

"We'd better get to bed, too."

"What time's your call?"

"Eight-thirty."

A squeal. "Watch it, it's slippery. I almost fell."

"Rue would shit if you showed up tomorrow with
bruises."

Cassidy withdrew his finger and found the distended heart
of her sexuality. Round and round he caressed the slippery
nubbin. Claire blinked frantically in an attempt to keep her
eyes open. Cassidy's image was blurring. She noted that his
hair was falling over his brows, that his features were set and
tense, and that his eyes were feverish.

Claire was seized by a purling climax. She fought it, but
it washed through her like a powerful, intravenous drug.
Instant warmth. A jolt of passion. A rush of sublimity.

The models' voices had faded, leaving only the sounds of
the storm and the silky rasp of heavy breathing. Cassidy
wrapped his arms around her and carried her to the bed, where

he laid her down before following with his own body. He removed her chemise, then his hands moved over her flushed breasts. His fingertips lingered on her nipples, and the sensations that concentrated there were so strong, Claire whimpered. He lowered his head and kissed them urgently but tenderly. She grasped handfuls of his hair, knowing she should stop this, but conceding that she might just as well try to stop the pounding rain.

He kissed her belly. Anxiously she murmured, "Cassidy?"

"Shh." He blew gently on her delta of hair.

"Cassidy?"

Disregarding her hesitancy, he scooped her hips in his hands and lifted her against his open mouth. His tongue investigated her sweet, wet center. He flicked it lazily, delved deeply. He nuzzled her affectionately, then kissed her intently, as though sucking the nectar from a piece of luscious fruit. With the tip of his tongue he reawakened that tiny seed of femininity.

The pleasure built until it was unendurable. "Please," she gasped.

He knelt between her thighs and thrust himself into her. His breathing was labored and hot against her neck. She heard him groan, "Oh, Christ. Christ." Then he began to move, stretching and stroking her until she became oblivious to everything except him.

The skin on his back was damp. His muscles rippled beneath her hands. She slid them inside his jeans and cupped his buttocks, drawing him deeper into her. He murmured with pleasure. They kissed. His lips tasted musky and forbidden. She licked them delicately, then greedily.

He gathered the fullness of her breast in his palm and brushed his thumb across the raised center, then lightly rolled it between his fingers. Claire's back arched off the mattress. She caught her breath sharply and spoke his name. The first climax had been only a harbinger. This time when she came she felt like part of a fireworks display. She was showered with fiery sparks and fell through space for what seemed eternity before the final glimmer was extinguished.

Moments later, Cassidy allowed himself to come. He embraced her tightly and filled her ear with erotic messages as she felt his warm, surging release deep inside her.

Replete, they rested, his head lying on the slopes of her breasts, her legs folded around him. Eventually he sat up and peeled off his jeans, then lay back down and gathered her close. Claire snuggled against his naked body.

The storm had passed, but it continued to rain. The distant thunder reminded her of the night Cassidy had first kissed her, the night they had gone to the Ponchartrain Hotel to pick up Mary Catherine.

With a shudder, Claire pushed away the thought. She didn't want to remember who they were and the opposing roles they were playing in a real-life drama.

Feeling her shudder, he tenderly kissed her temple. "What?"

"Nothing."

"Something."

She sighed, a smile playing about her lips. "That was the dirtiest sex I've ever had."

A chuckle started deep inside his chest, just below her ear. "Good."

She strummed his ribs, excited by the sensations conducted through her fingertips. "Cassidy?"

"Hmm?"

"What will happen tomorrow?"

He rolled her onto her back and leaned above her, laying his finger lengthwise against her lips. "If we talk about that, I'll have to leave. Is that what you want?" He stroked her lips, then kissed her, deeply, wetly, intimately, giving her his tongue. He nudged apart her thighs and moved against her suggestively. He was already hard again.

She sighed. "No. Don't leave."

Chapter Nineteen

✣ ✣

Andre Philippi was beside himself with excitement. Yasmine was in his hotel again. Yasmine! The most exquisite creature in the world.

He was taking a routine stroll through the lobby when he saw her come in. Even though the sun had already set, she was wearing opaque, wrap-around sunglasses. Obviously she didn't want to be recognized. If he weren't so familiar with her face, she might have escaped even his notice. But he spent more time staring into close-up photographs of her than he spent looking at himself in the mirror. Her face was better known to him than his own.

Her gait was purposeful as she strode toward the bank of elevators. One was standing open. Andre rushed to join her inside it before it began its ascent. "Yasmine. Welcome." He executed a quick bow.

"Hello, Andre." She smiled and removed her sunglasses, slipping them into her large shoulder bag. "How are you? It's been ages since I've seen you."

Claire had introduced them several years ago at a small

dinner party she had hosted. They had since been together on numerous occasions. However, it never failed to thrill and flatter Andre that she regarded him as a friend.

"I've been well. And you?"

"Can't complain." Her smile seemed to congeal around her words, as though they might not be wholly sincere.

"Are you in town to work on the catalog?"

"We're shooting pictures for the spring issue over in Mississippi. I just came back for the evening."

He never questioned a guest's reason for being in his hotel. That would have been a breach of his policy, which guaranteed absolute privacy above all else. "How is Claire?"

"Frankly, she was in a snit when I left her this afternoon," Yasmine replied.

"Oh, dear. Did Mary Catherine—"

"No, it had nothing to do with her mother."

He waited politely, hoping that Yasmine would expound upon their mutual friend's distress without his having to ask.

Yasmine rewarded his discretion. "I guess the pressure of the job got to her today. You know Claire. She never blows her top, which is the healthy way to get mad. She just simmers quietly and makes everybody around her feel like shit."

Sensing that there had been conflict between the two women he liked and admired so well, Andre responded diplomatically. "I'm confident that the catalog will be well worth the effort you've put into it."

"Yeah, I guess." Her lack of enthusiasm was evident.

"Isn't the creative aspect of the catalog always anxiety producing?" he inquired politely.

"This time more than usual."

"Why so?"

"Cassidy."

Andre blanched. "You mean he's *there?*"

"Yep. He followed Claire to Rosesharon and has practically become a permanent fixture on the sets."

He nervously wet his lips. "Why in heaven's name is he hounding her like that?"

The elevator had reached the designated floor. Andre stepped out with Yasmine, and they began walking together down the hotel corridor.

"He still suspects her of Wilde's murder."

"But that's preposterous!" Andre stumbled, as though his heart had dropped all the way to the floor and tripped him. "Oh dear. This is terrible. And it's all my fault." Perspiration broke out across his forehead. From his breast pocket he removed an immaculate linen handkerchief and blotted at the beads of sweat. "If I hadn't fallen for his trick and identified Claire as the caller on that recording—"

"Whoa!" Yasmine laid a commiserating hand on his shoulder. "Claire told me how upset you were when that happened. Listen, Cassidy is one smart cookie. One way or another, he would have found out that Claire was here at the Fairmont the night Jackson Wilde was shot. You didn't reveal anything that he wouldn't have discovered sooner or later."

She lowered her voice to a confidential pitch. "If you want to know what I think, I think Cassidy's more interested in proving Claire innocent than guilty."

"Which, of course, she is," Andre hastened to say. "Claire was here that night to pick up Mary Catherine, nothing more. I would swear to that in court. I would do anything to protect a friend."

"Your friends count on that."

Andre found that statement cryptic and unsettling. He wanted to reemphasize his belief in Claire's innocence, but Yasmine began moving away. "I'll look forward to a longer visit soon, Andre."

He reached for her hand, bowed over it, and kissed the back of it. "*Au revoir*, Yasmine. Your incandescent beauty lends light to everyone around you."

The smile that had made her famous broke across her face. "Why you little stinker! You're a poet!"

"I confess," he admitted sheepishly. She would never know about the hours he had spent composing odes to her beauty and charm.

She laid her palm against his cheek. "You're a real gentleman, Andre. Why can't all men be as kind and considerate and loyal as you?" Her smile became sad. She withdrew her hand, then turned and walked away from him. He didn't follow her. That would have been improper. But he waited until she was admitted into a room after knocking and speaking her name softly.

Andre didn't envy the man waiting for her on the other side of the door. His love for Yasmine wasn't sexual. Its origins were in his soul and it resided on a much higher plane than the physical realm. With all his heart, he wanted her to experience love and happiness in all their various forms and from whatever sources they could be derived.

He practically floated back to the elevator in a state of euphoria. Yasmine had touched his cheek with affection. Her hand had felt smooth and cool, like his *maman*'s caress when he was a boy. There had also been something in her eyes that had reminded him of his mother—a familiar poignancy that he remembered only too well. But he put that thought aside and didn't let it compromise the bubbling joy of the moment.

🦎

"You cocksucking bastard. You motherfucker." Yasmine lambasted Alister Petrie with a litany of obscenities.

"Charming language, Yasmine."

"Shut your lying mouth, you son of a fucking bitch."

Fury radiated from her like the red waves from a space heater. Her body was taut and bristling with rage. It burned in the depths of her eyes. "You never intended to leave your wife, did you?"

"Yasmine, I—"

"*Did you?*"

"During an election year, it would be political suicide. But that doesn't mean—"

"You goddamn liar. You slimy, stinking piece of rat shit. I could kill you."

"For God's sake." He ran his fingers through his hair. It was still tousled from their coupling, which had been almost as ferocious as their argument. They'd heaved and bucked and clutched and wrestled as if it were a contest rather than an act of love.

"You're overreacting," he said in a calming tone, trying to prevent another outburst of her violent shrieks. "This is only a temporary separation, Yasmine. It would be best—"

"Best for you."

"Best for both of us if we cooled it for a while, at least until after the election. I'm not breaking off the affair permanently. Jesus, do you think I want that? I don't. You're my life."

"Bullshit."

"I swear to you that once the election is over, I'll—"

"You'll what? You'll bless me with a few measly hours of screwing every week or so? For how long? For life? Fuck you, Congressman. I'm not putting up with that shit."

"I don't expect you to be happy about it. God, I'd be crushed if you were." He spread open his arms in a gesture of appeal. "What I do expect is a little understanding. My schedule is a nightmare, Yasmine. I'm under constant pressure."

"Sugar, you don't know pressure." Her voice thrummed with foreboding. "When I get finished with you, your skinny ass won't be worth shit in this state or any other. Your little nigger gal is through fuckin' around with you. The party is over, sugar. Now you gotta pay."

She headed for the door. He rushed after her. "Wait, Yasmine! Let me explain. You're not being reasonable." He caught her shoulders and turned her around. "Please." His voice cracked on a near sob. "Please."

She made no further attempt to leave, but her eyes contin-

ued to smolder like live coals. Alister gulped oxygen and
blinked rapidly, looking like a desperate man about to plead
for a stay of execution.

"Yasmine, darling," he began haltingly, "you've got to
cut me some slack. Promise me that you won't take this to
the media."

The words went through her like lances, opening up pockets of pain and outrage. "You don't give a shit about how I
feel, do you? You're only thinking of yourself and your
bloody campaign!"

"I didn't mean that. I—"

Issuing a savage cry, she lashed out, scraping her fingernails down his cheek and drawing blood from four long
gashes. With the other hand, she ripped out several strands
of his hair.

For a moment, Alister was too stunned to move. Then the
pain struck him and he cried out, raising his hand to his cheek.

"You're crazy!" he shouted when his hand came away
dripping blood. "You're a frigging lunatic."

Yasmine allowed herself several seconds to revel in his
astonishment and agony, then she stormed from the room.
On the way to the elevator, she encountered a man and a
woman in the hotel corridor. They stared at her and gave her
a wide berth. She realized then that tears were streaming from
her eyes and that her blouse was flapping open.

She buttoned it haphazardly and shoved it back into her
waistband as she rode the elevator down to the street level.
She also replaced her sunglasses. As she moved through the
Fairmont's lobby she kept her head down. She spotted Andre
from the corner of her eye, but didn't slow down or encourage
him to approach her as she left the building. She retrieved
Claire's rented van from the parking garage and headed across
Canal Street.

It was a mild evening. Many were getting a head start on
the weekend. The streets of the French Quarter were crowded
with tourists who tied up motor traffic and jammed the narrow

sidewalks. Yasmine had difficulty finding a parking place and finally left the van in a tow-away zone. She still had to walk several blocks down Rue Dumaine to reach her destination. She made eye contact with no one and drew as little attention to herself as possible.

The place was still open, but if she hadn't known it was there, she would never have noticed it. Several shoppers were browsing among the shelves of herbs that would find their way into gris-gris and potions.

"I'd like to see the priestess," Yasmine said, speaking softly to the attendant, who was smoking a joint. The aged hippie withdrew, then returned a moment later to signal Yasmine to follow her.

The Altar Room was separated from the shop by a dusty maroon velvet curtain. The walls were decorated with African masks and metal carvings, called vévé, which evoked powerful spirits. A large wooden cross stood in one corner, but it wasn't a traditional crucifix. Curled around the center post was Damballah, the snake, the most powerful spirit. Residing in a wire cage in the opposite corner was a python, representative of Damballah. The snake was used in the voodoo rituals conducted in the swamps outside the city. On the altar itself were statues of Christian saints, photographs of people who claimed to have been blessed by the spirits, flickering candles, burning sticks of incense, and ju-ju, the bones and skulls of animals.

The priestess was seated in the queen's chair adjacent to the altar. She was immense, her enormous breasts overlapping a belly comprised of several rolls of fat. Her large head was wrapped in a turban. Dozens of gold chains were suspended from her short, thick neck. On at least half of them were dangling charms, lockets, and other amulets. Her hands were as large as baseball gloves. Several rings glittered on each finger. She raised one of her giant hands and motioned Yasmine forward.

The priestess was Haitian, as black as ebony. Her wide,

round face was oily and shiny with sweat. In a trancelike state, she observed her visitor through heavy-lidded, slumberous eyes that were as small and brilliant as onyx buttons.

Yasmine addressed her with more reverence than a devout Catholic would address a cardinal. "I need your help." The dense smoke from the incense was intoxicating. Yasmine felt light-headed, but she always did whenever she visited this underworld of black magic. Dark powers seemed to emanate from the priestess, from her paraphernalia, from the murky shadows of every corner.

In a flat, monotonic voice, Yasmine told the priestess about her lover. "He's lied to me many times. He's an evil man. He must be punished."

The priestess nodded sagely. "Do you have something of his?"

"Yes."

The priestess raised one beringed hand and an assistant materialized. She offered Yasmine a small crockery bowl. Yasmine scraped the human tissue and specks of dried blood from beneath her fingernails and carefully dropped the particles into the bowl. Next she removed the strands of Alister's hair that were still wrapped around the fingers of her left hand and added them to the bowl.

Then she lifted her gaze to the priestess. Flickering candle-light was reflected in her agate eyes, making them appear animalistic. Her lips barely moved, but her sibilant message was clear. "I want him to suffer badly."

❦

Belle Petrie was waiting for Alister in the foyer when he arrived at their Greek revival home on the shore of Lake Ponchartrain. The children had been fed earlier and sent to bed. Before leaving for the day, the full-time housekeeper/ cook had set the formal dining table with the best china and added fresh flowers to the centerpiece.

Belle was dressed in purple silk lounging pajamas that swished against her legs as she moved forward to greet her husband. "My God. Did she do that to you?" As she examined the scratches on his cheek, there was no sympathy in her voice, merely surprise.

"Satisfied, Belle? These scratches should prove that I did what I promised."

"You told her that it was over for good and warned her not to bother us anymore?"

"Precisely that. Then she charged me like a goddamn panther."

Belle's gleaming page boy barely rippled as she made a tsking sound and shook her head. "Go upstairs and swab those scratches with peroxide while I pour our dinner wine."

"I'm not hungry."

"Of course you are, darling," she said with a fixed smile. "Run along and tend to your face. I'll expect you back down shortly."

Alister recognized her suggestion for what it was—a test to see if he would obey. In her subtle way, she was stating the terms under which she would stay with him, financially support his campaign, and decline to expose him for the unfaithful, lying husband that he was. From here on, she was the writer, producer, and director of this charade. If he wanted to play, he must accept his role and carry it out to the letter.

What choice did he have but to accept her conditions, no matter how unpalatable? Sure, he'd go along for a while. It would behoove him to toe the line until after the election. Then, if he wanted to resume his affair with Yasmine, or start a new one with somebody else, he'd damned well do it. Just because he'd been caught once didn't mean he intended to live the rest of his life as Belle's neutered lapdog. For the time being, however, it was prudent to pretend.

"I'll be down in a minute."

Upstairs, he inspected his face in the bathroom mirror. The gashes were still fresh, raw and bleeding How the hell would he explain them to his staff and campaign committee, much less the media and the voting public? Backlashing tree branches? A frisky new kitten? Who the hell would believe that?

On the other hand, in order to contradict him they'd have to accuse him of lying and prove it. So what was he worried about? They'd take his word for it because they'd have no alternative.

He wasn't even vaguely concerned that Yasmine would throw him out like a chunk of raw meat to the news hounds. True, he'd experienced a moment of trepidation when she'd looked at him in a way that had chilled his blood. But once she cooled down and her reason reasserted itself, she'd change her mind about seeking restitution. After all, she loved him. Her love had been a curse that might now turn out to be a blessing. She wouldn't do anything to destroy him politically because she probably still clung to the fantasy that one day she'd wind up being Mrs. Congressman Petrie.

Besides, she was proud to a fault. She couldn't publicize their affair without making herself look like a fool. She had a career to salvage, a business to protect, and creditors to pacify. The last thing Yasmine wanted or needed was a scandal.

But what if her desire for revenge was greater than her better judgement? What if she did squeal?

Alister shrugged at his reflection in the mirror. So what? The public outcry over such a notorious affair would work more against her than him. All he had to do was sit back, hold hands with Belle, and vehemently deny any allegations that Yasmine might make. Who'd believe a virtually bankrupt, morally depraved, hysterical woman from Harlem over an affluent, stable, happily married southern gentleman?

With all that resolved in his mind, his mood was almost buoyant as he went back downstairs. Belle kissed him gently and formed a moue of concern over his injured cheek. "It's all behind us now," she said as she extended him a glass of

perfectly chilled white wine. "Tell me about your day." She
served him a light supper of crab salad on toast points, sliced
cantaloupe, marinated cherry tomatoes, and raspberry sher-
bet.

They were lingering over their demitasse when something
smashed against the dining-room window. It landed hard,
making a horrific *crash* that caused the large pane of glass to
vibrate.

"What the hell was that?" Alister whipped his head
around.

Belle shot straight up from her chair, knocking it over
backward.

Alister gaped in horror at the blood and gore splattered on
the glass.

Belle covered her mouth with her hand to keep from gag-
ging.

"Jesus," Alister wheezed. "Stay inside."

"Alister—"

"Stay inside!"

He had never been inordinately brave, so it wasn't so much
courage as anger that propelled him through the front door of
his house and out onto his carefully manicured lawn. Down
the street, he heard the squeal of tires, but it was too far away
and too dark for him to see the make of the car or to read the
license plate.

He approached the dining-room window with caution and
fear. Looking at the blood-splattered glass from this side
made it even spookier, more real. He could smell the blood.
A Rorschach inkblot from hell.

He leaned across the flower bed to inspect it closer, lost
his balance, fell into the shrubbery beneath the window, and
landed on a dead chicken. Its throat had been slashed. The
cut was fresh, wide, and gaping. The feathers were wet and
shiny with dark blood.

The congressman screamed.

He scrambled to his feet, thrashed through the shrubbery.

and stumbled up the front steps. Once safely inside, he slammed the front door and slid home the bolts. Frantically he punched in the security alarm code on the panel.

Belle, having recovered from her initial shock, demanded an explanation. "Who made that disgusting mess on our front window? Do you realize what a chore it will be to get that stuff off?"

He wanted to shake her until her perfectly straight, white teeth rattled. "Don't you understand what this means? She wants me dead."

"Who?"

"*Her.*"

"Your former lover?"

He nodded, stuttering, "She . . . she's put a curse on me."

"For heaven's sake, Alister, get a grip on yourself. You're being ridiculous."

He shook his head furiously.

"This is a matter for the police." Belle, ever cool, headed for the hall telephone.

"No!" He lunged for the phone and yanked the cord from the wall jack. "No."

"Alister, you're not behaving rationally. What's got you so scared?"

He croaked a single word. "Voodoo."

Chapter Twenty

❧❧

Yasmine barged in on them a few minutes before six o'clock. She flung the bedroom door open, stomped in, then skidded to a halt when she saw Claire snuggled against Cassidy between the sheets of the twin bed.

"Oh, shit!"

The expletive woke Claire from a sound sleep. She sat up, shoved her hair out of her eyes, and groped for the corner of the sheet to raise against her breasts, which were rosy and tender from a night of lovemaking.

At her sudden movement, Cassidy rolled onto his back. "What's the matter?" He followed Claire's stunned stare to Yasmine, who looked down at them for several awkward seconds before turning on her heel and marching out, closing the door soundly behind her.

"Something's wrong." Claire reached for her chemise, which was draped over the footboard of the bed.

"What do you mean? What's wrong with what? What time

319

is it?'' Cassidy propped himself on his elbows and shook his head groggily.

"Something's wrong with Yasmine."

"Claire?"

She had pulled on a housecoat over her chemise. As she swept past the bed on her way to the door, his hand shot out and caught her arm. He gazed up at her from hooded eyes. She knew what the look meant, and it created flurries of delight in her tummy. "I can't," she whispered soulfully. "Yasmine needs me."

"I need you."

"You had me," she reminded him with a shy smile.

"Not nearly enough."

Torn between loyalty and desire, she glanced toward the door, then looked back at him. "I've got to check on her, Cassidy."

"Okay," he growled. "But I'm a sore loser." He raised her hand to his mouth and provocatively kissed the palm. "Hurry back."

"I promise."

The hallway was shrouded in the gray-violet light of dawn. She moved quickly to the staircase and tiptoed down, not wanting to rouse anyone. She gave the double parlors a swift glance but didn't see Yasmine. She was about to bypass the dining room when she noted movement near the wet bar. Reversing her direction, she joined Yasmine there.

The former model held up a decanter. "Want a drink?"

"Yasmine, what's the matter?"

"What do you care? By the looks of you, I'd say you had one hell of a night in your little twin bed. All cozied up nekkid with the detective, weren't you? Hmm-mmm. Imagine that."

"He's not a detective, and you're not being fair. Why should it matter to you if I sleep with Cassidy?"

She came around, holding a highball glass filled with vodka. "It doesn't. In fact, I don't give a fat rat's fart who you fuck."

"Whom I fuck," Claire corrected. "If you're going to insult me, at least be grammatically correct."

Yasmine set her drink on the bar with a hard thump. She tried to sustain her anger but couldn't. A smile tugged at the corners of her mouth. "Claire Louise Laurent. Always so bloody prim and proper." She grinned at Claire fleetingly, then her face crumpled like a soufflé. Lowering her head, she covered her face with her hands and began to sob.

Claire placed an arm around her and guided her down to one of the padded barstools. "What's wrong, Yasmine?" she asked, smoothing back her hair. "For you to be so nasty, something dreadful must have happened."

"The asshole dumped me."

Claire had been afraid of this. The inevitable had finally happened. She had believed all along that it was only a matter of time before Yasmine was jilted by her married lover, and she had dreaded this day. She drew her friend's head to her shoulder and let her use it as a cushion while she cried.

"The son of a bitch has been lying to me from the start," Yasmine said, her voice congested with tears. "He never intended to leave his wife. He never planned to marry me, or for us to have a life together. I've been so stupid, Claire. So goddamn stupid." She pounded the edge of the bar with her fists. "How could I have been played for such a fool?"

"Love distorts our judgment. It makes us do things we know are bad for us. We do them anyway."

Yasmine sat up and wiped her nose on the hem of her blouse. "He even made love to me last night before he broke the news. Can you believe the gall? When I got there, he practically fell on me. He told me that I was beautiful, that the days he spent without me were pure hell. We screwed like rabbits, hard and quick." Twin tears spilled over her lower eyelids and trickled down her flawless cheeks. "I loved him, Claire."

"I know. I'm sorry."

"Looking back, I can't believe I ever fell for his lies. Even though I fantasized about it, I can't see him actually flaunting me in Washington.''

"Washington?"

Yasmine snorted a laugh. "This might cost him a vote, but what the hell. Why shouldn't you know now? My mystery man was Congressman Alister Petrie."

Claire exhaled slowly. "Alister Petrie."

"Do you know him?"

"No, I never met him. But I know his wife, Belle. I made some things for her trousseau when they got married. I was doing commission work then. One of her friends recommended me to her."

"What's she like?"

"Oh, Yasmine, forget—"

"For God's sake, Claire, indulge me. What's she like?"

"Pretty. Blond. Slen—"

"That's not what I meant. I know what she looks like."

"You've met her?"

"I've seen her." Claire's brows arched inquisitively. "Yes, I spied on them a couple of times," Yasmine admitted impatiently. "I did everything a nice little mistress isn't supposed to do. I whined. I made demands. I issued ultimatums. I pleaded. I threw tantrums. I called their house in the middle of the night just to hear his voice when he answered the phone. All that crap.

"Since he began campaigning for reelection, he's had less time to spend with me. The less time we had together, the more I hounded him. That's one reason Alister got pissed, I think. I was taking chances with us getting caught. He was afraid Belle would find out. Or maybe she did find out. Who knows? Now I wouldn't believe a word the lying prick says."

"I can see why he'd be attracted to you. You're so different from her."

"In what way?"

"Every way," Claire replied. "I didn't like her. She comes from aristocracy and makes certain everyone knows it. She's cool and aloof. Snotty. Bigoted. And, I would guess, passionless.''

"Maybe he didn't lie about that," Yasmine murmured.

"It's premature to say this," Claire said hesitantly. "And you won't believe me, but it's true." She reached for Yasmine's hands and pressed them between hers. "The relationship wasn't good or you wouldn't have been so unhappy all the time. You're better off without him."

Yasmine shook her head. "No, Claire, you're wrong. I'm miserable. In fact, my entire life is in shambles."

"That's not true, Yasmine!"

"Obviously you've forgotten my financial straits. The money you'll pay me for those stock shares won't make a dent in what I owe creditors."

"That'll turn around. Give it time. You're beautiful and talented, Yasmine," she said, meaning it. "Thousands of women would trade places with you in an instant. Right now your heart is broken, but it will mend."

Yasmine's eyes narrowed and tilted up at the corners, giving her a calculating, feline look. "My heart is broken, but I'm not going to suffer alone." She withdrew her hands from Claire's grasp, reached into her shoulder bag, and withdrew an object that made Claire recoil.

"My God, Yasmine. What are you doing with that thing?"

The voodoo doll was a grotesque effigy of the congressman. She held the doll up and looked at it proudly. "See that hair on its head? That's really Alister's hair. That makes the spell more powerful. And this," she said, pointing to the exaggerated red felt penis thrusting from the doll's crotch, "well, you know what that represents."

Claire was appalled. "You're not serious, are you? A few candles and talismans, okay, that's harmless. But you can't seriously believe in spells and black magic."

Yasmine turned on her angrily. "Why not? You believe in a virgin birth, don't you?"

To argue religion was a futile pursuit. Claire wasn't going

to engage in it, especially now when her friend was emotionally fragile. She wisely kept quiet as she watched in horrified fascination as Yasmine lay the doll on the bar and reached into her blouse. She withdrew a silver charm suspended from a chain around her neck. The charm was a hollow, filigree sphere. It was filled with matter that Claire couldn't identify, but it had the odor of herbs.

"By wearing this close to my body," Yasmine said in a menacing voice, "I can control his thoughts. He won't be able to get me off his mind. I'll haunt him day and night. I'll drive him freaking nuts."

"Yasmine, you're frightening me."

She laughed low in her throat. "Yours is nothing compared to the fear Alister will experience before I'm finished."

"What do you mean 'finished'? Yasmine, what do you intend to do?"

Ignoring the question, she said, "Watch, Claire. Observe. Learn. In case you ever want to put a curse on someone."

Flipping back the collar of her shirt, she revealed a row of long, sinister pins. She pulled one from the fabric and laid it aside only long enough to strike a match from the matchbook lying on the bar. She ran the burning match along the pin until it became almost too hot for her to hold, then she plunged it into the repugnant red penis of the doll.

"Good morning, Alister," she whispered. "Sleep well? Don't even think of making love to your insipid wife. Even one of my famous blow-jobs couldn't get it up now, you limp dick." She lit another match, heated another pin, and jabbed it into the doll's torso.

Claire grabbed her by the shoulders and shook her hard. "Stop this! This is ridiculous. Practicing voodoo is dangerous and stupid and I won't have my best friend deluding herself with it." She shook her again. "Do you hear me, Yasmine?"

She blinked to clear her vision, as though Claire had snapped her out of a trance. "Of course I hear you." Smiling broadly, she asked, "You didn't think I was serious, did you?"

"I—" Claire began uncertainly.

Yasmine laughed. "I sure pulled one over on you, didn't I?" She dropped the charm back into her bodice and replaced the doll in her shoulder bag.

"Don't let Cassidy see that," Claire said. "He was interested in your Jackson Wilde doll, but I dismissed it as a gag. He might reconsider."

"Come on, Claire, relax. It's like having the gypsy lady at a carnival read your palm. You don't really believe in it, but it's fun."

Claire still wasn't convinced and her expression must have conveyed that. Yasmine shot her a retiring look as she picked up her drink. "This black magic hocus-pocus is all a hoax, but it's fun to pretend that I could really hurt Alister. Why should I be the only one agonizing? It makes me feel better to know that the bastard might be suffering a little, too." She sipped her drink. "Enough of my love life. Tell me how Cassidy sweet-talked himself into your pants."

❦

Quietly, Claire reentered the bedroom. Since it was on the west side of the house, it remained in semidarkness. Cassidy was still in bed, lying on his back with his hands stacked beneath his head, staring at the ceiling fan as it slowly rotated above him. He had an arresting profile, strong, masculine, each feature well defined. She loved the shape of his lips, and looking at them now, knowing how they tasted and felt against hers, whether supplicant or demanding, made her mouth water.

His biceps were as round and hard as apples. Soft dark hair lined his armpits and matted his chest, which rose above a flat, taut belly. It tapered into a narrow waist and an even trimmer pelvis. His sex was full and firm, and Claire knew it by touch, smell, and taste.

She tried to suppress the erotic memories as she closed the door behind her. He turned his head. "Hi."

"Hi."

"Everything all right?"

"It is now. It wasn't. She was awfully upset."

"About what?"

"Is that any business of yours?"

He eased his hands from beneath his head and propped himself on one elbow. "Don't get your stinger out, Claire. It was a politely curious question."

She sat on the edge of the bed but kept her back to him. "Her lover broke off their affair. And don't ask me who he was because I can't divulge that."

"I didn't intend to ask."

"So . . . good. We've got no problem."

"Really? Could have fooled me. From your tone of voice, I'd guess we do."

She stiffened her spine. "You should go back to your room now. Yasmine would like to shower and sleep for a couple of hours before we start working."

"This hasn't got anything to do with Yasmine."

'All right, it doesn't." Claire sprang to her feet and turned to confront him. She flung her hand toward the French doors. "In case you haven't noticed, Cassidy, the sun is up. It's morning."

"So what? Are you going to turn into a pumpkin?"

"No, but you're going to turn into an assistant district attorney who would love to pin a murder rap on me."

"Did you commit murder?"

"I don't have to answer that."

"I'd prefer you didn't, if it's going to be another lie."

"Just leave."

He threw off the sheet and sprang from the bed, naked and

sexy. Carnal recollections of last night elbowed their way into her consciousness. They were unwelcome, but they were there nevertheless and she was forced to make room for them. Seeing him like this, she longed to touch him again, to feel his powerful thighs against hers, to have his hands stroking her body.

She watched as he pulled on the old, faded jeans he'd worn into her room the night before. He didn't button them this time, either. They had molded to his body so well and so long ago that there was little risk of them falling down.

"Why don't you cut the bullshit about Yasmine and her secret lover and tell me what this is all about."

"I don't know what you're talking about."

"Don't." He aimed an index finger at the tip of her nose. "Don't retreat behind that lofty finishing-school disdain, Claire. I know now that it's an act you put on when it conveniently suits your purpose, when you want to avoid a confrontation. I met the real you last night. There," he said, pointing down at the rumpled bed.

"Is that why you took me to bed, so you could get to know me better?"

"Yes. In every sense."

"How romantic. Now what was the real reason?"

He grabbed her hand and shoved it into his open fly. "Drop this nonsense, kiss me, and in about twenty seconds your memory will be revived."

She pulled her hand free. "I'm sure you'll claim you only wanted to make love to me."

"That was the general idea, yeah."

"I don't believe you, Cassidy. You're always accusing me of lying. Now I think you are."

He snorted a laugh and shook his head in bafflement. "*What*? What happened during the half-hour you were gone?"

"I recaptured my sanity," she muttered, turning her head aside.

He took her chin between his fingers and drew her back around. "Don't talk to me in riddles."

"Okay, I'll be blunt," she said, lifting her chin off the perch of his fingertips. "Yasmine said some things that made me think."

"About what?"

"Sweet talk."

"Come again?"

Yasmine's question as to how Cassidy had wound up in her bed had yanked her from the warm, hazy glow of being in love and had plunged her into cold reality. Feeling tremulous but sounding intentionally hostile, she asked, "Why did you sleep with me last night?"

"Isn't that rather obvious, Claire?"

"You'd like me to think so."

"We wanted each other," he said.

"But you initiated it."

"You weren't coerced."

"No, you didn't come to me waving your ID, or with a satchel full of official documents, or issuing threats. You were much too clever for that because you know how I resent and resist authority. Instead you approached me as a man to a woman. You tapped into my jealousy. Yes," she said, slicing the air with her hands. "For whatever irrational reason, I was jealous of Yasmine yesterday. You took advantage of that and the sexual ambience that prevails over our sets.

"Yasmine talked about being a fool," she continued. "I comforted her by saying that, at one time or another, we all take departures from our better judgment and it's usually because of our libidos.

"That's when it occurred to me what a colossal fool I'd been. You wooed me into bed, hoping that by morning you'd have your killer. Maybe you were counting on breaking down my defenses and getting a confession before dawn."

"Oh for Christ's sake!" Having listened with diminishing patience, he now raked all ten fingers through his hair, then propped his hands on his hips. "Precisely when was this confession supposed to take place, Claire? During foreplay? Or at the moment of climax, did I expect you to scream, 'I'm guilty'? No, wait, I've got it. I was hoping that once we'd screwed ourselves senseless, you'd talk in your sleep, right?"

"This isn't funny."

"You're damn right it's not," he shouted.

"If you wanted to catch your murderer so badly, why be so insidious? Why didn't you just arrest me?"

"Hasn't it occurred to you what a conflict of interests this creates for me? For weeks I've been wrestling with it. Last night I wanted to make love to you more than I wanted an indictment."

"Liar."

He advanced on her, his stride long and angry. "If you think the reason I wanted to sleep with you had anything to do with this murder case, then your memory is shorter than the time it takes you to come."

Her palm connected hard with his bristly jaw, making a sharp, cracking sound. "Get out of my sight."

He caught her wrist and yanked her hard against him. Anger seethed in his eyes. For a moment Claire thought he might return her slap. Finally he spoke, but his lips were thin and hard and barely moved to form the words. "Gladly, Miss Laurent."

Before he went through the French doors, he turned. "You know what's really got your goat, Claire? You're mad at yourself for showing me the real you. You're angry because you let down your guard, because you liked everything we did so damn much. You loved it, from the first kiss to the last sigh. And the only one lying about it is you—to yourself."

"What do you want to hear?" she lashed out. "That you're a terrific lover? Does your male ego require morning-after accolades? Okay, I'll say it. It was bloody wonderful. You knew all the right buttons to push, when to be aggressive, when to be passive."

"Thanks."

"It's not a compliment. A technique as smooth as yours must have taken years of practice to develop. How many other female suspects have you bedded, hmm? Is that how you count coup? Not whether or not you send them to prison, but if you've managed to screw them first!"

"Listen," he said through clenched teeth, "I've never had to fuck my way into getting a conviction."

"Oh no?"

"No. I've never had to resort to tricks. I'm too good at what I do."

"Well, if you're so damn good, Mr. Cassidy, go about your business and get the hell out of my bedroom!"

Chapter Twenty-one

❧❧

"**Y**ou look fabulous." Joshua Wilde breezed into Ariel's hospital room pushing a wheelchair. The nursing staff had informed him that she was dressed and waiting to be escorted outside, where a throng of journalists was clambering to take pictures and question her about this latest episode in her dramatic life. "Your chariot awaits, madam."

Ariel snapped the latches on her suitcase. "Is the chariot necessary?"

"Hospital policy. Besides, it has such a biblical ring."

She frowned at him over her shoulder.

Josh accepted her foul disposition with equanimity. He looked inordinately handsome and dashing this morning. As usual, he was wearing his chic clothing with flair and his hair was well groomed and shiny, one long wave dipping low over his brow. But there was an uncharacteristic spring in his step. The last few days of rest and relaxation had rejuvenated him.

Even though Ariel was still dressed in unrelieved mourning black, she looked remarkably attractive for someone just discharged from the hospital. A beautician had been brought in to shampoo and blow-dry her long platinum hair. She'd applied her own cosmetics and had purposefully failed to put cover-up over the faint shadows beneath her large blue eyes. The haunting effect would remind her adoring public just how grueling her recent ordeal had been.

She wasn't especially glad to see Josh and was determined not to share his cheerful mood. "You're grinning like a goose. What about?"

"Nothing," he replied pleasantly. "Just generally happy."

"While I've been cooped up in here, you must have spent the entire time playing the piano."

"Practically around the clock." He pilfered a banana from a lavish fruit basket, peeled it, and bit off a large chunk. "Didn't play one gospel tune, either."

"All that classical junk," she muttered, as she checked her reflection one last time in her compact mirror. "I'm almost glad I wasn't there to hear it."

"I sounded pretty good, if I do say so myself."

She closed her compact with an economic flick of her wrist and dropped it into her handbag. "Keep your fingers limber because in a few days you won't be playing for pleasure anymore. You'll be pounding out gospel again."

Josh's smile faltered. He tossed the banana peel onto her bedtray. "What do you mean 'in a few days'? The doctors said you should have total rest for at least another month."

"I don't care what they said. By the end of next week I want another prayer meeting scheduled. We had so much momentum going, then this." She slapped her stomach as though punishing the child she carried. "We've got to get back on track. The sooner the better. I don't intend to let up until Cassidy, or whoever's in charge of the investigation now, puts somebody on trial for Jackson's murder.

"And that will be only the beginning. I plan to be present in the courtroom every day. The trial will be a hot news item for weeks, months. I want to be there for the duration. Visible. A tragic figure. I've got to make the most of the free publicity. Ready?"

While outlining her plans, she had been checking the bathroom, closet, and bureau drawers for anything she might have previously overlooked. Now she turned to Josh, who had remained quiet throughout her speech.

"Let me get this straight," he said tightly. "You haven't learned your lesson yet."

"I'm going to eat, all right? You can stop nagging me about that."

"But the bulimia was only half the problem, Ariel. You're going to drive yourself to the point of another collapse, is that the plan?"

"No, that's not the plan," she said with syrupy sweetness. "I don't intend to wind up in the hospital again, but I'm not going to retire from living just because I got a little overexerted and had a fainting spell."

"What about the baby?"

"What about it?"

"Is it mine?"

"No," she answered in a testy, clipped voice. "It's your dearly departed father's. He did this to me," she said, her eyes glinting with malice.

"Are you sure?"

"Yes. You always use a rubber. He didn't. The son of a bitch."

"You didn't want a child?"

"Hell no! Do you think I'm crazy? Why would I want to have a kid and give up everything I've worked for?"

"But Daddy wanted a child."

"Oh naturally," she said caustically. "You know how he was. Him and his monstrous ego. He wanted a little Jackson Wilde Junior who mirrored him to a tee." She regarded Josh with contempt. "His first son had been such a disappointment."

Josh lowered his eyes to his long, slender, musician's

hands; there was nothing he could say to refute the hateful truth.

"He'd been badgering me to have a kid," Ariel continued. "He said it would be good for our image and would strengthen the ministry. We'd be more popular than the First Family, he said.

"I kept putting him off, but, as always, the son of a bitch is having the last word. I'll bet he's having a good laugh on me right now." She glared down at the floor and stomped her foot, as though addressing her husband in hell. "I hate you, you bastard."

"When did you discover that you're pregnant, Ariel?"

She swung her hair over her shoulder and looked at her somber stepson. "I found out the night I collapsed, about an hour after they brought me here and examined me."

"You didn't know before then?"

She cocked her head, her eyes squinting shrewdly. "What are you getting at?"

"Did you suspect you were pregnant before Daddy . . . died?"

She turned her back on him and reached for her handbag. "What difference does it make? He knocked me up. If he were alive, I'd be stuck with a kid. Fortunately, he's in no position to prevent me from losing it."

Josh spun her around so quickly that her neck audibly popped. " 'Losing it'?"

She threw off his hands. "Don't be naïve, Josh. If you think I'm going to give up my career as a televangelist for dirty diapers and strained beets, you've got another think coming. I don't want a kid. I never did." She smiled smugly. "This is one argument Jackson is going to lose."

"Have you thought about how unpopular you'd become among your faithful flock if word leaked out that you'd had an abortion?"

"I'm not that stupid," she snapped. "Anyone who's seen a TV in the past week knows that I collapsed from exhaustion and grief. Soon it will be duly reported that in spite of my pregnancy, I'm dedicated to fulfilling Jackson's mission and denouncing his enemies. I won't rest until I see his killer captured and punished.

"For a while, I'll use the pregnancy to my benefit. Tears will flow every time I talk about how thrilled Jackson would be to know that he'd left his living seed in my womb. Talk about having a biblical ring!" she added with a coarse laugh.

"I'll reference Abraham and Sarah and how God finally rewarded their faithfulness with a child. Then, in a few weeks, I'll grieve myself into a miscarriage. Think of the avalanche of public sentiment we'll gain then. 'Robbed of her husband, robbed of her child, she courageously continues her crusade.' "

The fantasy caption made her eyes glow like blue flames. She glanced at Josh and laughed again. "Why, what's the matter, Josh? You look like you're about to blow chow."

"The thought of it makes me sick."

"Don't tell me you were excited about the baby. Is that why you've been so chipper lately? Did you fancy yourself a stand-in daddy for your little stepbrother?" She patted his cheek. "If you weren't so dumb, you'd be kind of cute."

He swatted her hand aside. "I'm not nearly as dumb as you mistakenly think, Ariel." With an irritable jerk of his head, he indicated the wheelchair. "Ready?"

"More than ready. But I'm walking, not riding." She reached for her suitcase.

"You shouldn't be carrying that."

"Why not? I'm anxious to free myself of Jackson's last shackle." Hoisting the heavy suitcase, she marched toward the door.

"It's open." Cassidy looked up from the mound of paperwork on his desk.

Detective Howard Glenn strolled in and nonchalantly plopped into a chair. "Welcome back."

"Thanks."

"How'd it go?"

"Just as I told you it probably would. Ms. Laurent cited that there are hundreds of cars like hers in this state, and she said that Yasmine has only a passing interest in voodoo. She's shown a fancy for several religions but isn't serious about any of them. One thing I did learn. Yasmine does have a mystery lover, but it wasn't Wilde. Her affair is currently on the skids. You might want to put a man on that."

"I'll do it. In the meantime, I've been checking out some other things."

"And?"

Glenn withdrew a small spiral notebook from the breast pocket of his tweed sports jacket. "So far—and I've still got a long way to go, mind you—I've got ten more very fishy parties that made contributions to Wilde's ministry. Substantial contributions."

"How substantial?"

"In the five-to twenty-five-thou range." He paused for Cassidy's reaction.

"I'm listening."

"Three of the ten own movie theaters of the triple x-rated variety. Two of them own and operate scummy bookstores. I've got two massage parlors and two titty bars." He shot Cassidy a man-to-man grin.

Cassidy remained unsmiling. "That's only nine. You said ten."

"There's a movie star that's generally thought to be the hottest thing in porno flicks since come shots."

Cassidy left his swivel desk chair and moved toward the windows. Pushing his hands into his pants pockets, he sightlessly stared outside. "Let me guess. After they made their 'offerings,' Wilde turned off the heat."

"I haven't had the manpower to verify that," Glenn said, "but that would be my first guess."

"Maybe Wilde had upped the price of his good graces and somebody didn't cotton to it."

"Maybe."

Cassidy turned around. "Were any of these people even remotely close to New Orleans the night he was killed?"

"Now you see, that's the bitch," the detective said, tugging thoughtfully on his earlobe. "They're scattered across the U.S. of A. None is really close to here."

"This city has an airport and a bus terminal, not to mention interstate highways."

"No need to get nasty, Cassidy."

"Sorry, but I'm in a nasty mood."

"You're entitled," Glenn said with an uncaring shrug. "Only the movie star claims to have ever visited New Orleans."

"When?"

"Long time ago. She was in Rome at the time of Wilde's murder."

"Rome, Italy?"

"That's the one."

"Does that check out?"

"She's got an Italian movie director who says she's been living with him in his villa since April."

A feeling of defeat settled over Cassidy with the weight of chain mail. "I suggest you stay with it, Glenn. Tell your men to go over those lists a hundred times if necessary. Sift out anyone who doesn't fit the profile of a fundamental, Bible-thumping disciple."

"I agree," he said, rolling off his spine to stand. "But it's gonna take time."

Brows furrowed, Cassidy asked, "What about the corporate contributors?"

"I've run across a few. Nothing interesting."

"Let's keep checking them out, too. Who's behind the company name? A business is good protection if somebody wants to remain anonymous. Let's start with the corporations that have connections in the South, particularly here, and fan out from there."

The detective nodded and shuffled out. Cassidy would have liked to give him a swift kick in the butt to see if he would move any faster. Right now, however, he couldn't afford to alienate anyone. His allies were scarce. Office politics being what they were, no one wanted to be chummy with a loser. Whenever he approached the coffee machine, his co-workers scattered like spilled BBs.

Upon his return to the city, he had reported to Crowder that the trip to Mississippi had yielded nothing. The D.A. hadn't taken well to the bad news. He was out of patience, he told Cassidy. "And you're out of time. I want something concrete from you by the end of this week or you're off the case."

"Whoever you assign in my place will run up against the same brick walls, Tony, and he wouldn't work as well with Glenn."

"Maybe not."

"I'm used to him." Crowder's expression remained stony. Cassidy sighed. "Look, there's no physical evidence beyond a few carpet fibers that could have come off any one of ten thousand cars in this parish."

"One of which belongs to Claire Laurent, who had both motive and opportunity."

"But I can't put her inside that hotel suite with Wilde at the time of the murder."

"The fibers might be enough."

"No way in hell," Cassidy said, shaking his head stubbornly. "I'm not going before the grand jury until I've covered my ass."

Crowder glowered at him. "Just make damn certain it's

your ass, and my ass, you're protecting and not Claire Laurent.''

The remark had made Cassidy mad enough to smash Crowder's face with his fists. Instead, however, he had stormed from Crowder's office. There had been no communication between them since, and that had been two days ago. The hours were ticking off.

The hell of it was that Crowder had hit the target at dead center. He *did* want to protect Claire. Although he was angry enough to strangle her himself, he didn't want to incarcerate her. But if she was guilty, he'd have no choice. He'd have to put her in prison for the rest of her life, without benefit of suspension, probation, or parole.

"Christ."

He dug the heels of his hands into his eyesockets and propped his elbows on his desk. It was in that vanquished posture that Joshua Wilde found him moments later.

Cassidy looked up when he heard the tentative knock on his office door. Josh stood hesitantly on the threshold. "The secretary said to come on in."

"What do you want?" Cassidy snarled.

"Are you still in charge of my father's murder case?"

"That's what the *Times Picayune* reported this morning. Come in. But I warn you that I'm in a pissy mood, so if you're here to jack me around, do yourself a favor and leave now."

"I didn't come to jack you around."

"Sit down." The younger man took a chair across the desk from him.

Cassidy nodded toward the front of the building. "Why aren't you down there lending support?"

Ever since his return from Rosesharon, each time Cassidy entered the building, he had to push his way through picket lines declaring him incompetent. It was a vocal and hostile crowd that paraded hour after hour, singing their theme song, and brandishing contentious pickets whenever they caught sight of him.

"That's my stepmother's latest brainstorm," Josh said of the well organized protest demonstration.

"I thought she just got out of the hospital."

"She did, but she dug right in. She's not going to give you a minute's peace until you convict a killer."

"She's not the only one," Cassidy muttered to himself. "Why don't you advise her to put a stop to that nonsense outside? It's serving no real purpose."

"It's getting her on the six-o'clock news. That's what she's after."

"It's only a matter of time before it turns ugly. Some pretty mean characters have business in this building, you know. Somebody's bound to get hurt. Surely Ariel doesn't want any adverse publicity."

"She'd figure a way to swing it to her advantage."

"She didn't fare too well with her picketers at French Silk. The Laurents made you look like goons."

"The way Claire Laurent turned that situation around made Ariel mad as hell." His snickering expression turned thoughtful. "She's an interesting lady. Most people would have resorted to mudslinging. She's got class. I admire her moxie."

Yeah, Cassidy thought dismally. *You gotta admire her moxie.*

"Anyway, back to Ariel," Josh said. "She doesn't listen to any advice from me. In fact, she doesn't listen to anyone's advice. Once she makes up her mind to do something, she's relentless, unstoppable."

"Are we talking about your stepmother or General Patton?"

"Believe me, Cassidy, you don't know her like I do. She's gone crazy, especially . . . especially since my father was killed."

Josh's eyes became shifty and skittered away from Cassidy's gaze, giving him a surge of hope. His no-fail instinct was telling him that he was on the brink of a breakthrough. It was tough to carry off, but he pretended to be unimpressed with what he'd heard so far. He raised his hand, indicating that Josh should continue.

"I'm sure you've heard about Ariel's pregnancy."

"Are congratulations in order?"

"You mean am I the father?" Josh shook his head. "She says Daddy was. That's why I'm here." Suddenly he came to his feet and began pacing along the edge of Cassidy's desk.

"Why don't you just relax and tell me what's eating you." Cassidy assumed a confidant's voice, the kind he hoped would inspire trust and give the late preacher's cowardly son courage.

"I lied to you," Josh blurted.

"About what?"

"About that night. About Ariel and me being together the whole time. The truth is . . . she . . . she left my suite and went back to theirs."

"When?"

"Earlier. Around midnight."

"For how long?"

"Fifteen, maybe twenty minutes."

"Did she speak to your father?"

"I don't know. Swear to God."

"Never mind God. Swear it to me."

Josh wet his lips. "I swear to you I don't know."

"Okay. Go on."

"She trumped up this excuse that she went looking for a piece of sheet music. She says Daddy was asleep. I didn't think anything of it until the following morning. She asked me not to mention that time lapse to you or to the police."

Cassidy's heart was thumping, but he knew better than to let his hopes soar on the word of a man who had already admitted to one crucial lie. This was only hearsay. It would never hold up in court. He still had no real evidence against the widow. However, this would give his investigation new focus and take the heat off Claire. After days of famine, this seemed like a bountiful harvest.

He asked, "Why'd you agree to lie about it, Josh?"

"I honestly didn't think it made any difference. Ariel was almost hysterical when she discovered his body. It was so, you know, bloody. I didn't think she could have had anything to do with the murder."

"What do you think now?"

Josh stopped pacing. Standing at the edge of Cassidy's desk, he faced him. "Now, I think she did."

Cassidy was afraid to swallow, to blink, afraid that the merest motion would shatter Joshua Wilde's fragile statement and it would disintegrate, that it would no longer be real. "What changed your mind?"

Josh was a man at war with himself. At least that's the impression he gave. He wiped his damp palms on his pants legs. "Contrary to what Ariel's saying to the media, she's unhappy about this pregnancy. In fact, she's livid over it. She plans to stage a miscarriage, which will serve a dual purpose—get rid of the baby and win more sympathizers."

Playing along, Cassidy registered shock. "She sounds like a monster."

"You don't know the half of it, Mr. Cassidy. She envisions herself a megastar, wielding influence over millions of people. You ought to hear the plans she has for the *Prayer and Praise Hour*. Outlandish stuff. For a start, she wants the pulpit to become a political forum for candidates who share her views on current issues. She's already extended invitations to several guest speakers. She's ambitious and shrewd, and determined not to let anything or anyone stand in her way. She's gone off the deep end, lost all touch with reality."

"Get back to the murder."

Josh resumed his seat. He linked his fingers between his knees and stared at them as he spoke. "My daddy was a tyrant. He played God over everybody, including Ariel and me. Especially Ariel and me. He teased her about her tendency to gain weight until she developed an eating disorder."

"The newspapers hinted that she'd been diagnosed bulimic, but it was never confirmed by the hospital staff in Kansas City."

"It's true. And this baby, she sees it as just another of Daddy's cruel jokes. See, it's like he's still got control over her. I think she knew she was pregnant long before that night she collapsed. I think she was furious with Daddy for forcing a child on her when she'd made it clear to him that she didn't want one. I think she killed him over it."

Cassidy decided to play devil's advocate by shooting holes in Josh's allegations, the way a defense attorney would shoot holes in a case no better corroborated than this. "It works in theory, Josh, but it's still circumstantial. Did you hear your father and Ariel arguing over this pregnancy?"

"No. I didn't know she was pregnant until the night she was rushed to the emergency room."

"Did you hear her threaten to kill your father?"

"No."

"Ever?"

"No. He wouldn't have tolerated that kind of talk."

"Does you stepmother own a gun?"

"No. At least not to my knowledge. But her brother is a convict."

Cassidy had uncovered that in his preliminary investigation. "According to prison records, Ariel hasn't had any contact with her brother for years, not even a postcard. I doubt he could have procured a weapon for her without somebody finding out."

Josh shrugged. "That was just a guess. She could have gotten a gun on the sly and disposed of it where it wouldn't be found."

"Maybe," Cassidy said noncommittally.

"Think of the wounds. A man gets a woman pregnant. She's furious with him for saddling her with an unwanted child. She shoots his balls off. Doesn't that make sense?"

Cassidy squinted one eye as though considering the viability of the hypothesis. He rubbed the back of his neck. "I have to tell you, Josh, it's shallow."

"I thought you'd be more excited," he said morosely.

"When she left your suite that night, was Ariel wearing shoes?"

"Shoes? No. She was barefoot, I think. She had taken off her shoes when we made love. I don't think she put them back on. Why?"

"We're still checking on some carpet fibers found in your father's bedroom." He paused for a moment. "Did either you or Ariel rent a car while you were here?"

"I did. I like having my own transportation."

"You drove around New Orleans?"

"Plenty. Every day. I rented a convertible and enjoyed driving with the top down."

That information could easily be checked out. "Did Ariel ever accompany you on these drives?"

"Once, I think. Twice maybe. Why?"

"Are you still sleeping with her?"

"No. Not for weeks now."

"What happened?"

Josh glanced up at him, then away. "I don't know. She got so carried away with being the leader of the ministry, there never seemed to be time. Or she'd be tired and cranky. Or I'd fuss at her about throwing up and she'd get mad. Now that I know about the baby . . ."

"What?"

"Well, I wouldn't feel right making love to her while she's carrying my stepbrother."

Cassidy leaned forward. "Do you see the irony in that.

Josh? It was okay to screw your father's wife while he was alive, but now that he's dead and she's pregnant with his baby, you've gone squeamish.''

Josh turned defensive. "That's how I feel."

"Okay." Cassidy leaned back in his chair. "For the moment, let's pretend it happened like this. Ready? Ariel left your company, returned to the suite she shared with your father, killed him with a gun no one knew she possessed and which hasn't been recovered, then came back for round two in bed with you, correctly assuming that you'd be her alibi."

"That's how I see it."

Cassidy smacked his lips with consternation. "What I'm having trouble with is your motivation for telling me this now."

"The lie has been on my conscience."

"Conscience?" Cassidy repeated skeptically.

Again, Josh took umbrage. "I might be an adulterer. I admit to cuckolding my own father. But I'm not going to share a murder rap with Ariel."

Indecisively, he gnawed on his lower lip. "Okay, it's more than conscience, Mr. Cassidy. You might not believe this, but I'm afraid of her."

Cassidy snorted.

Josh exclaimed, "It's true. Before all this, I knew she was ambitious and shrewd, but she's gone way overboard. She's ruthless. Mean. She stops at nothing to get her way. If somebody crosses her over the least little thing, she fires him. No mercy. No discussion. Zap," he said, smacking his fist against his opposite palm. "He's expunged."

He stared down at his shaky hands. "It's as though I've had blinders on. Maybe I was so focused on my father, I didn't see Ariel as she really is until now. I think she's capable of doing just about anything to protect her interests. I think she's unbalanced. Dangerously unbalanced."

Cassidy subjected him to a long, thoughtful stare, then stood, signaling an end to the interview. "Thanks, Josh." He extended his right hand. The young man shook it, looking bewildered.

"That's it? I thought you'd have a million questions to ask me."

"There'll be plenty later. I'm going to work on this immediately. In the meantime, act normally around your stepmother. Go about your business as usual. Don't do or say anything that might tip her that you've been to see me. Let her continue thinking that I eliminated her as a suspect weeks ago." Cassidy looked at Josh solemnly. "I know this wasn't easy for you."

"No, it wasn't. For years Ariel and I took refuge from my father in each other. I guess you could say we were codependent. We shared a common misery and relied on each other to make it bearable. Since his death, we haven't needed each other to exact petty revenge. Hating him was the only attraction that had drawn us together.

"I believe that Ariel has serious psychological problems that date back to her impoverished childhood. I get mad at her, but mostly I fear her. Still," he added, shaking his head sadly, "I can't let her get away with murder."

"Josh, because of your longstanding affair with Ariel, I have to know—would you be able to testify against her in court?"

Without a moment's hesitation Josh replied, "Yes."

They said their goodbyes. Josh had no sooner left his office than Cassidy pulled on his suit jacket and straightened his tie. As soon as he'd given Josh enough time to leave the building, he took the elevator up to the next floor and headed for Anthony Crowder's office. He didn't heed the secretary's warning that Crowder was terribly busy and had asked not to be disturbed. With a confidence he hadn't felt in days, he barged in unannounced.

"Before you start shouting at me, listen. I think I know who killed Jackson Wilde."

Crowder tossed down the ballpoint pen he'd been using. "Well?"

"His son."

Chapter Twenty-two

Practically verbatim, Cassidy repeated his conversation with Joshua Wilde. When he finished, Crowder stopped drumming his fingers. "I'm confused. You said you thought the son was the culprit, but he's claiming it's the widow."

"Out of pique. Tattling is a coward's way of getting even, and Josh has a yellow streak a yard wide down his back."

"Then where'd he get the courage to kill his father?"

"He caught Wilde at his most vulnerable. Naked. Lying on his back. Possibly even asleep. Josh knew his father's habits. He knew when to attack. Which would also apply to Ariel, for that matter," Cassidy mumbled as an afterthought. "Anyway, Josh shot Wilde in the balls to throw us off, to make it look like a woman had killed him. He even reminded me of that when we talked."

Crowder folded his meaty hands beneath his chin and ruminated on it a moment. "Why would Josh want his father dead? Jealousy?"

"Possibly. If Ariel's baby is his father's, as she claims. But I believe he had a stronger motivation."

"Stronger than jealousy? Money?"

"Not directly. No doubt Josh had a hankering to take over the ministry when his old man was no longer around. He figured he was heir apparent to the spotlight. For a young man who had been his father's apprentice, who had always lived in his giant shadow, that would be a reasonable ambition."

"Instead, Ariel seizes control."

"With both hands. Just as before, Josh is in the background. He's still second banana. But discounting the ministry as a factor, there's the personal one."

"Which is?"

"Josh admitted to me that Jackson Wilde was a tyrant who psychologically abused both of them. He had been Jackson's whipping boy all his adult life. He finally had had it up to here. So he gathered his meager courage and disposed of his old man, only to have his stepmother and lover elbow in and overshadow him. Talk about frustrating."

"He traded one despot for another."

"Right. To get rid of her, he makes her out the killer. Or maybe . . ." Now that he had opened a new channel of thought, other possibilities came to mind. "Maybe they plotted together to off Jackson. Then, for the reasons I cited before, Josh has turned into Judas."

"Sounds feasible either way. Have you discussed it with Glenn?

"Not yet, but he'll do backsprings. He figured all along it was either Ariel or Josh. He'll want to put them under a microscope and probe until we know them inside out. I'd like to put tails on them."

"The P.C. will shit if you ask for more men."

"You gave me until the end of the week, Tony. Play fair. Help us out. Run interference with the commissioner."

Cassidy returned to his office feeling as though he'd had

an internal battery recharged. For the first time in days, adrenaline was coursing through his veins. He had a purpose, a new plan of attack. He would stay with it until he'd exhausted all possibilities, as well as himself.

The first thing he did was make a series of telephone calls.

There was no need for Cassidy to identify himself on the first call. He simply asked, "Are you still feeding info to that TV reporter?"

The informant system was a two-way street. The D.A.'s office used the same sources as the media, sometimes transmitting information that, like a pistol firing blanks, was loaded with half-facts and innuendos that were intentionally misleading.

Cassidy said, "I had a lengthy and private conversation with Joshua Wilde this afternoon. He left my office looking angry and upset. That's it for now."

He dispatched a clerk to check all the car-leasing agencies in the city. "Find the one that leased a car to Joshua Wilde during the week of his father's murder. I want to know the make and model he rented, the mileage he put on it, and the condition it was in when he dropped it off. If it was a Chrysler product with blue carpet, I want the car chased down and taken immediately to the police lab. Thanks." Perhaps the lab boys would find a speck of dried blood that would turn out to be Jackson Wilde's and—bingo!—he'd have a bona fide suspect.

"This'll be the easiest stakeout ever," Cassidy told the police lieutenant who had been placed in charge of the surveillance team Crowder had weaseled out of the commissioner. "Joshua and Ariel Wilde are more visible than drag queens on Bourbon Street. They can't possibly give you the slip."

Once those responsibilities had been delegated, Cassidy sat back in his chair and sighed with a heightened sense of optimism. Something was bound to turn up. A piece of previously undisclosed evidence would point the accusing finger at either Josh or Ariel and away from Claire.

He had tried not to think about her since their bitter quarrel at Rosesharon, but to no avail. She remained uppermost in his mind—her body, her sweet lovemaking, and her angry allegations.

It was as if she had opened the closet of his soul and found the skeleton there, and she couldn't have rattled the bones of it any louder. She had accused him of deceit and manipulation. At one time that might have been true. As a defense attorney, he'd exercised whatever means were necessary to get an acquittal. He'd used theatrics, tears, laughter, scorn, whatever it took to have his clients walk from the courtroom cleared of all charges.

If his conscience ever pricked him, he justified his actions. Defending criminals was his duty, wasn't it? Even felons deserved their day in court. Somebody had to plead their cases before the judge and jury, so why not him? He was only doing his job, he told himself.

He had known those were justifications. There were ethical and reasonable ways to defend an accused without resorting to courtroom tricks, which he'd often used for no reason other than to show off.

Look at me, clever Robert Cassidy, the boy wonder who didn't go to an Ivy League prep school and didn't earn his law degree at Harvard. Turned out pretty damn well for a boy from rural Kentucky, didn't he?

Winning had been his ultimate goal, not seeking justice . . . until that one case he'd won, and the stakes had been far too high. When Claire had accused him of deceit and manipulation, she didn't know how close she was to being right about him, *as he'd once been.* But not as he was now. He brought the bad guys to justice and put them away where they could no longer hurt innocent people.

This case was no exception. He would go the distance to see that justice was done for whomever was found guilty by a jury of his peers of the murder of Jackson Wilde.

God help him if that person turned out to be Claire Laurent.

But it wouldn't, he told himself stubbornly. She was innocent. No woman who was that warm and giving in bed could have killed in cold blood. He'd touched not only her lips, and breasts, and thighs, and belly. He'd touched her soul. If it was poisoned, he would have known it.

But, contrary to what she believed, determining her guilt or innocence wasn't the reason he'd slept with her. That had been as inevitable as the tide. From the day they'd met, that part of their fate had been sealed.

As soon as she was vindicated, he'd go to her and humbly apologize for having put her through this awful ordeal. After all, she couldn't respect him if he didn't take his job as a public prosecutor seriously. Once they had apologized for their misgivings about each other, they'd make love again.

The thought stirred him physically, bringing him back into the present. Claire would be home from Mississippi by now. He stared at his desk telephone, tempted to call her. But no. She would still be angry. Best to give her a few more days to cool off.

In the meantime, he would dig diligently, looking for the missing element that would confirm someone else's guilt and exonerate Claire.

She was innocent.

🦎

Claire frowned at the unopened mail stacked in piles on her desk. There were bills to pay, memos to sort through, and a menacing envelope from the IRS to open. She lacked the energy to tackle the paperwork and attributed her ennui to the trip. She had worked very hard, on a rigid schedule, in oppressive, muggy heat. She needed and deserved a few days' rest before resuming her work. Then she realized that a few days' rest wasn't going to remedy her problem.

She warded off the depressing thought and pulled her mind back to the mess on her desk. In addition to the unopened mail were recent editions of the newspaper. According to an unidentified but reliable source, Assistant District Attorney Cassidy was readjusting his investigation to focus on Ariel and Joshua Wilde.

His name, printed in bold type face, captured her attention, and she stared at it until she lost track of time. In all likelihood she would have continued staring and remembering if her mother hadn't interrupted, appearing at her door carrying a tray.

"Would you like some tea, Claire Louise? You've looked so tired lately, I thought it might help perk you up."

"Thank you, Mama. That sounds wonderful. But only if you'll stay and share it."

"I was hoping you'd ask."

Claire smiled and, taking one of the newspapers with her, moved to the sitting area where she had first entertained Cassidy. It seemed that everything she said or did reminded her of him. She resented his intrusive power over her mind. He hadn't called or made any attempt to see her since the morning he'd left Rosesharon without a goodbye. She didn't know whether to be relieved, heartbroken, insulted, or a combination of the three.

Thoughts of him evoked every emotion she was acquainted with; some were blissful to experience, some miserable. She would catch herself grinning demurely, then in the next moment be on the verge of tears. Not since the social workers had dragged her from Aunt Laurel's house had anyone wielded that much power over her.

Mary Catherine set the silver service tray on the low coffee table. She passed Claire a hand-embroidered linen napkin, then poured them each a cup of fragrant tea from a china pot.

They chatted about inconsequential matters while they sipped their tea and nibbled on tea cakes Mary Catherine and Harry had baked that morning. The trip to Mississippi had been good for Mary Catherine. Claire noticed a healthy rosiness in her mother's cheeks that subtracted years from her appearance. Her eyes were clear and animated. They didn't have the vacancy that had always alarmed her, even as a child, because she recognized it as a harbinger of a "spell." Mary Catherine seemed more in tune with her surroundings. To Claire's knowledge, she hadn't had another lapse since taking Cassidy's fountain pen.

As though reading Claire's mind, she said, "I see you were reading the newspapers. It says Mr. Cassidy now believes that Jackson Wilde's son or widow killed him. Isn't that silly?"

"Silly?"

"They didn't do it. And I don't believe Mr. Cassidy thinks so either."

"How do you know they didn't do it, Mama?"

Ignoring the question, Mary Catherine asked one of her own. "And why are those people picketing in front of our building again?" Picket-toting Wilde disciples had kept vigil in front of French Silk since their return to the city.

"I wish they'd go away," Mary Catherine said with vexation. "It's difficult for Harry and me to go to the market in the mornings. I enjoy our outings, but having to get through that crowd ruins them."

To Mary Catherine's mind, the inability to get to the French Market without a hassle was more worrisome than having her daughter accused of murder. But that wasn't as disturbing to Claire as her mother's previous statements. "The pickets are a temporary inconvenience, Mama. Once they arrest somebody for killing Reverend Wilde, they will disband."

"Will he ever come back?"

For one heart-stopping instant, Claire thought she referred to Jackson Wilde. "Who, Mama?" she asked hoarsely.

"Mr. Cassidy."

Claire's shoulders relaxed as she slowly exhaled. "I don't know. Why?"

Tears suddenly welled up in Mary Catherine's eyes. Her lower lip began to tremble. "I was so hoping that when you fell in love, your young man wouldn't disappoint you like mine did me.''

She removed a monogrammed handkerchief from the pocket of her skirt. The linen was so sheer that it appeared to have been spun rather than woven. It smelled like the rose-scented sachets she kept in her bureau drawers.

As she blotted her eyes, Claire reached out and covered her hand. ''Don't cry, Mama. It was never . . . that way . . . with Mr. Cassidy and me.''

''Oh,'' she said with a soft, disconsolate sound. ''I thought it was. I hoped it was. I like him very much. He's such a handsome young man. And he knows how to treat a lady.''

Oh yes, Claire thought, *he's handsome*. Vividly she recalled seeing his face dark and intent with passion, his lips sensually caressing her breasts, his chest warmly, fuzzily naked. And he certainly knew how to treat a lady, especially in bed. He gave as much pleasure as he sought, maybe more. Such perfect lovemaking almost had to be calculated, didn't it?

She pushed aside the thought. It was too painful to think about. She was hopelessly in love with Cassidy, the key word being *hopelessly*. They could have no future together. Even if they weren't on opposite sides of a criminal investigation, he embodied the system that she feared and resented. As much as she loved Cassidy the man, she didn't believe she could ever completely trust Cassidy the prosecutor.

For Claire it was a heartbreaking conflict. When she dwelled on it, she was paralyzed by despair, so she kept this secret love locked away in her heart and pretended it wasn't there.

She extended her cup. ''Pour me some more tea, please, Mama. You make better tea than anyone.'' Claire directed their conversation to less disturbing topics. A half-hour later, Mary Catherine withdrew with the tray, leaving Claire alone again. She scanned the newspapers.

Joshua Wilde vehemently denied having had anything to do

with his father's slaying. Ariel accused Cassidy of implicating them only to cover his own ineptitude. She suggested that, for personal reasons, he was sheltering the most viable suspect. She had coyly declined to say who that suspect was, even when specifically asked if she referred to Claire Laurent. Her avoidance only confirmed the insinuation.

Claire was naturally relieved that she was no longer Cassidy's leading suspect, but she couldn't afford to get smug. She was temporarily in the eye of the hurricane and must still weather the second, and perhaps more ferocious, half of the storm. If Joshua Wilde became nervous over Cassidy's allegations, there was no telling what he might do or say to take the heat off himself. Instead of one foe, she would then have two.

Dwelling on that, she jumped when the telephone at her elbow rang. She didn't answer until the third ring. "Hello?"

"Claire, is that you?"

"Andre? *Bonsoir*. It's good to hear from you. How are you?"

"Fine, fine, I'm fine. No, actually . . ." He paused. "I'm terribly worried about Yasmine."

Claire frowned with full understanding of his concern. Since the breakup with her lover, Yasmine had been acting strangely. There was nothing that Claire could put her finger on, but something was amiss. On the surface, Yasmine was the same. As they wound up their work at Rosesharon, she had joked with the crew, bitched with Leon, and approached each catalog photograph with her customary imagination and flair. But her enthusiasm and laughter rang false.

Once they were finished in Mississippi, Claire had expected Yasmine to accompany the others back to New York, where the remainder of the catalog shots would be done in a studio. Instead, Yasmine had returned to New Orleans with her. Once ensconced in French Silk, she had dropped the pretense and become sullen and silent.

Yasmine said nothing about completing the catalog. Claire

was concerned from a business standpoint, but since their deadline with the printer was several weeks away, she was patiently biding her time. Yasmine stayed in her room all day, every day, then went out every night and didn't return until the wee hours. She never said where she was going or invited Claire to come along with her.

Claire guessed that she was spying on Congressman Petrie's house or making attempts to see him. She was tempted to caution Yasmine against such adolescent behavior, but Yasmine didn't invite conversation. In fact, she went out of her way to discourage it. The door to her room remained locked. She didn't join Claire and Mary Catherine for meals.

The old Yasmine surrounded herself with people, situating herself amid admirers and basking in their attention. Ordinarily, she hated being alone, so this reversal in behavior was disturbing. Claire had honored her friend's desire for solitude, as that was obviously the method Yasmine had chosen to heal her broken heart. But perhaps it was time to intervene.

Apparently Andre shared her concern. "Have you seen Yasmine recently?" she asked him.

"Not since last week when you were in Mississippi. She came to the hotel, stayed for about an hour, and left. Claire, you know I never divulge confidences, but knowing how close you are to Yasmine—"

"I don't dispute your loyalty, Andre. Nor your discretion. Both have served me on many occasions. Rest assured that I won't pump you for gossip."

"If I thought that, I wouldn't have called."

"Something prompted you to. I can hear the worry in your voice. I gather you spoke to Yasmine when you saw her?"

He told her about their conversation in the hotel corridor and how upset Yasmine had appeared when she left. "I've never seen her like that. She was quite distraught. Is she all right now?"

Claire, mindful of Yasmine's right to privacy, said, "Something very upsetting happened that night. She confided in me the following morning. I believe talking about it helped.''

"Did she return to New York?"

"No, she stayed. Probably because it's quieter here. Less hectic. I think she's trying to sort things through before she goes home.''

And Alister Petrie lives here, Claire thought, remembering seeing his picture on the front page of the morning newspaper. She didn't, however, mention the congressman to Andre. If he knew the identity of Yasmine's lover, he was being characteristically discreet. He wouldn't drop Petrie's name into the conversation. At the risk of placing Andre in a compromising position, neither would she.

"Do you think she's recovering from this . . . unpleasantness?" he asked.

That was a tough question. Although they were living under the same roof, Claire had had less contact with Yasmine than she did when Yasmine was in New York and calling her several nights a week for lengthy chats. Her reply was qualified: "She doesn't seem to be getting any worse."

"Ah, well, I'm relieved," he said. He gave a breathy little laugh. "It's no secret to you that I hold Yasmine in the highest regard.''

"No, it's no secret to me." Claire's teasing smile was soon replaced with another frown. "Maybe I've given her too much leeway. I think it's time we had another woman-to-woman talk.''

"Please let me know if there's anything I can do. Anything at all.''

"I will."

"Claire, you're . . . you're not angry with me? That matter with Mr. Cassidy—''

"Forget it, Andre. Please. You were unscrupulously tricked. As I've been," she added quietly. "Don't fret about it.''

She assured him that it would take more than Cassidy's

exploitation to affect their long-standing friendship. They agreed to have dinner together very soon. Shortly after saying goodbye and hanging up, she reached for the telephone again.

🦎

Cassidy sidled up to the undercover cop who'd been assigned to tail Joshua Wilde. As one stranger to another, he asked for a light.

"Didn't know you smoked," the cop said in a low, confidential voice. From his pocket he withdrew a lighter and flipped it open. It shot forth a blaze like a miniature flamethrower.

"I quit a couple of years ago," Cassidy said, choking on the smoke he inhaled.

"You taking it up again?"

"I just asked you for a light, okay? What else could I casually walk up and ask you for? A blow-job?"

The slender black man grinned. His long hair was pulled into a sleek queue at the back of his head and held there with a tight rubber band. He winked and gave Cassidy's shoulder a light squeeze. "I'm expensive. Can you afford me?"

Cassidy threw off the caress. "Fuck you."

"Oooh, sounds delicious, sweet thing."

Obviously the young cop, whom Cassidy knew was as straight as a plumb line, was enjoying himself at his expense. The guy was tall, slender, and good-looking, so he often worked the French Quarter in this cover. A study of insolence and nonchalance, he leaned against a gaslight post located across the street from The Gumbo Shop on St. Peter Street. Through the microphone hidden beneath the lapel of his flashy sharkskin suit, he'd reported to a central monitor that he'd tailed Josh to the popular restaurant. Cassidy, too keyed up to remain either in his downtown office or his stuffy, lonely apartment, had decided to participate actively in the surveillance.

"How long's he been in there?"

The cop checked the counterfeit Rolex on his wrist. "Thirty-two minutes."

"Is he having dinner?"

"Seems so."

Cassidy's eyes squinted against the smoke curling from between his lips. He peered through the blue-gray haze, trying to penetrate the windows of the restaurant. "How long does it take for a party of one to eat dinner?"

In character, the cop gave Cassidy an appraisal like a male prostitute sizing up a prospective client. Assuming the lilting lingo of his cover, he said, "Hey man, your ass is way too tight. If we're gonna have any fun, you gotta relax."

Cassidy shot him a baleful look and was about to move away when Josh appeared in the enclosed alley that served as the restaurant's entrance. Cassidy quickly turned his back and pretended to be shopping the T-shirts hanging in the doorway of the souvenir store. Taking glimpses of Josh over his shoulder, Cassidy could see that his jaw was set, his entire aspect angry.

"Uh-oh," the cop whispered. "Our man's good and pissed."

His mind was on what was going on behind him, but once again Cassidy pretended interest in a T-shirt with a ribald message spelled out in glittering letters. A smiling Asian clerk moved forward to give him a sales pitch. "No, thanks. Just looking."

"Might have known," the cop muttered. "Only a squeeze can get a man that pissed."

"A woman?" Cassidy glanced at the restaurant across the street, then whipped his head back around. "*Fuck!*" he exclaimed with soft but potent emphasis.

"Excuse?" the smiling Asian said.

The cop laughed beneath his breath.

The woman who had emerged from the restaurant with Josh didn't take notice of her surroundings. She said something to him, then turned and started walking down the sidewalk. Josh seemed on the verge of following her, but reconsidered and only glared at her retreating back. His long, musician's fingers flexed into fists. Then, with the bearing of an affronted prophet, he stalked off down the sidewalk in the opposite direction.

Cassidy tossed his cigarette into the gutter and bore down on the cop. "I thought you said he was alone."

"You're blowing my cover, man." He smiled and laid his hand on Cassidy's arm. Eyes smoldering, seductive grin in place, he cooed, "He was alone when he got here. He must've met her inside."

"You take him." Cassidy hitched his chin toward Josh, who had already reached the intersection with Royal Street.

"You going after the lady?"

"That's no lady," Cassidy said as he stepped off the curb and started across the street in pursuit. "That's Claire Laurent."

Chapter Twenty-three

Claire drew up short when she rounded the corner and saw Cassidy standing at the door of French Silk. It was the first time she'd seen him since the morning he'd stormed from her bedroom at Rosesharon. Seeing him so unexpectedly caused a catch in her breath. Her heart jumped. But she kept her expression impassive and tried to appear unruffled as she approached him. "Hello, Cassidy."

"Claire." He nodded. "Nice evening, isn't it?" He was perspiring and seemed to be suffering a shortness of breath more severe than her own.

"It's unseasonably warm. Autumn hasn't come to New Orleans yet."

He whisked off a bead of sweat that had made its way through his dense eyebrow and was trickling toward his eye. "Damn right. It's as hot and sticky as a cheap whore on Saturday night."

Claire's hackles rose. "I don't appreciate your crude analogy, Mr. Cassidy."

"Oh, we're back to *Mr.* Cassidy."

She wanted to slap the ingratiating grin off his face. Stiffly, she said, "I'm going in." Demonstrators were marching in front of the building. Their chorus of "Onward, Christian Soldiers" was slow and ponderous. Claire hoped they were growing tired and getting blisters on their feet.

Unnoticed, she slipped in through the side door. Before she could close it, Cassidy followed her inside. "What do you want?" she asked inhospitably. "I think we've exhausted the subject of the weather."

"I was in the neighborhood," he replied casually. "Thought I'd stop and say hi."

His chest was rising and falling rapidly, she noted. He hadn't yet caught his breath. Beneath his suit jacket, the front of his shirt was damp. "I appreciate the friendly gesture," she said. "Now, if you'll excuse—"

"Want to go for a bite of supper somewhere?"

"No, thank you. I ate earlier with Mama."

"Oh, you ate in tonight?"

"That's right."

"Then you were just out for an evening stroll?"

"I was busy at my desk all day. I needed to stretch my legs."

"Go any place in particular?"

"No. Just walked." She sidestepped him and tried to open the door for him. "I'm sorry, Cassidy, but I'd better get upstairs and check on Mama. I had to leave her al—"

Cassidy grabbed her shoulders and backed her up against the door. "You left her alone so you could keep your date with Joshua Wilde at the Gumbo Shop."

She had begun to smell a trap, but she was still astonished when the jaws of it sprang closed around her. She cast about for a logical explanation, but none came to her, so she responded with a counterattack.

"You were following me? Were the stories in the newspapers only decoys to throw me off guard?"

364 Sandra Brown

"You weren't under surveillance. We were tailing Josh. Imagine my surprise when you turned out to be his date."

"If you knew where I was and with whom, why the charade, Cassidy?"

"I took another route and sprinted back here. I wanted to see if you would level with me. As usual, you lied."

"Because I knew you wouldn't understand."

"You knew I wouldn't swallow any more of your lies." He leaned in closer and lowered his voice. "But give it a whirl, Claire. Try me. When did you first become acquainted with Joshua Wilde?"

"Tonight."

"You expect me to believe that bullshit?"

"I swear! I made several calls this afternoon until I located where he was staying. I asked him to meet me. He agreed to."

"Why?"

"Probably because he was curious to meet the scandalous owner of French Silk."

Cassidy shook his head. "I meant why did you want to meet with him? What could the two of you possibly have to talk about?"

"I offered him money."

"Money?" he repeated, taken aback.

"Yes. In exchange for his influence over Ariel. I asked him to try to persuade her to stop making allegations about me and my mother, to stop the picket lines, in general to call a truce to this whole mess. I told him I want to live my life and operate my business in peace, no matter what it costs me."

"You tried bribing him? Is that what you're telling me?"

"You're standing too close," Claire murmured. "I can't breathe."

Cassidy's eyes, which had been probing hers, blinked into awareness. He looked down, saw the white ridges of his knuckles where his fingers were still clenching her shoulders, saw that his body had hers tightly sandwiched between it and the door behind her, and backed away, lowering his hands to his sides.

"Thank you," she said quietly.

"You're not off the hook yet. Keep talking."

"That's essentially it. I know that Jackson, and probably Ariel and Josh, too, took payola from other publications in exchange for immunity."

"How do you know that?"

"It only makes sense, doesn't it? Publications that should have been on that list—Jackson Wilde's hit list, as you called it—were noticeably absent. What about *Lickety Split* and *Hot Pants*? Why was a lingerie catalog a target for Jackson Wilde's pulpit and not those porno magazines? It has to be because they were making certain that Wilde would leave them alone." She looked at Cassidy with dawning insight. "You've probably thought of this yourself."

"I've got people checking on it, yeah. What did Josh have to say?"

"He didn't admit that his father took bribes, but he didn't deny it either."

"Why have you waited until now to think up this alternative solution? You could have paid off Jackson a year ago and spared yourself all this hardship. Did you ever approach him about it?"

"No. Only in the form of the offering you already know about."

"Then why now, Claire?"

"I'm sick of it, that's why," she exclaimed. "Wouldn't you be? The signs the protesters carry make me out to be a twentieth-century Jezebel. My mother reads them and becomes upset. The people who carry them harass my employees when they report for work. They impede my business by creating traffic jams that make it difficult for us to receive deliveries or ship out goods. One trucking company has already threatened to increase their charges because their drivers have complained about it so much.''

She threw back her head as though imploring heaven for relief. ''For months before Jackson Wilde was killed, he was a thorn in my side. And now, weeks after his death, he still is. I want the specter of him out of my life. I want to be rid of him once and for all.''

She realized at once that her words had been ill chosen. She looked quickly at Cassidy, who was watching her closely. ''And killing him didn't quite do it.''

''That's not what I said.''

''Have I been barking up the wrong tree, Claire? Was it you and Josh who were in cahoots and not him and his stepmother?''

''Don't be ridiculous. I met Joshua Wilde for the first time tonight.''

''You're lying, Claire.''

''I'm not!''

Cassidy snorted a laugh. He moved away a few steps, turned his head, and studied a stack of shipping crates before swinging his gaze back to her. ''Give me a little credit. I know you significantly better now than I did a few weeks ago.''

All the excitement and passion that had seized them during the thunderstorm at Rosesharon enveloped them now. Claire was the first to draw her stare away from his. ''I'm not lying. I met with Joshua Wilde tonight and offered him a check in exchange for peace and quiet.''

''Maybe. But what aren't you telling me?''

''Nothing.''

''Claire!''

''_Nothing!_''

Cassidy swore beneath his breath. ''Okay, I'll play along. How'd Josh react?''

''He was incensed.''

''Turned you down?'' he asked incredulously.

"Flat. He said he isn't an extortionist." She gave Cassidy a level look, lifting her chin a notch. "I believe him."

"Then you're in the minority, because I'm not buying any of this crap. You offered Josh a bribe and he turned it down. Is that what I'm supposed to believe?"

"I don't give a damn what you believe."

"You'd better give a damn, Claire. Because I think you're concealing the real reason you made an appointment with Joshua Wilde."

"What other reason could I have?"

"I don't know, but I find it hard to swallow that you would offer anybody a bribe. First of all, you're too proud. Second, you don't care that much about the public's opinion of you. Finally, you told me yourself that this mess has been good for your business, so the Wildes aren't placing it in jeopardy. And I find it even harder to believe that Josh would refuse a bribe. In either case, it's suspicious as hell."

"You never give up, do you?"

"No. I can't. I'm paid not to."

"But you might be forced to. You're going to be replaced. Powerful people are calling for your head on a platter. Even your mentor, Anthony Crowder, won't defend you much longer."

"What's your point?" he said tightly.

"You're trying to build something from nothing. You're no closer to solving Wilde's murder than you were the morning following the crime."

"Don't be so sure."

"I'm sure of one thing. His son didn't kill him."

"Then that still leaves you, doesn't it, Claire?" He reached around her for the door and left without saying goodbye.

"Oh, Christ. Go away and leave me alone."

"Open up."

The hotel room door was closed momentarily so the chain lock could be released, then Josh opened it. "It's late," he grumbled.

Cassidy walked into the room and took a slow look around. The bed was still made, although the covers were rumpled. "You hadn't gone to bed yet. My guess is you'll have trouble sleeping tonight, Josh. I know I will."

Josh threw himself into one of the two easy chairs in the room and motioned Cassidy into its twin. "You're a bastard, Mr. Cassidy. I went to you of my own volition, spilled my guts, shared with you what I mistakenly assumed was privileged information. Next thing I know, it's front-page news. Ariel's gone ape-shit and will no longer speak to me. She fired me, you know. The moment the headlines hit the newsstands, Judas Iscariot here was history with the *Prayer and Praise Hour*. I think she fully expects me to go out and hang myself."

"Bet getting fired came as a blow."

Josh chuckled sourly. "Best thing that's ever happened to me. You'll probably find that hard to believe, but I swear to God it's the truth. I feel freer than I've ever felt in my life."

"Funny. You don't look like a guy sitting on top of the world," Cassidy remarked. "You look like you've been dunked in a tub of shit."

"I've got you to thank for that. The most recent stories I'm reading in the papers are strongly hinting that I might be a suspect again."

"By definition, Josh, suspect means someone whose actions are suspicious."

Josh raised his shoulders in an innocent shrug. "Like what?"

"Like trying to cast doubt on your stepmother/lover."

"I thought I was doing the right thing."

"Your conscience got the best of you?" Cassidy asked caustically.

"I didn't want to go down with her. I told you that."

"Okay. Explain this. Why'd you meet with Claire Laurent tonight?"

Josh's eyes sharpened on Cassidy. "How'd you know about that? Did you have me followed?"

"I saw you myself when you left The Gumbo Shop."

"You just happened to be passing by?" Josh asked angrily.

"Answer the question."

Cassidy's shout squelched Josh's brief, indignant outburst. He cast around for something to look at besides Cassidy's incisive stare. "She called and arranged that meeting, not me."

"You and the owner of French Silk make a very strange pairing."

Josh left his chair and began moving restlessly around the room. His motions were disjointed, jerky. "I nearly dropped the phone when she called and identified herself."

"You'd never met her before tonight?"

"Hell no. After all the dirty water that's gone under that bridge, she was the last person I ever expected to call and ask if I'd meet her for drinks."

Like Claire, Josh was lying or at the very least expurgating the truth. Cassidy went fishing. "Classy-looking lady."

"I guess," Josh replied warily.

"You appeared to be upset when you left the restaurant."

"I was."

"Let's stop dancing around it. What'd she want, Josh?"

"It has nothing to do with my father's murder."

"Let me decide that."

The younger man seemed to wrestle with himself for several moments before blurting out, "She offered me a check for twenty-five thousand dollars to call off our dogs."

Cassidy whistled. "Pretty steep price to pay to stop a protest demonstration."

"All that stuff. The picketing. The prank calls. The things Ariel's telling the papers. Ms. Laurent wants it to stop. Can't say that I blame her."

"So what'd you tell her?"

"I told her to piss off. What she obviously doesn't know is that I don't wield any influence over Ariel. Since Daddy died, she calls the shots, not me. I couldn't put a muzzle on her if I wanted to."

"So you declined Claire's offer?"

"I tore her check in two and symbolically threw it in her face. I told her that I had nothing to do with the ministry's operation. Never had. Never will. Never even wanted to. I play—played—the piano. That's it. That's all I ever wanted to do. I don't make the policies. I didn't cultivate my father's enemies. He was capable of doing that quite well all by himself. If he was accepting bribes, that was his business. I don't want any part of it."

"You're out of a job. You could have promised her what she wanted to hear, taken the check, and laughed about it all the way to the bank."

Josh gave him a cold, hostile stare. "You're full of shit, Cassidy. Get out."

"Not so fast. You were in there for more than half an hour. Is that all you and Claire talked about?"

"There were a lot of awkward silences."

"Oh, come on!"

"I'm serious. Once she got to the point, it was over in a matter of minutes. She picked up the pieces of the check, put them in her purse, and laid down enough money to cover our drinks. As we left, she said goodbye. That's all."

"You paused on the sidewalk as though you were tempted to go after her."

Josh raked back the wave that had fallen over his forehead. "I don't remember that."

"I do. Distinctly." Cassidy leaned forward. "Were you having second thoughts about taking the money?"

"No. I'm not a murderer and I'm not a thief."

Cassidy wanted to grab him by the collar and shake him. "There's something you're not telling me, Josh. I'm through screwing around with you. What are you holding back?"

Chapter Twenty-four

"S he—"

"What?" Cassidy demanded.

"I don't know." Josh grimaced with frustration.
"If I was staring after her as you say, it's because
I wasn't only mad but puzzled."

"About what?"

"About her. She has a way about her, you know?"

"No, I don't know. Explain it to me."

"I don't think I can."

"Try."

"It was like she could see into me," he cried. "But I felt
like I was looking at her through a veil. We were speaking
the same language, but the words didn't fit the messages I
was getting from her eyes. She freaked me out."

"What the hell are you talking about?"

Actually he knew exactly what Josh was talking about.
Every time he'd been with Claire, with the exception of those
moments when she had openly and freely shared her passion
with him, he'd felt totally exposed, while an essential element

of Claire always remained masked. It was like looking into the screened face of a fencing opponent. You knew who it was, but you couldn't distinctly see him.

"I knew you wouldn't believe me," Josh mumbled. "That's why I didn't bring it up myself."

Hoping to prize more information out of the troubled young man, Cassidy lied and said, "I think you're feeding me a bunch of bullshit to throw me off track."

Josh cursed and made a gesture as though trying to capture the correct words to express his thoughts. "I had never seen this woman face to face, but I got the eerie feeling that I knew her. Or, more to the point, that she knew me. Hell, I don't know. Daddy had people coming and going all the time. Maybe I bumped into her once and only my subconscious remembers."

He stopped pacing and spun around to face Cassidy. "Something just occurred to me. Maybe Claire Laurent tried the same tactic with my father, and when he refused her bribe, she bumped him off. Had you thought of that?"

Without answering, Cassidy stood and headed for the door, where he turned back and said in a menacing tone, "Josh, if you're lying to me, I'm going to come back and do you severe bodily harm. Then I'm going to pull your lower lip over your head, all the way down your back, and stuff it into your asshole." He aimed an index finger at him. "I'm going to ask one more time—had you met Claire Laurent before tonight?"

Josh swallowed visibly. "No. On my mother's grave, I swear it."

Outside, Cassidy dropped his tough demeanor. It was too exhausting to maintain. He trudged to his car. Fatigue settled over him heavily. During the drive to his condo, his eyes itched and burned, irritated by every pair of headlights he encountered, but he knew that as soon as he lay down to sleep, they would open and remain that way until dawn, when the whole unproductive routine would begin again.

Wearily he let himself into his airless living room, cursorily sorted through his mail, then plodded into the bedroom. As he regarded his haggard reflection in the mirror over the bathroom sink, he realized why he felt as depleted as a marathon runner following an uphill race. Claire had been cleared of one lie tonight, but in the process he had uncovered another possible motivation for her to kill Jackson Wilde.

Cassidy had left Claire very upset. Long after she had locked the door of French Silk behind him, she remained there, her head resting against the cool metal. She had wanted her meeting with Josh to be carried out in absolute secrecy. From now on, she must be doubly careful. She wouldn't again make the mistake of underestimating Mr. Cassidy's far-reaching arm. His resources outnumbered hers. He probably had plainclothesmen watching her around the clock.

That thought unnerved her for several reasons. First, her privacy was being violated. Second, regardless of the new slant to his investigation, she and everyone associated with French Silk were still suspects. Most upsetting was that a man she had been intimate with exercised tremendous authority over her.

His superiority defiled the tenderness and sweetness of their lovemaking, like a bed of flowers being trampled into the mud by someone uncaring and insensitive. The flowers were still flowers, but their beauty had been irreparably tarnished.

With that dismal thought, she pushed herself away from the door and walked toward the freight elevator. As she approached, she heard its clanking descent and saw Yasmine through the metal accordion doors as it ground to a stop on the first floor. "Hi," she said, trying to inject her voice with more spirit than she felt. Unfortunately, seeing Yasmine didn't cheer her. She was another source of worry. "Are you going out again tonight?"

"Yes, for a while."

"Want some company? I'd enjoy an evening out. I could call Harry to come sit with Mama."

Yasmine was already shaking her head. "I'm sorry, Claire, but I've made other plans."

Claire tried valiantly to keep her smile in place. "I'm glad to see you're putting yourself back in circulation. I was getting worried about you."

"You shouldn't have been. Everything's working out."

"Good. I knew it would. Do you need my car?"

"No, thanks. I'll take a cab."

At the risk of prying, Claire didn't ask where she was going or what her plans entailed. Yasmine's clothing gave her no clues. She was dressed in a semiconservative, plain silk dress. The melon color gave her complexion a special glow. Her hair had dried naturally, encircling her head in glossy, ebony curls. Large gold disks were clipped to her ears. The trademark bangles glittered on her slender wrists. She looked exceptionally beautiful and Claire told her so.

"Thank you. I wanted to look good tonight."

"Even on your worst days you look good." Acting on impulse, Claire embraced her.

Yasmine returned the tight hug. "Thanks for everything, Claire."

"No need to thank me. You've been going through a rough time."

"But you've stayed my friend when anyone else would have given up on me."

"Never. You can count on that." She squeezed her extra tight. "Take care tonight."

"You know me, sugar." As she broke the embrace, Yasmine winked and clucked her tongue. "Always on top of things."

Claire laughed. This was Yasmine at her sassy best. She wondered briefly if Alister Petrie had called her for a reconciliation. That would account for the special pains she had taken with her appearance tonight. "Shall I worry if you're late?"

"No, don't wait up. 'Bye-bye. I'll set the alarm on my way out."

"Thanks. 'Bye."

Claire waited until she had crossed the warehouse floor. At the door, she turned and gave Claire a jaunty little wave. Even from that distance, Claire could hear her bangles jangling.

Upstairs, Claire checked on Mary Catherine, who was sleeping peacefully. As she was pulling her mother's bedroom door closed, the smell of smoke brought her to a dead standstill.

When she'd had the old building renovated, she'd paid dearly for a state-of-the-art sprinkler system and smoke detectors, knowing that a fire would be costly, in merchandise and possibly in lives. Even with that safeguard, she was paranoid about fire.

She traced the faint whiffs to Yasmine's bedroom. She hadn't been there recently, but before her breakup with Alister, Yasmine had rarely kept the door closed. Claire had no qualms about opening it now to check for the source of smoke.

As she stepped across the threshold and entered the room, she received a shock to her sensibilities and to her nervous system. Reflexively clapping her right hand over her nose and mouth, she moved forward, reluctantly approaching the makeshift altar that had once been an ordinary nightstand.

Encircling the perimeter were smoky, sputtering candles that cast wavering shadows onto the walls. Unidentifiable herbs and oils had been sprinkled over the surface of the nightstand. They accounted for some of the malevolent odors permeating the room. But only some.

In the center of the altar was a crude crockery bowl. It was filled with what appeared to be the entrails of a small animal. At one time, organs might have been discernible. Now it was a mishmash of gore. The odor made Claire gag behind her hand.

Blood had been painstakingly dripped onto the surface to form symbolic patterns. The small effigy of Alister Petrie, the doll that Claire recognized as the one Yasmine had shown her, had been decapitated and emasculated. Like a stake through the heart, a vicious pin thrust up from the center of its chest.

"My God," Claire moaned, backing away from the grisly sight. "Oh my God, Yasmine. No!"

As soon as Harry arrived in response to her frantic call, Claire raced to her car and headed for the exclusive neighborhood along the shore of Lake Ponchartrain where Congressman Alister Petrie lived with his wife and children. She hoped she wouldn't arrive too late.

❧

"Want me to wait?" The cabbie slung one arm over the back of the seat and gaped at his stunning passenger.

"No, thanks." Yasmine passed him a twenty-dollar bill. "Keep the change."

"Thanks, miss. 'preciate it. Say, uh, do I know you? I mean, should I? Aren't you famous?"

"I was a model. Maybe you've seen my pictures in maga zines."

He slapped his forehead with the heel of his hand "Jesus H! I thought that was you." He grinned, revealing crooked, tobacco-stained teeth in the feeble dome light of his cab "Who'd've ever thought you'd ride in my cab? The only other celebrity I've ever hauled was that cooking lady on TV Julia somebody. Say, I'll be glad to come back for you later. I can give you my card. You can call when you're ready to be picked up."

Yasmine shook her head and alighted. "Thank you."

"Well, 'bye. It's been a pleasure."

He dropped the gear shift into drive, saluted her, and pulled away from the curb. Yasmine watched him drive way. She was smiling, glad she'd made his day. He would talk about her for months, maybe years, telling everybody he met that he'd had Yasmine in his cab the night she really made herself famous.

"Good luck to you, sugar," she whispered into the still evening air. Standing on the curb, she regarded the stately house across the street. It would have made a pretty picture for a postcard. Even the Spanish moss hanging from the branches of the live oaks was perfectly placed.

There was no blood on the dining room window, which was dark now. They'd washed it off the morning after she'd paid to have the dead chicken "delivered." She'd driven past the next day to see. There'd been no trace of the terror that she hoped her hex had caused the smug son of a bitch.

He didn't know what terror was. Not yet.

She stepped off the curb and started across the street. Reaching into her large leather shoulder bag, she took out the revolver. Even though she'd checked the cylinders a hundred times during the course of the long afternoon while she waited for nightfall, she checked them once again. All were loaded.

She started up the sidewalk that divided the front lawn into immaculately landscaped halves. Her stride was long and confident, as it had been for years on the runways of fashion houses all over the world. New York, Paris, Milan. No one walked like Yasmine. Her gait couldn't be imitated. Many had tried, but none had been able to combine that sensuous countermotion of hips and shoulders with elegance and grace the way she had mastered it.

She hesitated for only a heartbeat on the bottom step leading up to the porch, then strode to the wide front door and pressed the bell.

"Daddy, I've got a soccer game on Saturday. Do you think maybe you could come to this one? I'm playing goalie."

Alister Petrie reached across the corner of the kitchen dining table and ruffled his son's hair. "I'll try. That's all I can promise. But I'll try."

"Gee, that'd be great," the boy beamed.

Since the incident with the dead chicken, which had taken ten years off his life, Alister had turned over a new leaf. For days he'd lived in abject terror, venturing out of the house only when absolutely necessary and then only under the protection of the bodyguards Belle had insisted on hiring.

As he delivered his scheduled campaign speeches, his knees had knocked together behind the podiums because he feared an assassination. At night in his dreams, he envisioned a bullet coming at him at an unstoppable velocity and piercing his forehead, exploding his head like a watermelon. He always lived to witness his execution and woke up trembling and blubbering.

Belle was always beside him to render comfort and solace. Drawing his shivering body against hers, she crooned reassurances that his mistress had vented her spleen with that disgusting and savage display, and that was the end of it.

She did, however, manage to get in her sharp, vicious barbs. "You reap what you sow, Alister." "What goes around comes around." "Your sins find you out." She had a litany of adages, all with biblical overtones.

Like fishhooks, they stayed deeply embedded under his skin. It would be a while before he felt courageous enough to screw around. He'd learned his lesson. When he did feel the urge to stray, he'd make damn certain that the broad didn't have an affinity for voodoo. It might be harmless, but it fucked with your mind in the worst way.

Gradually, when it appeared that the dead chicken was indeed an isolated incident and the sum total of Yasmine's vengeance, Alister began to relax. He resumed his normal, hectic schedule. The bodyguards were dismissed. But the familial bliss was a lasting aftereffect. He was at home as frequently as possible now He kissed both children good-

night every night and took the time to exchange a few sentences with each of them at some point during the day.

Belle participated in his campaign more actively than before. They were rarely out of each other's sight. She kept him
on a very short leash, which for once he didn't resent, because
she had kept her promise not to reduce or suspend the campaign contributions that poured in from her private resources
and those of her extensive family.

They had not, however, eaten in the formal dining room
since that fateful night.

Tonight the Petries were gathered around the table that was
tucked into a cozy nook adjacent to the kitchen. Rockwell
couldn't have painted a scene more depictive of domestic
harmony. There had been fresh apple pie for dessert. The
aroma of cinnamon and baked Granny Smiths wafted through
the well-lighted room. They could have been any family in
America—except for the uniformed maid, who, at a silent
signal from Belle, began clearing away the dishes and carrying them to the dishwasher.

"Daddy?"

"Yes, sweetheart?" He gave his attention to his daughter.

"I colored a picture of you at school today."

"Did you?"

"Hmm. It's of you making a speech in front of the American flag."

"You don't say?" he said expansively. "Well, let's see
it."

"Mommy, may I be excused? It's in my school bag up in
my room."

Belle smiled indulgently. "Of course, darling."

The youngest Petrie slid from her chair and dashed out of
the kitchen. No sooner had she cleared the swinging door
than the front-door bell rang. "I'll get it!" Her high-pitched,
childish voice echoed through the rooms. They heard the
rubber soles of her sneakers striking the hardwood floors,
occasionally muted by area rugs.

The telephone rang. The maid answered the kitchen extension. "Petrie residence."

They heard the front door being opened.

"No," the maid said into the receiver. "There's no one here by that name."

"Who was it?" Belle asked as the maid hung up.

"Wrong number. A woman who sounded hysterical was looking for someone named Jasmine."

Alister blanched and surged to his feet. "Yasmine?"

Belle looked at him. Simultaneously the same chilling thought occurred to them. Belle said, "Is that—"

"Yes." Alister bounded through the swinging door.

"What's the matter, Mom?"

"Nothing, son."

"You look funny."

The maid said, "Miz Petrie? Anything wrong?"

"Don't be silly," Belle snapped. "What could be wrong?"

Then they heard the gunshot.

"No, don't hang up!" Claire shouted into the receiver of the public telephone. When she got a dial tone, she banged the receiver against the box. "I told you not to hang up!"

After becoming hopelessly lost in an area with which she wasn't familiar, she had stopped at a pay telephone to call the Petries. Unsure of exactly how to warn them, she clumsily punched out the number that directory assistance had given her. It had been answered on the first ring, but obviously the housekeeper to whom she had conveyed her hysteria dismissed her as a wrong number or a crank call.

She inserted another quarter and redialed. The line was busy. "Come on, please. Please." She put the quarter in and tried again. This time the phone rang repeatedly, but wasn't answered. Thinking that in her haste she must have misdialed, she repeated the process. It continued to ring.

Moments later, she became aware of approaching sirens. Dread, like a fist inside her chest, clutched at her heart. "Oh, no. Please, God, no."

But her prayers went unanswered. The emergency vehicles sped past, lights flashing. Claire dropped the telephone receiver, ran for her car, and struck out in pursuit. When they reached their destination, she bolted from her car, grabbed the arm of a pajama-clad neighbor, and asked, "Whose house is this?"

"Congressman Petrie's."

Policemen were already scrambling across the lawn and paramedics were rushing with a gurney toward the open door. Claire shoved aside the befuddled neighbor and plunged headlong up the sloping lawn. A policeman tried to halt her, but she ignored his shouted order to stop.

"My friend needs me."

Breathless, she reached the porch steps and ran up them toward the cluster of people huddled in the entrance. From within the house she could hear the hysterical screaming of a child. Behind her, police officers were ordering her to freeze.

Her worst fears were confirmed when she saw a draped from lying across the threshold. She was too late! Yasmine had killed him! She searched frantically for Yasmine among those stomping about in confusion and distress.

Suddenly Claire's eyes connected with Alister Petrie's. She almost laughed with relief. He seemed dazed, but unharmed.

Then she noticed that he was splattered with fresh blood that was not his own. He was standing in a puddle of it that was fed by the river flowing from beneath the plastic sheet.

Claire's eyes dropped to the body once again, and she saw something lying outside the sheet that she had missed the first time—a hand, beautifully shaped, long and slender, the color of café au lait.

And encircling the wrist were bright, gold bangles.

Chapter Twenty-five

W hen Claire exited the jetway, she was momentarily blinded by exploding flashbulbs and video lights. Reflexively, she threw her arm across her eyes. She wanted to flee, but there was nowhere to go. Other airline passengers were filing out behind her, cutting off that avenue of escape, and in front of her was a phalanx of reporters and photographers.

In New York she had endured the mad flurry of publicity caused by Yasmine's suicide. The media attention had been expected, so she had braced herself for it and met it head-on. But she had thought that by the time she returned to New Orleans it would be old news. She hadn't bolstered herself for this barrage and wasn't prepared for the reporters who surged toward her en masse.

"Ms. Laurent, what do you think of Yasmine's involvement—"

"Will the allegations stick?"

"What do you know about—"

"Please," she said, trying to push through them. But they

were like a solid rank of soldiers armed with cameras and microphones. They didn't give an inch. Without a statement, they weren't going to.

"My friend was obviously very unhappy." Claire spoke from behind her large sunglasses and tried to keep her face averted from the bright lights. "I grieve for her, but the contributions she made to me personally and those she made to the fashion industry will keep her memory alive for years to come. Excuse me."

Stoically she proceeded through the airport, refusing to acknowledge any more questions. Finally an airport security guard offered to claim her luggage and assisted her into a cab. When she arrived at French Silk, she was greeted not only by members of the media but by the dedicated disciples of Jackson Wilde who continued to picket. She hastily paid her fare and dashed inside.

She was gratified to see her employees going about their business, although they seemed unnaturally somber. Several murmured condolences, which she graciously accepted. In the elevator, she removed her sunglasses, hastily used a lipstick, and composed herself. She didn't want Mary Catherine to be any more upset by Yasmine's suicide than she already had been. When she had put her mother and Harry on a New Orleans–bound jet at La Guardia following the funeral, Mary Catherine had been vague and disoriented. Claire had been concerned for her mother's mental stability and despaired over the separation, but had felt that Mary Catherine would be better off in familiar surroundings than in New York, where Claire couldn't devote much time and attention to her.

Forcing herself to smile, she opened the main door of the apartment and breezed in. "Mama, I'm home!" She had taken only a few steps when she saw Mary Catherine in the living room, seated in the corner of a sofa, sniffing into a handkerchief. Harry was standing near the windows, rigid and unsmiling with disapproval.

After taking in the scene, Claire's eyes swung back to

Cassidy, who was seated beside her mother. "What the hell are you doing?"

"I told him this wasn't a good idea, but he insisted on speaking with her."

"Thank you, Harry. I know how persuasive Mr. Cassidy can be." Throwing daggers at him with her eyes, Claire quickly moved to the sofa and dropped to her knees in front of her mother. "Mama, I'm home. Aren't you glad to see me?"

"Claire Louise?"

"Yes, Mama?"

"Are they coming for you?"

"No. Nobody's coming for me."

"I don't want them to take you away on account of what I've done."

"They can't take me. I'm not going anywhere. I'm home now. We're together."

"I've tried to do better," Mary Catherine said between gentle hiccups. "Really, I have. Ask Aunt Laurel. It's just that . . ." She raised her hand to her temple and massaged it. "I get so distraught sometimes when I think of my sin. Mama and Papa were so angry with me when I told them about the baby."

Claire drew Mary Catherine against her and whispered, "Don't worry, Mama. I'm here now. I'll always take care of you." Claire held her until her weeping subsided, then pushed her away and smiled into the tear-streaked face. "Do you know what I'd love for supper? Some of your gumbo. Will you make some for me? Please."

"My roux is never as good as Aunt Laurel's," Mary Catherine said shyly, "but if you really want some . . ."

"I do." She motioned for Harry. "Why don't you start it now so it can simmer all day? Go with Harry. She'll help you." She assisted Mary Catherine to her feet.

Mary Catherine turned and extended her hand to Cassidy. "I've got to go now, Mr. Cassidy, but thank you so much for calling. Bring your folks with you one afternoon for a glass of sherry.'' He nodded. Harry ushered her into the kitchen.

"I'm not finished questioning her yet."

Claire rounded on him. "The hell you're not! How dare you sneak in here and upset her while I was away. What did you want with her?"

"I had some pertinent questions for her."

"To hell with your pertinent questions."

"As an assistant D.A., I have the right—"

"Right?" she repeated incredulously. "We've had a death in the family, or have you forgotten?"

"I'm sorry about Yasmine."

"I'll bet. That's one less suspect for you, isn't it?"

"You're not being fair. I didn't intend to upset your mother."

"Well, you did. And if you ever bully my mother again, I'll kill you. She doesn't know the answers to your bloody questions."

"But you do," he said. "That's why you're going downtown with me."

"What for?"

"I'll tell you when we get there." He took her arm in an inexorable grip.

"Are you going to have me arrested? What did you coerce my mother into saying?"

"Tell them goodbye, Claire, and go peaceably," he said, quietly by firmly. "Another scene will only upset Mary Catherine more."

At that moment Claire hated him. "You bastard."

"Get your purse and say goodbye."

In this skirmish, he was the uncontested winner. For her mother's sake, she wouldn't even compete. He knew that and was using it to his advantage. Claire stared him down, her loathing palpable. At last she said, "Harry, I'm going downtown with Mr. Cassidy for a while. Goodbye, Mama."

When they emerged from French Silk, it caused a furor among the reporters and the demonstrators. A dozen questions were hurled at Claire at once.

"Ms. Laurent has no comment," Cassidy tersely told the reporters.

"Cassidy, what do you think—"

"No comment."

"Do you believe you've found your killer?"

"No comment." Ignoring the microphones being poked into his face, he propelled Claire through the crowd. She was exhausted, bereaved, and confused, so she went docilely. At least Cassidy was a familiar adversary.

Cassidy's long stride soon broke them out of the pack. Two uniformed policemen closed ranks behind them. They started down the sidewalk, wasting no time.

"I'll drive her downtown in my car," Cassidy said to the patrolmen.

"Yes, sir."

"Thanks for your help."

"Yes, sir."

"Try your best to disperse that crowd, and keep a close watch on the place."

"Yes, sir."

The policemen peeled off to carry out his curt instructions. Never breaking stride, he escorted Claire to his car, which was illegally parked at the curb. He opened the passenger door for her and stepped aside. Too weary to war with him now, she slid into the seat.

"How'd you manage to keep the funeral off TV?" he asked once they were on their way uptown.

"I set up a decoy. A hearse with a fake coffin led the media hounds into New Jersey before they realized they'd been duped." She touched the gold bangle she was wearing on her wrist. It had been one of Yasmine's favorites. Claire knew she would have wanted her to have it. "I couldn't have borne it if her funeral had been a carnival attended by strangers."

It had been more than a week since she had arrived at Alister Petrie's house and seen her friend lying dead on his doorstep. In front of him and his daughter, Yasmine had shot herself through the back of the head, totally, almost vindictively, destroying her lovely face with the exit wound. Yasmine was unarguably dead. There were, however, moments when Claire almost forgot it. Then reality landed on her like an avalanche of bricks.

She'd barely had time to grieve. The days since the suicide had been filled with grim activity—forms to sign, arrangements to make, Yasmine's affairs to settle, media to dodge, questions to answer for which there were no answers. How did one explain why a woman who seemingly had everything would destroy herself in such a grotesquely poetic way?

Claire kept Yasmine's secrets to herself. She wouldn't betray her friend's confidence even now, when it no longer mattered. To mutual friends who had been shocked by the news and needed answers, Claire merely said that Yasmine had been extremely unhappy recently. She didn't divulge details of her failed love affair or of her financial difficulties.

Since all that remained of Yasmine's family were a few cousins sprinkled along the East Coast, to whom she had never been close, the responsibility of the funeral and burial had fallen to Claire. Yasmine had left no instructions, so Claire had followed her instincts and had the body cremated. The memorial service had been quiet and private, open to only a few invited guests. Now an urn sealed in a mausoleum was all that remained of her gorgeous, talented, vital friend who had possessed a zest for living until she fell in love with the wrong man.

Reminded of Petrie, Claire turned to Cassidy, who'd been driving in silence. "Petrie's little girl. Is she all right?"

"From what I read, she's coping. Still has nightmares, the papers said yesterday. She's under the care of a child psychologist."

"I can't imagine Yasmine doing something that ghastly in front of a child."

"Petrie was the lover who dumped her, right?"

"Lucky guess."

"I heard that afterward, they found all sorts of voodoo paraphernalia in her room."

"Yes."

"I also heard that you were on the scene, Claire."

"I found the altar in her room. I thought she was going to harm him. I went after her, but arrived too late."

"Dr. Dupuis told me that you refused to leave her side and accompanied her body to the morgue."

"She was my friend."

"You're to be commended."

"I don't need your praise."

"You're determined to alienate me, aren't you?"

"I thought it was decided the day we met that we couldn't be friends." They glanced at each other, then quickly away. After a while, Claire said, "This is bound to put a kink in Petrie's campaign. What does he have to say for himself?"

"You haven't read?"

"No. I've deliberately avoided reading anything about her suicide or the speculations on why she did it. They were certain to make me ill."

"Then I don't recommend the recent issues of any periodical. Everything from *The New York Times* to the *National Enquirer* has a theory."

"I was afraid of that. Give me an idea of what I'm up against."

"That she was strung out on drugs."

"I expected that one."

"That she held a racially founded grudge against Petrie."

"Yasmine was apolitical."

"That she was a spurned secret lover."

"Which I'm certain he's denied."

"Actually he hasn't said much. He's hiding behind his wife's skirts and letting her do all the talking. Pretty neat P.R. tactic when you think about it. If the wife's solidly behind him, he couldn't have been having an illicit affair, right?"

"Right. So they'll make Yasmine out to be a nut case."

"Basically." Cassidy wheeled his car into its designated parking slot at the side of the district attorney's office building.

"Why'd you bring me here?" Claire asked resentfully. "I'm travel grimy. I'm tired. I don't feel up to answering any questions. And I'm furious at you for badgering my mother. Besides, I thought you'd be off the case by now. Hasn't Crowder replaced you yet?"

"Not since there've been some late-breaking developments."

"Congratulations. But what could these late-breaking developments possibly have to do with me? I haven't even been here."

He turned to her, laying his arm across the back of the seat. "We ran a routine ballistics test on the bullet that killed Yasmine. It had the same markings as the ones that killed Jackson Wilde. All of them were fired from the .38 revolver that was removed from Yasmine's death grip."

Chapter Twenty-six

✻ ✻

Andre Philippi scoured his fingernails with a brush and liquid hand soap. It was the fifth time he'd washed his hands in that compulsive and meticulous manner since waking that morning. When his hands were clean to his satisfaction—temporarily—he rinsed them in water as hot as he could stand and blotted them dry with a fluffy white towel straight from the hotel's laundry.

He surveyed himself in the mirror over the basin. His clothes were immaculate, nary a speck or a wrinkle. The pink carnation in his lapel was fresh and dewy. There wasn't an oiled hair out of place. He should have felt splendid and well turned out, like a shiny new car on the showroom floor.

Instead he felt insecure, fearful, and miserable.

Leaving the bathroom and conscientiously switching off the light, he returned to his office. Measured by most standards, it was exceptionally tidy and well organized. To Andre it looked a mess. On his desk were stacks of correspondence that demanded his attention, in addition to employee time sheets, marketing memos, and customer questionnaires. All the paperwork he usually enjoyed sorting through and methodically completing had backed up during his period of mourning for Yasmine. He hadn't felt like working since he received the devastating news of her suicide. Considering his affinity for his work, this new attitude toward it was tantamount to sacrilege.

When Claire called to notify him of Yasmine's death, he had outright accused her of lying. The idea of that lovely creature destroying herself in that abhorrent fashion was too appalling to believe and too painful to contemplate. It was woefully reminiscent of the day he'd returned home from school to find his beautiful *maman* lying naked in an overflowing bathtub, dripping tepid water and warm blood onto the tile floor.

The two women he had loved and revered above all other of God's creation had chosen to die rather than live. Not only had they preferred a world without him, they hadn't even thought enough of him to say goodbye. As though it had physical qualities, grief compressed his chest until he couldn't breathe without experiencing excruciating pain around his heart.

He had declined to go to New York for the memorial service Claire had arranged. He had stood beside his *maman*'s tomb as it was being sealed, swearing then that he would never again acknowledge the finality of death until he himself died.

In order to cope with Yasmine's suicide he had tried consoling himself with familiar platitudes. "Extraordinary beauty can be a curse to the one who possesses it." "One pays a dear price for fame and fortune."

He had even dipped into some that he'd heard from his mother's friends when she took her own life. "Some angels," one well-meaning individual had told him, "are so beautiful that God can't bear to be separated from them for long.

They're destined to short lives before they're even born. Impatient with fate, they often hurry it along so they can return to a realm as blemishless as they are.'' Traditional of New Orleans, there'd been a parade, complete with a jazz band, through the French Quarter to celebrate his mother's passing into a world worthy of her.

He hadn't believed such nonsense when he was a teenager striving valiantly not to weep openly over his mother's body. He didn't believe it now. But it made him feel better to pay lip service to it. He'd also gone to mass every day and fervently prayed for Yasmine's soul.

As if her death weren't enough to cope with, he was upset by the way she was being maligned in the press. The accusations being made about her seemed grossly unfair, especially since she couldn't defend herself. He glared at the folded newspaper that he'd angrily stuffed into the wastepaper basket beneath his desk after reading the insulting headlines. Drivel. Lies. Wild speculations.

But Assistant District Attorney Cassidy believed them.

He'd called Andre early that morning. After reading the headlines, Andre wasn't surprised to hear from him. He had expected to. He'd almost looked forward to it so he could demonstrate his contempt for the disrespectful way Yasmine was being treated.

''The woman is dead, Mr. Cassidy,'' he'd said acidly. ''Like a vulture, you're circling over her corpse. The way you prey on the defenseless is obscene, disgraceful, and abominable.''

''Cut the crap, Andre. I'm a creep and I admit it. Unfortunately, the taxpayers, you included, pay me to be a creep. Now, I've got one question for you and you'd better tell me the truth or I'm coming over there and nip your bud right off the stem, and I'm not talking about the flower in your lapel. Was Yasmine in the Fairmont Hotel the night Jackson Wilde was killed?''

"Your language is offensive. I've a good mind to report you to—"

"Was she in the frigging hotel?" Cassidy had shouted through the telephone.

Andre collected himself, smoothed a damp palm over his head and said, "You saw the records. Was her name among our registered guests?"

"That's not what I asked you."

"I have nothing more to say."

"Look." Cassidy had tried another tack, in a much more conciliatory, much kinder voice. "I know Yasmine was your friend. I'm sorry she's dead. The short time I knew her was time enough for me to develop an admiration for her talent. She was gorgeous. Simply to look at her was like a religious experience. The planet is less beautiful because she's no longer a part of it. I'm sensitive to your feelings. Truly, I am. Her death was tragic and premature, and one can only speculate why she chose to end her life.

"If you've read the newspapers," he'd continued, "then you know that some of those speculations are way off base. Yasmine wasn't a dopehead. She wasn't a militant civil rights activist. She wasn't any of the things they've written about her. So in a very real sense, Andre, by confiding in me, you'll be sparing her a lot of garbage press. And think what this will mean to Claire."

"Don't play one of my friends against the other, Mr. Cassidy."

"I'm not trying to. But if Yasmine was guilty of killing Wilde, then that means Claire is innocent. Don't you want to clear her?"

"Not if it means indicting another friend who is equally innocent, who is dead, and who can't defend herself."

"Her guilt or innocence will probably be decided at an inquest," Cassidy had said, his impatience returning. "Just tell me if you saw Yasmine in your hotel that night."

"You paint a pretty word-picture, Mr. Cassidy, but your motivations are self-serving. You obviously have no case against Yasmine. If it's up to me, you never will. You tricked me once. That's one time too many. Goodbye."

"I can subpoena you," Cassidy had threatened.

"Do what you must. My responses to your questions will remain the same."

That's the way they'd left it. Andre had almost expected storm troopers from city hall to come crashing through his door with a subpoena. However, nothing Cassidy might do would faze him. Even brute force wouldn't sway him. The notion that Yasmine had killed Jackson Wilde was ridiculous. It was unfounded and untrue. In fact, Andre averred as he got up to wash his hands once more, it was impossible.

🦎

"That's impossible."

Claire kept trying to dig in her heels, but Cassidy practically dragged her through the side entrance of the district attorney's building. The front of it was besieged by Jackson Wilde's disciples, who were holding a prayer vigil. They were on the scent of fresh blood, this time Yasmine's, even though she was already dead.

Ariel Wilde had undoubtedly picked up the rumor that Yasmine's suicide and Jackson Wilde's murder were connected by a matching ballistics report. She had wasted no time in whipping her followers into a spiritual frenzy. Cassidy had remarked sourly to a cohort that she would be valuable to the Pentagon. She was a master strategist who knew how to launch a rapidly organized but highly effective attack. She also had the unshakable loyalty of her followers, who worshipped her right along with Jesus, which in Cassidy's opinion was the problem with televangelism. It made bigger celebrities of the preachers than of the deities.

"Are you suggesting that Yasmine killed Jackson Wilde?" Claire asked as Cassidy pushed her into an elevator and pressed the button for the second floor.

"Listen," he said crisply, "I didn't believe it either, until I studied those test results myself."

"There's been a mistake. Somebody made a terrible error."

"I had them checked and rechecked, Claire. The evidence is indisputable. The same weapon fired those bullets. Why the hell didn't you tell me Yasmine had a gun? If you had, your friend might still be alive."

With an injured sound, Claire flattened herself against the wall of the elevator as though to get as far from him as possible. "You're a mean-spirited bastard, Cassidy."

The elevator doors slid open. "After you," he said silkily. He waited, leaving her no option but to step out. "This way. We're going to sort this mess out once and for all." Inside the corner office, he slammed the door behind them, shrugged off his coat, and pointed her to a chair. "You'd might as well make yourself comfortable. You're not leaving here until I get to the bottom of this."

"You asked my mother if Yasmine could have killed Reverend Wilde. That's why she was upset."

"I asked her what she knew about Yasmine owning a gun. I asked her if Yasmine ever talked about shooting Wilde. Stuff like that. I swear to you I was as gentle as possible." Claire's expression remained reproachful. "I was only doing my job, Claire."

"Oh, yes, your bloody job." She scooped back a handful of hair. Even that reflexive gesture seemed to require a lot of energy. There were deep shadows beneath her eyes, and she appeared to be bone-weary. "May I at least call and check on her?"

He pointed to the telephone, then stuck his head through the door and bellowed an order for two coffees. By the time a scurrying clerk arrived with two steaming Styrofoam cups, Claire was concluding her brief call.

"The gumbo's on the stove. They're playing gin. Mama's winning."

Her smile would have looked at home on a madonna's face as she gazed at her sleeping child. Her lips looked soft and beautiful when she smiled that way. Cassidy tried not to think about how they tasted. "Coffee?"

"No, thank you."

"Drink it. You'll need it."

She pulled the cup toward her but didn't pick it up. She adjusted herself into a more comfortable position in the chair, crossing her legs and clasping her hands in her lap, then looked up at him. "Well? Ask away, counselor."

"Don't do this, Claire."

"Do what?"

"Don't make my job more difficult than it already is."

"I think the more difficult it is, the better you like it."

He leaned over her. "Do you think I enjoy asking you questions about Yasmine, knowing how close you two were, knowing how devastated you must be by her suicide."

"But that doesn't stop you, does it? You want a culprit to feed to the lions."

He slapped the desk with his palm. "Damn right. And I want it to be somebody, *anybody*, besides you!"

A long, taut moment stretched between them. His eyes conveyed more than he was permitted to speak, but she got the message. Her gaze fell away and with it her defiance.

"Yasmine couldn't have killed Jackson Wilde," she said with soft emphasis. "Surely you don't believe she did."

"Why shouldn't I believe it?"

"She didn't even know him on a personal level. What possible motive could she have had?"

"The same as you. She wanted to shut him up. He was endangering her livelihood and she was in hock with creditors. We discovered that when we checked out her offering to Wilde."

"Yasmine was having financial difficulties, but Wilde was

never a threat to French Silk. She thought it was hysterically funny that his objective had not only been defeated but had backfired. We were flourishing because of the publicity he gave us, and that tickled Yasmine. Anyway, whether or not she had motive is academic. She was in New York that night.''

''No, she wasn't.''

''I picked her up at the airport the following morning.''

''And I subpoenaed the airline records, Claire. Weeks ago. She wasn't on that morning flight. She arrived the evening before, more than twelve hours earlier.''

Claire stared at him in disbelief. ''Why didn't you tell me this?''

''I saw no reason to blow Yasmine's secret. I figured she came in early to see her lover and didn't want you to know because you disapproved of the affair. It was an issue between two friends, and I didn't want to be caught in the middle of it. But now her lie has taken on new significance.''

He sat down on the corner of his desk, facing her. ''Claire, did you know that Yasmine was in New Orleans that night?''

''No.''

''Did she borrow your car?''

''No. I didn't see her until the next morning.''

''Did you know that she carried a gun?''

She wavered. He could tell she was toying with the idea of lying and was relieved when she answered, ''Yes. I knew she owned a gun. She has since I've known her. I urged her several times to get rid of it.''

''Why didn't you tell me about it before?''

''Because . . . Yasmine said she had mislaid it.''

''You mean lost it?''

''For a while, yes. Later it turned up.''

''You mean it was lost and then suddenly reappeared?''

Claire nodded. ''She had to pack it in luggage whenever she flew so it wouldn't get confiscated by airport security. She said she had apparently overlooked it in a bag.''

''And you still didn't tell me?''

"Things get lost all the time," she said with irritation.

"We're talking about a lethal weapon, Claire. Again, why didn't you mention Yasmine's gun to me?"

"Because I didn't think it was important."

"That's a damn lie."

"All right!" she cried. "I was afraid you'd link that damn gun to Jackson Wilde's murder."

"It *is* linked to it."

"Yasmine didn't use that gun to kill Jackson Wilde."

"Somebody did."

"Not Yasmine."

"Who else had access to it?"

"No one that I know of."

"You did."

"I've never fired a gun. I wouldn't know how. I've told you that a dozen times."

"Which could be another dozen lies."

"I'm not lying."

"How did Yasmine say her gun got lost?"

"She didn't know."

"Where'd she lose it?"

"In her luggage I guess. I don't know."

"How long was it missing?"

"A couple or three weeks. I'm not sure."

"How'd she get it back?"

"She said it just reappeared in her handbag."

"Claire—"

"I don't know!"

"Cassidy?" A man knocked once abruptly before opening the door. Sensing the tension, he glanced uneasily at Claire, then back at Cassidy. "Crowder wants to see you."

"I'll check with him later."

Despite Cassidy's irritation, the young intern held his ground. "Excuse me, sir, but Mr. Crowder said now. Said it'd be my ass if I didn't bring you back. He's got somebody with him, and it's mandatory that you be there too."

Chapter Twenty-seven

❦ ❦

Cassidy, muttering curses, reached for his coat. As he was pulling it on, he said, "If Yasmine was in Wilde's room that night, she tracked in the carpet fibers from your car."

"For the hundredth time, I didn't see Yasmine that night. I was using my car." Claire kept her head down, her eyes averted, but her voice was steely. "I didn't see Yasmine until the following morning when I picked her up at the airport. If she was in New Orleans, she kept it a secret from me. In any event, she didn't have access to my car."

"I'll make this meeting with Crowder as brief as possible. Don't leave this room." He went out and pulled the door closed behind him.

On his way to the elevator, he met Howard Glenn. "Hey, Cassidy, I was on my way to see you."

"Anything?"

"Some pretty interesting stuff is coming out of those lists of Wilde's contributors."

"Thanks." Cassidy took the sheets of paper Glenn extended him, folded them twice, and slipped them into his breast pocket. "I'll get to it as soon as I can. Right now I'm due in Crowder's office. In the meantime, stay with it."

He stepped into the elevator. When he emerged, he didn't break stride until he was standing at the edge of Crowder's desk. "For Christ's sake, Tony, what's so damned important that it couldn't wait? I was questioning Claire Laurent. She's protecting Yasmine, but the more I pull out of her, the more apparent it is to me that Yasmine killed Wilde."

"That's what we wanted to talk to you about."

Cassidy, remembering that the intern had mentioned someone with Crowder, followed the direction of his gaze. Alister Petrie was complacently seated across the room in a leather wingback chair.

Cassidy had never liked Petrie, either as an individual or as a statesman. Having impressive political connections was his sole qualification to legislate. Petrie's family roots were sunk deep into delta dirt but weren't as deeply embedded as his wife's. Cassidy considered him a pompous nerd, who, through no achievement of his own, had enough money to buy a congressional seat. Because Cassidy had been weaned on the work ethic, he held Petrie in contempt, which he barely concealed. "Hello, Congressman."

"Mr. Cassidy," he replied coolly.

"Sit down, Cassidy," Crowder said, brusquely signaling him into a chair.

Cassidy's instincts were sizzling like exposed electrical wires. Something was afoot, and if his intuition was to be trusted, it was something he wasn't going to like. Tony Crowder was having a hard time looking him in the eye. That was a bad sign.

"I'll let Congressman Petrie explain why he asked us for this meeting." Tony coughed uncomfortably behind his fist.

"When you hear what he has to say, you'll realize its importance and urgency. Congressman?"

Petrie began by saying, "I was stunned by the headlines I read in this morning's newspaper, Mr. Cassidy."

"It's pretty stunning stuff. If a technician hadn't been on his toes, he wouldn't have noticed the similarities between the results of the ballistics test he ran on Yasmine's suicide bullet and the ones he'd recently conducted on the bullets we took out of Jackson Wilde. There was a deep groove running the length of the bullets that was worth remembering, he said. So he compared them. And bingo. Same weapon. He fired it just to make sure. There's no mistake."

"There has to be."

"There isn't."

"Nevertheless, your investigation into a possible connection between Yasmine's suicide and Jackson Wilde's murder must cease and desist. Immediately."

The command was issued so pedantically, and with such bald arrogance, that Cassidy's initial reaction was to laugh. He glanced at Tony Crowder, but there wasn't a trace of a smile on his superior's face. In fact, it looked as stern and indomitable as a totem hewn out of solid oak.

"What the hell is going on?" He faced Petrie again. "Where do you get off telling me to cease and desist my investigation?"

"Yasmine did not kill Jackson Wilde."

"How would you know?"

"Because she was with me that night. Throughout the night."

Silence stretched through the room. Again Cassidy turned to Tony, his hard stare demanding elaboration. The D.A. cleared his throat with obvious discomfort. Cassidy's respect for him slipped several notches. He was old enough to be Petrie's father, but he was kowtowing to the jerk like he was a frigging prince.

"Congressman Petrie came to me this morning and freely

admitted that he'd been having an . . . that is . . . he and this Yasmine had a relationship.''

"No shit," Cassidy said sarcastically. "I know all about his affair with her."

"Miss Laurent told you, I assume," Crowder said.

"That's right."

"Then you can appreciate the embarrassment that a lengthy and thorough investigation could cause Congressman Petrie and his family."

"He should have thought of that before he started screwing around."

Petrie bristled. "All this embarrassment would be for nothing, Mr. Cassidy, because, as I've informed you, I'm Yasmine's alibi. She was with me."

Cassidy looked at him scornfully. "And you get credit for her suicide, don't you, Petrie? She sprayed your walls with her brains because you're a lying cheat. What happened to make you call it quits? Did the new wear off? Or did you get cold feet over the upcoming election? Did you get scared that your white voters weren't going to look kindly upon your black mistress?"

"Cassidy!" Tony banged his fist on his desk.

Cassidy shot from his chair and turned his anger on Crowder. "This is the first piece of real evidence we've uncovered since we began investigating this crime. Do you really expect me to toss it away because it might get out that the woman implicated in the crime was our illustrious congressman's mistress?"

Petrie's previous nonchalance had vanished. Red-faced with indignation, he too came to his feet. "Yasmine was not my mistress. She had formed an unnatural attachment for me that was entirely one-sided. A fatal attraction."

"You're a liar. It was a two-way love affair until you turned gutless."

"She was a terribly disturbed young woman."

"That's bullshit."

"She was addicted to mind-altering drugs—"

"Dr. Dupuis's autopsy report says she didn't have so much as an aspirin in her system."

"Obviously Yasmine didn't agree with my position on—"

"Oh, I'll bet you agreed on most positions. Which one did you like best? On top or on bottom?"

"Cassidy, I won't have this!" Crowder bellowed, surging to his feet. "I won't have Congressman Petrie insulted in my office when he came here of his own accord and at great personal cost."

"I can't fuckin' believe this, Tony!" Cassidy exclaimed. "You're going to sweep this under the rug, pretend those ballistics tests don't exist?"

"You know as well as I do that those tests are inconclusive Besides, he makes good sense. Hear him out."

"Why, Tony?" Cassidy asked, seething.

"He's convinced me that the young woman had no motive to kill Wilde."

Cassidy swiveled his head and fixed a hard stare on Petrie. "You've got the floor. Make it good."

Petrie tugged on the hem of his suit jacket and composed himself. "Yasmine thought Jackson Wilde was a joke," he said. "Even though he called the French Silk catalog pornographic, she didn't take him seriously. To her he was a comic figure. That's all. She teased me about rolling out the red carpet to him while he was here."

"Oh, you're a specialist at kissing ass."

"Cassidy, shut up!"

He ignored Crowder and advanced on Petrie. "You looked right at home sitting on his podium. You're as full of shit as he was. In my opinion, Wilde was the Alister Petrie of clergymen. Like you he was a self-important, self-serving opportunist who's only talent was duping people."

Petrie's face turned even redder, but he kept his voice calm. "Insult me all you want. The facts remain the same.

Yasmine was with me the night Jackson Wilde was shot and killed.''

"Where?"

"At the Doubletree."

"You stayed overnight at the Doubletree and that didn't arouse Mrs. Petrie's suspicions?"

"I frequently stay downtown overnight if I'm going to be out late and have an early meeting scheduled for the next day. Sleeping over spares me a short night and a long commute the following morning."

"And gives you an opportunity to cheat on your wife."

"I'm trying to be up front with you," Petrie exclaimed angrily. "I've admitted to being with Yasmine at the Doubletree."

"I'll check on it."

"I'm sure you will."

"How do you explain her gun being used to kill Wilde if she didn't pull the trigger?"

"I may be able to shed some light on that."

"Then please do."

Following that sarcastic crack, Petrie addressed himself to Crowder. "I was with Yasmine when she rediscovered her gun."

"Rediscovered?"

"Yes. She was surprised to find it at the bottom of the handbag she was carrying at the time. She said it had been missing. She thought she'd lost it in transit between here and New York."

Mentally Cassidy cursed. It perfectly matched Claire's story and shot his case all to hell. His expression, however, remained pugnacious.

"I suggest you start questioning anyone who had access to Yasmine's handbag," Petrie said. "And put an end to investigating her activities that night."

"Which will be convenient as hell for you, won't it?"

Unruffled by Cassidy's snide remark, Petrie stooped down to retrieve his briefcase. "I leave the crime solving and prosecuting to you, Mr. Cassidy." He flashed a brittle smile. "Actually I'm sparing you hours of time, effort, and eventual public disgrace. I didn't have to come here and admit that I was with Yasmine that night. I felt it was my civic responsibility to do so. Now the taxpayers' money won't be wasted on another wild goose chase."

"The only one you're protecting is yourself," Cassidy said with a sneer. "You admitted to us that you and Yasmine were lovers only so you wouldn't have to admit it to your constituents."

Again Petrie gave him a fleeting smile. "You'd do well to take the advice of your mentor Mr. Crowder. Your ambition has been noted and duly recorded, Mr. Cassidy. But if you want to fill that chair," he said, nodding toward Crowder's desk, "you'd better learn to play the game."

"I don't shovel political bullshit, if that's what you mean."

"Everything is political, Mr. Cassidy. Most everything is also bullshit. If you're going to be in public office, get used to shoveling it."

Cassidy cocked his head to one side. "That's quite a speech, Petrie, but it sounds rehearsed. Did your wife write it for you?"

Petrie's arrogance collapsed like a dud parachute. He sputtered, "In this evening's *Times Picayune* I expect to read that the technician conducting the ballistics tests made a gross error, that Assistant District Attorney Cassidy's allegations regarding Yasmine were incorrect, that this office is retracting previous statements suggesting her possible involvement with the Wilde murder, and that you're redirecting your investigation. Let her suicide stand as the inexplicable action of an unbalanced woman, who, for reasons known only to her, chose to end her life on my doorstep, possibly in an attempt to make a radical political statement."

"Have you washed all the brain tissue off your wallpaper yet?"

"Cassidy."

"Or have you replaced the wallpaper altogether?"

"Cassidy!"

Once again, Crowder's reprimands were ignored. "Can you clean up that quickly, Petrie? A pail of water and some Spic 'n' Span, and *whoosh* she's expunged? Is that all her life meant to you?"

Using his words like a battering ram, Cassidy had hoped to smash the protective facade that was inherent to the public office Petrie held. He wanted to confront Petrie man to man, where he would have equal footing, if not the advantage. He wanted Petrie angry, scared, and upset. He finally got what he wanted.

"Yasmine wasn't worth the hell she put me through," Petrie smirked. "She was nothing but a whore with the hottest snatch I'd ever had. Too bad for you that you homed in on her cool friend, Claire Laurent, and not Yasmine."

Cassidy lunged at him, knocked him backward into the leather chair, and wound up with his forearm across Petrie's throat and his knee gouging his crotch.

"If Yasmine was a whore, what does that make you, you son of a bitch?" He increased the pressure against Petrie's windpipe and ground his knee into his vulnerable testicles. Petrie uttered a high-pitched squeal. Cassidy delighted in the terror he saw in his eyes.

But Cassidy's pleasure was short-lived. Crowder was almost thirty years older, but he was forty pounds heavier and as strong as a bull. His hands landed like sacks of wet concrete on Cassidy's shoulders, almost causing the leg supporting him to buckle. He pulled him off Petrie, who was clutching his throat and wheezing. He cowered from Cassidy and blubbered, "H-he's crazy."

"I apologize for my deputy's short temper," Crowder said.

He had one hand splayed against Cassidy's chest. Cassidy strained against it. Crowder shot him a warning look.

Petrie scooped up what was left of his dignity, straightened his suit jacket, smoothed a hand over his hair. "I intend to file assault charges. You'll be hearing from my attorney."

"No we won't," Crowder said curtly. "Not unless you want to expose the topic of our discussion here this morning. Right now, it's confidential. You litigate and it'll be a matter of public record."

Petrie was puffed up like an adder. Nevertheless, he took Crowder's subtle threat for what it was. Without another word, he stalked from the office.

For several moments after he left, neither of them moved. Finally, Cassidy reached up and angrily shoved Crowder's hand off his chest.

"I know what you're thinking," Crowder said.

"You couldn't begin to know." Cassidy's temper was momentarily corralled, but it was going to be a while before his anger subsided. He was still furious with the man he had respected and admired. Like a disillusioned child who spots weakness in a hero, he was as hurt as he was angry. "Why'd you do it, Tony?"

Crowder returned to his desk and sat down heavily. "I owed Petrie the favor. He endorsed me during the last election. He's a slimy, snot-nosed, cocky little bastard. But unfortunately he's got lots of political muscle and money behind him. He'll get reelected. I retire next year. I don't want Petrie's foot on my throat my last year in office. I want to go out peaceably, not embroiled in a political gumbo."

He looked up at Cassidy, silently asking for his understanding. Cassidy, saying nothing, moved to the windows. From there he could see Petrie on the street, surrounded by media, making a statement into microphones and cameras. He couldn't hear what the congressman was saying, but every lying, dulcet word was sure to be reported on *News at Five*.

The sad thing was that he'd be believed by a gullible public that was always inclined to trust a handsome face and sincere smile.

"Maybe at one time, when I was young and full of piss and vinegar like you, I'd have nailed his balls to the floor," Crowder was saying. "I'd have told him that criminal investigations were exempt from the bargaining table. That deals couldn't be struck when they conflicted with due process. That mutual back-scratching ended at that door." He pointed to his office door.

"There's no doubt I would have told him all that and sent him packing this morning if I had a strong case to back up my position. But at the bottom line, he's right, Cassidy. If he's willing to come in here and acknowledge having a mistress, we've got to believe him when he says she was with him that night."

Cassidy was still staring out the window, watching the pantomine being acted out below. Wilde's followers cheered Petrie as he left the area. His entourage packed him into a van and whisked him away. Motorcycle police provided escort.

"Fuck it," Cassidy muttered, turning back into the room. "Sometimes I think I dreamed Wilde's corpse, those three bullet wounds, the blood. He was murdered, wasn't he?"

"He was."

"Then, goddammit, somebody killed him."

"But it wasn't Yasmine. I already sent a policewoman over to the Doubletree to check out Petrie's story. Before you got here, she called in. Petrie was registered there that night. So far she's talked to four people who remember seeing him there. The doorman, a bellman—"

"Okay, okay. What about Yasmine?"

"No one claims to have seen her. But if they were having a tryst, she would naturally keep a low profile. And if you enter the hotel by the side door, you can get to the elevators without having to go through the lobby.''

Cassidy shoved his hands into his pants pockets. ''So it's back to square one.''

''Not really,'' Crowder said quietly.

''What do you mean?''

''It's so damn simple, Cassidy. It has been from the beginning. As we speak, your killer is sitting in your office.''

''Claire didn't do it.''

Crowder stabbed the surface of his desk with his index finger. ''She had the same motive as Yasmine, only stronger. She had opportunity because she can't account for all of her time that night. We've got her voice on tape asking her friend at the Fairmont to lie for her. The fibers found at the crime scene match the carpet in her car. She had access to Yasmine's gun and opportunity to replace it once she'd used it. My God, man, what more do you need?''

''She didn't do it,'' Cassidy said tightly.

''You're that sure of her innocence?''

''Yes.''

''Sure enough to stake your career on it?''

Crowder's secretary stuck her head around the door. ''I'm sorry, Mr. Crowder, but she insisted on—''

The secretary was pushed aside by Ariel Wilde. As she sailed in, her pale hair rippled over her shoulders. She was dressed in a white suit, reminiscent of the robe she wore on her television show.

''Well, Mrs. Wilde, how nice of you to stop by,'' Cassidy said caustically. ''Have you met District Attorney Anthony Crowder? Mr. Crowder, Mrs. Ariel Wilde.''

She turned her frigid blue glare on Cassidy. ''God is going to rain judgment on you. You've made a mockery of my husband's murder.''

Cassidy's eyebrows shot up. ''Mockery? You want to talk mockery? What about the mockery you made of your marriage by having an affair with your stepson?''

"I no longer have a stepson. Influenced by you, he turned out to be a Judas. God will punish him, too."

"How does God punish liars, Mrs. Wilde? Because you lied to me, didn't you? The night your husband was killed, you left Josh's room for a trip to your hotel suite around midnight."

"Cassidy, what are you getting at?" Crowder asked.

"I found out a few days ago that Josh leased a Chrysler LeBaron convertible while he was in New Orleans. Coincidentally, it is similar to Claire Laurent's and has the same type of carpet."

"I came here to tell you—"

Cassidy didn't give Ariel an opportunity to speak. "You rode in Josh's rental car. You could have tracked the carpet fibers into your husband's bedroom when you went in there to shoot him."

"I could have tracked it in there anytime," she cried. "Rather than finding my husband's killer, you persist in torturing me and my unborn child."

As though on cue, two reporters and one video photographer rushed past the flustered secretary and through the open door. Ariel cupped her abdomen with her hands. "If I lose my child, the guilt will rest on your head, Mr. Cassidy. From what I read in the newspapers, it appears as though my husband's death is connected to that filthy catalog and the whore who posed in it!"

"Yasmine wasn't a whore."

That calm statement came from Claire, who unexpectedly appeared in the doorway.

Cassidy's temper snapped again. "I told you to stay put."

"Harlot!" Ariel shouted, pointing a finger at Claire.

"Everyone, vacate this office at once!" Crowder yelled. "Who let the media in here?" The video camera swung around to get a shot of the D.A.'s flushed, angry face.

Ariel bore down on Claire. Her eyes narrowed to malicious slits. "Finally we meet face to face."

Chapter Twenty-eight

❦ ❦

From then on, everything happened so quickly that, later, Claire couldn't recall the exact sequence of events.

Ariel Wilde dropped to her knees, raised her clasped hands toward heaven, and began loudly thanking God for wielding his mighty sword of justice.

Crowder bellowed for the security guards to clear his office.

The reporters thrust microphones toward Claire and began firing questions.

The video photographer planted his soiled sneakers in the seat of an expensively upholstered chair in order to get a better camera angle on the unfolding scene.

The secretary behind Claire shrieked, "Oh my God!" when she turned to see a throng of Wilde disciples swarming toward the office.

When Claire had time to reflect on those first tumultuous moments following her confession, the recollections were blurred images as though she had experienced them from behind a foggy window pane. One memory, however, stood out with painfully stark clarity—the way Cassidy looked at her.

A myriad of emotions flickered across his face. Disbelief. Remorse. Guilt. Befuddlement. Disillusionment. Pain. Yet, this kaleidoscope of reactions didn't effect his stare, which remained steadfastly on her, glinting and hard.

It was broken only when one of Ariel's followers jostled Claire from behind, and, in order to keep her balance, she had to grab the door jamb. Unchecked by security guards who hadn't yet arrived, the crowd pressed in from behind.

Ariel ended her prayer and sprang to her feet, pointing an accusing finger at Claire. "She murdered my husband, one of this century's outstanding spiritual leaders!"

The video cameraman had a hard time capturing it all on tape. The reporters continued to shout their questions into Claire's face. Those outside the office undulated toward the door like a tidal wave, gaining momentum, going over and around the desks of secretaries, fighting Crowder's staff and each other for better vantage points.

Claire's name rippled through the crowd as word of her confession spread. It was repeated with mounting hatred. Within moments, the crowd resembled a lynch mob.

"It was her all along!" she heard a man shout.

"May her and French Silk be damned to eternal hell!"

The animosity escalated. The shouts became louder, the epithets meaner. Crowder ordered the reporters to leave. He yanked the video photographer from his perch. That unbalanced the camera on the man's shoulder. It crashed to the floor, and he began angrily accusing Crowder of infringing on his first amendment rights.

Since the camera was no longer operative and therefore undamaging, Crowder ignored him and turned his attention to Ariel Wilde. "Get your flock out of here!"

" 'Vengeance is mine, sayeth the Lord,' " she cried, her eyes fanatically bright.

Cassidy, apparently galvanized to action by the increasing

size of the crowd and their growing hostility, rushed toward Claire and wrapped his hand around her forearm. "If this keeps up they'll tear her to pieces." He had to shout to Crowder to make himself heard. "I'm getting her out of here."

"Where are you taking her? Cassidy!"

That was the last Claire saw or heard of Crowder, because Cassidy threw his arm across her shoulders, turned her around, and began battling a path through the wall of malcontents.

"Clear this area! Get these people out of here!"

The secretaries and clerks responded to the authoritative ring in Cassidy's voice and began making ineffectual attempts to disperse the crowd by nicely asking them to leave. The crowd wasn't listening. Uniformed security guards finally converged on the scene and joined the melee, barking orders and issuing threats of imminent arrest that went unheeded.

It became obvious to Claire that Cassidy was trying to get her to the stairwell. But when they reached the marked exit, a burly Bible-thumper wearing a T-shirt that read GOD IS LOVE blocked the door and sneered at Claire. "You'll burn in hell for what you did, sister."

"Get out of our way or you'll see hell a lot quicker than she does," Cassidy threatened.

The man snarled, reached out and grabbed a handful of Claire's hair, and pulled hard. Several strands were ripped from her scalp. Claire cried out in pain and instinctively raised her hands to protect her head.

Cassidy acted on instinct too. He rammed his fist into the man's gut, then, when he doubled over, caught him beneath the chin with a blow that sent his head crashing back into the wall.

The people nearest them began to scream. In a matter of seconds full-fledged panic broke out. Cassidy yanked open the door and gave the center of Claire's back a hard shove that sent her stumbling onto the landing.

He grabbed a security guard by the back of his collar and used him as a shield to block the exit. "Give me time to get her away from the building. Don't let anyone through this door," he shouted as he pulled the door closed. The guard, still unclear as to what was going on, nodded dumbly.

Cassidy gripped her hand and began running down the stairs. "Are you all right?"

Claire discovered that she was too frightened to speak. Like the bewildered guard, she nodded, but in his haste Cassidy didn't even look back.

The stairs served as a fire escape and opened to the outside, so they were able to avoid the chaos occurring in the atrium lobby of the building. It was crawling with Jackson Wilde's followers, confused employees, and those unfortunate enough to have business in the D.A.'s office that afternoon.

As soon as they were outside, Cassidy dragged her along behind him, around the rear of the building, toward where his car was parked on the opposite side. "Shit!" He halted so quickly, it jarred Claire's teeth. "My car keys are on my desk."

He didn't waste a moment to think about it, but went in search of something to break the window. He returned precious seconds later with a loose brick from a nearby construction site. "Turn your head."

He bashed the window with the brick, reached inside the shattered glass and unlocked the door, then barely gave Claire time to get in before slamming it behind her. She reached across the interior and opened the driver's door for him.

"How are you going to start it?"

"The way the thieves do."

While Claire brushed broken glass from the seat, he hotwired the car. Within minutes they had made their escape. Surrounding the city hall complex was a maze of one-way streets that required careful negotiation even by those who drove it every day. As he drove, Cassidy jerked his cellular phone off its stand and tossed the receiver into Claire's lap.

"Call French Silk. Tell them to shut down for the day. Tell everybody to get the hell out and away from there."

"They wouldn't dare—"

"You saw them back there. God only knows what these maniacs will do when they hear you've confessed."

Claire feared for her building and its costly inventory, but mostly for the safety of her employees. She fumbled with the rubberized digits on the transmitter. "My mother. I've got to get her to a safe place."

"I'm thinking," he said tautly as he raced through a yellow light.

Claire spoke to her secretary. "There's been a new development in the Wilde case." She cut her eyes to Cassidy; he glanced at her briefly. "It might be dangerous for French Silk to remain open today. Send everyone home. Yes, right now. Tell them not to report to work until notified, but assure them they'll receive full pay. Secure the building. Quickly. Now, please patch me into the apartment phone."

While that was being done, she said to Cassidy, "You have to take me home so I can see to my mother."

"I can't take you near that place, Claire. Ariel's got a communication system more effective than any public utility. But you're right, if they storm the building, it'll be unsafe for Mary Catherine to be there."

The thought filled Claire with panic. "You've got to take me to her now, Cassidy."

"I can't."

"The hell you can't."

"Could she go home with Harry?"

"I've got to—"

"Don't argue with me, goddammit! Can Harry take her home with her?"

He averted his eyes from the traffic long enough to look at her. Claire wanted to dispute him, but the suggestion was viable. She spoke tersely into the telephone. "Hello, Harry, it's me. Listen closely." Once she had made her request, she

said, "I know it's an imposition but I need to know that
Mama's safe and being well taken care of. Don't alarm her.
No, I'm sure you'll handle it beautifully. But timing is vital.
Get her out immediately. Yes, I'll be careful. I'll call later
and let you know where I am."

She replaced the telephone and sat stiffly, staring forward.
Cassidy weaved through traffic, taking the streets in a random, zigzag pattern. He drove well but fast. His eyes remained in constant motion, moving from side to side like a
mine sweeper.

"Shouldn't you be taking me to the police station?"

"Later. When they've scattered the crazies and I don't
have to worry about losing you to some fanatic who wants
an eye for an eye."

"Then where are we going?"

"I'm open to suggestions."

"You mean you don't have a destination in mind?"

"About a dozen so far. I've discarded them all. I can't take
you to French Silk. Once they figure out you're not there,
they'll look for you at my place."

"There are hundreds of hotels and motels."

"They'll be checking the registration desks."

"Even out of town?"

He shook his head no. "With a broken window, I can't
keep this car on the road for long. Too easy to spot."

"Take me back."

He made a scoffing sound. "Not likely. Even if you've got
a death wish, I don't."

"I've confessed to murder, Cassidy. A felony. Every police officer in the state will be out looking for me. I don't
want to make matters worse by becoming a fugitive."

"You're not a fugitive as long as you're in my custody.
As soon as we get where we're going, I'll call Crowder. Once
the coast is clear, I'll take you to the sheriff's office to be
booked. Hopefully we can get you in before the press gets
wind of it." He shot her a quick glance. "Between now and

then, I've got to make sure you're not taken out by some bastard with a Bible in one hand and a sawed-off shotgun in the other.''

He wasn't overdramatizing. She touched the sore spot on her scalp and shuddered when she remembered the hatred she had seen in the man's eyes.

"Any ideas?" he asked. "Unfortunately I don't own a fishing cabin, or a boat, or a place—''

"Aunt Laurel's house," Claire said suddenly. "It's been closed up for years. Only a few people know I still own it.''

"Have you got a key with you?"

"No, but I know where one is hidden.''

She found the latchkey beneath the rock under the third camellia bush in the flower bed on the left side of the porch, where it had been secreted for as long as Claire remembered. Cassidy had expressed concern about leaving his car on the street in front of the house, so they parked it in the rear alley.

Entering the old townhouse was like stepping through a time warp. Although it had the close, musty odor of any unoccupied dwelling, Claire's sense of smell was stirred by dozens of fond memories: Aunt Laurel's rose sachet, pomander balls made of dried oranges spiked with cloves, dusty old lace, jasmine tea, and Christmas candles.

The entryway catapulted Claire's childhood to the forefront of her mind. Some memories were as gauzy as the curtains that hung in the slender windows flanking the front door. Others were as vivid as the colors in the authentic Persian rug. Some were golden, like the butter-colored sunlight that cast dappled shadows on the walls. Others were as somber as the grandfather clock that had stopped ticking and stood tall and silent.

Cassidy shut the door behind them and relocked it, then peered through the curtains until he was satisfied that no one had followed them and that they hadn't aroused the curiosity of nosy neighbors. Turning his back to the window, he surveyed his surroundings. Claire watched closely for his reaction, realizing that she wanted him to like and appreciate the house as she did.

"How long has it been since you were here?" he asked.

"Yesterday." He shot her a stunned look and she smiled. "It seems that way."

His eyes took a more detailed inventory of the two-story entry. "It looks like a granny's house."

"Did you have a granny, Cassidy?"

"Only one. On my mother's side."

"Did you have aunts and uncles and lots of cousins?"

"Assorted."

"Hmm. I always wished for them." She gave him a wistful smile, then asked him to follow her. "Let me show you the courtyard. That's my favorite part of the house. Later I'll take you upstairs."

"What about a phone?"

"It was disconnected when we moved out."

"I'll have to use my car phone."

"This minute?" she asked with disappointment.

"Not this minute, but soon, Claire."

"I understand."

He followed her through a formal dining room and a quaint kitchen into what she called the sun room. It had windows on three sides and was furnished in white wicker with floral chintz cushions that were comfortably sagged in their centers. The sun room opened onto the courtyard. Claire unlocked the French door, pushed it open, and stepped outside onto the ancient bricks.

"Over there where the double French doors are is the living room," she said, pointing. "Or the parlor, as Aunt Laurel called it. Up above it, on the second floor, is my bedroom. Sometimes in the summer, when the mosquitoes weren't too bad, Mama and Aunt Laurel would let me make a pallet there on the balcony. I loved falling asleep to the sound of the water trickling in the fountain. And in the morning I could smell fresh coffee and honeysuckle before opening my eyes."

A struggling wisteria vine and one quick, shy chameleon were all that remained alive in the courtyard. The foundation of the fountain was cracked and crumbling. The basin around the naked cherub was filled with stagnant rainwater and dead leaves. The glider was rusty and squeaked when Claire gave it a gentle push.

"We used to have ferns hanging everywhere. When the airplane ferns made babies, we'd pinch them off and root them in water before planting them in clay pots. Every spring we'd plant perennials in the flower beds and they'd bloom sometimes through December. On mild evenings we'd eat supper out here. Before I started school, Mama used to sit in this chair and tell me fairy tales," she said, lovingly running her hand over the rusty wrought iron.

"Seeing it like this makes me sad. It's like viewing the corpse of someone you love." She gave the courtyard another poignant glance, then stepped back into the sun room. In the kitchen, she checked a tin in the pantry and found that it still contained Bigelow tea. "I made tea the last time I was here. Would you like some?"

Without waiting for his answer, she rinsed out the kettle and turned on the stove beneath it. She was reaching into the cabinet for china when Cassidy captured her busy hands and drew her around to face him.

This moment had been inevitable. She had known that eventually Cassidy would ask her about it and she would have to tell him. She had prolonged it for as long as possible but could delay no longer.

"Claire," he asked softly, "why did you kill Jackson Wilde?"

His eyes were gazing intently into hers. The time had come

"Jackson Wilde was my father."

Chapter Twenty-nine

⁂ ⁂

Spring 1958

It was hot in the Vieux Carré even though May was only a few days old. Blossoms had burst in such abundance that the air was heavily perfumed. Leaves were new and vibrantly green. The vitality of spring rushed through the veins of three schoolgirls, filling them with a lust for life that couldn't be appeased by English literature, geometry, French, or chemistry.

With energy pumping and looking for an outlet, they abandoned their studies to sneak off in search of the forbidden pleasures to be found in the French Quarter. They gorged on Lucky Dogs bought from a street vendor and had their palms read by a strolling gypsy lady with a parrot on her shoulder.

On a dare from Lisbet, Alice glanced inside one of the strip joints on Bourbon Street when a teasing barker swung the door open as she passed. Squealing, she raced back to where her friends were waiting. "What'd you see?"

"It was gross," Alice squealed.

"Was she naked?"

"Except for tassels. She was twirling them."

"Liar," Lisbet said.

"I swear."

"No one can really do that. It's anatomically impossible."

"It is if they're no bigger than yours," Alice taunted.

Mary Catherine Laurent diplomatically intervened. She often played the role of peacemaker, disliking strife of any kind, but particularly among her friends. "She didn't have on anything else?"

"Not a stitch. Well, she had a tiny triangle of glitter over you-know-what."

"Her pussy?" Dumbfounded, the two other girls gaped at Lisbet. "Well, that's what my big brother calls it." Lisbet's brother was a sophomore at Tulane and often inspired awe among his younger sister's friends.

Alice sniffed loftily. "That sounds like something he'd say. He's rude, crude, and socially unacceptable."

"And you're passionately in love with him," Mary Catherine teased.

"I am not."

"Are so."

"It doesn't matter," Lisbet said, striking off down the sidewalk, the pleats of her blue and gray plaid parochial-school skirt brushing against her calves. "He likes Betsy Bouvier. He told me he got his hand up her skirt on their last date." She glanced over her shoulder at Alice, who looked stricken. "Gotcha, Alice!"

"Oh!"

"Does cunt mean the same thing as pussy?" Mary Catherine asked as she skipped to catch up.

"Shh!" She was sprayed by the admonitions of her two friends. "My God, Mary Catherine. Don't you know anything?"

"Well, I don't have any brothers," she said defensively. "Does it mean the same thing?"

"Yes."

"But," Alice added, "if any man ever says that to you, you should slap his face."

"Or knee him hard right in the nuts."

"It's bad, then?"

"It's about the worst," Lisbet said, dramatically rolling her eyes.

"Yesterday you said 'fuck' was the worst."

The two girls looked at each other and shook their heads over Mary Catherine's ignorance and confusion. "She's hopeless."

They browsed in the gaudy souvenir shops lining both sides of Bourbon Street, pretending to admire the feathered, spangled Mardi Gras masks while actually studying a coffee mug with a detailed phallic handle.

"Do you think they really get that big when . . . you know, when you're doing it?" Alice whispered.

Lisbet answered with an air of superiority, "Oh, much bigger than that."

"How would you know?"

"I've heard."

"From who?"

"I can't remember, but she said it was huge and hurt like hell when he put it in."

Mary Catherine was aghast. "You know somebody who's actually done it?"

When pressed, Lisbet couldn't produce an actual name, so the accuracy of her statement was doubtful.

"I can't wait to do it," Alice admitted as they left the shop and continued down the sidewalk.

"Even though it hurts?" Mary Catherine thought the whole business of sex sounded unappealing and unladylike.

"It only hurts the first time, goose. After he busts your cherry, it's okay."

"What's a cherry?"

That sent the other two seventeen-year-olds careening into the exterior wall of a jazz joint, collapsing in a fit of giggles.

Invariably their conversations revolved around human sexuality. They were told by the nuns that it was a grievous sin to contemplate such matters, so that was largely what they contemplated. Mary Catherine and her two very best friends had speculated on everything from if the nuns shaved their pubic hair as well as their heads, to exactly how the male anatomy was constructed.

They sneaked copies of novels by James Joyce, James Baldwin and James Jones—Lisbet had remarked that there must be something to the name that made the men who had it highly sexual—and pored over the passages describing copulation, which had been conveniently underlined by previous readers. But sometimes even those were annoyingly euphemistic and vague.

It seemed to Mary Catherine that the more she learned about sex, the more there was to learn. To vent her frustration, she added each tidbit of knowledge to her diary. After her prayers each night, she faithfully confided everything to the leather-bound book with the small gold lock. Tonight, she would be able to fill pages with impressions and new vocabulary words.

She and her friends meandered through the Quarter, a trio of striking young women, whose ripe young bodies seemed out of place in the austere school uniforms. Their slender calves seemed designed to wear high heels and silk stockings rather than the despised oxfords and bobby socks.

They arrived at Jackson Square and paused to flirt with a sidewalk artist with a red goatee who was indolently soliciting business from the tourists. Of the samples displayed, his best work was a colored chalk portrait of Marilyn Monroe.

"He's probably done another one of her in the nude," Lisbet said knowingly. "He keeps it hidden away in his ratty little garret. At night he takes it out and jerks off while he's ogling it."

"Do you think any man will ever jerk off while ogling a picture of me?" Alice asked wistfully.

"You'd better go to confession twice this week," Lisbet said. "You've got sex on the brain."

"Me? You're the walking encyclopedia on the topic. Or at least you think you are."

"I've been exposed to much more than you have. I've seen my brother—"

"He's here again."

Mary Catherine's quiet observation brought the two other girls to a standstill. They followed her absorbed gaze to the statue of Andrew Jackson in the center of the square. More particularly, to the young man who was delivering a fiery sermon to a few pedestrians, one unconscious wino, and a flock of pigeons.

"The Lord is sick and tired of his children sinning," he declared, slapping the worn Bible in his hand. "He looks down here on Earth and sees the lying and the cheating and the gambling and the drinking and the fornicating—"

"That's another word for fuck," Lisbet informed Mary Catherine in a whisper.

Mary Catherine shrugged her off impatiently. She was drawn to the young preacher not so much by what he was saying, but by the passion with which he was saying it.

"His judgment is near, ladies and gentlemen. He ain't gonna stand for our sinning much longer. No, siree." He plucked a handkerchief from the breast pocket of his shiny navy blue suit and mopped his forehead, which was perspiring beneath a lock of dark blond hair.

"I weep for sinners to be *saved*." Gnashing his teeth and closing his eyes, he threw back his head and appealed to heaven. "Lord God, open their eyes. Sweet Jesus, have mercy on the weak. Give them strength to fight Satan and his wily, wicked ways."

The girls entered the gate and moved closer for a better look. "He's kind of cute," Lisbet said.

"You think so?" Alice asked, eyeing the preacher critically.

"I do."

Lisbet turned to Mary Catherine, who was still staring enraptured at the sidewalk preacher. "Hmm. I do believe Mary Catherine is smitten, Alice."

She blushed. "I've seen him here before. Last Saturday my daddy brought me to Café du Monde for breakfast. He was here then, too. There was a larger crowd. He laid hands on some of the people."

"On their what?" Alice asked, crowding in closer to Mary Catherine.

"On their heads, stupid," Lisbet said scornfully. "It *was* their heads, wasn't it?"

"Yes," Mary Catherine replied. "When you get saved, he lays his hands on you so you'll receive the Holy Spirit."

"Let's get saved," Lisbet suggested excitedly.

"We're already saved." Then with less conviction, Alice asked, "Aren't we?"

"Well, sure. We've been baptized. We go to mass. But he doesn't know that." Lisbet turned to Mary Catherine. "Go get saved."

"Yeah," Alice seconded. "We'll watch. Go on."

"No!"

"Chicken."

The preacher was extending an invitation for anyone within the sound of his voice to take his hand. It would be the same as accepting the Lord Jesus by the hand, he told his listeners. "Dear brothers and sisters, you don't want to go to hell, do you?"

"You don't want to go to hell, Mary Catherine,' Alice said seriously. "Go on. He's looking straight at you."

"No, he's not. He's looking at all of us."

"He's looking at *you*. Maybe he sees that you're truly a sinner. Go get saved." Lisbet gave her friend a firm push.

Mary Catherine demurred, but in ways she couldn't understand or explain, she was drawn to the young preacher's compelling voice. Years before, a young, good-looking priest had trained at their parish. She and all her friends had developed passionately sinful crushes on him. They attended nearly every mass that he conducted. Yet Mary Catherine hadn't felt moved by that young priest as she did by this shabbily dressed, marginally articulate, but positively dynamic sidewalk evangelist.

Urged on by her friends, she walked toward him, sending pigeons scuttling aside, drawn as though by a power beyond herself. When she was within several feet of him, he stepped forward and extended his hand. "Hello, sister."

"Hello."

"Do you want Jesus to come into your heart?"

"I . . . I think so. Yes. I do."

"Hallelujah! Take my hand."

She hesitated. His hand was perfectly formed, strong-looking, the smooth palm turned up invitingly. She stretched her hand forward and laid it in his. She thought she heard Alice and Lisbet gasp in disbelief of her courage, but all her senses were shocked by the sudden fist the preacher closed around her hand.

"Kneel now, sister." She did. The pavement was hard beneath her bare knees, but when he laid his hands on her head and invoked God's forgiveness and blessings, she didn't feel anything except the heat emanating from his fingers and palms. After a long prayer, he placed a hand beneath her elbow and assisted her to her feet.

"Just like Jesus told the woman taken in adultery, go and sin no more." Then he took a wooden offering plate out of a battered suitcase that was lying open at his feet and thrust it at her.

The gesture took her by surprise. "Oh." For a moment she was too flustered to think, then she hastily opened her purse, clumsily removed a five-dollar bill, and dropped it into the plate.

"Thank you kindly, sister. God's gonna reward you for your generosity."

He quickly replaced the offering plate with her five-dollar bill, along with his Bible, inside the suitcase and snapped it shut. Picking it up, he jauntily walked away.

"Uh, wait!" Mary Catherine couldn't believe her audacity, but to let him casually walk out of her life was unthinkable. "What's your name?"

"Reverend Jack Collins. But everybody calls me Wild Jack."

※

He'd been reared in a poverty-stricken rural town in Mississippi. About the only thing the town had going for it was the railroad. A section crew was headquartered there. For the most part, the men were single and lived in boardinghouses.

His mama provided evening entertainment for them.

Being the only whore in town, she did a lively business. She'd conceived and given birth to little Jack without ever knowing which of her customers had sired him. Jack's first memory was of toddling around their cramped room to fetch his mama her Lucky Strikes. By the time he was eight, they were fighting over the packs her gentlemen friends sometimes left behind.

He went to school only because the truant officer gave his mama hell if she neglected to get him up and send him off. She in turn gave him hell if he didn't go. Out of sheer stubbornness, he learned as little as possible, although he was a natural leader. Because he didn't give a damn about anything or anyone, because he never even whimpered when he got licks but looked at the principal eyeball to eyeball with open contempt, he earned the fear and admiration of his classmates. He used that to his advantage and wielded more authority on campus than did the faculty.

When he was thirteen, he called his mama a fat, stinking whore one time too many. She coaxed one of her johns to ambush and beat the hell out of him. The next day, he regained consciousness near the railroad tracks with a freight train barreling down it. Holding his broken ribs with one hand, he jumped the freight. He never went back and never saw his mama again. He hoped she died and rotted in hell.

He hoboed through the South for several years, taking odd jobs until he had enough money to get drunk, get laid, and get in a fight, and then he moved on.

One night the freight he was on stopped somewhere in Arkansas. It looked like a happening town, the kind that appealed to a wild young buck like him. But to his irritation the "happening" turned out to be a tent revival. The next freight wasn't due till morning, and that evening it came a downpour. He reasoned that the tent would at least provide shelter, so he attended the revival with everyone else in town.

He scorned everything about the service and everyone who listened with misplaced hope to the preacher who admonished his congregation to seek treasures in heaven, not on earth. What a dope, Jack thought.

He changed his mind when he saw how full the offering plate was when it was passed to him. Pretending to put a bill in, he took out a ten. But he looked upon the smug preacher standing on the podium with new respect.

Jack Collins made a career decision that rainy night in Arkansas. With a portion of that ten-dollar bill, he bought a Bible and struggled through a first reading. He attended more revival meetings. He listened and learned. To pass the hours in freight cars, he imitated the inflection and gestures of the preachers. When he felt ready, he stood on a street corner in a hick town in Alabama and preached his first sermon. The coins pitched to him added up to $1.37.

It was a start.

"Hello. You probably don't remember me."

Mary Catherine shyly intercepted him at the corner of the

Presbytere. He'd just finished his sermon and had cut across the square with his brisk, quick stride. Having observed him for several days, she had noticed that he always moved as though he were in a hurry to get where he was going.

He smiled at her. "Course I remember you."

"I got saved the other day."

"And you've been back twice since then. Without your friends."

She'd hung back at the edges of the crowd, afraid of appearing bold. He had seemed not to notice her. Flattered that he had, she blushed. "I don't want to bother you."

"No bother, sister. What's on your mind?"

"You said the Lord needed help in getting his work done."

"Yeah. So?"

"So I brought you this." She pushed a ten-dollar bill into his hand.

He stared down at it for a moment before raising his eyes to hers and saying emotionally, "God bless you, sister."

"Will it help?"

"More than you know." He cleared his throat. "Say, I'm hungry as a bear. Want a burger?"

Her previous dates had always come in the form of a telephone call. She'd never consented without first getting parental approval. It felt deliciously wicked to be asked out and to accept without anyone knowing, even Alice and Lisbet.

"That sounds lovely."

Grinning, he took her hand. "If we're gonna be friends, I gotta know your name."

When school was dismissed for summer vacation, it became easier for Mary Catherine to sneak off and meet Wild Jack Collins where he preached daily on the street corners of the French Quarter. They ate cheap suppers that, as often as not, Mary Catherine paid for. She didn't mind. He was the most fascinating person she'd ever met. People were naturally drawn to him, from the seediest ladies of the evening to the shrewdest con men who worked the streets.

Jack regaled her with anecdotes that had happened during his seven years in the ministry. He'd had more adventures than Mary Catherine could dream of as he'd traveled from city to city, spreading the gospel, preaching God's love and salvation to sinners.

"What I need is somebody who can sing," he told her one evening. "Do you have any musical talent, Mary Catherine?"

"No, I'm afraid not," she said woefully. How glorious it would be to join Jack's ministry and travel with him! His sermons didn't resemble the formal, ritualistic masses she was accustomed to. Although the underlying message of Christ's redemption was the same, she doubted that her parents would approve of Jack's rough street manners or the fanatical doctrine he preached. That's why her meetings with him remained secret, shared only with her diary.

As the summer heated up, so did their relationship. One night Jack suggested they pick up Chinese food and take it to his place to eat. Mary Catherine's conscience gnawed at her. Going into a young man's apartment without a chaperon led to disgrace and destruction. But when she saw the wounded look on Jack's face because of her hesitation, she accepted and paid for their Chinese food.

The squalid, roach-infested building in which he lived shocked her sensibilities. Even the colored people who did yard work for her family lived in much better housing. The wretchedness of the place demonstrated to her exactly how poor Jack was, how unselfishly dedicated he was to his mission, and how materialistic her upbringing had been. Out of shame and pity, she began to cry. When she explained to him the reason for her tears, he pulled her into his arms.

"There now, honey. Don't cry for me. Jesus was poor too."

That only made her cry harder. He held her tighter. And

soon his hands were skimming her slender back and his lips were moving in her hair, whispering how much he needed her, how sweet she was, how generous it was of her to contribute offerings to his ministry.

His lips eventually reached hers. When he kissed her, she whimpered. It wasn't the first time she'd been kissed. But it was the first time she'd been kissed with her mouth open and felt the urgent thrusting of a man's tongue against her own.

Confused and afraid, she struggled out of his arms and rushed for the door. He caught up with her there, took her into his arms again, and smoothed his hands over her hair. "That's never happened to me before, Mary Catherine," he said in a hushed, rapid voice. "When I kissed you, I felt the Holy Spirit moving between us. Didn't you?"

She had definitely felt something stirring inside her, but she wouldn't have guessed it was the Holy Spirit. "I've got to go home, Jack. My parents will start to worry."

She had reached the bottom of the dim, derelict staircase before he called down to her from his doorway. "Mary Catherine, I think Jesus wants us to be together."

Over the course of the next few days, she filled her diary with agonizing questions for which she had no answers. She certainly couldn't take her problem to her parents. Intuitively she knew they would take one look at Jack in his cheap, flashy suit, see his frayed cuffs and dingy collar, and dismiss him as white trash.

Involving her friends would force them to divide loyalties, and she couldn't risk them telling their parents, who in turn would tell hers. She considered confiding in her aunt Laurel, who had an understanding and kind heart, but she decided against it. Aunt Laurel might also feel duty-bound to inform her parents of her newfound love.

She was confronted with a grown-up problem, the first one of her life, and it must be resolved in a grown-up fashion. She was no longer a child. Jack spoke to her as one adult to another. He treated her as a woman.

But that was the most intimidating problem of all. Being made to feel like a woman was a scary prospect. From the nuns at school she had learned all about sex: Kissing led to petting. Petting led to sex. Sex was a sin.

But, she argued mentally, Jack had said he'd felt imbued by the Holy Spirit when they kissed. Since the nuns who condemned gratification of the flesh had never experienced it, how could they know what it was like? Maybe the light-headedness, the feverishness, and the yearning one felt when kissing weren't carnal reactions at all, but spiritual ones. When Jack's tongue had grazed hers, she'd felt transported. How much more spiritual could you get?

A few days after their first kiss, she was waiting in his apartment when he returned home. She had a supper laid out on the scarred table with the uneven legs. She'd stuck a candle in a pool of wax she melted in a saucer. Along with a bud vase of daisies, the candlelight helped to hide the ugly squalor of the room.

Feeling awkward, she said, "Hi, Jack. I wanted to surprise you."

"You did."

"I brought crawfish étouffée and . . . and a loaf of French bread. And this." She slid a folded twenty-dollar bill across the tabletop.

He looked at it but didn't pick it up. Instead, he pinched the bridge of his nose and closed his eyes. He bowed his head as though in prayer. Several moments passed.

"Jack?" Her voice wavered around his name. "What's the matter?"

He raised his head. Tears glistened in his eyes. "I thought you were mad at me because of the other night."

"No." She quickly rounded the table so that it wouldn't be a barrier between them. "I was startled when you kissed me, that's all."

He pulled her into a tight embrace. "O God, thank you. Sweet Jesus, thank you." He ran his hands over her hair. "I thought I'd lost you, Mary Catherine. I don't deserve somebody as sweet as you in my miserable life, but I prayed and prayed that God would send you back to me. Let's pray.''

He dropped to his knees, pulling her down with him. While they knelt on the grimy, peeling linoleum, facing each other, he offered up a prayer that praised her purity and beauty. The adjectives he used to describe her made her blush. Words of adoration poured from his lips, so that by the time he said, ''Amen,'' she was gazing at him with wonder and love.

''I had no idea you felt that strongly about me, Jack.''

He stared at her as though she were a vision. ''If you don't look like a angel with that candlelight shining through your hair, I pray that God'll strike me blind before my next heartbeat.''

God didn't, so he gingerly raised his hand and touched her hair. As he caressed it, he leaned forward and placed his lips on hers. Mary Catherine was disappointed that he didn't French kiss her again, but when he pressed his parted lips against her throat, she drew a catchy breath of surprise and delight.

Before she quite realized what was happening, he was nibbling her breasts through her thin cotton dress and undoing the pearl buttons.

''Jack?''

''You're right. We should move to the bed. God didn't ordain that I make love to you on the floor.''

He carried her to the bed and laid her down. Leaving her no time to protest, he kissed her mouth while undoing her dress to the waist. The fabric seemed to melt as quickly as cotton candy beneath his hot, anxious hands. She was wearing a full slip and a stiff white brassiere as impregnable as armor, but he deftly got rid of them. His hands moved over her bare flesh in a manner that could only be described as carnal. The caresses felt marvelous, and awfully sinful. But Jack was a preacher, so how could it be wrong? He led people away from sin, not toward it.

While removing the rest of her clothing, he murmured about the beauty and perfection of his Eve. "God created her for Adam. To be his helpmate, his partner in love. Now he's given you to me."

The biblical references quelled Mary Catherine's moral concerns. But when Jack's pants came off and she felt the hard, urgent probing of his sex, she looked up at him with alarm and fear. "Are you going to bust my cherry?"

He laughed. "I guess I am. You're a virgin, aren't you?"

"Of course, Jack, yes." Her breathless avowal became an outcry of pain.

Lisbet had been right. It hurt like hell. But the second time wasn't so bad.

&

It was a rainy afternoon in September when Mary Catherine informed Wild Jack Collins that he was going to be a father. She was waiting for him under the arches of the Cabildo, one of their several meeting places. He had stopped preaching early because the drizzle had become a cloudburst.

Sharing her umbrella, they ran to his apartment house, where the smell of stale food and unwashed bodies made her queasy. Once they were in his room, stripped of their wet clothes, huddled in bed beneath the drab linens, she whispered to him, "Jack, I'm going to have a baby."

His wandering lips ceased their exploration of her neck. His head snapped up. "What?"

"Didn't you hear me?"

Nervously she pulled her lower lip through her teeth, not wanting to repeat the words. For weeks she had anguished over the possibility. After her second missed period, coupled with morning nausea and a constant shortness of breath, there could be little doubt.

She lived in fear of her parents' noticing her swelling breasts and thickening waistline. She'd told no one. Months ago she'd forsaken her friends in favor of Jack's company, and she didn't feel she could go to them now with a problem of this magnitude. Besides, girls who got into trouble were scorned and shunned by everyone, including best friends. Even if Lisbet and Alice chose to remain her friends, their parents would never have permitted it.

She had made her confession at a church outside her own parish. While whispering to the disembodied voice behind the screen, her cheeks had flamed and her words had faltered when she admitted to the lustful things she and Jack had done together. Confessing them to a real person, face to face, would be too mortifying to consider. So she'd borne the guilty burden alone.

Now, she lay in stark terror of Jack's reaction.

He got up and stood at the side of the bed, looking down at her but saying nothing. His glibness seemed to have deserted him.

"Are you angry?" she asked in a feeble voice.

"Uh, no." Then stronger, "No." He sat down and took her damp, cold hand between his. "Did you think I'd be angry?"

Her relief was so vast, she could barely speak. Hot, salty tears flowed from her eyes. "Oh, Jack. I didn't know what you'd think. I didn't know what to do."

"Have you told your folks yet?" She shook her head. "Well, that's good. This is our baby. I don't want anybody horning in on our joy until it's time."

"Oh, Jack, I love you so much." She threw her arms around his neck and kissed his face ecstatically.

He indulged her, laughing, then set her away from him. "You know what this means, don't you?"

"What?"

"We've got to get married."

She clasped her hands beneath her chin. Her eyes were radiant and glowing. "I was hoping you'd say that. Oh, Jack, Jack, no one's ever been this happy."

They made love, then spent hours entangled beneath the covers, planning their future. "I've been wanting to leave New Orleans for several months, Mary Catherine. I haven't left before now because of you." He stroked her tummy. "But with the little one coming, I've got to consider our future in doing the Lord's work."

He outlined his plans for augmenting the ministry. "Maybe I can find somebody to play an instrument and sing hymns. Some preachers have several people working for them. These helpers go into the towns first and set things up, like the disciples used to do for Jesus. By the time the preacher gets there, they've got folks hyped up about him. That's what I want. I wasn't meant to preach for pennies on street corners. Someday I might even get on the radio. And then TV. Now wouldn't that be something?"

Mary Catherine was touched by the evangelical zeal that burned in his eyes. "I'll do whatever I can to help, Jack. You know that."

"Well, the kind of help I need right now . . . never mind."

"What?" She sat up and shook his shoulder. "Tell me."

He looked downcast. "I don't know what I'll do for money, especially now that I'll have two extra mouths to feed. I suppose my mission will have to be put on hold while I get a regular job."

"No! I won't hear of that. You must continue preaching, no matter what."

"I don't see how I can."

"Leave that to me. I've got some money."

Looking close to tears, he pulled her down onto his chest and held her tight. "I don't deserve you. You're a saint. Look at this crappy place. I've got to find better lodging in the next city." He gave the shabby room a look of rank disgust. "This place was all right for me. John the Baptist ate locusts and lived in the desert. But I can't ask my wife to make that kind of sacrifice."

The next day, she brought him twenty one-hundred-dollar

bills. "I took them out of my account at the bank. It's Christmas and birthday money that I've been saving for years."

"It's too much. I can't accept this, Mary Catherine."

"Of course you can," she said, pressing the bills back into his hands when he tried to return them. "I'm going to be your wife. What's mine is yours. It's for us. For our baby. For God's ministry."

They planned their elopement to take place three nights from then. "Why so long? Why not tomorrow?"

"I've got to make arrangements," he explained. "You don't get married without a bunch of red tape, you know."

"Oh," she said with disappointment. She hadn't known that. "Well, I'll leave all the legalities to you, Jack."

They kissed good-night, lingering over it, dreading the hours of separation. Mary Catherine went home, locked herself in her room, and wrote several pages in her diary. Later, unable to sleep due to a slight case of indigestion brought on by pregnancy and excitement, she went to her closet and planned what she would wear when she went to meet her groom.

Chapter Thirty

✤ ✤

"Of course when she went to meet him he wasn't there."

The shadows on the kitchen walls of Aunt Laurel's house were long. They stretched across the round table where Claire and Cassidy sat across from each other over cups of orange-flavored tea that had grown cold.

Claire spoke in a distant voice; her expression was melancholy. "At first Mama thought that in the excitement of the moment, she had mistaken the time and place of their rendezvous. She went to his apartment building, but he had cleared out. He'd left no forwarding address with the building manager. Or any mention of where God might send him next," she added sarcastically. "When a week went by and Mama received no word from him, she realized that he'd stolen her money and abandoned her." She glanced up at Cassidy. "Would you care for more tea?"

"No, thanks," he replied gruffly.

Claire continued her story. "Wild Jack Collins played his

hand extremely well. When Mama told him she was pregnant, he could have bolted. But he was too smart. Undoubtedly, he had discovered that the Laurents were well connected. For all he knew, Mama could have sicced the sheriff on him. He saw the advisability of proposing marriage instead. He made it all sound very romantic. Elopement. Running away together on a mission for the Lord. Remember, Mama was a devout Christian and believed in saving the lost. But she was also incredibly naïve.''

Her expression turned remote and cold. ''To the day he died—to the day I killed him—Wild Jack must have still been laughing at her and patting himself on the back for being such a clever chap. If he even remembered her, that is. It's anyone's guess how many other young women he left with illegitimate children in those early years of his traveling ministry.''

Cassidy scooted aside his teacup and saucer and rested his elbows on the table. ''How did you learn about all this Claire?''

''In Mama's diaries. They meticulously documented everything from that Saturday morning when her daddy took her to Café du Monde for breakfast and she saw Jack Collins preaching in the square. I found the diaries after Aunt Laurel died. She had continued the journal when Mama was no longer capable.''

''So she knew all along who your father was?''

Claire nodded. ''But only Aunt Laurel. When it became obvious to my mother that she'd been jilted, she confronted her parents and told them she was pregnant.''

''Did they make an attempt to apprehend Jack Collins?''

''No. Remember, she never identified her lover, but led my grandparents to believe that he was among their elite circle of acquaintances. The only person who knew the truth was Aunt Laurel. Mama had confided in her. So when Wild Jack Collins emerged years later as the televangelist Jackson Wilde—and his name change is doubtless due to the many tracks he had to cover—Aunt Laurel began to chronicle his rise to fame.

"Apparently he wooed Josh's mother the way he did mine Her family was Protestant, which made him slightly more acceptable to them than to staunch Catholics. They were also much wealthier than the Laurents. He saw a good thing and seized it. In her writings, Aunt Laurel surmised that he used his in-laws' money to expand his ministry into radio and television."

"This makes Josh—"

"My half-brother," she interrupted with a gentle smile.

"That's why you arranged to meet him."

"I wanted to see if he was like our father, or a man of integrity. He's weak, but, based on that one brief meeting, I think he's a respectable individual."

"Not too respectable. He was sleeping with his father's wife."

She didn't appreciate the mild rebuke and rushed to her step-brother's defense. "Josh was another victim of Jackson Wilde's emotional abuse. Having an affair with Ariel was his way of retaliating."

"And yours was to kill him."

"I did the world a service, Cassidy. Ariel pretends to be a grieving widow, but she's gotten out of Jackson's death what she wanted—the celebrity previously held by him. Josh has been released from his tormentor."

"Isn't that exaggerating it a bit? Wilde didn't keep Josh on a ball and chain."

"On an emotional level he did. Josh wanted to be a concert pianist. Wild Jack had other plans. He wanted a musician identifiable exclusively to his ministry, so he scoffed at Josh's ambition and disparaged his talent until Josh's self-confidence was in tatters. In the long run, he became what his father wanted him to be."

"Josh told you all this?"

"He told me that since Ariel has disassociated him from the ministry, he wants to resume his study of classical music his first love. I filled in the blanks."

"What about your mother?"

"What about her?"

"Did she ever connect Jackson Wilde to Wild Jack Collins?"

"No. Thank God. His appearance must have changed over the last thirty years. You know she can't hold a thought for long, so even if recognition flickered, it didn't register."

Cassidy frowned, his eyes squinting with skepticism. "Claire, I strongly advise you not to say anything more without an attorney present."

"I'm waiving my right to an attorney, Cassidy. I've made a public confession and a crowd of people witnessed it. I don't intend to retract it. I'll tell you anything you want to know. Although," she added, "you've already guessed most of it."

"What do you mean?"

"You guessed how I got into Jackson Wilde's room. Remember when we walked through the French Quarter, retracing the route I took the night of the murder?"

"You're about to tell me that that was an exercise in futility."

"Actually I did go for a walk that night. Afterward. It was when I returned to French Silk from my walk that I discovered Mama was gone."

"By a bizarre coincidence, she had wandered to the Fairmont Hotel that night."

"Yes."

"That's quite a hike for her."

"She might have taken a bus."

Cassidy declined to comment. "Go on," he said. "You were about to tell me how you got into Wilde's suite. Andre to the rescue?"

"No. Never," she said with an adamant shake of her head. "He's entirely innocent. I never lied about that. No one knew what I intended to do."

"Yasmine?"

"Not even her. I did this on my own. I would never compromise a friend."

"Heaven forbid. But you'd murder a man in cold blood."

"Do you want to hear this or not?"

Cassidy shot from his chair, rattling teacups. "What the hell do you think? Hell no, I don't want to hear it," he shouted. "And if you had an ounce of sense, you would call an attorney, who would insist that you not say 'God bless' if I sneezed."

He had removed his suit jacket when they came into the house, before the windows they'd opened had had a chance to air it out and cool it down. Gray suspenders criss-crossed his back. His shirtsleeves had been rolled to his elbows. Now, he loosened his tie.

Claire watched his nimble fingers working at the Windsor knot, knowing that she would never feel his touch on her skin again. The reminder created an ache in her lower body, a painful, gaping void. Rather than dwell on that yearning, she focused on his anger and used it to make him her adversary.

"While we were at Café du Monde," she said, "you guessed that the killer was waiting for Wilde when he returned to his suite. You were right."

"Don't tell me this, Claire."

Disregarding his advice, she continued. "I waited in an adjacent hallway. When the maid went in to turn down the beds, I sneaked into Wilde's suite and hid in a closet. I was there almost an hour before he came in."

"Alone?"

"Without Ariel, yes. He watched TV for a while. I could hear it from the closet. He showered, then went to bed. When I heard him snoring, I crept out and tiptoed into his bedroom. I shot him three times."

"Did you ever speak to him?"

"No. I was tempted to wake him. I wanted to see fear in his eyes. I would have liked him to know that he was going to die at the hand of his own child. I would have liked to speak Mama's name to see if it would elicit any response from him, trigger any memory at all. But he was a large man. I was afraid to wake him up. He could have overpowered me and taken the gun.

"But I stood at the foot of his bed for a long time. I stared down at him, hating him, hating the abuse he had inflicted on people who had loved him. Mama. Josh. Ariel. I did it for all of us.

"He lay there, sleeping so complacently, in a luxurious suite paid for by people who couldn't afford to send him offerings, but did so because they believed in him. There was a Rolex wristwatch lying on top of his Bible on the nightstand. The symbolism of that made me sick to my stomach. He profited from what martyrs through the centuries had died for, what they're still dying for."

Cassidy eagerly returned to his seat across from her. "You shot him three times. Why, Claire? Why three?"

"In the head for the way he deliberately distorted Christianity to serve his own purposes. In the heart to atone for all those he'd broken. In his manhood for the unconscionable way he seduced and then deserted a wholesome young woman who deserved to be loved."

"You blew him away, Claire."

"Yes." She swallowed hard. "It was messy. I didn't expect . . . When I saw all the blood, I ran."

"How'd you get out of the hotel?"

"The same way I got in. No one saw me on that floor because the only people registered to the rooms there were the Wildes. I took the elevator down to the lobby and walked out the University Street exit." She moistened her lips and glanced at him nervously. "And to help conceal my identity, in case I'd left clues, I dressed like Mama."

"You did what?"

"I wore one of her dresses, and her elopement hat, and carried her suitcase."

"Very clever. Later if a witness was asked who they'd seen in the hotel at that time of night, they would describe Mary Catherine. Then she would be immediately dismissed because she's known to behave strangely, and the hotel staff is accustomed to seeing her wandering through there, dressed that way, carrying a suitcase."

"Precisely. What I didn't count on was Mama actually going there that night."

"Without her hat and suitcase?"

The question threw her off for a moment. "Naturally she had them."

"I thought you said you had them."

"I did. But I returned home and changed clothes before going on my walk. That's when she went out."

"I'm not sure all that corresponds with the time of Wilde's death," Cassidy said, frowning. "If I were your defense attorney, I'd use those time discrepancies to establish reasonable doubt with the jury."

"There won't be a jury because there won't be a trial. I've confessed. Once I'm sentenced, that'll be the end to it."

"You sound as though you look forward to it," he said angrily. "Are you that eager to go to prison for the rest of your life? For the rest of my life?"

She looked away. "I just want to get it over with."

Swearing lavishly, he combed his fingers through his hair. "Why didn't you dispose of the gun, Claire? Why didn't you toss it in the river that night while you were on your walk?"

"I wish I had," she said miserably. "I never expected it to wind up in a police lab."

"The only fingerprints on that revolver were Yasmine's."

"I had on Mama's gloves."

"Which we can test for powder burns."

"I destroyed them and bought her new ones. You won't find anything."

"You're real smart, aren't you?"

"Well, my first choice would have been to get away with it!" she snapped. "But you're so damned persistent."

He ignored that and asked, "When did you sneak the gun out of Yasmine's purse?"

"The week before I used it. She came down for a quick overnight trip. She was so flighty and often careless with her possessions, I knew that when her gun turned up missing she'd shrug it off. I replaced it a few days later—after you'd questioned me about the weapon. Just as I expected, Yasmine passed it off as an oversight."

"That sounds out of character for you, Claire. By using her gun you implicated Yasmine in a murder."

"I didn't think the gun would ever be fired again. I certainly didn't expect Yasmine to take her own life with it." Tears formed in her eyes. Because of the events that had unfolded so quickly since her return from New York that morning, she still hadn't had an opportunity to grieve privately over the loss of her friend. "I wish I had disposed of the damn thing. Yasmine was in more emotional distress than I guessed. She was a disaster waiting to happen. I was too busy to notice, too caught up in my own crisis, too involved with—" Suddenly she broke off and glanced at Cassidy, then quickly lowered her eyes. "I was too involved with this murder investigation to realize that she was silently crying out for help. I failed her."

Cassidy said nothing for a moment. Then he asked, "That night, when you met Jackson Wilde face to face in the Superdome, what did you feel toward him?"

"Interesting," she said softly. "I didn't feel the unmitigated hatred that I expected I would. Believing me to be a new convert, he laid his hands on my head. There was no cosmic current. I felt no mystical attachment, either physical or emotional. When I looked into his eyes, I expected to experience a tug of recognition, a biological click, *something* deep inside me.

"Instead, I gazed into the eyes of a stranger. I felt no magnetic attraction to him. I didn't want to claim him as my father, any more than he had wanted to claim me thirty-two years ago." She raised her head slightly. "I'm glad he never knew me. After the heartache and mental illness he inflicted on my mother, he didn't deserve the privilege of knowing me."

"Bravo for you, Claire." He stared at her for a long moment, his gaze full of admiration. He even lifted his hand toward her cheek, but let it drop before touching her. Eventually he scraped back his chair and stood up. "I've got to go to my car and call Crowder. He's probably had a stroke or two by now. Is there anything to eat in the house?"

"I'm not hungry."

"You should eat anyway."

She shrugged indifferently. "There's a café around the corner. It doesn't look like much from the outside, but Mr. Thibodeaux makes good fried-oyster sandwiches."

"Sounds fine. Let's go."

"I'll stay here."

"Not a chance. Besides, you promised Harry you'd call."

Claire didn't have the energy to argue with him. His mouth was resolutely set, his stance unarguable. Feeling like she weighed a thousand pounds, she preceded him from the house.

"I'm trying to reach Assistant District Attorney Cassidy."

"You dialed the wrong number. You've called the NOPD, sir."

"I know that, but the D.A.'s office is closed for the day."

"That's right, it is. Call 'em tomorra."

"No, wait! Don't hang up."

Andre Philippi was in a tizzy. He'd finally worked up enough nerve to call Mr. Cassidy, but his attempts had been thwarted, first by the timeclock, now by an uncaring, dull-witted incompetent at the police station.

"It's imperative that I reach Mr. Cassidy tonight. There must be some way to contact him after hours. Does he have a pager?"

"I don't know."

"Then will you please check with your supervisor?"

"Do you wanna report a crime?"

"I want to speak to Mr. Cassidy!" Andre's naturally high-pitched voice rose to a full falsetto. Knowing he was reaching hysteria and realizing that his speech was conveying that, he willed himself to calm down. "It's about the Jackson Wilde case."

"The Jackson Wilde case?"

"That's right. And if you refuse to cooperate, you'll be obstructing justice." Andre hoped that was the correct term. He'd read the phrase once, and it seemed appropriate to use now. In any event, it was intimidating enough to get results.

"Hold on."

While Andre waited for the officer to return to the line, he scanned the front page of the evening papers again. According to the latest articles, Yasmine had been cleared of any involvement in the Wilde murder case. But beneath a blurry black-and-white photo of her, the caption suggested that she had participated in subversive activities and was very possibly deranged. The unfairness of the allegations struck Andre like a stinging slap in the face. Like his *maman*, Yasmine hadn't been properly appreciated or protected. He could no longer tolerate it.

To add insult to injury, the second headline declared Claire Laurent Jackson Wilde's confessed killer. Surely the report was inaccurate. Why in heaven's name would Claire confess to murder? It was preposterous. Moreover, it was untrue. His attempts to reach her for an explanation had gone unrewarded. No one was answering the phone at French Silk.

The entire world seemed to have gone haywire. He alone stood sane amid rampant insanity. To correct these grievous wrongs, he had no alternative but to contact Mr. Cassidy.

"Hey? You still there?"

"Yes," Andre replied eagerly. "Can you give me Mr. Cassidy's private number?"

"Sorry, no. I was told he had left for the day and was unavailable until tomorra mawnin', when he'll prob'ly make a statement."

"I'm not media."

"Sure. If you say so."

"I swear it."

"Tell you what, if you want, I'll give your name and number to a detective, name of Howard Glenn, who's been working with Cassidy."

Andre remembered the untidy brutes who had invaded his hotel the morning following the murder. "I'll speak only with Mr. Cassidy."

"Suit yourself, fella."

The policeman disconnected him, leaving Andre feeling adrift and agitated. He stewed over what he should do. He couldn't concentrate on his work. For the first time in his tenure as night manager, he neglected his responsibilities and his guests. Why wasn't the telephone at French Silk being answered? Where was Claire? Where was Mr. Cassidy?

And when he finally spoke with him, could he bring himself to tell him what he must?

Chapter Thirty-one

※ ※

From Cassidy's car, Claire had phoned her mother at Harry's house. For the time being, Mary Catherine was out of harm's way. Cassidy had been unable to reach Crowder and had become extremely upset about it.

"Call that detective you've been working with," Claire suggested after hearing a litany of curses.

"No. I know what he would want me to do."

"Bring me in handcuffed and shackled?"

"Something like that." Cassidy shook his head. "It's imperative that I speak to Tony first. I'm not taking you back until I do."

So she had been granted one night's reprieve. They had returned to Aunt Laurel's house. After eating the supper they had bought at Mr. Thibodeaux's café, Claire had pleaded exhaustion and retreated to her bedroom upstairs. She undressed and hung her clothes in the closet where some outdated garments were still stored. Now, she scooped cool water from the pedestal sink onto her face and neck.

The bathroom looked exactly as it had the day she moved from Aunt Laurel's house. She had designed the art deco bathroom in her new apartment, but she still loved the Victorian quaintness of this bathroom with its claw-footed tub, pedestal sink, and tile floors. She found towels and washcloths stored in the chiffonier. They smelled of floral potpourri.

She used one of the towels to blot her dripping face. When she straightened up, she saw Cassidy's reflection in the oval framed mirror above the sink. He was standing in the doorway, silent and still, watching her.

The lamplight in the bedroom behind him was dim, so half of his face was cast in shadow, heightening his intense predatory aspect. He was bare-chested, and his suspenders had slipped from his shoulders, forming loops against his hips. One forearm was raised, bracing him against the jamb. The other arm hung at his side. Although he hadn't moved, his stance conveyed power, strength, and a suggestion of latent violence.

Wearing nothing except an apricot satin bra and panties set, Claire felt more naked than if she'd been nude. She resisted the impulse to grab one of the towels to cover herself. The expression on Cassidy's shadowed face intimated that any attempt at modesty would be wasted effort. Besides, she didn't think she could move. His stare had captivated her.

He walked forward until he was a hair's breadth from touching her. They regarded each other in the mirror, their gazes hungry. He raised his hands, slipped them beneath her hair, and rested them on her bare shoulders.

"I'm going to make love to you."

Her shoulders slumped forward as though from the weight of his hands. "You can't. We can't." He brushed aside her hair and laid a tender kiss on her shoulder. "Don't, Cassidy," she murmured. "Don't." Belying her protests, when his lips moved to her nape, her head dropped forward in compliance.

"Claire," he whispered into her hair, "I've fallen in love with you."

"You can't say these things to me."

"I want you. Now."

"Stop, please. You'll regret this. I know you, Cassidy," she said with feeling. "I know how you think. You'll hate yourself for the rest of your life if you do this."

"No I won't."

"Yes, yes you will."

"Shh."

He massaged his way down her back and unhooked her bra. Claire moaned when his hands slipped beneath the lace-trimmed cups. He palmed her breasts, reshaping them with gentle squeezes. Then he caressed the nipples with his fingertips until they were stiff and distended. His mouth moved to the other side of her neck and took tender love bites.

"Cassidy, don't. I don't want to be a blot on your conscience. This isn't right. You know it. Please stop."

Her pleas sounded weak and insincere even to her own ears, and when his hand slid down her belly and into her panties, she stopped making them altogether. She could lie to him, but her body couldn't. At her center, she was creamy and warm.

He pushed down her underpants; she stepped out of them. He unfastened his trousers and moved closer to her, until she felt the firm pressure of his sex. When he sent it deep into her wet, silky heat, their sighs of gratification harmonized.

Bracing herself against the porcelain sink, Claire was able to meet his slow, deep thrusts. He took her hips between his strong hands and drew her against the warm fuzziness of his middle. Then splaying his hand over her abdomen, he held her motionless in place. She used her interior walls like a tight fist to squeeze him. He grimaced in ecstasy and turned his face into her neck.

"Oh, Jesus," he groaned. "I could never get too deep inside you."

Claire tilted her head and ground it against his. "Cassidy."

He reached around and laid his fingertips against her parted lips, then covered them with his hand. She kissed his palm, sponged the pads of his fingers with her tongue, sank her teeth into the fleshy base of his thumb. His thrusts grew faster, more urgent, animalistically possessive. Claire's passions, too, rose to a feverish pitch. She couldn't contain the cry she uttered when he slid his hand from her tummy to between her thighs and fondled the swollen, sensitive hood of her sex, which he so amply filled. At his stroking touch, a current of electricity shot through her body. It radiated through her thighs, and she clenched them tightly. It shimmied up through her belly and into her breasts and concentrated in their tight centers.

Cassidy folded both arms around her waist and leaned over her until she was bent over the sink and his chest was resting on her back. She was totally surrounded by, filled with, immersed in him. The glory of it made her heart soar. With a joyful sob, she submitted to a burst of love and fulfillment. When the hot rush of his climax filled her, she turned her head and captured his mouth in a deep, long, searching kiss that was seasoned with her tears.

❦

"You didn't have to say that you love me," Claire whispered as she threaded her fingers through his hair. It had been neglected and needed a trim. She liked it better this way, shaggy and unmanageable. "I would have succumbed to your charms anyway," she teased.

"I told you because that's the way it is." He adjusted his leg more comfortably against hers beneath the bed sheet. "I started falling in love with you from the minute I met you. Or maybe it was when you blew those damn bubbles at me from that vial you were wearing around your neck. It was symbolic and suggestive and erotic as hell."

"I didn't intend it to be."

"No? Maybe it was the way you held your mouth." He ran his finger over her lips, smiling wistfully, before his expression turned bleak. "Every time Crowder accused me of letting my feelings for you get in the way of my investigation, I denied it. But he's right." He squeezed his eyes shut for a moment. "I didn't want the killer to be you, Claire."

She burrowed her face in his chest hair. "I don't want to talk about it. Please. Let's talk about something else, something that ordinary lovers talk about."

"We aren't ordinary, Claire."

"But for an hour, let's pretend we are. This is Nawlins, where anything's possible. So let's make-believe that we met under normal circumstances. We were instantly attracted to each other. We've made love but are still in that magical getting-acquainted stage." She propped herself on her elbows and gazed down at him. "Tell me what hurt you so badly."

"What do you mean?"

"Don't insult my intelligence, Cassidy. There's something very painful in your past. I recognize the symptoms. What hurt you? What made you angry and determined to do well at all costs? Was it your wife? The divorce?"

"No. That was amicable. I didn't love her." He rubbed a strand of her hair between his fingers. "Not like I love you."

"You're changing the subject."

"I'm trying."

"It won't work. I'm as persistent as you."

He sighed with exasperation. "It doesn't make very good pillow talk, Claire."

"But I want to know."

"Why?"

"Because I've got so little time with you," she cried impatiently, all joking aside. Softening her tone, she added, "I want to make the most of it. You're the last lover I'll ever have, Cassidy. I want to know all I can about you. It's important to me."

His eyes stayed linked with hers for a suspended moment before he said, "You'll be sorry you insisted." She shook her head. Following a brief hesitation, he related the painful story he had recently told Tony Crowder.

Claire said nothing, giving him time to tell it in his own way. When he finished, he said, "Know where they found the bastard? Playing pool and drinking beer with his buddies. He'd left an eleven-year-old girl raped and murdered in a dry creekbed, and he was out partying with friends. He didn't fear arrest. He didn't think anything could touch him. I helped make him that arrogant."

She laid a gentling hand in the center of his chest. "His acquittal was determined by a twelve-person jury. You weren't responsible."

"I did my part," he said bitterly.

"You had an obligation to your client."

"I've tried a thousand different ways to justify it, Claire. There is no justification. If not for me and my grandstanding, he wouldn't have been on the streets. That little girl suffered and died on the altar of my conceit and ambition."

Claire's heart was breaking for him. He would carry the guilt with him to his grave. There was nothing she could say or do to change the past, but she wanted to make him see that he had atoned. "It was a hard lesson, Cassidy, but you learned from it. It's made you a better prosecutor."

He drew a deep sigh. "That's my only hope for redemption."

"I'm sorry," she said earnestly.

He looked at her with surprise. "Sorry?"

"Sorry that it happened to you."

"I thought you'd be put off."

"I'd only be put off if you hadn't taken it so hard."

Ducking her head, she kissed his chest, flicking it lightly with her swirling tongue as her lips continued on a downward path. She pecked soft kisses over his navel and inched her way down the silky strip of hair below it, then nuzzled that dark, dense thatch surrounding his sex.

When her lips grazed his cock, he rasped her name and took her head between his hands, tunneling all ten fingers through her hair. Daintily her tongue moistened the velvety tip and stroked the smooth shaft. She withheld nothing, did everything, tasted, teased, loved him thoroughly.

He pulled her up to straddle his lap and sheathed himself within her only heartbeats before his stunning climax. Crushing his face against her breasts, he sucked her nipple into his mouth. She clutched his head and rode his erection, which was still full and firm inside her. As light splintered through her, she mentally chanted what she couldn't speak out loud. *Cassidy, my love . . . my love . . . my love.*

Chapter Thirty-two

✿ ✿

When Claire awakened, she was alone. She hastily dressed in the clothes she'd worn from New York the day before and rushed downstairs. A policewoman and her male partner were waiting for her in the foyer. When she saw them, she drew up short and, using her fingers, nervously combed back her mussed hair. "Hello."

"Mr. Cassidy had to leave on urgent business," the policewoman told her. "We were dispatched to drive you downtown."

"Oh." She was vastly disappointed by the way Cassidy had chosen to handle this. Why hadn't he awakened her before he left so they could have one last private conversation?

"As soon as you're ready, Ms. Laurent," the policewoman said tactfully.

Claire secured Aunt Laurel's house, locking inside it memories of loving Cassidy along with the treasure trove of memories the rooms already held for her. It broke her heart to cross the porch for what would probably be the last time, but she couldn't nurse any regrets. This was only the first of many sacrifices she would be required to make.

"I'd like to shower and change, if that's possible. I haven't been home since I returned from New York yesterday."

The arresting officers agreed to stop at French Silk. When they pulled up in front, Claire was alarmed to see several patrolmen posted around the building. "What are they doing here?" Her first concern was for her mother, although Mary Catherine was safely ensconced with Harry.

"They're here to keep Ariel Wilde from doing any mischief."

"Oh. Thank you."

The officers rode in the elevator with her up to the third floor and waited while she bathed and dressed. Her vanity seemed misplaced, but she wanted to look her best and took pains with her makeup and hair. She dressed in a simple, elegant two-piece black suit with a slim, short skirt. The jacket had a white shawl collar. On the lapel, she pinned a marcasite brooch, a gift from Aunt Laurel. The silver cuff bracelet she slipped onto her wrist had belonged to Yasmine. In her purse, she carried one of Mary Catherine's hand-embroidered handkerchiefs.

Bolstered by the possessions of the people who had loved her, she left her bedroom and confidently announced, "I'm ready."

But her confidence flagged as she took one last look at her spectacular view of the river. Everything in the apartment testified to the hours of hard work she had dedicated to building a successful business. She had done very well for a girl who had grown up with an emotionally unstable mother, no father, and nothing in the way of commodities except a Singer sewing machine and a wealth of imagination.

When she crossed the warehouse floor for the last time, tears blurred her vision. What would happen to French Silk without her and Yasmine? The outstanding orders would be shipped. Receivables would be collected and invoices paid.

But there would be no new business. There wouldn't be another catalog. French Silk would cease to exist.

What an ironic twist—Jackson Wilde had achieved his goal.

Mentally, Claire squared her shoulders. She had done what was necessary. She had known the consequences of her decision and was willing to accept them.

The district attorney's building was still under siege by Wilde's disciples. "Onward, Christian Soldiers" was being sung by the marchers who carried pickets condemning Claire Laurent to eternal hellfire and damnation. She was escorted into the building under armed guard.

"I thought you'd take me directly to the sheriff's office," she remarked as she was being hustled into the elevator. "Isn't that where I'll be formally booked?"

"Mr. Cassidy instructed us to bring you to the D.A.'s office," the male cop informed her.

"Do you know why?"

"No, ma'am."

She was taken directly to Tony Crowder's office. The outer area seemed to have suffered no adverse effects from the chaos that had taken place there the day before. Secretaries were at their desks, going about their business. Crowder's personal secretary stood as they approached. She held open the door for Claire and closed it behind her immediately, leaving her alone with the district attorney.

He was seated behind his desk. His expression was grave. Annoyance showed in his eyes. Brusquely he said, "Good morning, Ms. Laurent."

"Good morning."

"Would you like some coffee?"

"No, thank you."

"Sit down." Once she was seated in the chair he indicated, he said, "I apologize for what happened in this office yesterday afternoon."

"I was partially responsible, Mr. Crowder."

"But your safety was placed in jeopardy. That's inexcusable. We beefed up the security this morning."

"I noticed. I also want to thank you for posting policemen at French Silk. Although my business no longer has a future, I'd hate for it to be destroyed by vandals."

"That was Cassidy's idea."

"I see," she said softly. "I must remember to thank him."

"He's due here in a matter of minutes. Don't ask me why."

"You don't know?"

"Haven't a clue. He called before I was even out of bed this morning and arranged this meeting." He clasped his hands on the edge of his desk and leaned toward her. "Ms. Laurent, did you kill Jackson Wilde?"

"Yes."

"With your friend's gun?"

"Yes."

"How long has Cassidy known this for fact?"

The door behind her opened with gust of air and a blast of energy that was palpable. She quickly turned. Cassidy's stride was long and confident as he advanced into the office. His hair had been washed and neatly combed. He had shaved recently. His dark suit was wrinkle-free from the fitted vest hugging his torso to the hem of his trousers that broke the vamp of his shoes in exactly the right spot.

"Good morning, Tony."

Claire was taken aback. She didn't know this Cassidy. This wasn't the Cassidy who had made love to her with matching degrees of tenderness and fervency, who whispered words of passion in her ear while his body moved within hers, who had touched her in ways, both emotionally and physically, that no one else ever had. This Cassidy was a stranger.

"Good morning, Claire."

His voice was the same. His handsome features were dear and beloved to her. It was the well-tailored suit that put her off. That bureaucratic uniform had made him her adversary from the moment he walked in the door.

"Good morning, Mr. Cassidy," she replied in a husky undertone.

"Can I get either of you some coffee before we begin?"

"Forget the coffee," Crowder said crossly. "What's this about? As a courtesy, shouldn't Glenn be in on this?"

"He's otherwise occupied. I'll get to that later." Cassidy wasted no time but came straight to the point. "Claire's confession was phony. She didn't kill Jackson Wilde."

"Oh for Christ's sake!" Crowder exploded. "She sat right there not thirty seconds before you breezed in here and admitted to me that she did."

"She's lying." Cassidy looked down at Claire with a trace of a smile. "She has a bad habit of that."

"She appears to be in full control of her faculties. Why would she confess to a felony homicide she didn't commit?" Crowder demanded to know.

"To protect someone else from prosecution."

"That's not true!" Claire exclaimed.

"She says that's not true," Crowder echoed.

"Bear with me, Tony," Cassidy said. "Give me five minutes."

"I'm counting."

"Last night I had Claire re-create the crime for me."

"Without a lawyer present? Jesus." Crowder dragged his hands down his face.

"Just shut up and listen," Cassidy said impatiently. "Claire waived her right to have an attorney present, but it doesn't matter. She didn't kill Wilde. She wasn't even there."

"You mean at the murder scene?"

"That's exactly what I mean." He fished something from his breast pocket and handed it to Claire. "Read the part that's underlined."

"What is it?" Crowder asked.

"It's a portion of the press release we issued to the media the morning following the murder."

Claire scanned the underlined sentences. They described the scene of the crime. "I don't understand."

"The statement is inaccurate," Cassidy told her. "Deliberately so. I planted a bogus fact to weed out the crazies and chronic confessors who invariably surface after a sensational murder."

Claire's heart began to beat hard against her ribs. She reread the sentences, frantically trying to pinpoint which detail might be a decoy.

Cassidy bent over her chair and lowered his voice. "Last night when you recounted the murder, you quoted this almost verbatim, Claire. You got your facts from the newspaper, not from the scene itself."

"I was there. I killed him."

"If that's so, then show me the discrepancy," he challenged.

"I—"

"You can't, can you?"

"No. Yes." She groped blindly for a way out. "I can't remember every little detail."

"You remembered them last night."

"You're confusing me."

"You're confusing me, too, Cassidy," Crowder said. "If she said she did it, she did it."

"You just want to end this thing," Cassidy shouted.

"And you want to continue sleeping with Ms. Laurent."

"Damn you, Tony!"

"Then deny it!"

"I can't. I don't even want to. But whether I'm sleeping with her or not, do you want to sentence a woman to life imprisonment for something she didn't do?"

The question momentarily silenced Crowder, although he continued to fume. Cassidy knelt in front of Claire and covered her hands where they were tightly clenched in her lap.

"Claire, last night you said that when you stood at the foot of Wilde's bed, you noticed his Rolex wristwatch lying on top of his Bible on the nightstand. You said the symbolism of that made you sick.''

''Wait! It wasn't a Rolex. It was an expensive wristwatch, but it might not have been a Rolex. I've never placed much importance on labels, so when I said 'Rolex' I meant it in a generic sense. After I read the newspaper accounts, it probably stuck in my mind that his watch was a Rolex.''

''So now you're saying that the watch lying on top of the Bible wasn't a Rolex?''

''It might have just looked like one to me.''

A smile spread slowly across Cassidy's face. ''It was a Rolex, all right. But there was no Bible.''

Claire gasped softly.

Crowder grunted.

Cassidy leaned in closer to her. ''Claire, you didn't kill Jackson Wilde, did you? Before yesterday, you had dozens of opportunities to confess.''

''But I never denied it, did I? Think back. You accused me of it repeatedly, but I never once denied it.''

''In principle. That's like you. It's also like you to confess in order to protect someone else.''

''No,'' she said, shaking her head. ''I killed him.''

''You've got to trust me. For once, dammit, you've got to trust me enough to tell the truth.''

She tried to concentrate only on the earnestness in his voice and the compelling facets of his eyes, but what he represented blocked out everything else. He reminded her of the social workers who had claimed to be doing what was best for little Claire Louise. They had asked for her trust even while dragging her from Aunt Laurel's house with her mother screaming and in tears.

''Claire, do you love me?''

Tears spilled over her eyelids and ran down her cheeks, but she refused to answer him because the truth might trap her.

"You can't really love me if you can't trust me. You were right last night, you know. I could never have made love to you if I were convinced you were the killer. But I'm convinced that you're not. I swear to you that everything will turn out all right if you'll tell me the truth now."

The words wanted to be spoken. They were dammed up in her throat. But she was afraid. By telling him the truth, she would be entrusting her life to him. More important, she'd be entrusting the life of one she loved to him. Those one loved were more important than the truth, weren't they? People were more valuable than ideals. People were more valuable than anything.

"Claire." He squeezed her fingers until the bones ached. "Trust me," he whispered urgently. "Trust me. Did you kill Jackson Wilde?"

She was perched on a precipice and he was urging her take a leap into the unknown. If she loved him, she had to believe that her landing would be gentle and safe. If she loved him, she had to trust him.

And looking into his face, she knew unequivocally that she loved him.

"No, Cassidy," she said, her voice cracking emotionally. "I did not."

His tension snapped. His head dropped forward between his shoulders, and he remained bent over their clasped hands for several silent moments. Finally Crowder asked, "Why did you confess to a murder you didn't commit, Ms. Laurent?"

Cassidy raised his head. "She was protecting her mother."

"*No!*" Claire's wide, disbelieving eyes followed him as he stood up. "You said—"

"Everything will be all right, Claire," he said, touching her cheek. "But I have to tell Tony everything you told me last night."

Claire hesitated, then nodded. Cassidy turned to Crowder and bluntly stated, "Jackson Wilde was Claire's father."

Crowder listened in stunned, absorbed silence while Cassidy related the story of Mary Catherine's seduction and abandonment by the sidewalk preacher Wild Jack Collins.

"As the investigation progressed, Claire came to believe that in a lucid moment, Mary Catherine had recognized Wilde and connived to kill him. Her suspicions were confirmed when we determined that Yasmine's .38 had been the murder weapon. Mary Catherine had access to it, and she sometimes 'borrows' things and later replaces them." He told Crowder about the incident with his fountain pen at Rosesharon.

"Yesterday Claire was afraid I would remember that and put two and two together, just as she had, so she quickly confessed to throw me off track."

Crowder exhaled a deep breath and leaned back in his chair. He fixed his most intimidating frown on Claire. "Is Cassidy's assumption correct?"

She glanced up at Cassidy, who gave her a terse nod. Trusting him came more easily this time. She reached for his hand. He firmly clasped hers.

"Yes, Mr. Crowder," she admitted quietly. "Shortly after the murder, Yasmine mentioned to me that her gun had been missing but had mysteriously reappeared. That was when it first occurred to me that Mama might have taken it, used it, then replaced it. She had been in the Fairmont Hotel that night and showed more than a passing interest in the news stories about Jackson Wilde and the murder case."

"But you didn't tell Cassidy any of this."

"No. In fact, each time Ariel Wilde brought my mother's name up, I panicked. I was afraid that someone, particularly Mr. Cassidy, might discover that Jackson Wilde was her long lost lover, which would certainly provide her with motivation to kill him. I thought of taking legal action to silence Mrs. Wilde, but was advised by an attorney that litigation would only spark more interest. I wanted to avoid that at all costs."

"You could be charged with obstruction of justice."

"I would protect my mother with my dying breath, Mr. Crowder. She poses no threat to the rest of society, and I don't sit in judgment of her for taking her revenge on Wild Jack Collins.''

''You figured that after a while Cassidy would give up, call off the investigation, and the case would go unsolved.''

''I was hoping that's the way it would be.''

''What if we'd convicted somebody else?''

''It would never have happened. You had no evidence.''

''You had it all thought out, I see,'' he said, regarding her with a degree of admiration.

''All but one element. I didn't think that Yasmine's gun would ever be fired again.'' She glanced down and touched the bracelet around her wrist. ''When Cassidy told me that it was the weapon that had been used to kill Wilde, I confessed so that my mother wouldn't fall under suspicion.''

She looked at Crowder imploringly. ''She can't be held accountable. She doesn't even realize she's done anything wrong. It would be like a child killing a scorpion that's stung him and caused tremendous pain. She probably doesn't even remember now that—''

''Claire, you don't have to worry about Mary Catherine,'' Cassidy said. ''She didn't kill Wilde.'' His confident statement took them by surprise.

''How do you know?'' Crowder asked.

''Because he was shot by Congressman Alister Petrie.''

Chapter Thirty-three

$\sim$

"**T**his is getting silly."

Belle Petrie, who was making her bed, gave her husband a quizzical glance. "What's silly, dear?"

Petrie felt an almost overwhelming urge to piss on the carpet, send the étagère full of Baccarat crystal crashing to the floor, or place his hands around her throat and choke the life out of her. He wanted to do something rash to destroy the cool scorn with which his wife had been treating him.

"I'm getting tired of sleeping in the guest room, Belle," he said testily. "How much longer am I going to be condemned to marital Siberia? I've admitted to being a naughty boy, so when will you permit me to sleep in my own goddamn bed?"

"Lower your voice. The children will hear you."

He lunged at her, knocked the decorative bolster pillow from her hand, and took her roughly by the shoulders. "I've apologized a thousand times. What more do you want?"

"I want you to let go of me." The words were as sharp

468

and brittle as icicles. Coupled with the arctic glint in her eyes, they served to dismantle Alister's temper tantrum. He released her and stepped back.

"I'm sorry, Belle. This last month has been a living nightmare."

"Yes. I imagine that having your mistress blow her brains out in front of your daughter could put a wrinkle in your month."

"Christ. You won't give an inch, will you?"

He'd apologized repeatedly for his affair and its ghastly denouement. So far, his apologies hadn't made a dent in Belle's tough armor. The marital harmony that had been briefly reestablished when he broke off the affair with Yasmine had been shattered again by her sensationalized suicide. When her revolver was linked to the Wilde murder, he'd panicked and thrown himself on Belle's mercy, pleading for her help.

"I've done everything you told me to do, Belle," he said now. "I confessed my affair to Tony Crowder and that Cassidy character." Petrie's eyes turned dark. "If I can help it, he'll never get that D.A.'s office. Smug son of a bitch. You should have heard the way he talked to me. He attacked me physically!"

She appeared singularly unsympathetic.

"Okay, so I got myself in a mess. We had to stop Cassidy's investigation before my affair with Yasmine became public. In order to do that, I called in a favor from Crowder. I didn't like standing there in front of them with my pants down, but I did it because you advised me to, and, in retrospect, I think it was good advice. Crowder ordered Cassidy to redirect his investigation, pronto. In a day or two no one will remember Yasmine's suicide because everyone's attention will be on that Laurent broad's confession. Now, can't we drop this subject once and for all? Can I sleep in my own bed tonight?"

"You never told me she was black."

"What?"

"Your mistress was *black*." Belle's fists were clenched at her sides. Her nostrils flared with indignation and disgust. "It's humiliating to both of us that you had to find your fun outside this bedroom. But to think of the father of my children sleeping with a . . . Did you kiss her on the mouth? Oh, God!" She rubbed the back of her hand across her lips in a scrubbing motion. "The thought of it makes me sick. You make me sick. That's why I don't want you in my bed."

Alister didn't like being upbraided like a twelve-year-old caught jerking off. He'd suffered enough humiliation yesterday in the D.A.'s office, so he struck back. "If you knew just half the sex tricks Yasmine did, I wouldn't have had a mistress in the first place. Black, white, or any other color."

Belle's eyes drilled into his. She didn't raise her voice, but her soft-spoken tone was more sinister than a shout. "Watch yourself, Alister. You've committed a series of monumental blunders. Left to your own devices, you probably would have dug yourself in so deep you couldn't get out. But thanks to my quick thinking, you walked away from your mistakes unscathed."

She turned and took something from the nightstand drawer. "I'm curious about the misdeeds you've committed that haven't yet come to light." She tossed the small object in the air, flipping it end over end like a coin. "You see, I know that you had words with Reverend Wilde the day of his death. Despite appearances, the two of you weren't on the best of terms when you joined him on the podium that night.'

She caught the object in her hand and looked down at it musingly as she continued. "If I discovered your mistress, perhaps the reverend had, too. You're not smart enough to hire someone discreet to do your dirty work for you. You might have been stupid enough to take matters into your own hands, tried to solve your problem without guidance, which we both know you desperately need."

Alister watched as she replaced the matchbook, bearing the logo of the Fairmont Hotel, in her bedside drawer. "I hope

I'm wrong, but I suspect that you eagerly grasped my idea to confess to your mistress only to cover up an uglier transgression.

"If that's so, then heed this warning. I'm through with covering up for your mistakes, Alister. For instance, if Mr. Cassidy came to me with questions about that night, I would be forced to tell him that I had called your room at the Doubletree repeatedly and received no answer. To protect myself and my children, I would be pressed to show him that matchbook."

Her voice turned cold. She pointed her finger at him. "I'm giving you fair warning—if you get out of line again, I'll divorce, disgrace, and disinherit you. Once my family and I are finished with you, you'll be lucky to get a job skimming out cesspools.

"You're being placed on probation, dear," she said with saccharine sarcasm. "In public, you'll be the shining example of truth, justice, and the American way. You'll be a devoted husband and a doting father, a smiling, sterling pillar of virtue and integrity.

"After a while, you might earn back your place in my bed. Until the time I deem you worthy, don't even ask to rejoin me there. I can't bear the thought of having your hands on me. Do I make myself clear?"

"As a bell," he replied flippantly. "No pun intended."

He marched from the room, slamming the door behind him. Who needed her arid, sterile bed, he asked himself angrily as he returned to the guest room to finish dressing. She was so stiff and dry, he'd just as soon fuck a corn husk.

He relished his anger. It kept him from acknowledging his fear, which was insidiously lurking in the dark shadows of his mind like a rat, waiting for an opportune time to dart out and seize him.

Not for a single second did he doubt Belle's threat of exposure and desertion if he messed up again. Nor did he question her ability to ruin him if she so desired. She had not only the impetus of a woman scorned to motivate her, she had the muscle and the money behind her to make good her threats.

She liked being a congressman's wife. It elevated her, gave her prestige. But, hell, with her fortune, she could buy herself a judge or a governor or even a senator if she wanted one. In other words, Alister Petrie could be replaced. What if Cassidy hadn't bought his story? What if he did question Belle?

That possibility made his knees weak and his bowels loose. He stumbled to his unmade bed and sat down on the edge of it, holding his throbbing head in his hands. Belle had him by the short and curlies, and she damn well knew it. The bitch.

What could he do about it?

For the time being, nothing except wait. He'd had several close calls. Belle was still on his side, but for how long? Only as long as her cushy position in the world wasn't threatened. God forbid it ever was.

All he could do now was hope to sweet Jesus that Claire Laurent's phony confession stuck.

⚓

Cassidy's stunning statement brought Crowder to his feet. "Have you lost your frigging mind? Pardon me, Ms. Laurent."

Claire didn't notice his crude language. She was in shock, coupled with profound relief. Her mother wasn't a suspect! But *Alister Petrie*?

"I know it sounds crazy," Cassidy said, "but when I lay out all the facts, you'll begin to see, as I did, that Petrie is guilty of killing Jackson Wilde."

"You're just pissed off at him," Crowder said. "A word of advice, Cassidy—don't mess with him. He's poison."

"You're making my case for me, Tony."

"Petrie's got enough money supporting him to float a battleship."

Cassidy held up both hands. "His *wife* has the money. And Petrie was using it to pay off Wilde."

Crowder resettled his bulk in his chair. "Pay off Wilde? You mean Wilde was blackmailing him?"

"Look at this." Cassidy produced the list of Wilde's contributors. "Glenn gave this to me yesterday right before all hell broke loose. I forgot about it when Claire confessed and didn't have an opportunity to look at it until early this morning. But by then it only proved what I'd already figured out."

"It doesn't prove a damn thing," Crowder said, grouchily flicking his hand at the sheets of paper.

"Listen to me, Tony. Several people, and more than a handful of companies, were funneling 'offerings' into Wilde's ministry. Glenn has found several who'll testify that it was hush money."

"Joshua virtually admitted to me that his father took bribes in exchange for absolution," Claire told Crowder.

"He admitted it to me, too," Cassidy said. "This Block Bag and Box Company is a pissant business owned by Petrie's wife's family. Right after they married, he was made president of the corporation, but it's a figurehead position from which he draws a handsome monthly salary. It also gives him access to the company books and the authorization to sign checks."

Cassidy pointed to the printed material lying on Crowder's desk. "Why in hell would Block Bag and Box Company contribute over a hundred thousand dollars to a televangelist's ministry, Tony? It started with a check for five thousand dollars, dated almost a year ago. The amounts increased in increments."

"Somebody else would have reviewed the books."

"If anybody questioned him about it, Petrie probably passed off the contributions as needed tax deductions. Who's going to cross the owner's son-in-law?"

Crowder gnawed his lower lip. "What was Wilde blackmailing him for? They kissed each other's ass."

"Publicly. Because it behooved both of them. My guess is that Wilde knew about Petrie's affair with Yasmine and threatened to expose it."

Claire said, "Yasmine told me several times that Petrie secretly disliked Jackson Wilde. He only used him to win votes."

"Petrie had access to Yasmine's gun, Tony. He could have taken it, used it that night, and then replaced it during a rendezvous. I'm sure he'd be smart enough to wear gloves or wipe off the fingerprints."

"How'd he get into Wilde's suite?"

"Maybe Wilde was expecting Petrie to deliver another 'offering,' " Cassidy said caustically. "He would have had no qualms about admitting Petrie to his room late at night."

"Naked?" Claire asked.

"It was documented in the newspapers that they had exercised together at a local health club that afternoon. Wilde wouldn't have been self-conscious about his nudity." Cassidy turned to Crowder. "Yesterday, I moved to that window," he said, pointing. "I watched as Petrie left the building. His entourage hustled him into a van. It's white with blue interior. It's a Chrysler van, Tony."

Claire's mind was clicking along faster than Crowder's. "The carpet in that van would match my LeBaron's," she said excitedly.

"Most probably. Petrie had been in that van the night Wilde was killed. He tracked the fibers into Wilde's bedroom. If we get carpet fibers from that van, I'm betting they'll match those taken from the scene."

Crowder's wide fingertips were doing pushups against each other. "It's all interesting, but it's not enough. What else have you got?"

"Petrie's cunning. He'd be smart enough to place the wounds so it would look like a woman shot Wilde."

"It worked. It threw you off from day one."

"Yeah," Cassidy admitted grimly. "Petrie probably

thought Ariel would become our chief suspect. He'd been around the Wildes enough to know that they didn't have a marriage made in heaven. He might even have known about her affair with Josh."

"Why'd he come to us yesterday?"

"He was covering his ass. Our investigation into Yasmine's involvement would have eventually exposed their affair, but it also could have implicated him in the murder. He confessed to one sin in order to throw up a smokescreen to hide the other."

"But he's got alibis at the Doubletree who will testify that he was there that night," Crowder reminded him.

"He *was* there. He checked in at the registration desk and made certain he was seen. But he spent a good deal of the night at the Fairmont."

Crowder stubbornly shook his head. "It's still guesswork and circumstantial, Cassidy. A defense attorney—and he can afford the best—will chase your ass out of the courtroom unless you can substantiate that Petrie was in the Fairmont Hotel that night."

"I can."

"You can?"

"I have an eyewitness."

Crowder's eyebrows sprang up. "Who?"

"Andre Philippi."

"Andre?" Claire gasped.

Cassidy nodded. "He tried to reach me several times last night, and when he couldn't, he relented and spoke with Glenn, who hasn't let him out of his sight since. As soon as I got the message this morning, I joined them. Claire will understand this. You will after you meet him, Tony. He has this *thing* about safeguarding the privacy of his guests. It's like a code of honor to him. He's passionate about it. He kept Claire's secret until we caught him at it, remember? Likewise, he was keeping Petrie's. Until this morning."

"Why's he blowing the whistle on Petrie now?"

"It seems that Andre's second passion was Yasmine."

"That's true," Claire said. She told them about Andre's mother and the parallels between the two women. "Andre grew up resenting the distance his father kept from his mother, even though he supported her financially. A few days before Yasmine's suicide, he called me, terribly worried about her. He's sure to have seen the correlation between her tragic ending and his mother's."

Cassidy elaborated. "He knows that Yasmine killed herself over Petrie. And since Petrie's letting her name be dragged through the muck and circulating vicious lies about her, Andre no longer feels obligated to protect him. He swears on his mother's grave that Petrie spent the night at the Fairmont with Yasmine. He arrived shortly after eleven and left around seven the following morning, before Ariel discovered Wilde's body and we sealed the doors. Andre himself called Yasmine a cab. She went to the airport in time to meet Claire at the designated time. I'll bet no one at the Doubletree can swear under oath that they saw Petrie between eleven P.M. and seven A.M."

"Why would a jury believe this Andre fellow?"

"They'll believe him," Cassidy said confidently. "Furthermore, they'd believe Belle."

"His wife?" Crowder exclaimed.

"Right. It wouldn't surprise me if she knew about the murder. She's covered Alister's tracks this far, but somehow I don't think she'd go out on a limb if it involved murder."

"I don't think so either," Claire said quietly. "I only met her a few times, years ago, but she impressed me as a woman who values her own skin."

Crowder tugged on his lower lip. "Petrie might toss it back and say it was Yasmine who killed Wilde. She had motivation, and the murder weapon belonged to her. He might even accuse Ms. Laurent."

"He might." Cassidy said, grinning craftily. "But he'd still have to answer to spending the night at the Fairmont

Hotel with his mistress. Either way, he's screwed. At the very least, he's guilty of ducking out when he had information pertinent to the investigation of a murder."

Cassidy leaned over Crowder's desk. "I want the bastard, Tony. I want to launch a full-fledged but covert investigation. He's got to be puzzling over why Claire made a confession and probably reasons correctly that she's doing it to protect either Yasmine or Mary Catherine. In any event, he thinks he's gotten away with murder. He hasn't."

Tony Crowder held Cassidy's stare for several moments, glanced at Claire, then returned his gaze to his deputy prosecutor. "Proceed with caution and absolute secrecy, but nail the son of a bitch."

※

Ariel Wilde answered Cassidy's knock with the cordiality of a rattlesnake poised to strike. Whatever she'd been about to say died on her lips when she saw who accompanied him.

"I thought she'd be behind bars by now."

"I asked Mr. Cassidy to arrange this meeting," Claire said. "May we come in?"

Radiating a hostile aura, the widow stepped aside and admitted them into her hotel room. Without specifying why, Cassidy had called an hour earlier, telling her that he wanted to see her and Joshua alone.

Josh, who'd been sprawled on a sofa and looking very unhappy about being there, rose to his feet when they came in. His eyes bounced between them, curious and wary in equal proportions.

"I'm waiting." Ariel crossed her arms over her middle. "I'm very busy this afternoon."

"Organizing more demonstrations?" Cassidy asked pleasantly.

"They're working, aren't they? They got her to confess."

"I didn't kill your husband, Mrs. Wilde."

"What!" Ariel rounded on Cassidy. "You're sleeping with her, right? So you're not letting her confession stick. Wait'll the media gets hold of this. You won't—"

"Mrs. Wilde." Claire spoke softly, but with such authority that Ariel fell silent. "I confessed because I thought I was protecting my mother. I thought she had killed your husband."

"Why would you think that? Your mother's a loony tune."

Claire pulled herself up to her full height and struggled to keep a reign on her temper. "My mother has emotional problems, yes. Their origins date back to over thirty years ago, when she fell in love with a young street preacher named Jack Collins, who went by the nickname of Wild Jack. He seduced her, robbed her of money, and deserted her, leaving her pregnant with his baby. Wild Jack Collins was Jackson Wilde. And I was the baby."

Ariel barked a harsh laugh. "What the hell are you trying to pull? Do you—"

"Shut up, Ariel." The unexpected rebuke came from Josh, who was staring closely at Claire. "I knew there was something . . . When I met you, I . . . You're my half-sister."

"Yes. Hello again, Josh." Smiling, Claire extended her hand. He reached out and shook it, but his eyes never wavered from hers. "I hope you'll forgive me for testing your character by offering you a bribe. You didn't disappoint me by refusing."

"This is all very touching," Ariel sneered, "but I'll be damned before I believe this crap."

"This much is true," Josh said. "Before he married my mother, Daddy was known as Wild Jack Collins. I once overheard my grandfather referring to him by that name, and it made Daddy mad as hell."

Claire gave Josh's hand a light squeeze before releasing it and turning to Ariel again. "I have no intention of disclosing my relationship to Jackson Wilde. Frankly, I'm not at all proud of it, and it would focus attention on my mother, which I hope to avoid.''

"Then what are you doing here?"

"To strongly suggest that you forget you ever heard of French Silk or anyone connected to it.''

"Or what?"

"Or I'll reveal to the world the real Jackson Wilde. I'm sure you don't want your late husband exposed as a seducer of young girls, a fornicator, a thief, a liar, and a child deserter. It wouldn't be good for the ministry, would it?"

Ariel's wide blue eyes blinked rapidly. She was obviously afraid, but not yet ready to concede. "You can't prove it.''

"You can't disprove it. And people always believe the worst, don't they, Ariel? In fact, you've used that human trait to your advantage each time you've spoken my name to the media.''

Ariel opened her mouth, but no words came out.

"I was certain you'd see the wisdom in my argument," Claire said. "I think it would be best for both of us if we let this matter drop. I want nothing of Jackson Wilde's. Not even his hateful name. If I'm allowed to pursue my interests without any further interference from you, your husband's treachery will remain a secret. However, if you continue your crusade against me and French Silk, I would be forced to reconsider my position." Claire smiled. "But I'm confident I won't.''

She looked at Josh. "Goodbye for now. I'll be in touch soon." She turned and moved toward the door.

Cassidy paused to deliver a parting shot. "I'm continuing my investigation into your husband's murder, Mrs. Wilde. I have new evidence which I'm certain will result in a conviction. In the meantime, I advise you to stay out of my business, keep out of my way, get your butt back to Nashville, and concentrate on winning lost souls.''

"I'd like to help Josh further his music career. I know a lot of people in New York. I could introduce him around, get him in the right circles. He should have the opportunity to cultivate his talent as he always wanted to."

Claire and Cassidy were cuddled together on the glider in the courtyard of Aunt Laurel's house. Late that afternoon, news that she had retracted her confession reached the media. Every reporter in the country wanted statements from her and Cassidy. Crowder had told them to "clear the hell out, lay low for a couple of days," and let him handle it.

He intended to hold a press conference and announce that Claire Laurent had made a false confession in order to spare herself, her business, and her family any further distress. He planned to dismiss her confession completely, as it had been induced by harassment from the media and the Jackson Wilde Ministry, and bereavement over the loss of her friend and business associate, Yasmine. He would also suggest that the joint investigative forces were in possession of evidence that negated any involvement on Ms. Laurent's part and that opened up a whole new avenue of investigation. That was stretching it a bit, but Crowder was first and foremost a politician.

After leaving him, Claire and Cassidy had gone to Harriett York's house to see Mary Catherine. She had beaten Harry in every game of gin they'd played and proudly showed them the eighty-two cents she'd won.

"Harry's a perfect hostess, but when will we be going home, Claire Louise?"

"Consider this a vacation, Mama. In a few days, we'll all go home." She drew her mother close and hugged her tight.

"You've always been such a wonderful daughter," Mary Catherine said, stroking Claire's cheek. "When we get home,

I'll bake you one of Aunt Laurel's famous French Silk pies. Do you like chocolate pie, Mr. Cassidy?''

"Love it.''

Her face lit up. "Then we must have one very soon for you to share with us.''

"I'd like that. Thanks for the invitation.''

Now, Claire nestled her head on Cassidy's shoulder, content to be in this quiet retreat. They'd thrown a quilt over the weather-worn canvas cushions of the glider. It squeaked rustily each time it rocked, but Claire had never been as comfortable.

"Is Josh going to be another of your adoptees?'' Cassidy asked with a smile in his voice.

"What do you mean?''

"You have a habit of adopting people and assuming their problems as your own. Mary Catherine. To an extent, Andre. Yasmine.''

"Not Yasmine. She took me on.''

"Maybe at first. But you were the strong one, Claire. The backbone of French Silk. The creative genius and the one with the business sense to market your product effectively. Her name might have helped to launch you, but she had come to need French Silk more than it needed her.''

Claire knew that what he said was true, but it seemed disloyal to her friend to agree. "I'm going to miss her. I find myself trying to remember what day she's coming in from New York before I remember that she won't be coming.''

"That's natural. It'll take a while.''

"A long while.''

They were quiet for a moment, the silence broken only by the squeaking of the glider. Finally Cassidy said, "What about me?''

Claire raised her head and looked at him quizzically. "What about you?''

"Are you going to adopt me, too?''

"I don't know," she said airily. "The last thing I need is another adoptee. What would I do with you?"

"You could acquaint me with the Vieux Carré, which you love, which is as much a part of you as your heartbeat. Teach me French. Talk over ideas for French Silk. Discuss my more interesting cases. Listen to me gripe. Go out for ice cream. Neck in public places."

"In other words be your companion and lover."

"Exactly."

They kissed in the balmy twilight. Several blocks away, a saxophone bleated out the blues. Someone living nearby was cooking with filé and cayenne pepper. The spicy aromas permeated the air.

Cassidy opened her suit jacket and covered her breast with a possessive hand. Their kiss deepened. Claire rubbed her bent knee against his fly, and he murmured her name with arousal.

When they paused for breath, he said, "You're a fascinating woman, Claire Louise Laurent. The most intriguing. The most mystifying."

"Not any longer, Cassidy." She took his face between her hands. "You know all my secrets now. Everything. I hope that you can understand and appreciate why I lied to you so many times. I had to. I had to protect Mama from any more pain."

He assumed that darkly intense expression that she associated with him and had come to love. "I've never known a woman—or a man, for that matter—who had such a capacity to love that she would sacrifice her life. I know that's the way it's supposed to be, but until I met you I thought it was an unattainable ideal. What I want to know is, does that love extend to me?"

She kissed him softly. "I've loved you from the day I met you, Cassidy. I was afraid of you and contemptuous of the system you represented, but I loved you."

"I haven't got much to offer you," he said ruefully. "What

I mean is, I'm not as wealthy as you. I love my work. I'm good at it, but I'm not an entrepreneur. As long as I'm in public service, there'll be a ceiling on my earning capacity.'' His eyes moved over her face, scanning every feature. Then he whispered, ''But I love you, Claire. God knows I do. Will you marry me?''

''How unfair,'' she said breathlessly, when he bent his head to her breasts. ''You're asking me at a weak moment.''

''Will you?''

''Yes.''

Anxiously and clumsily, they grappled with clothing until she was astride his lap. When she sank upon his hard shaft, their sighs rose into the evening air.

The saxophone began another soulful song. Someone named Desiree was called to supper. A blue jay flew into the courtyard, perched on the basin of the fountain, and drank from the puddle of rainwater. On a breath of breeze, the leaves of the clinging wisteria rustled against the ancient brick wall and startled the chameleon into taking cover.

And the glider's rhythmic squeaking escalated until, with a shudder and a sweet sigh, it fell silent and settled into repose.

More
Sandra Brown!

Please turn this page
for a
bonus excerpt from
Where There's Smoke
a new
Warner Books hardcover
available at
bookstores everywhere

Chapter One

He'd never particularly liked cats.

His problem, however, was that the woman lying beside him purred like one. Deep satisfaction vibrated through her from her throat to her belly. She had narrow, tilted eyes and moved with sinuous, fluid motion. She didn't walk, she stalked. Her foreplay had been a choreographed program of stretching and rubbing herself against him like a tabby in heat, and when she climaxed, she had screamed and clawed his shoulders.

Cats seemed sneaky and sly and, to his way of thinking, untrustworthy. He'd always been slightly uncomfortable turning his back to one.

"How was I?" Her voice was as sultry as the night beyond the pleated window shades.

"You don't hear me complaining, do you?"

Key Tackett also had an aversion to postcoital evaluation. If it was good, chatter was superfluous. If it wasn't, well, the less said the better.

She mistook his droll response as a compliment and slithered off the wide bed. Naked, she crossed the room to her cluttered dressing table and lit a cigarette with a jeweled lighter. "Want one?"

"No, thanks."

"Drink?"

"If it's handy. A quick one." Bored now, he gazed at the crystal chandelier in the center of the ceiling. The fixture was gaudy and distinctly ugly. It was too large for the bedroom even with the light bulbs behind the glass teardrops dimmed to a mere glimmer.

The shocking pink carpet was equally garish, and the portable brass bar was filled with ornate crystal decanters. She poured him a shot of bourbon. "You don't have to rush off," she told him with a smile. "My husband's out of town, and my daughter's spending the night at a friend's house."

"Male or female?"

"Female. For chrissake, she's only sixteen."

It would be unchivalrous of him to mention that she had acquired her reputation for being an easy lay long before reaching the age of sixteen. He remained silent, mostly from indifference.

"My point is, we've got till morning." Handing Key the drink, she sat down beside him, nudging his hip with hers.

He raised his head from the silk-encased pillow and sipped the straight bourbon. "I gotta get home. Here I've been back in town for . . " he checked his wristwatch, "three and a half hours, and have yet to darken the door of the family homestead."

"You said they weren't expecting you tonight."

"No, but I promised to get home as soon as I could manage it."

She twined a strand of his dark hair around her finger. "But you didn't count on running into me at The Palm the minute you hit town, did you?"

He drained his drink and thrust the empty tumbler at her. "Wonder why they call it The Palm. There isn't a palm tree within three hundred miles of here. You go there often?"

"Often enough."

Key returned her wicked grin. "Whenever your old man's out of town?"

"And whenever the boredom of this wide place in the road gets unbearable, which, God knows, is practically every day. I can usually find some interesting company at The Palm."

He glanced at her abundant breasts. "Yeah, I bet you can. Bet you enjoy getting every man in the place all worked up and sporting a hard-on."

"You know me so well." Laughing huskily, she bent down to brush her damp lips across his.

He turned his head away. "I don't know you at all."

"Why that's not true, Key Tackett." She sat back, looking affronted. "We went through school together."

"I went through school with a lot of kids. Doesn't mean I knew all of them beyond saying hello."

"But you kissed me."

"Liar." Chivalry aside, he added, "I didn't like standing in line, so I never even asked you out."

Her feline eyes squinted with malice that vanished in an instant. As quickly as she extended her claws, they were retracted. "We never actually went on a date, no," she purred. "But one Friday night after a victory against Gladewater, you and the rest of the football team came strutting off the field. My friends and me—with just about everybody else in Eden Pass—lined up along the sideline to cheer as you went past on your way to the field house.

"You," she emphasized, digging her fingernail into his bare chest, "were the outstanding stud among all the studs. You were the sweatiest, and your jersey was the dirtiest, and of course all the girls thought you were the handsomest. You thought so too, I think."

She paused for him to comment, but Key regarded her impassively. He was remembering dozens of Friday nights like the one she had just described. Pregame jitters and postwin exhilaration. The glare of the stadium lights. The cadence of the marching band. The smell of fresh popcorn. The pep squad. The cheering crowds.

And Jody, cheering louder than anybody. Cheering for him. That had been a long time ago.

"When you went past me," she continued, "you grabbed me around the waist, lifted me clean off the ground, hauled me up against you, and kissed me smack on the mouth. Hard. Kinda barbariclike."

"Hmm. You sure?"

"Sure I'm sure. I creamed my panties." She leaned over him, pressing her nipples against his chest. "I waited a long time to have you finish what you started then."

"Well, I'm glad to have been of service." He swatted her fanny and sat up. "Scoot." Reaching around her, he retrieved his jeans.

"You really are leaving?" she asked, surprised.

"Yep."

Frowning, she ground out her cigarette in a nightstand ashtray. "Son of a bitch," she muttered. Then, taking a different tack, she came off the bed and swept aside his jeans before he could step into them. She bumped against his middle seductively.

"It's late, Key. Everybody out at your mama's house will be sound asleep. You'd just as well stay with me tonight." She reached between his strong thighs and fondled him, with audacity and know-how, boldly looking into his face as her fingers coaxed a response. "You haven't lived until you've partaken of one of my breakfast specialties."

Key's lips twitched with amusement. "Served in bed?"

"Damn straight. With all the trimmings. I even—" She broke off suddenly, her hands reflexively clenching hard enough to cause him to grimace.

"Hey, watch out. Them's the family jewels."

"Shh!" Releasing him, she ran on tiptoe toward the open bedroom door. As she reached it, a male voice called out. "Sugar pie, I'm home."

"*Shit!*" No longer languid and seductive, she turned toward Key. "You've got to get out of here," she hissed. "Now!"

Key had already stepped into his jeans and was bending

6

down to search for his boots. "How do you suggest I do that?" he whispered.

"Sugar? You upstairs?" Key heard footsteps on the marble tiles of the entry below, then on the carpet of the stairs. "I got away early and decided to come on home tonight instead of waiting for morning."

She frantically motioned Key toward the French doors on the far side of the room. Scooping up his boots and shirt, he pulled open the doors and slipped through them. He was outside on the balcony before he remembered that the master bedroom was on the second floor of the house. Peering over the wrought-iron railing, he saw no easy way down.

Swearing beneath his breath, he quickly reviewed his options. What the hell? He'd faced worse situations. Typhoons, bullets, an earthquake or two, acts of God, and manmade mayhem. A husband coming home unexpectedly wasn't a new experience for him, either. He'd just have to bluff his way through and hope for the best.

He stepped back into the bedroom but pulled up short on the threshold of the French doors. The nightstand drawer was open. His lover was now reclining in bed clutching the satin sheet to her chin with one hand. With the other, she was aiming a pistol straight at him.

"What the hell are you doing?"

Her piercing scream stunned him. A second later, a blast from her pistol shattered his eardrums. It was a few pounding heartbeats later before he realized that he'd been hit. He gazed down at the searing wound in his left side, then raised his incredulous eyes back to her.

The running footsteps had now reached the hallway. "Sugar pie!"

Again she screamed, a bloodcurdling sound. Again she aimed the gun.

Galvanized, Key spun around just as she fired. He thought she missed but couldn't afford the time to check. He tossed his boots and shirt over the railing, threw his left leg over, then his right, and balanced on an inch of support before leaping through the darkness to the ground below.

He landed hard on his right ankle. Pain shimmied up through his shin, thigh, and groin before slamming into his gut. Blinking hard, he gasped for breath, prayed he wouldn't vomit, and strove to remain conscious as he swept up his boots and shirt and ran like hell.

Lara jumped at the sound of hard knocking on her back door.

She'd been absorbed in a syrupy Bette Davis classic. Muting the television with the remote control, she listened. The knocking came again, harder and more urgent. Throwing off the afghan covering her legs, she left the comfort of her living room sofa and hurried down the hallway, switching on lights as she went.

When she reached the back room of the clinic, she saw the silhouette of a man leaning against the partially open miniblinds on the door. Cautiously she crept forward and peered through a crack in the blinds.

Beneath the harsh glare of the porch light his face looked waxy and set. The lower half of it was shadowed by a day-old beard. Sweat had plastered several strands of unruly dark hair to his forehead. Beneath dense, dark eyebrows, he squinted through the blinds.

"Doc?" He raised his fist and pounded on the door again. "Hey, Doc, open up! I'm making a hell of a mess on your back steps." He wiped his forehead with the back of his hand, and Lara saw blood.

Putting aside her caution, she disengaged the alarm system and unlocked the door. As soon as the latch gave way, he shouldered his way through and stumbled, barefoot, into the room.

"You took long enough," he mumbled. "But all's forgiven if you still keep a bottle of Jack Daniel's stashed in here." He moved straight to a white enamel cabinet and bent down to open the bottom drawer.

"There's no Jack Daniel's in there."

At the sound of her voice, he spun around. He gaped at her

for several seconds. Lara gaped back. He had an animalistic quality that both attracted and repelled her, and although she was inured to the smell of fresh blood, she could smell his.

Instinctively she wanted to recoil, but not from fear. Her impulse was a feminine one of self-defense. She held her ground, however, subjecting herself to his disbelieving and disapproving stare.

"Who the hell are you? Where's Doc?" He was scowling darkly and holding the bloodied tail of his unbuttoned shirt against his side.

"You'd better sit down. You're hurt."

"No shit, lady. Where's Doc?"

"Probably asleep in his bed at his fishing cabin on the lake. He retired and moved out there several months ago."

He glared at her. Finally, in disgust, he said, "Great. That's just fuckin' great." He muttered curses as he shoved his fingers through his hair. Then he took a few lurching steps toward the door and careened into the examination table.

Reflexively Lara reached for him. He staved her off but remained leaning against the padded table. Breathing heavily and wincing in pain, he said, "Can I have some whiskey?"

"What happened to you?"

"What's it to you?"

"I didn't just move into Dr. Patton's house. I took over his medical practice."

His sapphire eyes snapped up to meet hers. "You're a doctor?"

She nodded and spread her arms to indicate the examination room.

"Well I'll be damned." His eyes moved over her. "You must be a real hit at the hospital wearing that getup," he said, lifting his chin to indicate her attire. "Is that the latest thing in lady doctor outfits?"

She had on a long white shirt over a pair of leggings that ended at her knees. Despite her bare feet and legs, she assumed an authoritarian tone. "I don't generally wear my lady doctor outfits past midnight. It's after hours, but I'm still licensed to practice medicine, so why don't you forget how I'm dressed and let me look at your wound. What happened?"

"A little accident."

As she slipped his shirt from his shoulders, she noticed that his belt was unbuckled and only half the buttons of his fly were fastened. She prised his bloody hand away from the wound on his left side, about waist level.

"That's a gunshot!"

"Naw. Like I told you, I had a little accident."

Clearly, he was lying, something he seemed accustomed to doing frequently and without repentance. "What kind of 'accident'?"

"I fell on a pitchfork." He motioned down at the wound. "Just clean it out, put a Band-Aid on it, and tomorrow I'll be fine."

She straightened up and unsmilingly met his grinning face. "Cut the crap, all right? I know a bullet wound when I see one," she said. "I can't take care of this here. You belong in the county hospital."

Turning her back on him, she moved to the phone and began punching out numbers. "I'll make you as comfortable as I can until the ambulance arrives. Please lie down. As soon as I've completed the call, I'll do what I can to stop the bleeding. Yes, hello," she said into the receiver when her call was answered. "This is Dr. Mallory in Eden Pass. I have an emer—"

His hand came from behind her and broke the connection. Alarmed, she looked at him over her shoulder.

"I'm not going to any damn hospital," he said succinctly. "No ambulance. This is nothing. Nothing, understand? Just stop the bleeding and slap a bandage on it. Easy as pie. Have you got any whiskey?" he asked for the third time.

Stubbornly, Lara began redialing. Before she completed the sequence of numbers, he plucked the receiver from her hand and angrily yanked it out of the phone, leaving the cord dangling from his fist.

She turned and confronted him, but, for the first time since opening the door, she was afraid. Even in this small

East Texas town, drug abuse was a problem. Shortly after moving into the clinic, she had installed a burglar alarm system to prevent thefts of prescription drugs and narcotic painkillers.

He must have sensed her apprehension. With a clatter, he dropped the telephone receiver onto a cabinet and smiled grimly. "Look, Doc, if I'd come here to hurt you, I'd have already done it and gotten the hell out. I just don't want to involve a bunch of people in this. No hospital, okay? Take care of me here, and I'll be on my merry way." Even as he spoke, his lips became taut and colorless. He drew an audible breath through clenched teeth.

"Are you about to pass out?"

"Not if I can help it."

"You're in a lot of pain."

"Yeah," he conceded, slowly nodding his head. "It hurts like a son of a bitch. Are you going to let me bleed to death while we argue about it?"

She studied his resolute face for a moment longer and reached the conclusion that she either had to do it his way or he'd leave. The former was preferable to the latter, in which case she would be risking the patient's health and possibly his life. She ordered him to lie down and lower his jeans.

"I've used that same line a dozen times myself," he drawled as he eased himself onto the table.

"That doesn't surprise me." Unimpressed by his boast, she moved to a basin and washed her hands with disinfectant soap. "If you know Doc Patton well enough to know where he stashed his Jack Daniel's, you must live here."

"Born and raised."

"Then why didn't you know he'd retired?"

"I've been away for a while."

"Were you a regular patient of his?"

"All my life. He got me through chicken pox, tonsillitis, two broken ribs, a broken collarbone, a broken arm, and an altercation with a rusty tin can that was serving as second base. Still got the scar on my thigh where I landed when I slid in."

"Were you called out?"

"Hell no," he replied, as though that were beyond the realm of possibility. "More than once I've come through that back door in the middle of the night, needing Doc to patch me up for one reason or another. He wasn't as stingy with the medicinal whiskey as you are. What's that your fixing there?"

"A sedative." She calmly depressed the plunger of a syringe and sent a spurt of medication into the air.

She then set it down and swabbed his upper arm with a cotton ball soaked in alcohol. Before she knew what he was about to do, he picked up the syringe, pushed the plunger with his thumb and squirted the fluid onto the floor.

"Do you think I'm stupid, or what?"

"Mr.—"

"If you want me anesthetized, get me a glass of whiskey. You're not pumping anything into my bloodstream that'll knock me out and give you an opportunity to call the hospital."

"And the sheriff. I'm required by law to report a gunshot wound to the authorities."

He struggled to sit up and when he did, the open wound gushed bright red blood. He groaned. Lara hastily slipped on a pair of surgical gloves and began stanching the flow with gauze pads so that she could determine how serious the wound was.

"Afraid I'll give you AIDS?" he asked, nodding at her gloved hands.

"Professional precaution."

"No worry," he said with a slow grin. "I've been real careful all my life."

"You weren't so careful tonight. Were you caught cheating at poker? Flirting with the wrong woman? Or were you cleaning your pistol when it accidentally went off?"

"I told you, it was a—"

"Yes. A pitchfork. Which would have punctured instead of tearing off a chunk of tissue." She worked quickly and effectively. "Look, I've got to trim off the rough edges of the wound and put in some deep sutures. It's going to be painful. I must anesthetize you."

"Forget it." He hitched his hip over the side of the table as though to leave.

Lara stopped him by placing the heels of her hands on his shoulders. The fingers of her gloves were bloody. "Lidocaine? Local anesthetic," she explained. She took a vial from her cabinet and let him read the label. "Okay?"

He nodded tersely and watched as she prepared another syringe. She injected him near the wound. When the surrounding tissue was deadened, she clipped the debris from around the wound, irrigated it with a saline solution, sutured the interior, and put in a drain.

"What the hell is that?" he asked. He was pale and sweating profusely, but he had watched every swift and economic movement of her hands.

"It's called a penrose drain. It drains off blood and fluid and helps prevent infection. I'll remove it in a few days." She closed the wound with sutures and placed a sterile bandage over it.

After dropping the bloody gloves into a marked metal trash can that designated contaminated materials, Lara returned to the sink to wash her hands. She then asked him to sit up while she wrapped an Ace bandage around his trunk to keep the dressing in place.

She stepped away from him and looked critically at her handiwork. "You're lucky he wasn't a better marksman. A few inches to the right and the bullet could have penetrated several vital organs."

"Or a few inches lower, and I couldn't have penetrated anything ever again."

Lara gave him a retiring look. "How lucky for you."

She had remained professionally detached, although each time her arms had encircled him while bandaging his wound, her cheek had come close to his wide chest. He had a lean, sunbaked, hair-spattered torso. The Ace bandage bisected

13

his hard, flat belly. She'd worked the emergency rooms of major city hospitals; she'd stitched up shady characters before—but none quite this glib, amusing, and handsome.

"Believe it, Doc. I've got the luck of the devil."

"Oh, I believe it. You appear to be a man who lives on the edge and survives by his wits. When did you last have a tetanus shot?"

"Last year." She looked at him skeptically. He raised his right hand as though taking an oath. "Swear to God."

He eased himself over the side of the examination table and stood with his hip propped against it while he rebuttoned his jeans. He left his belt unbuckled. "What do I owe you?"

"Fifty dollars for the after-hours office call, fifty for the sutures and dressing, twelve each for the injections, including the one you wasted, and forty for the medication."

"Medication?"

She removed two plastic bottles from a locked cabinet and handed them to him. "An antibiotic and a pain pill. Once the lidocaine wears off, it'll hurt."

He withdrew a money clip from the front pocket of his snug jeans. "Let's see, fifty plus fifty, plus twenty-four, plus forty comes to—"

"One sixty-four."

He cocked an eyebrow, seeming amused by her prompt tabulation. "Right. One hundred and sixty-four." He extracted the necessary bills and laid them on the examination table. "Keep the change," he said when he put down a five-dollar bill instead of four ones.

Lara was surprised that he had that much cash on him. Even after paying her, he still had a wad of currency in high denominations. "Thank you. Take two of the antibiotic capsules tonight, then four a day until you've taken all of them."

He read the labels, opened the bottle of pain pills and shook out one. He tossed it back and swallowed it dry. "It'd go down better with a shot of whiskey." His voice rose on a hopeful, inquiring note.

She shook her head. "Take one every four hours. Two if

14

absolutely necessary. Take them with water," she emphasized, seriously doubting that he'd stick to those instructions.
"Tomorrow afternoon around four-thirty, come in and I'll
change your dressing."

"For another fifty bucks, I guess."

"No, that's included."

"Much obliged."

"Don't be. As soon as you leave, I'm calling Sheriff Baxter."

Crossing his arms over his bare chest, he regarded her
indulgently. "And get him out of bed at this time of night?"
He shook his head remorsefully. "I've known poor old Elmo
Baxter all my life. He and my daddy were buddies. They were
youngsters during the oil boom, see? It was kinda like going
through a war together, they said.

"They used to hang out around the drilling sites, came to
be like mascots to the roughnecks and wildcatters. Ran er-
rands for them to buy hamburgers, cigarettes, moonshine,
whatever they wanted. He and my daddy probably procured
some things that old Elmo would rather not recall," he said
with a wink.

"Anyway, go ahead and call him. But once he gets here,
he'll be nothing but glad to see me. He'll slap me on the
back and say something like, 'Long time no see,' and ask
what the hell I've been up to lately." He paused to gauge
Lara's reaction. Her stony stare didn't faze him.

"Elmo's overworked and underpaid. Calling him out this
late over this piddling accident of mine will get him all out
of sorts, and he's already cantankerous by nature. If you ever
have a real emergency, like some crazy dopehead breaking in
here looking for something to stop the little green monsters
from crawling out of his eye sockets, the sheriff'll think twice
before rushing to your rescue.

"Besides," he added, lowering his voice, "folks won't take
kindly to you when they hear that you can't be trusted with
their secrets. People in a small town like Eden Pass put a lot
of stock in privileged information."

"I doubt that many even know the definition of privileged

information," Lara refuted dryly. "And contrary to what you say, in the time I've been here, I've learned just how far-reaching and accurate the grapevine is. A secret has a short life span in this town.

"But your message to me about Sheriff Baxter came through loud and clear. What you're telling me is that he enforces a good ol' boy form of justice and that even if I reported your bullet wound, that would be the end of it."

"More'n likely," he replied honestly. "Around here, if the sheriff investigated every shooting, he'd be plumb worn out in a month."

Realizing that he probably was right, Lara sighed. "Were you shot while committing a crime?"

"A few sins, maybe," he said, giving her a slow, lazy smile. His blue eyes squinted mischievously. "But I don't think they're illegal."

She finally relinquished her professional posture and laughed. He didn't appear to be a criminal, although he was almost certainly a sinner. She doubted that he was dangerous, except perhaps to a susceptible woman.

"Hey, the lady doctor's not so stuffy after all. She can smile. Got a real nice smile, too." Narrowing his eyes, he asked softly, "What else have you got that's real nice?"

Now it was her turn to fold her arms across her chest. "Do these come-on lines usually work for you?"

"I've always thought that where boys and girls are concerned, talk is practically unnecessary."

"Really?"

"Saves time and energy. Energy better spent on doing other things."

"I don't dare ask 'Like what?' "

"Go ahead, ask. I don't embarrass easily. Do you?"

It had been a long time since a man had flirted with her. Even longer since she had flirted back. It felt good. But only for a few seconds. Then she remembered why she couldn't afford to flirt, no matter how harmlessly. Her smile faltered, then faded. She drew herself up and resumed her professional demeanor. "Don't forget your shirt," she said curtly.

16

"You can throw it away." He took a step away from the table, but fell back against it, his face contorted in pain. "Shitfire!"

"What?"

"My goddamn ankle. I twisted it when I . . . Hell of a sprain, I think."

She knelt down and as gently as possible worked up the right leg of his jeans. "Good Lord! Why didn't you show me this sooner?" The ankle was swollen and discolored.

"Because I was bleeding like a stuck hog. First things first. It'll be all right." He bent over, pushed aside her probing hands, and pulled down his pants leg.

"You should have it X-rayed. It could be broken."

"It isn't."

"You're not qualified to give a medical opinion."

"No, but I've had enough broken bones to know when one's broken, and this one isn't."

"I can't take responsibility if—"

"Relax, will you? I'm not going to hold you responsible for anything." Shirtless, shoeless, he hopped toward the door through which he'd entered.

"Would you like to wash your hands before you go?" she offered.

He looked down at the bloodstains and shook his head. "They've been dirtier."

Lara felt derelict in her duties as a physician treating him this way. But he was an adult, accountable for his own actions. She'd done as much as he had permitted.

"Don't forget to take your antibiotics," she cautioned as she slipped under his right arm and fit her left shoulder into his armpit. She placed her left arm around him for additional support as he hopped through the door, his right arm across her shoulders. A pickup truck was parked a few yards from the back steps. Its front tires had narrowly missed her bed of struggling petunias.

"Do you have some crutches?"

"I'll find some if I need them."

"You'll need them. Don't put any weight on your ankle

17

for several days. When you get home, put an ice pack on it and keep it elevated whenever possible. And remember to come in at—"

"Four-thirty tomorrow. I wouldn't miss it."

She looked up at him. He tilted his head down to look at her. Their gazes came together and held. Lara felt the heat emanating from his body. He was muscular and fit, and she was certain that his vital body would heal quickly. He was a physical specimen, which she had tried, not entirely successfully, to regard through purely professional eyes.

His eyes scanned her, looking intently at her face, her hair, her mouth. In a low, rough voice he said, "You sure as hell don't look like any doctor I've ever seen." His hand slid from her shoulder to her hip. "You don't feel like one either."

"What is a doctor supposed to feel like?"

"Not like this," he rasped, gently squeezing her.

He kissed her then. Abruptly and impertinently, he stamped her lips with his.

Gasping in surprise, Lara disengaged herself. Her heart was knocking and she felt hot all over. A thousand options on how to react flashed through her mind, but she considered that the best one was to pretend the kiss hadn't happened. Taking issue with it would only give it importance. She would be forced to acknowledge it, discuss it with him, and that, she hastily reasoned, should be avoided.

So, she assumed a cool, haughty tone as she asked, "Would you like me to drive you somewhere?"

He was grinning from ear to ear, as though he saw straight through her attempt to conceal her discomposure. "No, thanks," he replied cockily. "This truck's got automatic transmission. I'll manage with my left foot."

She nodded brusquely. "If I hear of any crimes that occurred tonight, I'll have to report this incident to Sheriff Baxter."

Laughing even as he grimaced in pain, he climbed into the cab of the pickup. "Don't worry. You're not obstructing justice." He drew an imaginary X over his left breast. "Cross my heart and hope to die, stick a cross-tie in my eye." The engine sputtered to life. He dropped the gear shift into reverse. "Bye-bye, Doc."

"Be careful, Mr.—"

"Tackett," he told her through the open window. "But call me Key."

Everything inside Lara went very still. It seemed her heart, which had been racing only moments earlier, ceased to beat at all. Blood drained from her head, making her dizzy. She must have gone drastically pale, but it was too dark for him to notice as he backed the pickup to the end of the driveway. He tapped his horn twice and saluted her with the tips of his fingers as the truck rumbled away into the darkness.

Lara plopped down onto the cool concrete steps, which were speckled with drying drops of blood. She covered her face with damp, trembling hands. The night was seasonally warm and balmy, but she shivered inside her loose white shirt. Goose bumps broke out along her bare legs. Her mouth had gone dry.

Key Tackett. Clark's younger brother. He'd finally come home. This was the day she'd been anticipating. He was essential to the daring plan she'd spent the past year developing and cultivating. Now, he was here. Somehow, someway, she must enlist his help. But how?

Dr. Lara Mallory was the last person Key Tackett wanted to know.